I0788556

The Complete Story of the Christ Jesus

Peter Ng

Complete Story of the Christ Jesus

Dedication

Acknowledgment

Thank you to the WEB Bible Translation team providing a better version of the Scriptures that this book is using.

About the Author

I am not a pastor or a faculty of a seminary, but a self-employed businessman. I graduated from Multnomah University in Church Leadership. Actively Served in the church for over thirty years as a member. Served in different Christian gospel sharing organizations and participated in many discussions on the social media to lead the lost ones to the truth of God.

The confusion and misunderstanding of many people about the difference between the four gospels fused me to study into the harmony of the four gospels. I believe this complete story about Christ Jesus will give answer to the confusion and misunderstanding persons.

Table of Contents

Preface

There are many attempts to compile the canonical gospels of the Christian New Testament into a single account by merging narrative or a tabular format. Technically known as harmony. There are four main types of harmony: radical, synthetic, sequential, and parallel. This book included all four types of harmony.

All Christians believe that the four gospels tell the story of Jesus, which is one story, but the four gospels are described in four different viewpoints and not four different stories. There are events recorded in one gospel but not in other gospels. Some events or teachings are recorded in all four gospels, but one has information the others do not have. Most Bibles have parallel harmony references to link all similar Scriptures. These links helped me a lot in creating this book.

This book is a sharing of my Bible Study exercise, in which I tried to compile a Gospel Harmony. The book is one hundred percent from the four gospels of the New Testament with minimal change besides a few word changes for better sentence structure, with no change in meaning of the Scripture. I am just the one to arrange it and merge it together from the four gospels. It started as my own study, but I was excited to see how well the merging was and wanted to share it with others. I learned many new, in-depth facts of the life of Jesus by seeing it in one gospel harmony story as it should be. The reference part is showing how the story is chosen from the four gospels. Some Scriptures chosen for the story and the Scriptures with similar descriptions are included in a box.

We know the four Gospels are four viewpoints of the four Gospel writers—Matthew, Mark, Luke, and John. They wrote down what they knew and heard from others. Some were recorded from their memory or from other eyewitnesses, and some were recorded from the notes they wrote down themselves or from others. The gospel of Matthew, chapters 5 to 7, is long, and it could be a copy from a note from one of the listeners when Jesus taught them; and Chapter 5 of the Gospel of Luke is only a little more than half of chapter 5 can be written down from memory of the writer or one of the persons who listened to the teaching of Jesus. Therefore, I chose the longer and more detailed version of the recording for the book and put the other scriptures as a reference.

Apostle John was also a note-taker. He wrote down many of Jesus's teachings, which were recorded in chapters 10, 14, 15, 16, and 17 of the Gospel of John. Apostle John was also one of the first few disciples who followed Jesus right after Jesus was baptized by John the Baptist. He witnessed the first and second miracles Jesus did by turning water into wine and healing the son of the Official who was close to death. These miracles weren't recorded in other gospel books. These miracles are done right after Jesus was baptized; therefore, Jesus logically did those miracles before being tempted by the devil in the wilderness, as stated in this book. I use logic to set the sequential harmony of the Scriptures and find some unrecorded facts.

There were a few disciples who followed Jesus right after Jesus was baptized, but when Jesus went to the wilderness for temptation, those disciples didn't wait long enough until Jesus returned. They gave up waiting and went back to their home. This is an example of my logic for the sequential harmony of the book. Jesus later had to go look for His disciples in their hometown. Jesus called Peter, Andrew, James, and John when they were fishing in their hometown. This calling should be just calling them back to follow Him, and not the first time they saw and know each other.

The gospel of Luke has many details about the mother of Jesus and about the birth of John the Baptist, whose mother was a relative of Mary. The Genealogy of Jesus in the Gospel of Luke is different than the genealogy in the Gospel of Matthew. They both show that Jesus is the descendant of King David, but the Gospel of Matthew is from Solomon as the son of David; in the Gospel of Luke, the son of David was Nathan. This Nathan was one of the sons of King David and could be the prophet Nathan who showed King David that he committed the sin of adultery. Many scholars believe that the genealogy in the Gospel of Luke is the Genealogy of Mary's family. Joseph is the son-in-law of Heli and the son of Jacob, as shown in the gospel of Matthew. This is Synthetic Harmony.

When joining the four gospels together, I found a funny story. In Chapter 18 of the Gospel of Luke, Jesus ordered His disciples to bring the blind man to Him, but in Mark Chapter 10, the blind man seems to jump up and go to Jesus by himself. If so, he might have walked in the wrong direction. Jesus had to stop and call His disciples to bring the blind man to Him. It is just my imagination. The blind man may not have walked to Jesus by himself. It is parallel harmony because many readers believe that in Mark Chapter 10, the blind man went to Jesus by himself.

We heard about the seven last words Jesus said on the cross, but while merging the four gospels together, I couldn't find all seven words the first time I looked for them. It took me a while to find all seven. Merging the four gospels gives us the opportunity to see all seven words together instead of pieces from different gospels. This is radical harmony because we all know Jesus said seven words when he was on the cross.

The most exciting part is merging the four gospels from the triumphant entry into Jerusalem to the last supper, the trials, and the resurrection. It all comes together like puzzles with a perfect fit. Even though the verses are from different gospels, they come together just as they were planned to fit together. The story has a logical and smooth flow.

The reference part is to prove this book is one hundred percent from the Scriptures. The Scriptures, which are put in boxes in the reference part, are Scriptures not selected to put in the book because they tell a similar story to the selected Scriptures presented. It is also a good resource for Bible Study because it includes all the verses in the reference part, which is one event or teaching, by putting all the cross-reference verses in one place.

Many people believe that merging the four gospels is impossible. It is true that there are many places I cannot merge. The place I worried most was the part when Jesus prophesied about the end time. I have no confidence that I put the verse together in the correct order. I pray that the Holy Spirit guided me and put the verses in the order they should be. When quoting the prophecy, please quote from the Gospels and not from this book.

The other problem of merging is whether James and John went to Jesus themselves to request sitting at the left and right of Jesus, or their mother did it. Or they went to Jesus themselves first, and then their mother went later. Did the Centurion himself go to ask Jesus to heal his servant, or did he send the elders to do it? I chose the mother of James and John because their mother did the same as they did. The same way the elders asked is the same as the centurion himself wondered. Or the elder went first, and then the centurion also went to meet Jesus.

There are other cans of worms that I am not willing to open. Jesus died on a special Sabbath Preparation Day. What does special Sabbath Preparation Day mean? The trial of Jesus by Pilate was at about the sixth hour, according to John 19:14, but the crucifixion of Jesus started at the third hour, according to Mark 15:25. The explanation can be that it was on a different day, or it can be that the recording of the time is estimated only and not accurate. I will let the reader decide what explanation is correct.

This book is not a complete Gospel Harmony book, but it is one of the best complete stories of Christ Jesus. The different recordings between the four gospels remain as is. This book cannot replace the Four Gospel Books but can only be used as a reference book in Bible study. There are many improvements needed, and I pray that if it is His will,

God will help me to write a complete Gospel Harmony
Book.

Chapter One:
The Beginning of the Good News

The Beginning of the Good News
Mk 1: 1 / Luke 1:1-4 / Jn 1:1-14

The beginning of the Good News of Jesus Christ, the Son of God.

Since many have undertaken to set in order a narrative concerning those matters which have been fulfilled among us, even as those who from the beginning were eyewitnesses and servants of the word delivered them to us, it seemed good to me also, having traced the course of all things accurately from the first, to write to you in order, most excellent Theophilus; that you might know the certainty concerning the things in which you were instructed.

In the beginning was the Word, and the Word was with God, and the Word was God. The same was in the beginning with God. All things were made through him. Without him, anything made that has been made. In him was life, and the life was the light of men. The light shines in the darkness, and the darkness hasn't overcome it.

There came a man, sent from God, whose name was John. The same came as a witness that he might testify about the light, that all might believe through him. He was not the light but was sent that he might testify about the light. The true light that enlightened everyone was coming into the world.

He was in the world, and the world was made through him, and the world didn't recognize him. He came to his own, and those who were his own didn't receive him. But as many as received him, to them he gave the right to become God's children, to those who believe in his name: who were born not of blood, nor of the will of the flesh, nor of the will of man, but of God. The Word became fresh and lived among us. We saw his glory, such glory as of the one and only Son of the Father, full of grace and truth.

The birth of John the Baptist
Lk 1 : 5-25

There was in the days of Herod, the king of Judea, a certain priest named Zacharias of the priestly division of Abijah. He had a wife, the daughters of Aaron, and her name was Elizabeth. They were both righteous before God, walking blamelessly in all the commandments and ordinances of the Lord. But they had no child because Elizabeth was barren, and they both were well advanced in years.

Now it happened, while he executed the priest's office before God in the order of his division, according to the custom of the priest's office, his lot was to enter into the temple of the Lord and burn incense. The whole multitude of the people were praying outside at the hour of incense.

An angel of the Lord appeared to him, standing on the right side of the incense altar. Zacharias was troubled when he saw him, and fear fell upon him. But the angel said to him, "Don't be afraid, Zacharias, because your request has been heard, and your wife, Elizabeth, will bear you a son, and you shall call his name John. You will have joy and gladness, and many will rejoice at his birth. For he will be great in the sight of the Lord, and he will drink no wine nor strong drink. He will be filled with the Holy Spirit, even from his mother's womb. He will turn many of the children of Israel to the Lord, their God. He will go before him in the spirit and power of Elijah, to turn the hearts of the fathers to the children,' and the disobedient to the wisdom of the just; to prepare a people prepared for the Lord."

Zacharias said to the angel, "How can I be sure of this? For I am an old man, and my wife is well advanced in years."

The angel answered him, "I am Gabriel, who stands in the presence of God. I was sent to speak to you and to bring you this good news. Behold, you will be silent and not able to speak until the day that these things will happen because you didn't believe my words, which will be fulfilled in their proper time."

The people were waiting for Zacharias, and they marveled that he was delayed in the temple. When he came out, he could not speak to them, and they perceived that he had seen a vision in the temple. He continued making signs to them and remained mute. It happened when the days of his service were fulfilled, and he departed to his house.

After these days, Elizabeth, his wife, conceived, and she hid herself for five months, saying, "Thus has the Lord done to me in the days in which he looked at me, to take away my reproach among men."

The Birth of Jesus
Lk 1 : 26-38

Now, in the sixth month, the angel Gabriel was sent from God to a city in Galilee named Nazareth, to a virgin who had pledged to be married to a man whose name was Joseph, of the house of David. The virgin's name was Mary.

Editor Footnote: Joseph is the son of Jacob and son-in-law of Heli. Mary's husband, Joseph, was the descendant of King David from the line of Solomon. Mary is the daughter of Heli. Heli is the descendant of King David, but from the line of Nathan, who was one of the sons of King David; he could be the prophet Nathan who talked with King David when he sinned.

The angel Gabriel appeared to Mary outside of her house.

Having come in, the angel said to her, "Rejoice, you highly favored one! The Lord is with you. Blessed are you among women!"

But when she saw him, she was greatly troubled by the saying and considered what kind of salutation this might be.

The angel said to her, "Don't be afraid, Mary, for you have found favor with God. Behold, you will conceive in your womb, and give birth to a son, and will call his name Jesus.' He will be great and will be called the Son of the Most High. The Lord God will give him the throne of his father, David, and he will reign over the house of Jacob forever. There will be no end to his Kingdom."

Mary said to the angel, "How can this be, seeing I am a virgin?"

The angel answered her, "The Holy Spirit will come on you, and the power of the Most High will overshadow you. Therefore, the holy one who is born from you will also be called the Son of God. Behold, Elizabeth, your relative, also has conceived a son in her old age, and this is the sixth month with her, who was called barren. For everything spoken by God is possible."

Mary said, "Behold, the handmaid of the Lord; be it to me according to your word."

The angel departed from her.

Mary went to meet the mother of John the Baptist Lk 1 : 39-80

Mary arose in those days and went into the hill country with haste, into the city of Judah, and entered into the house of Zacharias and greeted Elizabeth. It happened when Elizabeth heard Mary's greeting, and the baby leaped in her womb. Elizabeth was filled with the Holy Spirit.

She called out with a loud voice and said, "Blessed are you among women, and blessed is the fruit of your womb! Why am I so favored that the mother of my Lord should come to me? For behold, when the voice of your greeting came into my ears, the baby leaped in my womb for joy! Blessed is she who believed, for there will be a fulfillment of the things which have been spoken to her from the Lord!"

Mary said, "My soul magnifies the Lord. My spirit has rejoiced in God, my Savior, for He has looked at the humble state of his handmaid. For behold, from now on, all generations will call me blessed, for He who is mighty has done great things for me. Holy is His name. His mercy is for generations of those who fear Him. He has shown strength with His arm. He has scattered the pride in the imagination of their hearts. He has put down princes from their thrones. And has exalted the lowly. He has filled the hunger with good things. He has sent the rich away empty. He has given help to Israel, His servant, so that He might remember mercy, as He spoke to our fathers, to Abraham and his seed forever."

Mary stayed with her for about three months and then returned to her house. Now, the time that Elizabeth should have given birth was fulfilled, and she gave birth to a son. Her neighbors and her relatives heard that the Lord had magnified his mercy towards her, and they rejoiced with her.

It happened on the eighth day that they came to circumcise the child, and they would have called him Zacharias after the name of the father.

His mother answered, "Not so, but he will be called John."

They said to her, "There is no one among your relatives who is called by this name."

They made signs to his father of what he would have him call. He asked for a writing tablet and wrote, "His name is John."

They all marveled. His mouth was opened immediately, and his tongue freed, and he spoke, blessing God. Fear came on all who lived around them, and all these sayings were talked about throughout all the hill country of Judea.

All who heard them laid them up in their hearts, saying, "What then will this child be?"

The hand of the Lord was with him.

His father, Zacharias, was filled with the Holy Spirit and prophesied, saying, "Blessed be the Lord, the God of Israel, for he has visited and worked redemption for his people; and has raised up a horn of salvation for us in the house of his servant David (as he spoke by the mouth of his holy prophets who have been from of old), salvation from our enemies, and from the hand of all who hate us; to show mercy towards our fathers, to remember his holy covenant, the oath which he spoke to Abraham, our father, to grant to us that we, being delivered out of the hand of our enemies, should serve him without fear, In holiness and righteousness before him all the days of our life. And you, child, will be called a prophet of the Most High, for you will go before the face of the Lord to prepare his ways, to give knowledge of salvation to his people by the remission of their sins, because of the tender mercy of our God, whereby the dawn from on high will visit us, to shine on those who sit in darkness and the shadow of death; to guide our feet into the way of peace."

The child was growing and becoming strong in spirit, and he was in the desert until the day of his public appearance in Israel.

God told Joseph to accept Mary, who was pregnant by the Holy Spirit
Mt 1 : 19-25

> Editor Footnote: Joseph found out that Mary was pregnant by the Holy Spirit.

Joseph, her husband, being a righteous man and not willing to make her a public example, intended to put her away secretly. But when he thought about these things, behold, an angel of the Lord appeared to him in a dream, saying, "Joseph, son of David, don't be afraid to take to yourself Mary, your wife, for that which is conceived in her is of the Holy Spirit. She shall give birth to a son. You shall call his name Jesus, for it is he who shall save his people from their sins."

Now all this has happened, that it might be fulfilled which was spoken by the Lord through the prophet, saying, "Behold, the virgin shall be with child, and shall give birth to a son. They shall call His name Immanuel," which is being interpreted, "God with us."

Joseph arose from his sleep and did as the angel of the Lord commanded him, and took his wife to himself, and didn't know her sexually until she had given birth to her firstborn son. He named him Jesus.

Jesus was born in Bethlehem.
Lk 2 : 1-39

Now, it happened in those days that Caesar Augustus passed a decree that all the world should be enrolled. This was the first enrollment made when Quirinius was governor of Syria. All went to enroll themselves, and everyone went to his own city.

Joseph also went up from Galilee, out of the city of Nazareth, into Judea, to the city of David, which is called Bethlehem, because he was of the house and family of David, to enroll himself with Mary, who was pledged to be married to him as wife, being pregnant. It happened, while they were there, that the day had come that she should give birth.

She gave birth to her firstborn son. She wrapped him in bands of cloth and laid him in a feeding trough because there was no room for them in the inn. There were shepherds in the same country staying in the field and keeping watch by night over their flock. Behold, an angel of the Lord stood by them, and the glory of the Lord shone around them, and they were terrified.

The angel said to them, "Don't be afraid, for behold, I bring you good news of great joy which will be to all the people, for there is born to you, this day, in the city of David, a Savior, who is Christ the Lord. This is the sign to you: you will find a baby wrapped in strips of cloth lying in a feeding trough."

Suddenly, there was with the angel a multitude of the heavenly army praising God and saying, "Glory to God in the highest, on earth peace, goodwill toward men."

It happened when the angels went away from them into the sky, and the shepherds said one to another, "Let's go to Bethlehem, now, and see this thing that has happened, which the Lord has made known to us."

They came with haste and found both Mary and Joseph, and the baby was lying in the feeding trough. When they saw it, they publicized widely the saying that was spoken to them about this child. All who heard it wondered at the things which were spoken to them by the shepherds. But Mary kept all these sayings, pondering them in her heart.

The shepherds returned, glorifying and praising God for all the things that they had heard and seen, just as it had told them.

When eight days were fulfilled for the circumcision of the child, his name was called Jesus, which was given by the angel before he was conceived in the womb.

When the days of their purification according to the law of Moses were fulfilled, they brought him up to Jerusalem to present him to the Lord (as it is written in the law of the Lord, "Every male who opens the womb shall be called holy to the Lord"), and to offer a sacrifice according to that which is said in the law of the Lord, "A pair of turtledoves, or two young pigeons."

Behold, there was a man in Jerusalem whose name was Simeon. This man was righteous and devout, looking for the consolation of Israel, and the Holy Spirit was on him. It had been revealed to him by the Holy Spirit that he should not see death before he had seen the Lord's Christ. He came in the Spirit into the temple.

When the parents brought in the child, Jesus, that they might do concerning him according to the custom of the law, then he received him into his arms, and blessed God, and said, "Now you are releasing your servant, Master, according to your word, in peace; for my eyes have seen your salvation, which you have prepared before the face of all peoples; a light for revelation to the nations, and the glory of your people Israel."

Joseph and his mother were marveling at the things that were spoken concerning him, and Simeon blessed them and said to Mary, his mother, "Behold, this child is set for the falling and the rising of many in Israel, and for a sign which is spoken against. Yes, a sword will pierce through your own soul, that the thoughts of many hearts may be revealed."

There was one Anna, a prophetess, the daughter of Phanuel, of the tribe of Asher (she was of a great age, having lived with a husband seven years from her virginity, and she had been a widow for about eighty-four years), who didn't depart from the temple, worshiping with fasting and petitions night and day. Coming up at that very hour, she gave thanks to the Lord and spoke of him to all those who were looking for redemption in Jerusalem.

The Wise Men came to see Jesus
Mt 2 : 1-14

Now, when Jesus was born in Bethlehem of Judea in the days of King Herod, behold, wise men from the east came to Jerusalem, saying, "Where is he who is born King of the Jews? For we saw his star in the east and have come to worship him."

When King Herod heard it, he was troubled and all Jerusalem with him. Gathering all the chief priests and scribes of the people, he asked them where Christ would be born.

They said to him, "In Bethlehem of Judea, for this is written through the prophet, You Bethlehem, land of Judah, are in no way least among the princes of Judah: for out of you shall come a governor, who shall shepherd my people, Israel."

Then Herod secretly called the wise men and learned from them exactly what time the star appeared.

He sent them to Bethlehem and said, "Go and search diligently for the young child. When you have found him, bring me a word so that I also may come and worship him."

They, having heard the king, went their way, and behold, the star, which they saw in the east, went before them until it came and stood over where the young child was. When they saw the star, they rejoiced with exceedingly great joy.

They came into the house and saw the young child with Mary, his mother, and they fell down and worshipped him. Opening their treasures, they offered him gifts: gold, frankincense, and myrrh. Being warned in a dream that they shouldn't return to Herod, they went back to their own country another way.

Now, when they had departed, behold, an angel of the Lord appeared to Joseph in a dream, saying, "Arise and take the young child and his mother, and flee into Egypt, and stay there until I tell you, for Herod will seek the young child to destroy him."

He arose and took the young child and his mother by night and departed into Egypt.

King Herod ordered to kill the children
Mt 2:15-18

And was there until the death of Herod; that it might be fulfilled which was spoken by the Lord through the prophet, saying, "Out of Egypt I called my son."

Then Herod, when he saw that the wise men mocked him, was exceedingly angry and sent out and killed all the male children who were in Bethlehem and in all the surrounding countryside, from two years old and under, according to the exact time which he had learned from the wise men.

Then that which was spoken by Jeremiah the prophet was fulfilled, saying, "A voice was heard in Ramah, lamentation, weeping and great mourning, Rachel weeping for her children; she wouldn't be comforted, because they are no more."

Joseph returned to Galilee
Mt 2:19-22

But when Herod was dead, behold, an angel of the Lord appeared in a dream to Joseph in Egypt, saying, "Arise and take the young child and his mother, and go into the land of Israel, for those who sought the young child's life are dead."

He arose and took the young child and his mother and came into the land of Israel. But when he heard that Archelaus was reigning over Judea in the place of his father, Herod, he was afraid to go there. Being warned in a dream, he withdrew into the region of Galilee.

The boy Jesus
Mt 2:15-18

The child was growing and becoming strong in spirit, filled with wisdom, and the grace of God was upon him. His parents went every year to Jerusalem at the feast of the Passover. When he was twelve years old, they went up to Jerusalem according to the custom of the feast, and when they had fulfilled the days, as they were returning, the boy Jesus stayed behind in Jerusalem. Joseph and his mother didn't know it, but supposing he was in the company, they went on a day's journey and looked for him among their relatives and acquaintances.

When they didn't find him, they returned to Jerusalem, looking for him. It happened after three days; they found him in the temple, sitting in the midst of the teachers, both listening to them and asking them questions. All who heard him were amazed at his understanding and his answers.

When they saw him, they were astonished, and his mother said to him, "Son, why have you treated us this way? Behold, your father and I were anxiously looking for you."

He said to them, "Why were you looking for me? Didn't you know that I must be in my Father's house?"

They didn't understand the saying that he said to them.

And he went down with them and came to Nazareth. He was subject to them, and his mother kept all these sayings in her heart. And Jesus increased in wisdom and stature, and in favor with God and men. And came and lived in a city called Nazareth; that might be fulfilled, as spoken through the prophets: "He will be called a Nazarene."

Chapter Two:
John the Baptist

The beginning of John the Baptist ministry
Lk 3:1-18/ Mk 1:2-18/ Mt 3:1-12

Now in the fifteenth year of the reign of Tiberius Caesar, Pontius Pilate being governor of Judea, Herod being tetrarch of Galilee, and his brother Philip tetrarch of the region of Ituraea and Trachonitis, and Lysanias tetrarch of Abilene, in the high priesthood of Annas and Caiaphas, the word of God came to John, the son of Zacharias, in the wilderness. John came baptizing in the wilderness and preaching the baptism of repentance for forgiveness of sins. All the country of Judea and all those of Jerusalem went out to him. He baptized them in the Jordan River, confessing their sins.

"Repent, for the Kingdom of Heaven is at hand!"

He came into all the regions around the Jordan, preaching the baptism of repentance for the remission of sins. As it is written in the book of the words of Isaiah the prophet,

"The voice of one crying in the wilderness,

Make ready the way of the Lord.

Make his paths straight.

Every valley will be filled.

Every mountain and hill will be brought low.

The crooked will become straight,

and the rough ways smooth.

All flesh will see God's salvation.'"

Now, John himself wore clothing made of camel hair and a leather belt around his waist. His food was locusts and wild honey.

Then, people from Jerusalem, all of Judea, and all the region around the Jordan went out to him.

He baptized them in Jordan, confessing their sins.

But when he saw many of the Pharisees and Sadducees coming for his baptism, he said to them, "You offspring of vipers, who warned you to flee from the wrath to come?

Therefore, produce fruit worthy of repentance! Don't think to yourselves, we have Abraham for our father,' for I tell you that God is able to raise up children to Abraham from these stones.

Even now, the axe also lies at the root of the trees. Every tree, therefore, that doesn't produce good fruit is cut down and thrown into the fire."

The multitudes asked him, "What then must we do?"

He answered them, "He who has two coats, let him give to him who has none. He who has food, let him do likewise."

Tax collectors also came to be baptized, and they said to him, "Teacher, what must we do?"

He said to them, "Collect no more than that which is appointed to you."

Soldiers also asked him, saying, "What about us? What must we do?"

He said to them, "Extort from no one by violence, neither accuse anyone wrongfully. Be content with your wages."

As the people were in expectation, and all men reasoned in their hearts concerning John, whether perhaps he was the Christ,

John answered them all, "I indeed baptize you with water, but he comes who is mightier than I, the strap of whose sandals I am not worthy to loosen. He will baptize you in the Holy Spirit and fire, whose fan is in his hand, and he will thoroughly cleanse his threshing floor and will gather the wheat into his barn, but he will burn up the chaff with unquenchable fire."

Then, with many other exhortations, he preached good news to the people.

Jesus got baptism by John the Baptist
Mt 3:13-17 / Mk 1:9-11/Lk 3:21-22

Then Jesus came from Galilee to the Jordan to John to be baptized by him.

But John would have hindered him, saying, "I need to be baptized by you, and you come to me?"

But Jesus, answering, said to him, "Allow it now, for this is the fitting way for us to fulfill all righteousness."

Then he allowed him. In those days, Jesus came from Nazareth of Galilee and was baptized by John in the Jordan.

Immediately coming up from the water, he saw the heavens parting and the Spirit descending on him like a dove.

A voice came out of the sky, "You are my beloved Son, in whom I am well pleased."

John the Baptist testified about Jesus
Jn 1:15-18

John testified about him. He cried out, saying, "This was he of whom I said, He who comes after me has surpassed me, for he was before me.'"

We all received grace upon grace from his fullness, for the law was given through Moses. Grace and truth were realized through Jesus Christ. No one has seen God at any time. The one and only Son, who is in the bosom of the Father, he has declared him.

John the Baptist Denies Being the Christ
Jn 1:19-28

This is John's testimony when the Jews sent priests and Levites from Jerusalem to ask him, "Who are you?"

He declared and didn't deny, but he declared, "I am not the Christ."

They asked him, "What then? Are you Elijah?"

He said, "I am not."

"Are you the prophet?"

He answered, "No."

They said, therefore, to him, "Who are you? Give us an answer to take back to those who sent us. What do you say about yourself?"

He said, "I am the voice of one crying in the wilderness, make straight the way of the Lord,' as Isaiah the prophet said."

The ones who had been sent were from the Pharisees.

They asked him, "Why then do you baptize if you are not the Christ, nor Elijah, nor the prophet?"

John answered them, "I baptize in water, but one whom you don't know stands among you.

He is the one who comes after me, who prefers before me, whose sandal strap I'm not worthy to loosen." These things were done in Bethany beyond the Jordan, where John was baptizing.

The beginning of Jesus's ministry
Lk 3:23 / John 1:29-36

Jesus himself, when he began to teach, was about thirty years old, being the son (as was supposed) of Joseph, the son of Heli.

The next day, he saw Jesus coming to him and said, "Behold, the Lamb of God, who takes away the sin of the world! This is he of whom I said, "After me comes a man who is preferred before me, for he was before me. I didn't know him, but I came baptizing in water for this reason: that he would be revealed to Israel."

John testified, saying, "I have seen the Spirit descending like a dove out of heaven, and it remained on him. I didn't recognize him, but he who sent me to baptize in water said to me, On whomever you will see the Spirit descending, and remaining on him, the same is he who baptizes in the Holy Spirit.' I have seen and have testified that this is the Son of God."

Again, the next day, John was standing with two of his disciples, and he looked at Jesus as he walked and said, "Behold, the Lamb of God!"

Two disciples of John the Baptist followed Jesus
Jn 1:37-42

The two disciples heard him speak, and they followed Jesus. Jesus turned, and saw them following, and said to them, "What are you looking for?"

They said to him, "Rabbi" (which is to say, being interpreted as Teacher), "Where are you staying?"

He said to them, "Come and see."

They came and saw where he was staying and stayed with him that day. It was about the tenth hour. One of the two who heard John and followed him was Andrew, Simon Peter's brother. He first found his own brother, Simon, and said to him, "We have found the Messiah!" (which is, being interpreted, Christ).

He brought him to Jesus.

Jesus looked at him and said, "You are Simon, the son of Jonah. You shall be called Cephas" (which is by interpretation, Peter).

Chapter Three:
Jesus Started His Ministry

Jesus called Philip
Jn 1:43-44

The next day, he was determined to go out into Galilee and find Philip.

Jesus said to him, "Follow me."

Now Philip was from Bethsaida, of the city of Andrew and Peter.

Jesus met Nathanael
Jn 1:45-51

Philip found Nathanael and said to him, "We have found him, of whom Moses in the law and the prophets wrote: Jesus of Nazareth, the son of Joseph."

Nathanael said to him, "Can any good things come out of Nazareth?"

Philip said to him, "Come and see."

Jesus saw Nathanael coming to him and said about him, "Behold, an Israelite indeed, in whom is no deceit!"

Nathanael said to him, "How do you know me?"

Jesus answered him, "Before Philip called you, when you were under the fig tree, I saw you."

Nathanael answered him, "Rabbi, you are the Son of God! You are King of Israel!"

Jesus answered him, "Because I told you, 'I saw you underneath the fig tree,' do you believe? You will see greater things than these!"

He said to him, "Most certainly, I tell you, hereafter you will see heaven opened and the angels of God ascending and descending on the Son of Man."

Jesus turns water into wine.
Jn 2:1-12

On the third day, there was a marriage in Cana of Galilee. Jesus' mother was there. Jesus also was invited, with his disciples, to the marriage.

When the wine ran out, Jesus' mother said to him, "They have no wine."

Jesus said to her, "Woman, what does that have to do with you and me? My hour has not yet come." His mother said to the servants, "Whatever he says to you, do it."

Now there were six water pots of stone set there after the Jews' way of purifying, containing two or three metretes apiece.

Jesus said to them, "Fill the water pots with water."

They filled them up to the brim.

He said to them, "Now draw some out and take it to the ruler of the feast."

So, they took it. When the ruler of the feast tasted the water now became wine and didn't know where it came from (but the servants who had drawn the water knew), the ruler of the feast called the bridegroom and said to him, "Everyone serves the good wine first, and when the guests have drunk freely, then that which is worse. You have kept the good wine until now!"

This is the beginning of the signs Jesus did in Cana of Galilee, and it revealed his glory; his disciples believed in him.

After this, he went down to Capernaum, he and his mother, his brothers, and his disciples, and they stayed there a few days.

Jesus cleaned out the temple court in Jerusalem for the first time
Jn 2:13-25 / (Mk 11:15-18 / Mt 21:12-17 / Lk 19:45-48)

The Passover of the Jews was at hand, and Jesus went up to Jerusalem. He found in the temple those who sold oxen, sheep, and doves, as well as the changers of money sitting.

He made a whip of cords and threw all out of the temple, both the sheep and the oxen, and he poured out the changers' money and overthrew their tables.

He said to those who sold the doves, "Take these things out of here! Don't make my Father's house a marketplace!"

His disciples remembered that it was written, "Zeal for your house will eat me up."

The Jews, therefore, answered him, "What sign do you show us, seeing that you do these things?"

Jesus answered them, "Destroy this temple, and in three days, I will raise it up."

The Jews, therefore, said, "It took forty-six years to build this temple! Will you raise it up in three days?"

But he spoke of the temple of his body. When he was raised from the dead, his disciples remembered that he said this, and they believed the Scripture, and the word which Jesus had said.

Now, when he was in Jerusalem at the Passover, during the feast, many believed in his name, observing his signs, which he did.

But Jesus didn't trust himself to them because he knew everyone and didn't need anyone to testify concerning man, for he knew what was in man.

Jesus met and talked with Nicodemus
Jn 3:1-21

Now, there was a man of the Pharisees named Nicodemus, a ruler of the Jews.

He came to Jesus by night and said to him, "Rabbi, we know that you are a teacher who has come from God, for no one can do these signs that you do, unless God is with him."

Jesus answered him, "Most certainly, I tell you, unless one is born anew, he can't see the Kingdom of God."

Nicodemus said to him, "How can a man be born when he is old? Can he enter a second time into his mother's womb and be born?"

Jesus answered, "Most certainly I tell you, unless one is born of water and spirit, he can't enter into the Kingdom of God! That which is born of the flesh is flesh. That which is born of the Spirit is Spirit. Don't marvel that I said to you, you must be born anew.' The wind blows where it wants to, and you hear its sound but don't know where it comes from and where it is going. So is everyone who is born of the Spirit."

Nicodemus answered him, "How can these things be?"

Jesus answered him, "Are you the teacher of Israel and don't understand these things? Most certainly, I tell you, we speak that which we know and testify that which we have seen, and you don't receive our witness. If I told you earthly things and you don't believe it, how will you believe if I tell you heavenly things? No one has ascended into heaven, but he who descended out of heaven, the Son of Man, who is in heaven.

As Moses lifted up the serpent in the wilderness, even so must the Son of Man be lifted up, that whoever believes in him should not perish but have eternal life.

For God so loved the world, that he gave his one and only Son, that whoever believes in Him should not perish, but have eternal life. For God didn't send His Son into the world to judge the world, but that the world should be saved through Him. He who believes in Him is not judged. He who doesn't believe has been judged already because he has not believed in the name of God's one and only Son. This is the judgment that the light has come into the world, and men loved the darkness rather than the light, for their works were evil.

For everyone who does evil hates the light and doesn't come to the light, lest his works would be exposed. But he who does the truth comes to the light, that his works may be revealed, that they have been done in God."

The disciples of Jesus did baptizing
Jn 3:22-36

After these things, Jesus came with his disciples into the land of Judea. He stayed there with them and baptized them.

John was also baptized in Enon near Salim because there was a lot of water there. They came and were baptized.

For John had not yet been thrown into prison.

There arose, therefore, a questioning on the part of John's disciples with some Jews about purification.

They came to John and said to him, "Rabbi, he who was with you beyond the Jordan, to whom you have testified, behold, the same baptizes, and everyone is coming to him."

John answered, "A man can receive nothing unless it has been given him from heaven. You yourselves testify that I said, I am not the Christ,' but I have been sent before him.'

He who has the bride is the bridegroom, but the friend of the bridegroom, who stands and hears him, rejoices greatly because of the bridegroom's voice. This, my joy, therefore, is made full. He must increase, but I must decrease. He who comes from above is above all. He who is from the earth belongs to the earth and speaks of the earth. He who comes from heaven is above all. He testifies what he has seen and heard; no one receives his witness. He who has received his witness has set his seal to this, that God is true.

For he whom God has sent speaks the words of God; for God gives the Spirit without measure. The Father loves the Son and has given all things into his hand. One who believes in the Son has eternal life, but one who disobeys the Son won't see life, but the wrath of God remains on him."

Jesus met and talked with the Samaritan woman Jn 4:1-42

Therefore, when the Lord knew that the Pharisees had heard that Jesus was making and baptizing more disciples than John (although Jesus himself didn't baptize, but his disciples), he left Judea and departed into Galilee. He needed to pass through Samaria.

So he came to a city of Samaria, called Sychar, near the parcel of ground that Jacob gave to his son, Joseph. Jacob's well was there. Therefore, being tired from his journey, Jesus sat down by the well. It was about the sixth hour. A woman from Samaria came to draw water.

Jesus said to her, "Give me a drink."

For his disciples had gone away into the city to buy food.
The Samaritan woman, therefore, said to him, "How is it that you, being a Jew, ask for a drink from me, a Samaritan woman?" (For Jews have no dealings with Samaritans.)

Jesus answered her, "If you knew the gift of God, and who it is who says to you, Give me a drink,' you would have asked him, and he would have given you living water."

The woman said to him, "Sir, you have nothing to draw with, and the well is deep. From where, then, have you that living water? Are you greater than our father, Jacob, who gave us the well and drank of it himself, as did his children and his livestock?"

Jesus answered her, "Everyone who drinks of this water will thirst again, but whoever drinks of the water that I will give him will never thirst again; but the water that I will give him will become in him a well of water springing up to eternal life."

The woman said to him, "Sir, give me this water so that I don't get thirsty, nor come all the way here to draw."

Jesus said to her, "Go, call your husband, and come here."

The woman answered, "I have no husband."

Jesus said to her, "You said well, 'I have no husband,' for you have had five husbands, and he whom you now have is not your husband. This you have said truly."

The woman told him, "Sir, I perceive you as a prophet. Our fathers worshiped in this mountain, and you Jews say that in Jerusalem is the place where people ought to worship."

Jesus said to her, "Woman, believe me, the hour comes when neither in this mountain nor in Jerusalem will you worship the Father. You worship that which you don't know.

We worship that which we know, for salvation is from the Jews. But the hour comes, and now is when the true worshipers will worship the Father in spirit and truth, for the Father seeks such to be his worshipers. God is spirit, and those who worship him must worship in spirit and truth."

The woman said to him, "I know that Messiah comes" (he who is called Christ). "When he comes, he will declare to us all things."

Jesus said to her, "I am He, the One who speaks to you."

At this, his disciples came. They marveled that he was speaking with a woman, yet no one said, "What are you looking for?" or, "Why do you speak with her?"

So the woman left her water pot and went away into the city and said to the people,

"Come, see a man who told me everything that I did. Can this be the Christ?"

They went out of the city and were coming to him. Meanwhile, the disciples urged him, saying, "Rabbi, eat."

But he said to them, "I have food to eat that you don't know about."

The disciples, therefore, said to one another, "Has anyone brought him something to eat?"

Jesus said to them, "My food is to do the will of him who sent me and to accomplish his work. Don't you say there are yet four months until the harvest?' Behold, I tell you, lift up your eyes and look at the fields, which are already white for harvest. He who reaps receives wages and gathers fruit for eternal life; that both he who sows and he who reaps may rejoice together. The saying is true in this: One sows, and another reaps.' I sent you to reap that for which you haven't labored. Others have labored, and you have entered into their labor."

From that city, many of the Samaritans believed in him because of the word of the woman, who testified, "He told me everything that I did."

So when the Samaritans came to Him, they begged Him to stay with them. He stayed there for two days. Many more believed because of His word.

They said to the woman, "Now we believe, not because of your speaking; for we have heard for ourselves, and know that this is indeed the Christ, the Savior of the world."

Jesus healed the son of a royal official, His second miracle
Jn 4:43-54

After two days, he left and went into Galilee. Jesus himself testified that a prophet has no honor in his own country. So, when he came into Galilee, the Galileans received him, having seen all the things that he did in Jerusalem, at the feast, for they also went to the feast. Jesus came, therefore, again to Cana of Galilee, where he made the water into wine.

There was a certain nobleman whose son was sick at Capernaum. When he heard that Jesus had come out of Judea into Galilee, he went to him and begged him that he would come down and heal his son, for he was at the point of death.

Jesus, therefore, said to him, "Unless you see signs and wonders, you will in no way believe."

The nobleman said to him, "Sir, come down before my child dies."

Jesus said to him, "Go your way. Your son lives."

The man believed the word that Jesus spoke to him, and he went his way. As he went down, his servants met him and reported, saying, "Your child lives!"

So he inquired about them the hour when he began to get better. They said, therefore, to him, "Yesterday at the seventh hour, the fever left him."

So, the father knew that it was at that hour in which Jesus said to him, "Your son lives."

He believed, as did his whole house. This is again the second sign that Jesus did, having come out of Judea into Galilee.

The Healing at the Pool
Jn 5:1-15

After these things, there was a feast for the Jews, and Jesus went up to Jerusalem. Now, in Jerusalem, by the sheep gate, there is a pool, which is called in Hebrew, "Bethesda," having five porches. In these lay a great multitude of those who were sick, blind, lame, or paralyzed, waiting for the moving of the water, for an angel went down at certain times into the pool and stirred up the water. Whoever stepped in first after the stirring of the water was healed of whatever disease he had.

A certain man was there, who had been sick for thirty-eight years. When Jesus saw him lying there and knew that he had been sick for a long time, He asked him, "Do you want to be made well?"

The sick man answered him, "Sir, I have no one to put me into the pool when the water is stirred up, but while I'm coming, another steps down before me."

Jesus said to him, "Arise, take up your mat, and walk."

Immediately, the man was made well and took up his mat and walked.

Now, it was the Sabbath on that day.

So the Jews said to him who was cured, "It is the Sabbath. It is not lawful for you to carry the mat."

He answered them, "He who made me well, the same said to me, Take up your mat, and walk.'"

Then they asked him, "Who is the man who said to you, Take up your mat and walk?"

But he who was healed didn't know who it was, for Jesus had withdrawn, a crowd being in the place.

Afterward, Jesus found him in the temple and said to him, "Behold, you are made well. Sin no more so that nothing worse happens to you."

The man went away and told the Jews that it was Jesus who had made him well.

The Authority of the Son
Jn 5: 16-30

For this cause, the Jews persecuted Jesus and sought to kill him because he did these things on the Sabbath. But Jesus answered them, "My Father is still working, so I am working, too."

For this cause, the Jews sought all the more to kill him because he not only broke the Sabbath but also called God his own Father, making Himself equal with God.

Jesus, therefore, answered them, "Most certainly, I tell you, the Son can do nothing of Himself but what He sees the Father doing. For whatever things He does, the Son also does likewise. For the Father has affection for the Son and shows Him all things that He Himself does. He will show Him greater works than these, that you may marvel.

For as the Father raises the dead and gives them life, even so, the Son also gives life to whom He desires. For the Father judges no one, but he has given all judgment to the Son, that all may honor the Son, even as they honor the Father. He who doesn't honor the Son doesn't honor the Father who sent Him.

"Most certainly, I tell you, he who hears my word and believes Him who sent me has eternal life and doesn't come into judgment but has passed out of death into life.

Most certainly, I tell you, the hour comes, and now is when the dead will hear the Son of God's voice, and those who hear will live, for as the Father has life in himself. Even so, he gave to the Son also to have life in himself. He also gave him the authority to execute judgment because he was a son of man. Don't marvel at this, for the hour comes, in which all that are in the tombs will hear his voice and will come out; those who have done good, to the resurrection of life; and those who have done evil, to the resurrection of judgment.

I can, of myself, do nothing. As I hear, I judge, and my judgment is righteous because I don't seek my own will but the will of my Father who sent me.

Testimonies About Jesus
Jn 5:31-47

"If I testify about myself, my witness is not valid. It is another who testifies about me. I know that the testimony that he testifies about me is true. You have sent to John, and he has testified to the truth. But the testimony that I received was not from a man. However, I say these things so that you may be saved. He was the burning and shining lamp, and you were willing to rejoice for a while in his light. But my testimony is greater than that of John, for the works which the Father gave me to accomplish, the very works that I do, testify about me, that the Father has sent me. The Father himself, who sent me, has testified about me. You have neither heard his voice at any time nor seen his form.

You don't have his word living in you because you don't believe him whom he sent.

"You search the Scriptures because you think that in them you have eternal life, and these are they which testify about me. Yet you will not come to me, that you may have life.

I don't receive glory from men. But I know that you don't have God's love in yourselves. I have come in my Father's name, and you don't receive me. If another comes in his own name, you will receive him. How can you believe those who receive glory from one another, and you don't seek the glory that comes from the only God?

"Don't think that I will accuse you before the Father. There is one who accuses you, even Moses, on whom you have set your hope. For if you believed Moses, you would believe me, for he wrote about me. But if you don't believe his writings, how will you believe my words?"

Jesus was tempted by the devil
Mt 4:1-11/Mk 1:12-13/ Lk 4:1-13

Then Jesus was led up by the Spirit into the wilderness to be tempted by the devil. He was hungry afterward when he had fasted forty days and forty nights.

The tempter came and said to him, "If you are the Son of God, command that these stones become bread."

But he answered, "It is written, Man shall not live by bread alone, but by every word that proceeds out of the mouth of God."

Then, the devil took him into the holy city. He set him on the temple's pinnacle and said, "If you are the Son of God, throw yourself down, for it is written, He will put his angels in charge of you.' And on their hands, they will bear you up so that you don't dash your foot against a stone.'"

Jesus said to him, "Again, it is written, You shall not test the Lord, your God.'"

Again, the devil took Him to an exceedingly high mountain and showed Him all the kingdoms of the world and their glory. He told him, "I will give you all of these things if you fall down and worship me."

Then Jesus said to him, "Get behind me, Satan! For it is written, You shall worship the Lord your God, and you shall serve Him only.'"

Then the devil left Him, and behold, angels came and served Him.

Editor Footnote: The disciples waited a few days after Jesus went to the wilderness. They didn't see Jesus return, and they went back to their home.

Chapter Four:
Jesus called the Disciples back

Jesus was teaching in the Synagogues
Lk 4:14-30

Jesus returned in the power of the Spirit into Galilee, and news about Him spread through all the surrounding area. He taught in their synagogues, being glorified by all. He came to Nazareth, where He had been brought up. He entered, as was his custom, into the synagogue on the Sabbath day, and stood up to read. The book of the prophet Isaiah was handed to him. He opened the book and found the place where it was written.

"The Spirit of the Lord is on me,

because he has anointed me

to preach good news to the poor.

He sent me to heal the broken-hearted,

to proclaim release to the captives,

recovering sight to the blind,

to deliver those who are crushed,

and to proclaim the acceptable year of the Lord."

He closed the book, gave it back to the attendant, and sat down. The eyes of all in the synagogue were fastened on him. He began to tell them, "Today, this Scripture has been fulfilled in your hearing."

All testified about him, and wondered at the gracious words which proceeded out of his mouth, and they said, "Isn't this Joseph's son?"

He said to them, "Doubtless you will tell me this parable, Physician, heal yourself! Whatever we have heard done at Capernaum, do also here in your hometown.'"

He said, "Most certainly I tell you, no prophet is acceptable in his hometown. But truly I tell you, there were many widows in Israel in the days of Elijah, when the sky was shut for three years and six months, when a great famine came over all the land. Elijah was sent to none of them, except to Zarephath, in the land of Sidon, to a woman who was a widow. There were many lepers in Israel in the time of Elisha the prophet, yet not one of them was cleansed, except Naaman, the Syrian."

They were all filled with wrath in the synagogue, as they heard these things. They rose up, threw him out of the city, and led him to the brow of the hill on which their city was built, hoping they might throw him off the cliff. But he, passing through their midst, went his way.

Jesus ordered the Impure Spirit to come out
Lk 4:31-37

He came down to Capernaum, a city of Galilee. He was teaching them on the Sabbath day, and they were astonished at his teaching, for his word was with authority. In the synagogue, there was a man who had a spirit of an unclean demon, and he cried out with a loud voice, saying, "Ah! What have we to do with you, Jesus of Nazareth? Have you come to destroy us? I know who you are: the Holy One of God!"

Jesus rebuked him, saying, "Be silent, and come out of him!"

When the demon had thrown him down in their midst, he came out of him, having done him no harm.

Amazement came on all, and they spoke together, one with another, saying, "What is this word? For with authority and power he commands the unclean spirits, and they come out!"

News about him went out into every place of the surrounding region.

John the Baptist was put in Prison by Herod
Lk 3:19-20

But Herod the tetrarch, being reproved by him for Herodias, his brother's wife, and for all the evil things Herod had done, added this to them all, that he shut up John in prison.

Jesus went to Galilee
Mt 4:12-17 / Mk 1:14-15

Now when Jesus heard that John was delivered up, he withdrew into Galilee. Leaving Nazareth, he came and lived in Capernaum, which is by the sea, in the region of Zebulun and Naphtali, that it might be fulfilled which was spoken through Isaiah the prophet, saying,

"The land of Zebulun and the land of Naphtali,

toward the sea, beyond the Jordan,

Galilee of the Gentiles,

The people who sat in darkness saw a great light,

to those who sat in the region and shadow of death,

to them light has dawned."

From that time, Jesus began to preach, and to say, "Repent! For the Kingdom of Heaven is at hand."

Jesus called Peter, Andrew, James and John
Lk 5:1-11 / Mt 4:18-22 / Mk 1:16-20

Now it happened, while the multitude pressed on him and heard the word of God, that he was standing by the lake of Gennesaret. He saw two boats standing by the lake, but the fishermen had gone out of them and were washing their nets. He entered one of the boats, which was Simon's, and asked him to put out a little from the land. He sat down and taught the multitudes from the boat.

When he had finished speaking, he said to Simon, "Put out into the deep, and let down your nets for a catch."

Simon answered him, "Master, we worked all night and took nothing; but at your word I will let down the net."

When they had done this, they caught a great multitude of fish, and their net was breaking. They beckoned to their partners in the other boat, and they came and helped them. They came, and filled both boats, so that they began to sink. But Simon Peter, when he saw it, fell down at Jesus' knees, saying, "Depart from me, for I am a sinful man, Lord."

For he was amazed, and all who were with him, at the catch of fish which they had caught; and so also were James and John, sons of Zebedee, who were partners with Simon.

Jesus said to Simon, "Don't be afraid. From now on, you will be catching people alive."

When they had brought their boats to land, they left everything and followed him.

Going on from there, he saw two other brothers, James the son of Zebedee, and John his brother, in the boat with Zebedee, their father, mending their nets.

He called them. They immediately left the boat and their father and followed him.

Jesus casted out the Demon Processed Man
Mk 1:21-27

They went into Capernaum, and immediately on the Sabbath day he entered the synagogue and taught. They were astonished at his teaching, for he taught them as having authority, and not as the scribes. Immediately, a man with an unclean spirit was in their synagogue, and he cried out, saying, "Ha! What do we have to do with you, Jesus, you Nazarene? Have you come to destroy us? I know who you are: the Holy One of God!"

Jesus rebuked him, saying, "Be quiet, and come out of him!"

The unclean spirit, convulsing him and crying with a loud voice, came out of him.

They were all amazed, so that they questioned among themselves, saying, "What is this? A new teaching? For with authority he commands even the unclean spirits, and they obey him!"

Jesus healed Peter's Mother-in-Law
Mk 1:28-31 / Mt 8"14-15 / Lk 4:38-39

The report went out immediately everywhere into all the regions of Galilee and its surrounding area. Immediately, when they had come out of the synagogue, they came into the house of Simon and Andrew, with James and John. Now Simon's wife's mother lay sick with a fever, and immediately they told him about her. He came and took her by the hand and raised her up. The fever left her, and she served them.

Jesus healed People and drove out Demons and healed the Sicks
Mk 1:32-34 / Mt 8:16-17 / Mt 4:23-25 / Lk 4:40-44

In the evening, when the sun had set, they brought to him all who were sick, and those who were possessed by demons. All the city was gathered at the door. He healed many who were sick with various diseases and cast out many demons. He didn't allow the demons to speak, because they knew him.

That it might be fulfilled which was spoken through Isaiah the prophet, who said: "He took our infirmities, and bore our diseases."

Jesus went about in all Galilee, teaching in their synagogues, preaching the Good News of the Kingdom, and healing every disease and every sickness among the people.

The report about him went out all over Syria.

They brought to him all who were sick, afflicted with various diseases and torments, possessed by demons, epileptics, and paralytics; and he healed them. Great multitudes from Galilee, Decapolis, Jerusalem, Judea, and from beyond the Jordan followed him.

When the sun was setting, all those who were sick with various diseases were brought to him; and he laid his hands on every one of them and he healed them. Demons also came out of many, crying out, and saying, "You are the Christ, the Son of God!"

Rebuking them, he didn't allow them to speak, because they knew that he was the Christ. When it was day, he departed and went into an uninhabited place, and the multitudes looked for him, and came to him, and held on to him, so that he wouldn't go away from them.

But he said to them, "I must preach the good news of the Kingdom of God to the other cities also. For this reason, I have been sent."

He was preaching in the synagogues of Galilee.

Jesus went to Pray Alone
Mk 1:35-39

Early in the morning, while it was still dark, He rose up and went out, and departed into a deserted place, and prayed there. Simon and those who were with Him followed after Him; and they found Him, and told Him, "Everyone is looking for you."

He said to them, "Let's go elsewhere into the next towns, that I may preach there also, because I came out for this reason."

He went into their synagogues throughout all Galilee, preaching and casting out demons.

Jesus healed a Leper Man
Mk 1:40-45 / Lk 5:12-16 / Mt 8:1-4

A leper came to him, begging Him, kneeling down, and saying, "If you want to, you can make me clean."

Being moved with compassion, He stretched out His hand, and touched him, and said to him, "I want to. Be clean."

When He said this, the leprosy immediately departed from him, and he was made clean. He strictly warned him, and immediately sent him out, and said, "See you say nothing to anybody, but go show yourself to the priest, and offer for your cleansing the things which Moses commanded, for a testimony to them."

But he went out, and began to proclaim it much, and spread the matter so that Jesus could no more openly enter into a city but was outside in desert places: and they came to Him from everywhere.

Jesus healed the Paralyzed Man
Mk 2:1-12 / Lk 5:17-26 / Mt 9:1-8

When He entered Capernaum again after some days, it was heard that He was in the house. Immediately, many were gathered together, so that there was no more room, not even around the door; and He spoke the word to them. Four people came, carrying a paralytic to Him. When they could not come near to Him because of the crowd, they removed the roof where He was. When they broke it up, they let down the mat that the paralytic was lying on.

Jesus, seeing their faith, said to the paralytic, "Son, your sins are forgiven."

But some of the scribes were sitting there, and reasoning in their hearts, "Why does this man speak blasphemies like that? Who can forgive sins but God alone?"

Immediately Jesus, perceiving in his spirit that they so reasoned within themselves, said to them, "Why do you reason these things in your hearts? Which is easier, to tell the paralytic, your sins are forgiven; or to say, Arise, and take up your bed, and walk?' But that you may know that the Son of Man has authority on earth to forgive sins," he said to the paralytic

"I tell you, arise, take up your mat, and go to your house."

He arose, immediately took up the mat, and went out in front of them all; so that they were all amazed. He glorified God, saying, "We never saw anything like this!"

Jesus called Levi, the Tax Collector
Mk 2:13-17 / Lk 5:27-32 / Mt 9:9-13

He went out again to the seaside. All the multitude came to Him, and He taught them. As He passed by, He saw Levi, the son of Alphaeus, sitting at the tax office, and He said to him, "Follow me." And he arose and followed Him.

It happened that he was reclining at the table in his house, and many tax collectors and sinners sat down with Jesus and His disciples, for there were many, and they followed Him.

The scribes and the Pharisees saw that He was eating with the sinners and tax collectors. They said to His disciples, "Why is it that He eats and drinks with tax collectors and sinners?"

When Jesus heard it, He said to them, "Those who are healthy have no need for a physician, but those who are sick. I came not to call the righteous, but sinners to repentance."

But you go and learn what this means: I desire mercy, and not sacrifice, 'for I came not to call the righteous, but sinners to repentance."

Question about Fasting
Lk 5:33-39 / Mk 2:18-22 / Mt 9:14-17

They said to him, "Why do John's disciples often fast and pray, likewise also the disciples of the Pharisees, but yours eat and drink?"

He said to them, "Can you make the friends of the bridegroom fast, while the bridegroom is with them? But the days will come when the bridegroom will be taken away from them. Then they will fast in those days."

He also told a parable to them. "No one puts a piece from a new garment on an old garment, or else he will tear the new, and also the piece from the new will not match the old. No one puts new wine into old wineskins, or else the new wine will burst the skin, and it will be spilled, and the skins will be destroyed. But new wine must be put into fresh wineskins, and both are preserved. No man having drunk old wine immediately desires new, for he says, the old is better.'"

Jesus Is Lord of the Sabbath
Mt 12:1-14 / Mk 2:23-28 & Mk 3:1-6 / Lk 6:1-12

Jesus went on the Sabbath day through the grain fields at that time. His disciples were hungry and began to pluck heads of grain and to eat.

But the Pharisees, when they saw it, said to Him, "Behold, your disciples do what is not lawful to do on the Sabbath."

But He said to them, "Haven't you read what David did, when he was hungry, and those who were with him; how he entered into God's house, and ate the show bread, which was not lawful for him to eat, neither for those who were with him, but only for the priests? Or have you not read in the law that on the Sabbath day, the priests in the temple profane the Sabbath and are guiltless? But I tell you that one greater than the temple is here. But if you had known what this means, I desire mercy, and not sacrifice,' you would not have condemned the guiltless. For the Son of Man is Lord of the Sabbath."

He departed there and went into their synagogue.

And behold, there was a man with a withered hand. They asked him, "Is it lawful to heal on the Sabbath day?" that they might accuse Him.

He said to them, "What man is there among you, who has one sheep, and if this one falls into a pit on the Sabbath day, won't he grab on to it, and lift it out? How much more value is a man than a sheep! Therefore, it is lawful to do good on the Sabbath day."

Then He told the man, "Stretch out your hand."

He stretched it out, and it was restored whole, just like the other. But the Pharisees went out, and conspired against Him, to find out how they might destroy Him.

Jesus taught People and drove out Demon
Mk 3:7-12 / Lk 6:17-19

Jesus withdrew to the sea with His disciples, and a great multitude followed Him from Galilee, Judea, Jerusalem, Idumaea, beyond the Jordan, and those from around Tyre and Sidon. Hearing what great things He did, a great multitude came to Him.

He told His disciples that a little boat should stay near Him because of the crowd, so that they wouldn't press on Him, for he had healed many, so that as many as had diseases pressed on Him that they might touch Him. Whenever the unclean spirits saw Him, they fell down before Him, and cried, "You are the Son of God!"

He sternly warned them that they should not make Him known.

The Twelve Disciples of Jesus
Mk 3:13-19 / Lk 6:13-16

He went up into the mountain, and called to Himself those whom He wanted, and they went to Him. He appointed twelve, that they might be with Him, and that He might send them out to preach, and to have authority to heal sicknesses and to cast out demons:

Simon, to whom he gave the name Peter; James the son of Zebedee; John, the brother of James, and He called them Boanerges, which means, Sons of Thunder; Andrew; Philip; Bartholomew; Matthew; Thomas; James, the son of Alphaeus; Thaddaeus; Simon the Zealot; and Judas Iscariot, who also betrayed Him.

Chapter Five:
Sermon on the Mount

The Beatitudes
Mt 5:1-12 / Lk 6:20-26

Seeing the multitudes, He went up onto the mountain. When He had sat down, His disciples came to Him. He opened His mouth and taught them, saying,

"Blessed are the poor in spirit,

for theirs is the Kingdom of Heaven.

Blessed are those who mourn,

for they shall be comforted.

Blessed are the gentle,

for they shall inherit the earth.

Blessed are those who hunger

and thirst after righteousness,

for they shall be filled.

Blessed are the merciful, for they shall obtain mercy.

Blessed are the pure in heart, for they shall see God.

Blessed are the peacemakers,

for they shall be called children of God.

Blessed are those who have been persecuted

for righteousness' sake,

for theirs is the Kingdom of Heaven.

"Blessed are you when people reproach you, persecute you, and say all kinds of evil against you falsely, for my sake.

Rejoice, and be exceedingly glad,

for great is your reward in heaven.

For that is how they persecuted the prophets

who were before you.

"But woe to you who are rich!

For you have received your consolation. Woe to you, you who are full now, for you will be hungry.

Woe to you who laugh now, for you will mourn and weep. Woe, when men speak well of you, for their fathers did the same thing to the false prophets.

Salt and Light
Mt 5:13-16 / Mk 4:21-25

"You are the salt of the earth, but if the salt has lost its flavor, with what will it be salted? It is then good for nothing, but to be cast out and trodden under the feet of men. You are the light of the world. A city located on a hill can't be hidden. Neither do you light a lamp, and put it under a measuring basket, but on a stand; and it shines to all who are in the house.

Even so, let your light shine before men; that they may see your good works, and glorify your Father who is in heaven.

He said to them, "Take heed what you hear. With whatever measure you measure, it will be measured to you, and more will be given to you who hear. For whoever has, to him will more be given, and he who doesn't have, even that which he has, will be taken away from him."

The Fulfillment of the Law
Mt 5:17-20

"Don't think that I came to destroy the law or the prophets. I didn't come to destroy, but to fulfill. For most certainly, I tell you, until heaven and earth pass away, not even one smallest letter or one tiny pen stroke shall in any way pass away from the law, until all things are accomplished. Whoever, therefore, shall break one of these least commandments, and teach others to do so, shall be called least in the Kingdom of Heaven; but whoever shall do and teach them shall be called great in the Kingdom of Heaven. For I tell you that unless your righteousness exceeds that of the scribes and Pharisees, there is no way you will enter into the Kingdom of Heaven.

Murder
Mt 5:21-26

"You have heard that it was said to the ancient ones, You shall not murder,' and whoever shall murder shall be in danger of the judgment.' But I tell you, that everyone who is angry with his brother without a cause shall be in danger of the judgment; and whoever shall say to his brother, Raca!' shall be in danger of the council; and whoever shall say, You fool!' shall be in danger of the fire of Gehenna.

"If therefore you are offering your gift at the altar, and remember that your brother has anything against you, leave your gift there before the altar, and go your way. First be reconciled to your brother and then come and offer your gift. Agree with your adversary quickly, while you are with him on the way; lest perhaps the prosecutor deliver you to the judge, and the judge deliver you to the officer, and you be cast into prison. Most certainly I tell you, you shall by no means leave, until you have paid the last penny.

Adultery
Mt 5:27-30

"You have heard that it was said, You shall not commit adultery.' But I tell you that everyone who gazes at a woman to lust after her has committed adultery with her already in his heart. If your right eye causes you to stumble, pluck it out and throw it away from you. For it is more profitable for you that one of your members should perish, than for your whole body to be cast into Gehenna. If your right hand causes you to stumble, cut it off, and throw it away from you. For it is more profitable for you that one of your members should perish, than for your whole body to be cast into Gehenna.

Divorce
Mt 5:31-32

"It was also said, whoever shall put away his wife, let him give her a writing of divorce.' But I tell you that whoever puts away his wife, except for the cause of sexual immorality, makes her an adulteress; and whoever marries her when she is put away commits adultery.

Oaths
Mt 5:33-37

"Again you have heard that it was said to them of old time, You shall not make false vows, but shall perform to the Lord your vows,' but I tell you, don't swear at all: neither by heaven, for it is the throne of God; nor by the earth, for it is the footstool of his feet; nor by Jerusalem, for it is the city of the great King. Neither shall you swear with your head, for you can't make one hair white or black. But let your Yes' be Yes' and your No' be No.' Whatever is more than these is of the evil one.

Love for Enemies
Mt 5:38-48 / Lk 6:27-36

"You have heard that it was said, An eye for an eye, and a tooth for a tooth.' But I tell you, don't resist him who is evil; but whoever strikes you on your right cheek, turn to him the other also. If anyone sues you to take away your coat, let him have your cloak also. Whoever compels you to go one mile, go with him two. Give to him who asks you, and don't turn away him who desires to borrow from you.

"But I tell you who hear; love your enemies, do good to those who hate you, bless those who curse you, and pray for those who mistreat you. Give to everyone who asks you, and don't ask him who takes away your goods to give them back again.

"As you would like people to do to you, do exactly so to them. If you love those who love you, what credit is that to you? For even sinners love those who love them. If you do good to those who do good to you, what credit is that to you? For even sinners do the same.

If you lend to those from whom you hope to receive, what credit is that to you? Even sinners lend to sinners, to receive back as much.

But love your enemies, and do good, and lend, expecting nothing back; and your reward will be great, and you will be children of the Most High; for he is kind toward the unthankful and evil. "Therefore, be merciful, even as your Father is also merciful. Therefore, you shall be perfect, just as your Father in heaven is perfect."

Giving to the Needy
Mt 6:1-4

"Be careful that you don't do your charitable giving before men, to be seen by them, or else you have no reward from your Father who is in heaven. Therefore, when you do merciful deeds, don't sound a trumpet before yourself, as the hypocrites do in the synagogues and in the streets, that they may get glory from men. Most certainly I tell you, they have received their reward. But when you do merciful deeds, don't let your left hand know what your right hand does, so that your merciful deeds may be in secret, then your Father who sees in secret will reward you openly.

Prayer
Mt 6:5-15 / Lk 11:1-4

"When you pray, you shall not be as the hypocrites, for they love to stand and pray in the synagogues and in the corners of the streets, that they may be seen by men. Most certainly, I tell you, they have received their reward. But you, when you pray, enter into your inner room, and having shut your door, pray to your Father who is in secret, and your Father who sees in secret will reward you openly. In praying, don't use vain repetitions, as the Gentiles do; for they think that they will be heard for their much speaking. Therefore, don't be like them, for your Father knows what things you need, before you ask Him.

Pray like this: Our Father in heaven,

May your name be kept holy.

Let your Kingdom come.

Let your will be done, as in heaven, so on earth.

Give us today our daily bread.

Forgive us our debts, as we also forgive our debtors.
Bring us not into temptation,

but deliver us from the evil one.

For yours is the Kingdom, the power,

and the glory forever. Amen.

"For if you forgive men their trespasses, your heavenly Father will also forgive you. But if you don't forgive men their trespasses, neither will your Father forgive your trespasses.

Fasting
Mt 6:16-18

"Moreover, when you fast, don't be like the hypocrites, with sad faces. For they disfigure their faces, that they may be seen by men to be fasting. Most certainly I tell you, they have received their reward. But you, when you fast, anoint your head, and wash your face; so that you are not seen by men to be fasting, but by your Father who is in secret, and your Father, who sees in secret, will reward you.

Treasures in Heaven and the Lamp of the Body
Mt 6:19-24 / Lk 11: 33-36

"Don't lay up treasures for yourselves on the earth, where moth and rust consume, and where thieves break through and steal; but lay up for yourselves treasures in heaven, where neither moth nor rust consume, and where thieves don't break through and steal; Where your treasure is, there your heart will be also."

"The lamp of the body is the eye. If therefore your eye is sound, your whole body will be full of light. But if your eye is evil, your whole body will be full of darkness. If therefore the light that is in you is darkness, how great is the darkness! No one can serve two masters, for either he will hate the one and love the other; or else he will be devoted to one and despise the other. You can't serve both God and Mammon."

Do Not Worry
Mt 6:25-34 / Lk 12:22-34

He said to his disciples, "Therefore I tell you, don't be anxious for your life, what you will eat, nor yet for your body, what you will wear. Life is more than food, and the body is more than clothing. Consider the ravens: they don't sow, they don't reap, they have no warehouse or barn, and God feeds them. How much more valuable are you than birds!"

"Which of you, by being anxious, can add one moment to his lifespan? If then you aren't able to do even the least things, why are you anxious about the rest? Why are you anxious about clothing? Consider the lilies of the field, how they grow. They don't toil, neither do they spin, yet I tell you that even Solomon in all His glory was not dressed like one of these.

But if God so clothes the grass of the field, which today exists, and tomorrow is thrown into the oven, won't He much more clothe you, you of little faith?

"Therefore don't be anxious, saying, What will we eat?', What will we drink?' or, With what will we be clothed?'

Don't seek what you will eat or what you will drink; neither be anxious. For the Gentiles seek after all these things; for your heavenly Father knows that you need all these things. But seek first God's Kingdom, and His righteousness; and all these things will be given to you as well.

Therefore, don't be anxious for tomorrow, for tomorrow will be anxious for itself. Each day's own evil is sufficient. Don't be afraid, little flock, for it is your Father's good pleasure to give you the Kingdom.

Sell that which you have, and give gifts to the needy. Make for yourselves purses which don't grow old, a treasure in the heavens that doesn't fail, where no thief approaches, neither moth destroys. For where your treasure is, there will your heart be also.

Do not Judge
Lk 6:37-47 / Mt 7:1-6

Don't judge, and you won't be judged. Don't condemn, and you won't be condemned. Set free, and you will be set free.

"Give, and it will be given to you: good measure, pressed down, shaken together, and running over, will be given to you. For with the same measure you measure it will be measured back to you."

He spoke a parable to them. "Can the blind guide the blind? Won't they both fall into a pit?

A disciple is not above his teacher, but everyone, when he is fully trained, will be like his teacher. Why do you see the speck of chaff that is in your brother's eye, but don't consider the beam that is in your own eye? Or how can you tell your brother, Brother, let me remove the speck of chaff that is in your eye,' when you yourself don't see the beam that is in your own eye? You hypocrite! First remove the beam from your own eye, and then you can see clearly to remove the speck of chaff that is in your brother's eye. For there is no good tree that produces rotten fruit; nor again a rotten tree that produces good fruit. For each tree is known by its own fruit. For people don't gather figs from thorns, nor do they gather grapes from a bramble bush.

The good man out of the good treasure of his heart brings out that which is good, and the evil man out of the evil treasure of his heart brings out that which is evil, for out of the abundance of the heart, his mouth speaks.

"Don't give that which is holy to the dogs, neither throw your pearls before the pigs, lest perhaps they trample them under their feet, and turn and tear you to pieces.

"Why do you call me, Lord, Lord,' and don't do the things which I say? Everyone who comes to me, and hears my words, and does them, I will show you what he is like.

Ask, Seek, Knock
Lk 11:5-13 / Mt 7:7-12

He said to them, "Which of you, if you go to a friend at midnight, and tell him, Friend, lend me three loaves of bread, for a friend of mine has come to me from a journey, and I have nothing to set before him,' and he from within will answer and say, Don't bother me. The door is now shut, and my children are with me in bed. I can't get up and give it to you?

I tell you, although he will not rise and give it to him because he is his friend, yet because of his persistence, he will get up and give him as many as he needs.

"Ask, and it will be given to you. Seek, and you will find. Knock, and it will be opened for you.

For everyone who asks receives. He who seeks finds. To him who knocks it will be opened. Or who is there among you, who, if his son asks him for bread, will give him a stone?

Or if he asks for a fish, who will give him a serpent? If you then, being evil, know how to give good gifts to your children, how much more will your Father who is in heaven give good things to those who ask Him! Therefore, whatever you desire for men to do to you, you shall also do to them; for this is the law and the prophets.

The Narrow and Wide Gates
Mt 7: 13-14 / (Lk 13:22-35)

"Enter in by the narrow gate; for wide is the gate and broad is the way that leads to destruction, and many are those who enter in by it. How narrow is the gate, and restricted is the way that leads to life! Few are those who find it.

True and False Prophets
Mt 7:15-20

"Beware of false prophets, who come to you in sheep's clothing, but inwardly are ravening wolves. By their fruits you will know them. Do you gather grapes from thorns, or figs from thistles? Even so, every good tree produces good fruit; but the corrupt tree produces evil fruit. A good tree can't produce evil fruit, nor can a corrupt tree produce good fruit. Every tree that doesn't bear good fruit is cut down and thrown into the fire.

Therefore, by their fruits you will know them.

True and False Disciples
Mt 7:21-23

Not everyone who says to me, Lord, Lord,' will enter the Kingdom of Heaven; but he who does the will of my Father who is in heaven. Many will tell me on that day, Lord, Lord, didn't we prophecy in your name, in your name cast out demons, and in your name do many mighty works?' Then I will tell them, I never knew you. Depart from me, you who work iniquity.'

The Wise and Foolish Builders
Mt 7:24-29 / Lk 6:48-49

"Everyone therefore who hears these words of mine, and does them, I will liken him to a wise man, who built his house on a rock. The rain came down, the floods came, and the winds blew, and beat on that house; and it didn't fall, for it was founded on the rock.

Everyone who hears these words of mine, and doesn't do them, will be like a foolish man, who built his house on the sand. The rain came down, the floods came, and the winds blew, and beat on that house; and it fell and great was its fall." It happened, when Jesus had finished saying these things, that the multitudes were astonished at His teaching, for He taught them with authority, and not like the scribes.

Chapter Six:
Jesus Teaches About God Through Healing and Driving Out Demons

Jesus healed the servant of the Centurion
Lk 7: 1-10 / Mt 8:5-13

After He had finished speaking in the hearing of the people, He entered Capernaum. A certain centurion's servant, who was dear to him, was sick and at the point of death. When he heard about Jesus, he sent to him the elders of the Jews, asking Him to come and save his servant.

When they came to Jesus, they begged Him earnestly, saying, "He is worthy for you to do this for him, for he loves our nation, and he built our synagogue for us."

Jesus went with them. When He was now not far from the house, the centurion sent friends to him, saying to him, "Lord, don't trouble yourself, for I am not worthy for you to come under my roof. Therefore, I didn't even think myself worthy to come to you; but say the word, and my servant will be healed. For I also am a man placed under authority, having under myself soldiers. I tell this one, Go!' and he goes; and to another, come!' and he comes; and to my servant, do this,' and he does it."

When Jesus heard these things, he marveled at him and turned and said to the multitude who followed him, "I tell you, I have not found such great faith, no, not in Israel."

I tell you that many will come from the east and the west, and will sit down with Abraham, Isaac, and Jacob in the Kingdom of Heaven, but the children of the Kingdom will be thrown out into the outer darkness. There will be weeping and gnashing of teeth."

Jesus said to the centurion, "Go your way. Let it be done for you as you have believed."

His servant was healed at that hour.

Jesus Raises a Widow's Son
Lk 7:11-17

It happened soon afterwards that he went to a city called Nain. Many of His disciples, along with a great multitude, went with Him. Now, when He drew near to the gate of the city, behold, one who was dead was carried out, the only son of his mother, and she was a widow. Many people of the city were with her. When the Lord saw her, He had compassion on her, and said to her, He came near and touched the coffin, and the bearers stood still. He said, "Young man, I tell you, arise!"

He who was dead sat up and began to speak. And He gave him to his mother.

Fear took hold of all, and they glorified God, saying, "A great prophet has arisen among us!" and, "God has visited His people!"

This report went out concerning Him in the whole of Judea, and in all the surrounding regions.

Jesus and John the Baptist
Mt 11:1-19 / Lk 7:18-35

It happened that when Jesus had finished directing His twelve disciples, He departed from there to teach and preach in their cities. Now, when John heard in the prison the works of Christ, he sent two of his disciples and said to him, "Are you He who comes, or should we look for another?"

Jesus answered them, "Go and tell John the things which you hear and see: the blinds receive their sight, the lame walk, the lepers are cleansed, the deaf hear, the dead are raised up, and the poor have good news preached to them. Blessed is he who finds no occasion for stumbling in me."

As these went their way, Jesus began to say to the multitudes concerning John, "What did you go out into the wilderness to see? A reed shaken by the wind? But what did you go out to see? A man in soft clothing? Behold, those who wear soft clothing are in the king's houses.

But why did you go out? To see a prophet? Yes, I tell you, and much more than a prophet.

For this is he, of whom it is written, Behold, I send my messenger before your face, who will prepare your way before you.' Most certainly I tell you, among those who are born of women there has not arisen anyone greater than John the Baptizer; yet he who is least in the Kingdom of Heaven is greater than he. From the days of John the Baptizer until now, the Kingdom of Heaven suffers violence, and the violent take it by force, for all the prophets and the law prophesied until John. If you are willing to receive it, this is

Elijah, who is to come. He who has ears to hear, let him hear.

"But what shall I compare this generation? It is like children sitting in the marketplaces, who call to their companions and say, We played the flute for you, and you didn't dance. We mourned you, and you didn't lament.' For John came neither eating nor drinking, and they say, he has a demon.' The Son of Man came eating and drinking, and they say, Behold, a gluttonous man and a drunkard, a friend of tax collectors and sinners!' But wisdom is justified by her children."

Jesus Anointed by a Sinful Woman
Lk 7:36-50

One of the Pharisees invited Him to eat with him. He entered the Pharisee's house and sat at the table. Behold, a woman in the city who was a sinner, when she knew that He was reclining in the Pharisee's house, she brought an alabaster jar of ointment.

Standing behind, at his feet weeping, she began to wet His feet with her tears, and she wiped them with the hair of her head, kissed His feet, and anointed them with the ointment.

Now, when the Pharisee who had invited Him saw it, he said to himself, "This man, if he were a prophet, would have perceived who and what kind of woman this is who touches him, that she is a sinner."

Jesus answered him, "Simon, I have something to tell you."

He said, "Teacher, say on." "A certain lender had two debtors. The one owed five hundred denarii, and the other fifty. When they couldn't pay, he forgave them both. Which of them, therefore, will love him most?"

Simon answered, "He, I suppose, to whom he forgave the most."

He said to him, "You have judged correctly."

Turning to the woman, he said to Simon, "Do you see this woman? I entered your house, and you gave me no water for my feet, but she has wet my feet with her tears and wiped them with the hair of her head. You gave me no kiss, but she, since the time I came in, has not ceased to kiss my feet. You didn't anoint my head with oil, but she has anointed my feet with ointment. Therefore, I tell you, her sins, which are many, are forgiven, for she loved much. But to whom little is forgiven, the same loves little."

He said to her, "Your sins are forgiven."

Those who sat at the table with Him began to say to themselves, "Who is this who even forgives sins?"

He said to the woman, "Your faith has saved you. Go in peace."

Women who followed Jesus
Lk 8 :1-3

It happened soon afterwards that He went about through cities and villages, preaching and bringing the good news of the Kingdom of God. With Him were the twelve, and certain women who had been healed of evil spirits and infirmities:

Mary who was called Magdalene, from whom seven demons had gone out; and Joanna, the wife of Chuzas, Herod's steward; Susanna; and many others, who served them from their possessions.

The Parable of the Growing Seed
Mk 4:26-29 / Lk 8:16-18

He said, "The Kingdom of God is as if a man should cast seed on the earth, and should sleep and rise night and day, and the seed should spring up and grow, he doesn't know how. For the earth bears fruit: first the blade, then the ear, then the full grain in the ear. But when the fruit is ripe, immediately he puts in the sickle, because the harvest has come."

Mother and Brothers of Jesus
Mk 3:31-35 / Mt 12:46-50 / Lk 8:19-21

His mother and His brothers came, and standing outside, they sent to Him, calling Him. A multitude was sitting around Him, and they told Him, "Behold, your mother, your brothers, and your sisters are outside looking for you."

He answered them, "Who are my mother and my brothers?"

Looking around at those who sat around Him, He said, "Behold, my mother and my brothers! For whoever does the will of God, the same is my brother, and my sister, and my mother."

Jesus Calms the Storm
Mk 4:35-41 / Lk 8:22-25 / Mt 8:23-27

On that day, when evening had come, He said to them, "Let's go over to the other side."

Leaving the multitude, they took Him with them, even as He was, in the boat. Other small boats were also with Him. A big windstorm arose, and the waves beat into the boat, so much that the boat was already filled. He Himself was in the stern, asleep on the cushion, and they woke Him up, and told Him, "Teacher, don't you care that we are dying?"

He awoke, and rebuked the wind, and said to the sea, "Peace! Be still!" The wind ceased, and there was a great calm.

He said to them, "Why are you so afraid? How is it that you have no faith?"

They were greatly afraid, and said to one another, "Who then is this, that even the wind and the sea obey him?"

Jesus Restores a Demon-Possessed Man
Lk 8:26-39 / Mk 5:1-20 / Mt 8:28-34

They arrived at the country of the Gadarenes, which is opposite Galilee. When Jesus stepped ashore, a certain man out of the city who had demons for a long time met Him. He wore no clothes, and didn't live in a house, but in the tombs. When he saw Jesus, he cried out, and fell down before Him, and with a loud voice said, "What do I have to do with you, Jesus, you Son of the Most High God? I beg you, don't torment me!"

For Jesus was commanding the unclean spirit to come out of the man. For the unclean spirit had often seized the man. He was kept under guard and bound with chains and fetters. Breaking the bands apart, he was driven by the demon into the desert.

Jesus asked him, "What is your name?"

He said, "Legion," for many demons had entered into him. They begged Him that he would not command them to go into the abyss.

Now there was there a herd of many pigs feeding on the mountain, and they begged Him that he would allow them to enter into those. He allowed them.

The demons came out of the man, and entered into the pigs, and the herd rushed down the steep bank into the lake, and were drowned. When those who fed them saw what had happened, they fled and told it in the city and in the country.

People went out to see what had happened. They came to Jesus and found the man from whom the demons had gone out, sitting at Jesus' feet, clothed and in his right mind; and they were afraid. Those who saw it told them how he who had been possessed by demons was healed. All the people of the surrounding country of the Gadarenes asked Him to depart from them, for they were very much afraid. He entered into the boat and returned.

But the man from whom the demons had gone out begged Him that he might go with Him, but Jesus sent him away, saying, "Return to your house and declare what great things God has done for you."

He went his way, proclaiming throughout the whole city what great things Jesus had done for him.

Jesus Raises a Dead Girl and Heals a Sick Woman Mk 5:21-43 / Lk 8:40-56 / Mt 9:18-26

When Jesus had crossed back over in the boat to the other side, a great multitude was gathered to him, and he was by the sea. Behold, one of the rulers of the synagogue, Jairus by name, came; and seeing Him, he fell at His feet, and begged Him much, saying, "My little daughter is at the point of death. Please come and lay your hands on her, so that she may be made healthy, and live."

He went with him, and a great multitude followed Him, and they pressed upon Him on all sides.

A certain woman, who had an issue of blood for twelve years, and had suffered many things by many physicians, and had spent all that she had, and was no better, but rather grew worse, having heard the things concerning Jesus, came up behind Him in the crowd, and touched His clothes. For she said, "If I just touch His clothes, I will be made well."

Immediately, the flow of her blood dried up, and she felt in her body that she was healed of her affliction. Immediately, Jesus, perceiving in Himself that the power had gone out from Him, turned around in the crowd, and asked, "Who touched my clothes?"

His disciples said to Him, "You see the multitude pressing against you, and you say, Who touched me?'"

He looked around to see who had done this thing. But the woman, fearing and trembling, knowing what had been done to her, came and fell down before Him, and told Him all the truth.

He said to her, "Daughter, your faith has made you well. Go in peace and be cured of your disease."

While He was still speaking, people came from the synagogue ruler's house saying, "Your daughter is dead. Why bother the Teacher any more?"

But Jesus, when He heard the message spoken, immediately said to the ruler of the synagogue, "Don't be afraid, only believe."

He allowed no one to follow Him, except Peter, James, and John, the brother of James. He came to the synagogue ruler's house, and he saw an uproar, weeping, and great wailing. When He had entered in, He said to them, "Why do you make an uproar and weep? The child is not dead but is asleep."

They ridiculed Him.

But He, having put them all out, took the father of the child, her mother, and those who were with Him, and went in where the child was lying. Taking the child by the hand, He said to her, "Talitha cumi!" which means, being interpreted, "Girl, I tell you, get up!"

Immediately, the girl rose up and walked, for she was twelve years old. They were amazed with great amazement. He strictly ordered them that no one should know this, and commanded that something should be given to her to eat.

Jesus healed the Blind Men and the Mute Person
Mt 9:27-34

As Jesus passed by from there, two blind men followed Him, calling out and saying, "Have mercy on us, son of David!"

When He had come into the house, the blind men came to Him. Jesus said to them, "Do you believe that I am able to do this?"

They told Him, "Yes, Lord."

Then He touched their eyes, saying, "According to your faith be it done to you."

Their eyes were opened. Jesus strictly commanded them, saying, "See that no one knows about this."

But they went out and spread abroad His fame in all that land. As they went out, behold, a mute man who was demon-possessed was brought to Him. When the demon was cast out, the mute man spoke. The multitudes marveled, saying, "Nothing like this has ever been seen in Israel!"

But the Pharisees said, "By the prince of the demons, he casts out demons."

Chapter Seven:
Jesus sent Disciples to share the Gospel

The Harvest is Plentiful, but the Workers are Few
Mt 9:35-38

Jesus went about all the cities and the villages, teaching in their synagogues, and preaching the Good News of the Kingdom, and healing every disease and every sickness among the people. But when He saw the multitudes, He was moved with compassion for them, because they were harassed and scattered, like sheep without a shepherd.

Then He said to his disciples, "The harvest indeed is plentiful, but the laborers are few. Pray therefore that the Lord of the harvest will send out laborers into his harvest."

Jesus Sends Out the Twelve
Mt 10:1-42 / Mk 6:7-13 / Lk 9:1-6

He called to Himself His twelve disciples, and gave them authority over unclean spirits, to cast them out, and to heal every disease and every sickness. Now the names of the twelve apostles are these. The first, Simon, who is called Peter; Andrew, his brother; James the son of Zebedee; John, his brother; Philip; Bartholomew; Thomas; Matthew the tax collector; James the son of Alphaeus; Lebbaeus, who was also called Thaddaeus;

Simon the Canaanite; and Judas Iscariot, who also betrayed him.

Jesus sent these twelve out, and commanded them, saying, "Don't go among the Gentiles, and don't enter into any city of the Samaritans. Rather, go to the lost sheep of the house of Israel. As you go, preach, saying, The Kingdom of Heaven is at hand!' Heal the sick, cleanse the lepers, and cast out demons. Freely you received, so freely give.

Don't take any gold, nor silver, nor brass in your money belts. Take no bag for your journey, neither two coats, nor shoes, nor staff: for the laborer is worthy of his food. Into whatever city or village you enter, find out who in it is worthy; and stay there until you go on.

As you enter into the household, greet it. If the household is worthy, let your peace come on it, but if it isn't worthy, let your peace return to you. Whoever doesn't receive you, nor hear your words, as you go out of that house or that city, shake off the dust from your feet.

Most certainly I tell you, it will be more tolerable for the land of Sodom and Gomorrah in the day of judgment than for that city.

"Behold, I send you out as sheep in the midst of wolves. Therefore be wise as serpents, and harmless as doves. But beware of men: for they will deliver you up to councils, and in their synagogues, they will scourge you. Yes, and you will be brought before governors and kings for my sake, for a testimony to them and to the nations. But when they deliver you up, don't be anxious how or what you will say, for it will be given you in that hour what you will say. For it is not you who speak, but the Spirit of your Father who speaks in you.

"Brother will deliver up brother to death, and the father his child. Children will rise up against parents, and cause them to be put to death. You will be hated by all men for my name's sake, but he who endures to the end will be saved. But when they persecute you in this city, flee into the next, for most certainly I tell you, you will not have gone through the cities of Israel, until the Son of Man has come.

"A disciple is not above his teacher, nor a servant above his lord. It is enough for the disciple that he be like his teacher, and the servant like his lord. If they have called the master of the house Beelzebul, how much more those of his household! Therefore, don't be afraid of them, for there is nothing covered that will not be revealed; and hidden that will not be known. What I tell you in the darkness, speak in the light; and what you hear whispered in the ear, proclaim on the housetops. Don't be afraid of those who kill the body, but are not able to kill the soul. Rather, fear him who is able to destroy both soul and body in Gehenna.

"Aren't two sparrows sold for an assarion coin? Not one of them falls on the ground apart from your Father's will, but the very hairs of your head are all numbered. Therefore, don't be afraid. You are of more value than many sparrows. Everyone therefore who confesses me before men, him I will also confess before my Father who is in heaven. But whoever denies me before men, him I will also deny before my Father who is in heaven.

"Don't think that I came to send peace on the earth. I didn't come to send peace, but a sword. For I came to set a man at odds against his father, and a daughter against her mother, and a daughter-in-law against her mother-in-law. A man's foes will be those of his own household. He who loves father or mother more than me is not worthy of me; and he who loves son or daughter more than me isn't worthy of me.

He who doesn't take his cross and follow after me, isn't worthy of me. He who seeks his life will lose it; and he who loses his life for my sake will find it. He who receives you receives me, and he who receives me receives him who sent me. He who receives a prophet in the name of a prophet will receive a prophet's reward. He who receives a righteous man in the name of a righteous man will receive a righteous man's reward. Whoever gives one of these little ones just a cup of cold water to drink in the name of a disciple, most certainly I tell you he will in no way lose his reward."

Woe on Unrepentant Towns
Mt 11:20-24

Then Jesus began to denounce the towns in which most of his miracles had been performed, because they did not repent.

"Woe to you, Chorazin! Woe to you, Bethsaida! For if the mighty works had been done in Tyre and Sidon which were done in you, they would have repented long ago in sackcloth and ashes. But I tell you, it will be more tolerable for Tyre and Sidon on the day of judgment than for you. You, Capernaum, who are exalted to heaven, you will go down to Hades. For if the mighty works had been done in Sodom which were done in you, it would have remained until this day. But I tell you that it will be more tolerable for the land of Sodom, on the day of judgment, than for you."

The Father Revealed in the Son
Mt 11:25-30

At that time, Jesus answered, "I thank you, Father, Lord of heaven and earth, that you hid these things from the wise and understanding, and revealed them to infants. Yes, Father, for so it was well-pleasing in your sight. All things have been delivered to me by my Father. No one knows the Son, except the Father; neither does anyone know the Father, except the Son, and he to whom the Son desires to reveal him.

Come to me, all you who labor and are heavily burdened, and I will give you rest. Take my yoke upon you, and learn from me, for I am gentle and lowly in heart; and you will find rest for your souls. For my yoke is easy, and my burden is light."

God's Chosen Servant
Mt 12:15-21

Jesus, perceiving that, withdrew from there. Great multitudes followed him; and he healed them all, and commanded them that they should not make him known: that it might be fulfilled which was spoken through Isaiah the prophet, saying,

"Behold, my servant whom I have chosen;

my beloved in whom my soul is well pleased:

I will put my Spirit on him.

He will proclaim justice to the nations.

He will not strive, nor shout;

neither will anyone hear his voice in the streets.

He won't break a bruised reed.

He won't quench a smoking flax,

until he leads justice to victory.

In his name, the nations will hope."

Jesus and Beelzebul
Mt 12:22-37 / Mk 3:20-30 / Lk 11:14-23 & Lk 11:27-28

Then one possessed by a demon, blind and mute, was brought to Him and He healed him, so that the blind and mute man both spoke and saw.

All the multitudes were amazed, and said, "Can this be the son of David?"

But when the Pharisees heard it, they said, "This man does not cast out demons, except by Beelzebul, the prince of the demons."

Knowing their thoughts, Jesus said to them, "Every kingdom divided against itself is brought to desolation, and every city or house divided against itself will not stand. If Satan casts out Satan, he is divided against himself. How then will his kingdom stand? If I by Beelzebul cast out demons, by whom do your children cast them out? Therefore they will be your judges. But if I by the Spirit of God cast out demons, then the Kingdom of God has come upon you. Or how can one enter into the house of the strong man, and plunder his goods, unless he first bind the strong man? Then he will plunder his house.

The unclean spirit, when he has gone out of the man, passes through dry places, seeking rest, and finding none, he says, I will turn back to my house from which I came out.'

When he returns, he finds it swept and put in order. Then he goes, and takes seven other spirits more evil than himself, and they enter in and dwell there. The last state of that man becomes worse than the first."

"He who is not with me is against me, and he who doesn't gather with me, scatters. Therefore, I tell you, every sin and blasphemy will be forgiven men, but the blasphemy against the Spirit will not be forgiven men. Whoever speaks a word against the Son of Man, it will be forgiven him; but whoever speaks against the Holy Spirit, it will not be forgiven him, neither in this age, nor in that which is to come.

"Either make the tree good, and its fruit good, or make the tree corrupt, and its fruit corrupt; for the tree is known by its fruit. You offspring of vipers, how can you, being evil, speak good things? For out of the abundance of the heart, the mouth speaks. The good man out of his good treasure brings out good things, and the evil man out of his evil treasure brings out evil things. I tell you that every idle word that men speak, they will give account of it in the day of judgment. For by your words you will be justified, and by your words you will be condemned."

It came to pass, as he said these things, a certain woman out of the multitude lifted up her voice, and said to Him, "Blessed is the womb that bore you, and the breasts which nursed you!"

But He said, "On the contrary, blessed are those who hear the word of God, and keep it."

The Sign of Jonah
Mt 12:38-45 / Lk 11:29-32 & Lk 11:24-26 / (Mt 16:1-4) / (Mk 8:11-13)

Then certain of the scribes and Pharisees answered, "Teacher, we want to see a sign from you."

But He answered them, "An evil and adulterous generation seeks after a sign, but no sign will be given it but the sign of Jonah the prophet. For as Jonah was three days and three nights in the belly of the whale, so will the Son of Man be three days and three nights in the heart of the earth. The men of Nineveh will stand up in the judgment with this generation, and will condemn it, for they repented at the preaching of Jonah; and behold, someone greater than Jonah is here. The queen of the south will rise in the judgment with this generation, and will condemn it, for she came from the ends of the earth to hear the wisdom of Solomon; and behold, someone greater than Solomon is here.

But the unclean spirit, when he is gone out of the man, passes through waterless places, seeking rest, and doesn't find it. Then he says, 'I will return into my house from which I came out,' and when he has come back, he finds it empty, swept, and put in order. Then he goes and takes with himself seven other spirits more evil than he is, and they enter in and dwell there. The last state of that man becomes worse than the first. Even so will it be also to this evil generation."

Parable of Seed Sowing
Mt 13:1-23 / Mk 4:1-20 / Lk 8:4-15

On that day Jesus went out of the house and sat by the seaside. Great multitudes gathered to Him, so that He entered into a boat, and sat, and all the multitude stood on the beach.

He spoke to them many things in parables, saying, "Behold, a farmer went out to sow.

As he sowed, some seeds fell by the roadside, and the birds came and devoured them.

Others fell on rocky ground, where they didn't have much soil, and immediately they sprang up, because they had no depth of earth. When the sun had risen, they were scorched. Because they had no root, they withered away. Others fell among thorns. The thorns grew up and choked them. Others fell on good soil, and yielded fruit: some one hundred times as much, some sixty, and some thirty. He who has ears to hear, let him hear."

The disciples came, and said to Him, "Why do you speak to them in parables?"

He answered them, "To you it is given to know the mysteries of the Kingdom of Heaven, but it is not given to them. For whoever has, to him will be given, and he will have abundance, but whoever doesn't have, from him will be taken away even that which he has. Therefore, I speak to them in parables, because seeing they don't see, and hearing, they don't hear, neither do they understand. In them the prophecy of Isaiah is fulfilled, which says,

By hearing you will hear,

and will in no way understand;

Seeing you will see,

and will in no way perceive:

for this people's heart has grown callous,

their ears are dull of hearing,

they have closed their eyes;

or else perhaps they might perceive with their eyes,

hear with their ears, understand with their heart,

and should turn again; and I would heal them.'

"But blessed are your eyes, for they see; and your ears, for they hear. For most certainly I tell you that many prophets and righteous men desired to see the things which you see, and didn't see them; and to hear the things which you hear, and didn't hear them.

"Hear, then, the parable of the farmer. When anyone hears the word of the Kingdom, and doesn't understand it, the evil one comes and snatches away that which has been sown in his heart. This is what was sown by the roadside. What was sown on the rocky places, this is he who hears the word, and immediately with joy receives it; yet he has no root in himself but endures for a while. When oppression or persecution arises because of the word, immediately he stumbles.

What was sown among the thorns, this is he who hears the word, but the cares of this age and the deceitfulness of riches choke the word, and he becomes unfruitful. What was sown on the good ground, this is he who hears the word, and understands it, who most certainly bears fruit, and produces, some one hundred times as much, some sixty, and some thirty."

The Parable of the Weeds
Mt 13:24-30

He set another parable before them, saying, "The Kingdom of Heaven is like a man who sowed good seed in his field, but while people slept, his enemy came and sowed darnel weeds also among the wheat, and went away. But when the blade sprang up and produced fruit, then the darnel weeds appeared also.

The servants of the householder came and said to him, Sir, didn't you sow good seed in your field? Where did this darnel come from?'

"He said to them, an enemy has done this.'

"The servants asked him, 'Do you want us to go and gather them up?'

"But he said, No, lest perhaps while you gather up the darnel weeds, you root up the wheat with them. Let both grow together until the harvest, and in the harvest time I will tell the reapers, "First, gather up the darnel weeds, and bind them in bundles to burn them; but gather the wheat into my barn."""

The Parable of the Weeds Explained
Mt 13:36-43

Then Jesus sent the multitudes away and went into the house. His disciples came to Him, saying, "Explain to us the parable of the darnel weeds of the field."

He answered them, "He who sows the good seed is the Son of Man, the field is the world; and the good seed, these are the children of the Kingdom; and the darnel weeds are the children of the evil one. The enemy who sowed them is the devil. The harvest is the end of the age, and the reapers are angels. As therefore the darnel weeds are gathered up and burned with fire; so, will it be at the end of this age. The Son of Man will send out his angels, and they will gather out of his Kingdom all things that cause stumbling, and those who do iniquity, and will cast them into the furnace of fire. There will be weeping and the gnashing of teeth. Then the righteous will shine like the sun in the Kingdom of their Father. He who has ears to hear, let him hear.

The Parables of the Hidden Treasure and the Pearl
Mt 13:44-46

"Again, the Kingdom of Heaven is like a treasure hidden in the field, which a man found, and hid. In his joy, he goes and sells all that he has and buys that field.

"Again, the Kingdom of Heaven is like a man who is a merchant seeking fine pearls, who having found one pearl of great price, he went and sold all that he had and bought it.

The Parable of the Net
Mt 13:47-52

"Again, the Kingdom of Heaven is like a dragnet, that was cast into the sea, and gathered some fish of every kind, which, when it was filled, they drew up on the beach. They sat down, and gathered the good into containers, but the bad they threw away. So will it be in the end of the world. The angels will come and separate the wicked from among the righteous and will cast them into the furnace of fire. There will be the weeping and the gnashing of teeth."

Jesus said to them, "Have you understood all these things?"

They answered Him, "Yes, Lord."

He said to them, "Therefore every scribe who has been made a disciple in the Kingdom of Heaven is like a man who is a householder, who brings out of his treasure new and old things."

A Prophet Without Honor
Mt 13:53-58 / Mk 6:1-6

It happened that when Jesus had finished these parables, He departed from there. Coming into his own country, He taught them in their synagogue, so that they were astonished, and said, "Where did this man get this wisdom, and these mighty works?

Isn't this the carpenter's son? Isn't His mother called Mary, and His brothers, James, Joses, Simon, and Judas?

Aren't all of His sisters with us? Where then did this man get all of these things?"

They were offended by Him. But Jesus said to them, "A prophet is not without honor, except in his own country, and in his own house."

He could do no mighty work there, except that He laid His hands on a few sick people and healed them. He marveled because of their unbelief. He went around the villages teaching.

Chapter Eight:
Jesus continue His Ministry after the Death of John the Baptist

John the Baptist Beheaded
Mk 6:14-29 / Lk 9:7-9 / Mt 14:1-12

King Herod heard this, for his name had become known, and he said, "John the Baptizer has risen from the dead, and therefore these powers are at work in Him."

But others said, "He is Elijah."

Others said, "He is a prophet, or like one of the prophets."

But Herod, when he heard this, said, "This is John, whom I beheaded. He has risen from the dead."

For Herod himself had sent out and arrested John, and bound him in prison for the sake of Herodias, his brother Philip's wife, for he had married her.

For John said to Herod, "It is not lawful for you to have your brother's wife."

Herodias set herself against him, and desired to kill him, but she couldn't, for Herod feared John, knowing that he was a righteous and holy man, and kept him safe. When he heard him, he did many things, and he heard him gladly. Then a convenient day came, that Herod on his birthday made a supper for his nobles, the high officers, and the chief men of Galilee. When the daughter of Herodias herself came in and danced, she pleased Herod and those sitting with him. The king said to the young lady, "Ask me whatever you want, and I will give it to you."

He swore to her, "Whatever you shall ask of me, I will give you, up to half of my kingdom."

She went out, and said to her mother, "What shall I ask?"

She said, "The head of John the Baptizer."

She came in immediately with haste to the king, and asked, "I want you to give me right now the head of John the Baptizer on a platter."

The king was exceedingly sorry, but for the sake of his oaths, and of his dinner guests, he didn't wish to refuse her. Immediately the king sent out a soldier of his guard, and commanded to bring John's head, and he went and beheaded him in the prison, and brought his head on a platter, and gave it to the young lady; and the young lady gave it to her mother.

When his disciples heard this, they came and took up his corpse and laid it in a tomb.

Jesus Feeds the Five Thousand
Mk 6:30-44 / Jn 6:1-15 / Mt 14:13-21 / Lk 9:10-17

The apostles gathered themselves together to Jesus, and they told him all things, whatever they had done, and whatever they had taught.

He said to them, "You come apart into a deserted place, and rest awhile."

For there were many coming and going, and they had no leisure so much as to eat. They went away in the boat to a deserted place by themselves. They saw them going, and many recognized Him and ran there on foot from all the cities. They arrived before them and came together to Him. Jesus came out, saw a great multitude, and He had compassion on them, because they were like sheep without a shepherd, and He began to teach them many things. Jesus went up into the mountain, and He sat there with His disciples.

Now the Passover, the feast of the Jews, was at hand. When it was late in the day, His disciples came to Him, and said, "This place is deserted, and it is late in the day."

Jesus therefore lifting up His eyes, and seeing that a great multitude was coming to Him, said to Philip, "Where are we to buy bread, that these may eat?"

This He said to test him, for He Himself knew what He would do.

Philip answered Him, "Two hundred denarii worth of bread is not sufficient for them, that every one of them may receive a little. Send them away, that they may go into the surrounding country and villages, and buy themselves bread, for they have nothing to eat."

But He answered them, "You give them something to eat."

They asked Him, "Shall we go and buy two hundred denarii worth of bread, and give them something to eat?"

One of His disciples, Andrew, Simon Peter's brother, said to Him, "There is a boy here who has five barley loaves and two fish, but what are these among so many?"

Jesus said, "Have the people sit down."

Now there was much grass in that place. So the men sat down, in number about five thousand. He commanded them that everyone should sit down in groups on the green grass. They sat down in ranks, by hundreds and by fifties. He took the five loaves and the two fish, and looking up to heaven, He blessed and broke the loaves, and He gave to His disciples to set before them, and He divided the two fish among them all.

When they were filled, He said to His disciples, "Gather up the broken pieces which are left over, that nothing be lost."

So they gathered them up and filled twelve baskets with broken pieces from the five barley loaves, which were left over by those who had eaten. When therefore the people saw the sign which Jesus did, they said, "This is truly the prophet who comes into the world."

Jesus therefore, perceiving that they were about to come and take Him by force, to make Him king, withdrew again to the mountain by Himself.

Jesus Walks on the Water
Mt 14:22-36 / Jn 6:16-24 / Mk 6:45-56

Immediately Jesus made the disciples get into the boat, and to go ahead of Him to the other side, while He sent the multitudes away. After He had sent the multitudes away, He went up into the mountain by Himself to pray. When evening had come, He was there alone. But the boat was now in the middle of the sea, distressed by the waves, for the wind was contrary. In the fourth watch of the night, Jesus came to them, walking on the sea.

When the disciples saw Him walking on the sea, they were troubled, saying, "It's a ghost!"

And they cried out for fear.

But immediately Jesus spoke to them, saying "Cheer up! It is I! Don't be afraid."

Peter answered Him and said, "Lord, if it is you, command me to come to you on the waters."

He said, "Come!"

Peter stepped down from the boat and walked on the waters to come to Jesus. But when he saw that the wind was strong, he was afraid, and beginning to sink, he cried out, saying, "Lord, save me!"

Immediately Jesus stretched out His hand, took hold of him, and said to him, "You of little faith, why did you doubt?"

When they got up into the boat, the wind ceased. Those who were in the boat came and worshiped Him, saying, "You are truly the Son of God!"

When they had crossed over, they came to the land of Gennesaret.

On the next day, the multitude that stood on the other side of the sea saw that there was no other boat there, except the one in which His disciples had embarked, and that Jesus hadn't entered with His disciples into the boat, but His disciples had gone away alone. However, boats from Tiberias came near to the place where they ate the bread after the Lord had given thanks.

When the multitude therefore saw that Jesus wasn't there, nor His disciples, they themselves got into the boats, and came to Capernaum, seeking Jesus. When the people of that place recognized Him, they sent into all that surrounding region, and brought to Him all who were sick, and they begged Him that they might just touch the fringe of His garment. As many as touched it were made whole.

Jesus the Bread of Life
Jn 6:25-59

When they found Him on the other side of the sea, they asked him, "Rabbi, when did you come here?"

Jesus answered them, "Most certainly I tell you, you seek me, not because you saw signs, but because you ate of the loaves, and were filled. Don't work for the food which perishes, but for the food which remains to eternal life, which the Son of Man will give to you. For God the Father has sealed him."

They said therefore to Him, "What must we do, that we may work the works of God?"

Jesus answered them, "This is the work of God, that you believe in Him whom He has sent."

They said therefore to Him, "What then do you do for a sign, that we may see, and believe you? What work do you do? Our fathers ate the manna in the wilderness. As it is written, He gave them bread out of heaven to eat.'"

Jesus therefore said to them, "Most certainly, I tell you, it wasn't Moses who gave you the bread out of heaven, but my Father gives you the true bread out of heaven. For the bread of God is that which comes down out of heaven, and gives life to the world."

They said therefore to him, "Lord, always give us this bread."

Jesus said to them, "I am the bread of life. He who comes to me will not be hungry, and he who believes in me will never be thirsty. But I told you that you have seen me, and yet you don't believe. All those whom the Father gives me will come to me. He who comes to me I will in no way throw out. For I have come down from heaven, not to do my own will, but the will of Him who sent me. This is the will of my Father who sent me, that of all he has given to me I should lose nothing, but should raise him up at the last day. This is the will of the one who sent me, that everyone who sees the Son, and believes in Him, should have eternal life; and I will raise him up at the last day."

The Jews therefore murmured concerning Him, because He said, "I am the bread which came down out of heaven."

They said, "Isn't this Jesus, the son of Joseph, whose father and mother we know? How then does He say, I have come down out of heaven?'"

Therefore, Jesus answered them, "Don't murmur among yourselves. No one can come to me unless the Father who sent me draws him, and I will raise him up in the last day. It is written in the prophets, They will all be taught by God.' Therefore, everyone who hears from the Father, and has learned, comes to me. Not that anyone has seen the Father, except He who is from God. He has seen the Father. Most certainly, I tell you, he who believes in me has eternal life. I am the bread of life. Your fathers ate the manna in the wilderness, and they died. This is the bread which comes down out of heaven, that anyone may eat of it and not die. I am the living bread which came down out of heaven. If anyone eats this bread, he will live forever. Yes, the bread which I will give for the life of the world is my flesh."

The Jews therefore contended with one another, saying, "How can this man give us His flesh to eat?"

Jesus therefore said to them, "Most certainly I tell you, unless you eat the flesh of the Son of Man and drink His blood, you don't have life in yourselves. He who eats my flesh and drinks my blood has eternal life, and I will raise him up at the last day. For my flesh is food indeed, and my blood is drink indeed. He who eats my flesh and drinks my blood lives in me, and I in him. As the living Father sent me, and I live because of the Father; so he who feeds on me, he will also live because of me. This is the bread which came down out of heaven not as our fathers ate the manna, and died. He who eats this bread will live forever."

He said these things in the synagogue, as He taught in Capernaum.

Many Disciples Desert Jesus
Jn 6:60-71

Therefore, many of his disciples, when they heard this, said, "This is a hard saying! Who can listen to it?"

But Jesus knowing in himself that His disciples murmured at this, said to them, "Does this cause you to stumble? Then what if you would see the Son of Man ascending to where He was before? It is the spirit who gives life. The flesh profits nothing. The words that I speak to you are spirit and are life. But there are some of you who don't believe."

For Jesus knew from the beginning who they were who didn't believe, and who it was who would betray him. He said, "For this cause have I said to you that no one can come to me, unless it is given to him by my Father."

At this, many of his disciples went back, and walked no more with Him.

Jesus said therefore to the twelve, "You don't also want to go away, do you?"

Simon Peter answered him, "Lord, to whom would we go? You have the words of eternal life. We have come to believe and know that you are the Christ, the Son of the living God."

Jesus answered them, "Didn't I choose you, the twelve, and one of you is a devil?"

Now He spoke of Judas, the son of Simon Iscariot, for it was he who would betray him, being one of the twelve.

Jesus Goes to the Festival of Tabernacles
Jn 7:1-13

After these things, Jesus was walking in Galilee, for He wouldn't walk in Judea, because the Jews sought to kill Him. Now the feast of the Jews, the Feast of Booths, was at hand.

His brothers therefore said to Him, "Depart from here, and go into Judea, that your disciples also may see your works which you do. For no one does anything in secret, and himself seeks to be known openly. If you do these things, reveal yourself to the world."

For even His brothers didn't believe in Him. Jesus therefore said to them, "My time has not yet come, but your time is always ready.

The world can't hate you, but it hates me, because I testify about it, that its works are evil.

You go up to the feast. I am not yet going up to this feast, because my time is not yet fulfilled."

Having said these things to them, he stayed in Galilee. But when his brothers had gone up to the feast, then He also went up, not publicly, but as it were in secret.

The Jews therefore sought Him at the feast, and said, "Where is He?"

There was much murmuring among the multitudes concerning Him. Some said, "He is a good man."

Others said, "Not so, but He leads the multitude astray."

Yet no one spoke openly of Him for fear of the Jews.

Jesus Teaches at the Festival
Jn 7:14-24

But when it was now the midst of the feast, Jesus went up into the temple and taught. The Jews therefore marveled, saying, "How does this man know letters, having never been educated?"

Jesus therefore answered them, "My teaching is not mine, but His who sent me. If anyone desires to do His will, he will know about the teaching, whether it is from God, or if I am speaking from myself. He who speaks from himself seeks his own glory, but he who seeks the glory of Him who sent Him is true, and no unrighteousness is in Him. Didn't Moses give you the law, and yet none of you keeps the law? Why do you seek to kill me?"

The multitude answered, "You have a demon! Who seeks to kill you?"

Jesus answered them, "I did one work, and you all marvel because of it. Moses has given you circumcision (not that it is of Moses, but of the fathers), and on the Sabbath you circumcise a boy. If a boy receives circumcision on the Sabbath, that the law of Moses may not be broken, are you angry with me, because I made a man completely healthy on the Sabbath? Don't judge according to appearance but judge righteous judgment."

Division Over Who Jesus Is
Jn 7:25-44

Therefore, some of them of Jerusalem said, "Isn't this He whom they seek to kill? Behold, He speaks openly, and they say nothing to Him. Can it be that the rulers indeed know that this is truly the Christ? However, we know where this man comes from, but when the Christ comes, no one will know where He comes from."

Jesus therefore cried out in the temple, teaching and saying, "You both know me, and know where I am from. I have not come of myself, but He who sent me is true, whom you don't know. I know Him, because I am from Him, and He sent me."

They sought therefore to take Him; but no one laid a hand on Him, because His hour had not yet come. But of the multitude, many believed in Him.

They said, "When the Christ comes, He won't do more signs than those which this man has done, will He?"

The Pharisees heard the multitude murmuring these things concerning Him, and the chief priests and the Pharisees sent officers to arrest Him.

Then Jesus said, "I will be with you a little while longer, then I go to Him who sent me. You will seek me, and won't find me; and where I am, you can't come."

The Jews therefore said among themselves, "Where will this man go that we won't find Him? Will He go to the Dispersion among the Greeks, and teach the Greeks? What is this word that He said, You will seek me, and won't find me; and where I am, you can't come'?"

Now on the last and greatest day of the feast, Jesus stood and cried out, "If anyone is thirsty, let him come to me and drink! He who believes in me, as the Scripture has said, from within him will flow rivers of living water."

But He said this about the Spirit, which those believing in Him were to receive. For the Holy Spirit was not yet given, because Jesus wasn't yet glorified. Many of the multitude therefore, when they heard these words, said, "This is truly the prophet."

Others said, "This is the Christ."

But some said, "What, does the Christ come out of Galilee? Hasn't the Scripture said that the Christ comes of the seed of David, So there arose a division in the multitude because of him. Some of them would have arrested him, but no one laid hands on him.

Unbelief of the Jewish Leaders
Jn 7:45-53

The officers therefore came to the chief priests and Pharisees, and they said to them, "Why didn't you bring him?"

The officers answered, "No man ever spoke like this man!"

The Pharisees therefore answered them, "You aren't also led astray, are you? Have any of the rulers believed in him, or of the Pharisees? But this multitude that doesn't know the law is accursed."

Nicodemus (he who came to him by night, being one of them) said to them, "Does our law judge a man, unless it first hears from him personally and knows what he does?"

They answered him, "Are you also from Galilee? Search and see that no prophet has arisen out of Galilee."

Everyone went to his own house,

A Woman Caught in Adultery
Jn 8:1-11

But Jesus went to the Mount of Olives. Now very early in the morning, he came again into the temple, and all the people came to him. He sat down, and taught them.

The scribes and the Pharisees brought a woman taken in adultery. Having set her in the midst, they told him, "Teacher, we found this woman in adultery, in the very act. Now in our law, Moses commanded us to stone such women. What then do you say about her?"

They said this testing him, that they might have something to accuse him of. But Jesus stooped down, and wrote on the ground with his finger.

But when they continued asking him, he looked up and said to them, "He who is without sin among you, let him throw the first stone at her."

Again he stooped down, and with his finger wrote on the ground. They, when they heard it, being convicted by their conscience, went out one by one, beginning from the oldest, even to the last. Jesus was left alone with the woman where she was, in the middle.

Jesus, standing up, saw her and said, "Woman, where are your accusers? Did no one condemn you?"

She said, "No one, Lord."

Jesus said, "Neither do I condemn you. Go your way. From now on, sin no more."

Dispute Over Jesus' Testimony
Jn 8:12-20

Again, therefore, Jesus spoke to them, saying, "I am the light of the world. He who follows me will not walk in the darkness, but will have the light of life."

The Pharisees therefore said to him, "You testify about yourself. Your testimony is not valid."

Jesus answered them, "Even if I testify about myself, my testimony is true, for I know where I came from, and where I am going; but you don't know where I came from, or where I am going. You judge according to the flesh. I judge no one. Even if I do judge, my judgment is true, for I am not alone, but I am with the Father who sent me. It's also written in your law that the testimony of two people is valid. I am one who testifies about myself, and the Father who sent me testifies about me."

They said therefore to him, "Where is your Father?"

Jesus answered, "You know neither me, nor my Father. If you knew me, you would know my Father also."

Jesus spoke these words in the treasury, as he taught in the temple. Yet no one arrested him, because his hour had not yet come.

Dispute Over Who Jesus Is
Jn 8:21-30

Jesus said therefore again to them, "I am going away, and you will seek me, and you will die in your sins. Where I go, you can't come."

The Jews therefore said, "Will he kill himself, that he says, Where I am going, you can't come?'"

He said to them, "You are from beneath. I am from above. You are of this world. I am not of this world. I said therefore to you that you will die in your sins; for unless you believe that I am he, you will die in your sins."

They said therefore to him, "Who are you?"

Jesus said to them, "Just what I have been saying to you from the beginning. I have many things to speak and to judge concerning you. However he who sent me is true; and the things which I heard from him, these I say to the world."

They didn't understand that he spoke to them about the Father.

Jesus therefore said to them, "When you have lifted up the Son of Man, then you will know that I am he, and I do nothing of myself, but as my Father taught me, I say these things. He who sent me is with me. The Father hasn't left me alone, for I always do the things that are pleasing to him."

As he spoke these things, many believed in him.

Dispute Over Whose Children Jesus'
Opponents Are
Jn 8:31-47

Jesus therefore said to those Jews who had believed him, "If you remain in my word, then you are truly my disciples. You will know the truth, and the truth will make you free."

They answered him, "We are Abraham's seed, and have never been in bondage to anyone. How do you say, You will be made free?'"

Jesus answered them, "Most certainly I tell you, everyone who commits sin is the bondservant of sin. A bondservant doesn't live in the house forever. A son remains forever.

If therefore the Son makes you free, you will be free indeed. I know that you are Abraham's seed, yet you seek to kill me, because my word finds no place in you.

I say the things which I have seen with my Father; and you also do the things which you have seen with your father."

They answered him, "Our father is Abraham."

Jesus said to them, "If you were Abraham's children, you would do the works of Abraham.

"If you were Abraham's children," said Jesus, "then you would do what Abraham did.

But now you seek to kill me, a man who has told you the truth, which I heard from God. Abraham didn't do this. You do the works of your father."

They said to him, "We were not born of sexual immorality. We have one Father, God."

Therefore Jesus said to them, "If God were your father, you would love me, for I came out and have come from God. For I haven't come of myself, but he sent me.

Why don't you understand my speech? Because you can't hear my word. You are of your father, the devil, and you want to do the desires of your father. He was a murderer from the beginning, and doesn't stand in the truth, because there is no truth in him. When he speaks a lie, he speaks on his own; for he is a liar, and its father. But because I tell the truth, you don't believe me. Which of you convicts me of sin? If I tell the truth, why do you not believe me? He who is of God hears the words of God. For this cause you don't hear, because you are not of God."

Jesus' Claims About Himself
Jn 8:48-59

Then the Jews answered him, "Don't we say well that you are a Samaritan, and have a demon?"

Jesus answered, "I don't have a demon, but I honor my Father, and you dishonor me. But I don't seek my own glory. There is one who seeks and judges. Most certainly, I tell you, if a person keeps my word, he will never see death."

Then the Jews said to him, "Now we know that you have a demon. Abraham died, and the prophets; and you say, If a man keeps my word, he will never taste of death.' Are you greater than our father, Abraham, who died? The prophets died. Who do you make yourself out to be?"

Jesus answered, "If I glorify myself, my glory is nothing. It is my Father who glorifies me, of whom you say that he is our God. You have not known him, but I know him. If I said, I don't know him,' I would be like you, a liar. But I know him and keep his word. Your father Abraham rejoiced to see my day. He saw it and was glad."

The Jews therefore said to him, "You are not yet fifty years old, and have you seen Abraham?"

Jesus said to them, "Most certainly, I tell you, before Abraham came into existence, I AM."

Therefore, they took up stones to throw at him, but Jesus was hidden, and went out of the temple, having gone through their midst, and so passed by.

Eating with Unclean Hands
Mk 7:1-23 / Mt 15:1-20

Then the Pharisees, and some of the scribes gathered together to him, having come from Jerusalem. Now when they saw some of his disciples eating bread with defiled, that is, unwashed, hands, they found fault.

(For the Pharisees, and all the Jews, don't eat unless they wash their hands and forearms, holding to the tradition of the elders. They don't eat when they come from the marketplace, unless they bathe themselves, and there are many other things which they have received to hold to: washings of cups, pitchers, bronze vessels, and couches.) The Pharisees and the scribes asked him, "Why don't your disciples walk according to the tradition of the elders, but eat their bread with unwashed hands?"

He answered them, "Well did Isaiah prophesy of you hypocrites, as it is written,

These people honor me with their lips,

but their heart is far from me.

But in vain do they worship me,

teaching as doctrines the commandments of men.' "For you set aside the commandment of God and hold tightly to the tradition of men the washing of pitchers and cups, and you do many other such things."

He said to them, "Full well do you reject the commandment of God, that you may keep your tradition. For Moses said, 'Honor your father and your mother;' and, He who speaks evil of father or mother, let him be put to death.' But you say, If a man tells his father or his mother, "Whatever profit you might have received from me is Corban, that is to say, given to God";' then you no longer allow him to do anything for his father or his mother, making void the word of God by your tradition, which you have handed down. You do many things like this."

He called all the multitude to himself, and said to them, "Hear me, all of you, and understand. There is nothing from outside of the man, that going into him can defile him; but the things which proceed out of the man are those that defile the man. If anyone has ears to hear, let him hear!"

When he had entered into a house away from the multitude, his disciples asked him about the parable.

He said to them, "Are you thus without understanding also? Don't you perceive that whatever goes into the man from outside can't defile him, because it doesn't go into his heart, but into his stomach, then into the latrine, thus purifying all foods?"

He said, "That which proceeds out of the man, that defiles the man. For from within, out of the hearts of men, proceed evil thoughts, adulteries, sexual sins, murders, thefts, coveting, wickedness, deceit, lustful desires, an evil eye, blasphemy, pride, and foolishness. All these evil things come from within and defile the man."

The Faith of a Canaanite Woman
Mt 15:21-28 / Mk 7:24-30

Jesus went out from there and withdrew into the region of Tyre and Sidon.

Behold, a Canaanite woman came out from those borders, and cried, saying, "Have mercy on me, Lord, you son of David! My daughter is severely possessed by a demon!"
But he answered her not a word. His disciples came and begged him, saying, "Send her away; for she cries after us."

But he answered, "I wasn't sent to anyone but the lost sheep of the house of Israel."

But she came and worshiped him, saying, "Lord, help me."

But he answered, "It is not appropriate to take the children's bread and throw it to the dogs."

But she said, "Yes, Lord, but even the dogs eat the crumbs which fall from their masters' table."

Then Jesus answered her, "Woman, great is your faith! Be it done to you even as you desire."

And her daughter was healed from that hour.

Jesus Heals a Deaf and Mute Man
Mk 7:31-37

Again he departed from the borders of Tyre and Sidon, and came to the sea of Galilee, through the midst of the region of Decapolis. They brought to him one who was deaf and had an impediment in his speech. They begged him to lay his hand on him.

He took him aside from the multitude, privately, and put his fingers into his ears, and he spat, and touched his tongue.

Looking up to heaven, he sighed, and said to him, "Ephphatha!" that is, "Be opened!"

Immediately his ears were opened, and the impediment of his tongue was released, and he spoke clearly. He commanded them that they should tell no one, but the more he commanded them, so much the more widely they proclaimed it.

They were astonished beyond measure, saying, "He has done all things well. He makes even the deaf hear, and the mute speak!"

Jesus feed the Four Thousand
Mk 8:1-10 / Mt 15:29-39

In those days, when there was a very great multitude, and they had nothing to eat, Jesus called his disciples to himself, and said to them, "I have compassion on the multitude, because they have stayed with me now three days, and have nothing to eat.

If I send them away fasting to their home, they will faint on the way, for some of them have come a long way."

His disciples answered him, "From where could one satisfy these people with bread here in a deserted place?"

He asked them, "How many loaves do you have?"

They said, "Seven."

He commanded the multitude to sit down on the ground, and he took the seven loaves. Having given thanks, he broke them, and gave them to his disciples to serve, and they served the multitude. They had a few small fish. Having blessed them, he said to serve these also. They ate and were filled. They took up seven baskets of broken pieces that were left over. There were about four thousand people who had eaten. Then he sent them away.

Immediately he entered into the boat with his disciples, and came into the region of Dalmanutha.

The Demand for a Sign
Mt 16:1-4 / Mk 8:11-13 / (Mt 12:38-45) / (Lk 11:29-32 & Lk 11:24-26)

The Pharisees and Sadducees came, and testing him, asked him to show them a sign from heaven. But he answered them, "When it is evening, you say, It will be fair weather, for the sky is red.' In the morning, It will be foul weather today, for the sky is red and threatening.'

Hypocrites! You know how to discern the appearance of the sky, but you can't discern the signs of the times! An evil and adulterous generation seeks after a sign, and there will be no sign given to it, except the sign of the prophet Jonah."

He left them, and departed.

The Yeast of the Pharisees and Herod
Mk 8:14-21

They forgot to take bread; and they didn't have more than one loaf in the boat with them. He warned them, saying, "Take heed: beware of the yeast of the Pharisees and the yeast of Herod."

They reasoned with one another, saying, "It's because we have no bread."

Jesus, perceiving it, said to them, "Why do you reason that it's because you have no bread? Don't you perceive yet, neither understand? Is your heart still hardened? Having eyes, don't you see? Having ears, don't you hear? Don't you remember? When I broke the five loaves among the five thousand, how many baskets full of broken pieces did you take up?"

They told him, "Twelve."

"When the seven loaves fed the four thousand, how many baskets full of broken pieces did you take up?"

They told him, "Seven."

He asked them, "Don't you understand, yet?"

Jesus Heals a Blind Man at Bethsaida
Mk 8:22-26 / Mt 16:5-12

He came to Bethsaida. They brought a blind man to him, and begged him to touch him. He took hold of the blind man by the hand, and brought him out of the village. When he had spit on his eyes, and laid his hands on him, he asked him if he saw anything.

He looked up, and said, "I see men; for I see them like trees walking."

Then again he laid his hands on his eyes. He looked intently, and was restored, and saw everyone clearly.

He sent him away to his house, saying, "Don't enter into the village, nor tell anyone in the village."

Peter Declares That Jesus Is Jesus the Christ
Mt 16:13-20 / Mk 8:27-30 / Lk 9:18-20

Now when Jesus came into the parts of Caesarea Philippi, he asked his disciples, saying, "Who do men say that I, the Son of Man, am?"

They said, "Some say John the Baptizer, some, Elijah, and others, Jeremiah, or one of the prophets."

He said to them, "But who do you say that I am?"

Simon Peter answered, "You are the Christ, the Son of the living God."

Jesus answered him, "Blessed are you, Simon Bar Jonah, for flesh and blood has not revealed this to you, but my Father who is in heaven. I also tell you that you are Peter, and on this rock I will build my assembly, and the gates of Hades will not prevail against it.

I will give to you the keys of the Kingdom of Heaven, and whatever you bind on earth will have been bound in heaven; and whatever you release on earth will have been released in heaven."

Then he commanded the disciples that they should tell no one that he was Jesus the Christ.

Chapter Nine:
Jesus knew His Death was Coming Soon

Jesus Predicts His Death
Mk 8:31-33 / Mt 16:21-23 / Lk 9:21-22

He began to teach them that the Son of Man must suffer many things, and be rejected by the elders, the chief priests, and the scribes, and be killed, and after three days rise again. He spoke to them openly.

Peter took him, and began to rebuke him.

But he, turning around, and seeing his disciples, rebuked Peter, and said, "Get behind me, Satan! For you have in mind not the things of God, but the things of men."

The Way of the Cross
Mk 8"34-38 & Mk 9:1 / Mt 16:24-28 / Lk 9:23-27

He called the multitude to himself with his disciples, and said to them, For whoever wants to save his life will lose it; and whoever will lose his life for my sake and the sake of the Good News will save it. For what does it profit a man, to gain the whole world, and forfeit his life? For what will a man give in exchange for his life? For whoever will be ashamed of me and of my words in this adulterous and sinful generation, the Son of Man also will be ashamed of him, when he comes in the glory of his Father with the holy angels."

He said to them, "Most certainly I tell you, there are some standing here who will in no way taste death until they see the Kingdom of God come with power."

The Transfiguration
Mk 9:2-13 / Mt 17:1-13 / Lk 9:28-36

After six days Jesus took with him Peter, James, and John, and brought them up onto a high mountain privately by themselves, and he was changed into another form in front of them. His clothing became glistening, exceedingly white, like snow, such as no launderer on earth can whiten them. Elijah and Moses appeared to them, and they were talking with Jesus.

Peter answered Jesus, "Rabbi, it is good for us to be here. Let's make three tents: one for you, one for Moses, and one for Elijah."

For he didn't know what to say, for they were very afraid. A cloud came, overshadowing them, and a voice came out of the cloud, "This is my beloved Son. Listen to him."

Suddenly looking around, they saw no one with them any more, except Jesus only.

As they were coming down from the mountain, he commanded them that they should tell no one what things they had seen, until after the Son of Man had risen from the dead.

They kept this saying to themselves, questioning what the "rising from the dead" meant.

They asked him, saying, "Why do the scribes say that Elijah must come first?"

He said to them, "Elijah indeed comes first, and restores all things. How is it written about the Son of Man, that he should suffer many things and be despised? But I tell you that Elijah has come, and they have also done to him whatever they wanted to, even as it is written about him."

Then the disciples understood that he spoke to them of John the Baptizer.

Jesus Heals a Boy Possessed by an Impure Spirit
Mk 9:14-29 / Mt 17:14-21 / Lk 9:37-43

Coming to the disciples, he saw a great multitude around them, and scribes questioning them. Immediately all the multitude, when they saw him, were greatly amazed, and running to him greeted him.

He asked the scribes, "What are you asking them?"

One of the multitude answered, "Teacher, I brought to you my son, who has a mute spirit; and wherever it seizes him, it throws him down, and he foams at the mouth, and grinds his teeth, and wastes away. I asked your disciples to cast it out, and they weren't able."

He answered him, "Unbelieving generation, how long shall I be with you? How long shall I bear with you? Bring him to me."

They brought him to him, and when he saw him, immediately the spirit convulsed him, and he fell on the ground, wallowing and foaming at the mouth.

He asked his father, "How long has it been since this has come to him?"

He said, "From childhood. Often it has cast him both into the fire and into the water, to destroy him. But if you can do anything, have compassion on us, and help us."

Jesus said to him, "If you can believe, all things are possible to him who believes."

Immediately the father of the child cried out with tears, "I believe. Help my unbelief!"

When Jesus saw that a multitude came running together, he rebuked the unclean spirit, saying to him, "You mute and deaf spirit, I command you, come out of him, and never enter him again!"

Having cried out, and convulsed greatly, it came out of him. The boy became like one dead; so much that most of them said, "He is dead."

But Jesus took him by the hand and raised him up; and he arose.

When he came into the house, his disciples asked him privately, "Why couldn't we cast it out?"

He said to them, "This kind can come out by nothing, except by prayer and fasting."

Jesus Predicts His Death a Second Time
Mk 9:30-32 / Mt 17:22-23 / Lk 9:44-45

They went out from there and passed through Galilee. He didn't want anyone to know it. For he was teaching his disciples, and said to them, "The Son of Man is being handed over to the hands of men, and they will kill him; and when he is killed, on the third day he will rise again."

But they didn't understand the saying and were afraid to ask him.

The Temple Tax
Mt 17:24-27

When they came to Capernaum, those who collected the didrachma coins came to Peter, and said, "Doesn't your teacher pay the didrachma?"

He said, "Yes." When he came into the house,

Jesus anticipated him, saying, "What do you think, Simon? From whom do the kings of the earth receive toll or tribute? From their children, or from strangers?"

Peter said to him, "From strangers."

Jesus said to him, "Therefore the children are exempt. But lest we cause them to stumble, go to the sea, cast a hook, and take up the first fish that comes up. When you have opened its mouth, you will find a stater coin. Take that and give it to them for me and you."

The Greatest in the kingdom of God
Lk 9:46-48 / Mk 9:33-37 / Mt 18:1-5

There arose an argument among them about which of them was the greatest.

He came to Capernaum, and when he was in the house, he asked them, "What were you arguing among yourselves on the way?"

But they were silent, for they had disputed one with another on the way about who was the greatest. He sat down and called the twelve.

and he said to them, "If any man wants to be first, he shall be last of all, and servant of all."

Jesus called a little child to himself, and set him in their midst,

and said, "Most certainly I tell you, unless you turn, and become as little children, you will in no way enter into the Kingdom of Heaven. Whoever therefore humbles himself as this little child, the same is the greatest in the Kingdom of Heaven."

And said to them, "Whoever receives this little child in my name receives me. Whoever receives me receives him who sent me. For whoever is least among you all, this one will be great."

Whoever Is Not Against Us Is for Us
Mk 9:38-41 / Lk 9:49-50

John said to him, "Teacher, we saw someone who didn't follow us casting out demons in your name; and we forbade him, because he doesn't follow us."

But Jesus said, "Don't forbid him, for there is no one who will do a mighty work in my name and be able quickly to speak evil of me. For whoever is not against us is on our side. For whoever will give you a cup of water to drink in my name, because you are Christ's, most certainly I tell you, he will in no way lose his reward.

Causing Stumble
Mk 9:42-50 / Mt 18:6-9

Whoever will cause one of these little ones who believe in me to stumble, it would be better for him if he were thrown into the sea with a millstone hanging around his neck.

If your hand causes you to stumble, cut it off. It is better for you to enter life maimed, rather than having your two hands to go into Gehenna, into the unquenchable fire, where their worm doesn't die, and the fire is not quenched.' If your foot causes you to stumble, cut it off. It is better for you to enter into life lame, rather than having your two feet cast into Gehenna, into the fire that will never be quenched where their worm doesn't die, and the fire is not quenched.'

If your eye causes you to stumble, cast it out. It is better for you to enter into the Kingdom of God with one eye, rather than having two eyes to be cast into the Gehenna of fire, where their worm doesn't die, and the fire is not quenched.' For everyone it will be salted with fire, and every sacrifice will be seasoned with salt. Salt is good, but if the salt has lost its saltiness, with what will you season it? Have salt in yourselves and be at peace with one another."

Dealing With Sin in the Church
Mt 18:15-20

"If your brother sins against you, go, show him his fault between you and him alone. If he listens to you, you have gained back your brother. But if he doesn't listen, take one or two more with you, that at the mouth of two or three witnesses every word may be established. If he refuses to listen to them, tell it to the assembly. If he refuses to hear the assembly also, let him be to you as a Gentile or a tax collector. Most certainly I tell you, whatever things you bind on earth will have been bound in heaven, and whatever things you release on earth will have been released in heaven. Again, assuredly I tell you, that if two of you will agree on earth concerning anything that they will ask, it will be done for them by my Father who is in heaven. For where two or three are gathered together in my name, there I am in their midst."

The Parable of the Unmerciful Servant
Mt 18:21-35

Then Peter came and said to him, "Lord, how often shall my brother sin against me, and I forgive him? Until seven times?"

Jesus said to him, "I don't tell you until seven times, but, until seventy times seven. Therefore, the Kingdom of Heaven is like a certain king, who wanted to reconcile accounts with his servants. When he had begun to reconcile, one was brought to him who owed him ten thousand talents. But because he couldn't pay, his lord commanded him to be sold, with his wife, his children, and all that he had, and payment to be made.

The servant therefore fell down and kneeled before him, saying, Lord, have patience with me, and I will repay you all!'

The lord of that servant, being moved with compassion, released him, and forgave him the debt.

"But that servant went out, and found one of his fellow servants, who owed him one hundred denarii, and he grabbed him, and took him by the throat, saying, pay me what you owe!'

"So, his fellow servant fell down at his feet and begged him, saying, have patience with me, and I will repay you!' He would not, but went and cast him into prison, until he should pay back that which was due.

When his fellow servants saw what was done, they were exceedingly sorry and came and told their lord all that was done. Then his lord called him in, and said to him, You wicked servant! I forgave you all that debt, because you begged me. Shouldn't you also have had mercy on your fellow servant, even as I had mercy on you?'

His lord was angry, and delivered him to the tormentors, until he should pay all that was due to him. So my heavenly

Father will also do to you, if you don't each forgive your brother from your hearts for his misdeeds."

Samaritan Opposition
Lk 9:51-56

It came to pass, when the days were near that he should be taken up, he intently set his face to go to Jerusalem and sent messengers before his face. They went and entered a village of the Samaritans, so as to prepare for him. They didn't receive him, because he was traveling with his face set towards Jerusalem.

When his disciples, James and John, saw this, they said, "Lord, do you want us to command fire to come down from the sky, and destroy them, just as Elijah did?"

But he turned and rebuked them, "You don't know what kind of spirit you are. For the Son of Man didn't come to destroy men's lives, but to save them."

They went to another village.

The Cost of Following Jesus
Lk 9:57-62 / Mt 8:18-22

As they went on the way, a certain man said to him, "I want to follow you wherever you go, Lord."

Jesus said to him, "The foxes have holes, and the birds of the sky have nests, but the Son of Man has no place to lay his head."

He said to another, "Follow me!"

But he said, "Lord, allow me first to go and bury my father."

But Jesus said to him, "Leave the dead to bury their own dead, but you go and announce the Kingdom of God."

Another also said, "I want to follow you, Lord, but first allow me to say good-bye to those who are at my house."

But Jesus said to him, "No one, having put his hand to the plow, and looking back, is fit for the Kingdom of God."

Jesus sent out Seventy-Two
Lk 10:1-24

Now after these things, the Lord also appointed seventy others and sent them two by two ahead of him into every city and place, where he was about to come.

Then he said to them, "The harvest is indeed plentiful, but the laborers are few. Pray therefore to the Lord of the harvest, that he may send out laborers into his harvest.

Go your ways. Behold, I send you out as lambs among wolves. Carry no purse, nor wallet, nor sandals. Greet no one on the way. Into whatever house you enter, first say, Peace be to this house.' If a son of peace is there, your peace will rest on him; but if not, it will return to you. Remain in that same house, eating and drinking the things they give, for the laborer is worthy of his wages. Don't go from house to house. Into whatever city you enter, and they receive you, eat the things that are set before you. Heal the sick who are therein, and tell them, The Kingdom of God has come near to you.'

But into whatever city you enter, and they don't receive you, go out into its streets and say, even the dust from your city that clings to us, we wipe off against you. Nevertheless, know this, that the Kingdom of God has come near to you.' I tell you, it will be more tolerable in that day for Sodom than for that city.

"Woe to you, Chorazin! Woe to you, Bethsaida! For if the mighty works had been done in Tyre and Sidon which were done in you, they would have repented long ago, sitting in sackcloth and ashes. But it will be more tolerable for Tyre and Sidon in the judgment than for you. You, Capernaum, who are exalted to heaven, will be brought down to Hades. Whoever listens to you listens to me, and whoever rejects you rejects me. Whoever rejects me rejects him who sent me."

The seventy returned with joy, saying, "Lord, even the demons are subject to us in your name!"

He said to them, "I saw Satan having fallen like lightning from heaven. Behold, I give you authority to tread on serpents and scorpions, and over all the power of the enemy. Nothing will in any way hurt you. Nevertheless, don't rejoice in this, that the spirits are subject to you, but rejoice that your names are written in heaven."

In that same hour Jesus rejoiced in the Holy Spirit, and said, "I thank you, O Father, Lord of heaven and earth, that you have hidden these things from the wise and understanding, and revealed them to little children. Yes, Father, for so it was well-pleasing in your sight."

Turning to the disciples, he said, "All things have been delivered to me by my Father. No one knows who the Son is, except the Father, and who the Father is, except the Son, and he to whomever the Son desires to reveal him."

Turning to the disciples, he said privately, "Blessed are the eyes which see the things that you see, for I tell you that many prophets and kings desired to see the things which you see, and didn't see them, and to hear the things which you hear, and didn't hear them."

The Parable of the Good Samaritan
Lk 10:25-37

Behold, a certain lawyer stood up and tested him, saying, "Teacher, what shall I do to inherit eternal life?"

He said to him, "What is written in the law? How do you read it?"

He answered, "You shall love the Lord your God with all your heart, with all your soul, with all your strength, and with all your mind; and your neighbor as yourself."

He said to him, "You have answered correctly. Do this, and you will live."

But he, desiring to justify himself, asked Jesus, "Who is my neighbor?"

Jesus answered, "A certain man was going down from Jerusalem to Jericho, and he fell among robbers, who both stripped him and beat him, and departed, leaving him half dead. By chance a certain priest was going down that way. When he saw him, he passed by on the other side. In the same way a Levite also, when he came to the place, and saw him, passed by on the other side. But a certain Samaritan, as he traveled, came where he was. When he saw him, he was moved with compassion, came to him, and bound up his wounds, pouring on oil and wine. He set him on his own animal, and brought him to an inn, and took care of him. On the next day, when he departed, he took out two denarii, and gave them to the host, and said to him, Take care of him. Whatever you spend beyond that, I will repay you when I return.' Now which of these three do you think seemed to be a neighbor to him who fell among the robbers?"

He said, "He who showed mercy on him."

Then Jesus said to him, "Go and do likewise."

At the Home of Martha and Mary
Lk 10:38-42

It happened as they went on their way, he entered into a certain village, and a certain woman named Martha received him into her house. She had a sister called Mary, who also sat at Jesus' feet, and heard his word. But Martha was distracted with much serving, and she came up to him, and said, "Lord, don't you care that my sister left me to serve alone? Ask her therefore to help me."

Jesus answered her, "Martha, Martha, you are anxious and troubled about many things, but one thing is needed. Mary has chosen the good part, which will not be taken away from her."

Woes on the Pharisees and the Experts in the Law Lk 11:37-54

Now as he spoke, a certain Pharisee asked him to dine with him. He went in and sat at the table. When the Pharisee saw it, he marveled that he had not first washed himself before dinner.

The Lord said to him, "Now you Pharisees cleanse the outside of the cup and of the platter, but your inward part is full of extortion and wickedness. You, foolish ones, didn't he who made the outside make the inside also? But give gifts to the needy those things which are within, and behold, all things will be clean to you.

But woe to you Pharisees! For you tithe mint and rue and every herb, but you bypass justice and the love of God. You ought to have done this, and not to have left the other undone.

Woe to you Pharisees! For you love the best seats in the synagogues, and the greetings in the marketplaces. Woe to you, scribes and Pharisees, hypocrites! For you are like hidden graves, and the men who walk over them don't know it."

One of the lawyers answered him, "Teacher, in saying this you insult us also."

He said, "Woe to you lawyers also! For you load men with burdens that are difficult to carry, and you yourselves won't even lift one finger to help carry those burdens.

Woe to you! For you build the tombs of the prophets, and your fathers killed them.

So you testify and consent to the work of your fathers. For they killed them, and you build their tombs. Therefore also the wisdom of God said, I will send to them prophets and apostles; and some of them they will kill and persecute, that the blood of all the prophets, which was shed from the foundation of the world, may be required of this generation; from the blood of Abel to the blood of Zachariah, who perished between the altar and the sanctuary.' Yes, I tell you, it will be required of this generation.

Woe to you, lawyers! For you took away the key to knowledge. You didn't enter in yourselves, and those who were entering in, you hindered."

As he said these things to them, the scribes and the Pharisees began to be terribly angry, and to draw many things out of him; lying in wait for him and seeking to catch him in something he might say, that they might accuse him.

Warnings and Encouragements
Lk 12:1-12

Meanwhile, when a multitude of many thousands had gathered, so much so that they trampled on each other,

he began to tell his disciples first, "Beware of the yeast of the Pharisees, which is hypocrisy. But there is nothing covered up, that will not be revealed, nor hidden, that will not be known. Therefore, whatever you have said in the darkness will be heard in the light. What you have spoken in the ear in the inner rooms will be proclaimed on the housetops.

"I tell you, my friends, don't be afraid of those who kill the body, and after that have no more that they can do. But I will warn you whom you should fear. Fear him, who after he has killed, has power to cast into Gehenna. Yes, I tell you, fear him.

"Aren't five sparrows sold for two assaria coins? Not one of them is forgotten by God.

But the very hairs of your head are all numbered. Therefore, don't be afraid. You are of more value than many sparrows.

"I tell you, everyone who confesses me before men, him will the Son of Man also confess before the angels of God; but he who denies me in the presence of men will be denied in the presence of the angels of God.

Everyone who speaks a word against the Son of Man will be forgiven, but those who blaspheme against the Holy Spirit will not be forgiven.

When they bring you before the synagogues, the rulers, and the authorities, don't be anxious how or what you will answer, or what you will say; for the Holy Spirit will teach you in that same hour what you must say."

Chapter Ten:
The Teaching about the Kingdom of God

The Parable of the Rich Fool
Lk 12:13-21

One of the multitude said to him, "Teacher, tell my brother to divide the inheritance with me."

But he said to him, "Man, who made me a judge or an arbitrator over you?"

He said to them, "Beware! Keep yourselves from covetousness, for a man's life doesn't consist of the abundance of the things which he possesses."

He spoke a parable to them, saying, "The ground of a certain rich man produced abundantly. He reasoned within himself, saying, What will I do, because I don't have room to store my crops?'

He said, This is what I will do. I will pull down my barns, and build bigger ones, and there I will store all my grain and my goods.

I will tell my soul, "Soul, you have many goods laid up for many years. Take your ease, eat, drink, be merry."'

"But God said to him, You foolish one, tonight your soul is required of you. The things which you have prepared whose will they be?'

So is he who lays up treasure for himself and is not rich toward God."

Watchfulness
Lk 12:35-48 / (Mt 24:36-51 / Mk 13:32-36)

"Let your waist be dressed and your lamps burning. Be like men watching for their lord, when he returns from the marriage feast; that, when he comes and knocks, they may immediately open to him. Blessed are those servants, whom the lord will find watching when he comes. Most certainly I tell you that he will dress himself, and make them recline, and will come and serve them. They will be blessed if he comes in the second or third watch and finds them so. But know this, that if the master of the house had known in what hour the thief was coming, he would have watched and not allowed his house to be broken into. Therefore, be ready also, for the Son of Man is coming in an hour that you don't expect him."

Peter said to him, "Lord, are you telling this parable to us, or to everybody?"

The Lord said, "Who then is the faithful and wise steward, whom his lord will set over his household, to give them their portion of food at the right times? Blessed is that servant whom his lord will find doing so when he comes. Truly I tell you, that he will set him over all that he has. But if that servant says in his heart, My lord delays his coming,' and begins to beat the menservants and the maidservants, and to eat and drink, and to be drunken, then the lord of that servant will come in a day when he isn't expecting him, and in an hour that he doesn't know, and will cut him in two, and place his portion with the unfaithful. That servant, who knew his lord's will, and didn't prepare, nor do what he wanted, will be beaten with many stripes, but he who didn't know, and did things worthy of stripes, will be beaten with few stripes. To whomever much is given, of him much will be required; and to whom much was entrusted, of him more will be asked.

Not Peace but Division
Lk 12:49-53 / (Mt 10:34-36)

"I came to throw fire on the earth. I wish it were already kindled. But I have a baptism to be baptized with, and how distressed I am until it is accomplished!

Do you think that I have come to give peace to the earth? I tell you, no, but rather division.

For from now on, there will be five in one house divided, three against two, and two against three. They will be divided, father against son, and son against father; mother against daughter, and daughter against her mother; mother-in-law against her daughter-in-law, and daughter-in-law against her mother-in-law."

Interpreting the Times
Lk 12:54-59

He said to the multitudes also, "When you see a cloud rising from the west, immediately you say, A shower is coming,' and so it happens. When a south wind blows, you say, there will be a scorching heat,' and it happens.

You hypocrites! You know how to interpret the appearance of the earth and the sky, but how is it that you don't interpret this time? Why don't you judge for yourselves what is right?

For when you are going with your adversary before the magistrate, try diligently on the way to be released from him, lest perhaps he drags you to the judge, and the judge deliver you to the officer, and the officer throw you into prison. I tell you, you will by no means get out of there, until you have paid the very last penny."

Repent or Perish
Lk 13:1-9

Now there were some present at the same time who told him about the Galileans, whose blood Pilate had mixed with their sacrifices.

Jesus answered them, "Do you think that these Galileans were worse sinners than all the other Galileans, because they suffered such things? I tell you, no, but unless you repent, you will all perish in the same way. Or those eighteen, on whom the tower in Siloam fell, and killed them; do you think that they were worse offenders than all the men who dwell in Jerusalem? I tell you, no, but, unless you repent, you will all perish in the same way."

He spoke this parable. "A certain man had a fig tree planted in his vineyard, and he came seeking fruit on it, and found none.

He said to the vine dresser, Behold, these three years I have come looking for fruit on this

He answered, Lord, leave it alone this year also, until I dig around it, and fertilize it. If it bears fruit, fine; but if not, after that, you can cut it down.'"

Jesus Heals a Crippled Woman on the Sabbath Lk 13:10-17

He was teaching in one of the synagogues on the Sabbath day. Behold, there was a woman who had a spirit of infirmity eighteen years, and she was bent over, and could in no way straighten herself up.

When Jesus saw her, he called her, and said to her, "Woman, you are freed from your infirmity."

He laid his hands on her, and immediately she stood up straight, and glorified God.

The ruler of the synagogue, being indignant because Jesus had healed on the Sabbath, said to the multitude, "There are six days in which men ought to work. Therefore come on those days and be healed, and not on the Sabbath day!"

Therefore the Lord answered him, "You hypocrites! Doesn't each one of you free his ox or his donkey from the stall on the Sabbath, and lead him away to water? Ought not this woman, being a daughter of Abraham, whom Satan had bound eighteen long years, be freed from this bondage on the Sabbath day?"

As he said these things, all his adversaries were disappointed, and all the multitude rejoiced for all the glorious things that were done by him.

The Parable of the Mustard Seed
and Leavened Flour
Mk 4:30-34 / Lk 13:18-21 / Mt 13:31-35

He said, "How will we liken the Kingdom of God? Or with what parable will we illustrate it? It's like a grain of mustard seed, which, when it is sown in the earth, though it is less than all the seeds that are on the earth, yet when it is sown, grows up, and becomes greater than all the herbs, and puts out great branches, so that the birds of the sky can lodge under its shadow."

With many such parables he spoke the word to them, as they were able to hear it.

Without a parable he didn't speak to them; but privately to his own disciples he explained everything. That it might be fulfilled which was spoken through the prophet, saying, "I will open my mouth in parables; I will utter things hidden from the foundation of the world."

Again, he said, "To what shall I compare the Kingdom of God? It is like yeast, which a woman took and hid in three measures of flour, until it was all leavened."

The Narrow Door
Lk 13:22-30 / (Mt 7: 13-14)

He went on his way through cities and villages, teaching, and traveling to Jerusalem. One said to him, "Lord, are they few who are saved?"

He said to them, "Strive to enter in by the narrow door, for many, I tell you, will seek to enter in, and will not be able. When once the master of the house has risen up, and has shut the door, and you begin to stand outside, and to knock at the door, saying, Lord, Lord, open to us!' then he will answer and tell you, I don't know you or where you come from.' Then you will begin to say, we ate and drank in your presence, and you taught in our streets.'

He will say, I tell you, I don't know where you come from. Depart from me, all you workers of iniquity.' There will be weeping and gnashing of teeth, when you see Abraham, Isaac, Jacob, and all the prophets, in the Kingdom of God, and yourselves being thrown outside. They will come from the east, west, north, and south, and will sit down in the Kingdom of God.

Behold, there are some who are last who will be first, and there are some who are first who will be last."

Jesus' Sorrow for Jerusalem
Lk 13:31-35

On that same day, some Pharisees came, saying to him, "Get out of here, and go away, for Herod wants to kill you."

He said to them, "Go and tell that fox, Behold, I cast out demons and perform cures today and tomorrow, and the third day I complete my mission. Nevertheless I must go on my way today and tomorrow and the next day, for it can't be that a prophet perish outside of Jerusalem.'

"Jerusalem, Jerusalem, that kills the prophets, and stones those who are sent to her! How often I wanted to gather your children together, like a hen gathers her own brood under her wings, and you refused! Behold, your house is left to you desolate. I tell you, you will not see me, until you say, Blessed is he who comes in the name of the Lord!'"

Healing on Sabath day
Lk 14:1-6

It happened, when he went into the house of one of the rulers of the Pharisees on a Sabbath to eat bread, that they were watching him. Behold, a certain man who had dropsy was in front of him. Jesus, answering, spoke to the lawyers and Pharisees, saying, "Is it lawful to heal on the Sabbath?"

But they were silent. He took him, and healed him, and let him go.

He answered them, "Which of you, if your son or an ox fell into a well, wouldn't immediately pull him out on a Sabbath day?"

They couldn't answer him regarding these things.

The Parable of being humble in a Banquet
Lk 14:7-14

He spoke a parable to those who were invited, when he noticed how they chose the best seats, and said to them,

"When you are invited by anyone to a marriage feast, don't sit in the best seat, since perhaps someone more honorable than you might be invited by him, and he who invited both of you would come and tell you, Make room for this person.' Then you would begin, with shame, to take the lowest place. But when you are invited, go and sit in the lowest place, so that when he who invited you comes, he may tell you, Friend, move up higher.' Then you will be honored in the presence of all who sit at the table with you.

For everyone who exalts himself will be humbled, and whoever humbles himself will be exalted."

He also said to the one who had invited him, "When you make a dinner or a supper, don't call your friends, nor your brothers, nor your kinsmen, nor rich neighbors, or perhaps they might also return the favor, and pay you back. But when you make a feast, ask the poor, the maimed, the lame, or the blind; and you will be blessed, because they don't have the resources to repay you. For you will be repaid in the resurrection of the righteous."

The Parable of the Great Banquet
Lk 14:15-24 / Mt 22:1-14

When one of those who sat at the table with him heard these things, he said to him, "Blessed is he who will feast in the Kingdom of God!"

But he said to him, "A certain man made a great supper, and he invited many people.

He sent out his servant at supper time to tell those who were invited, come, for everything is ready now.' They all as one began to make excuses.

"The first said to him, I have bought a field, and I must go and see it. Please have me excused.:

"Another said, I have bought five yokes of oxen, and I must go try them out. Please have me excused.'

"Another said, I have married a wife, and therefore I can't come.'

"That servant came, and told his lord these things. Then the master of the house, being angry, said to his servant, Go out quickly into the streets and lanes of the city, and bring in the poor, maimed, blind, and lame.'

"The servant said, Lord, it is done as you commanded, and there is still room.'

"The lord said to the servant, Go out into the highways and hedges, and compel them to come in, that my house may be filled. For I tell you that none of those men who were invited will taste of my supper.'"

But when the king came in to see the guests, he saw there a man who didn't have on wedding clothing, and he said to him, Friend, how did you come in here not wearing wedding clothing?'

He was speechless.

Then the king said to the servants, Bind him hand and foot, take him away, and throw him into the outer darkness; there is where the weeping and grinding of teeth will be.' For many are called, but few chosen."

The Cost of Being a Disciple
Lk 14:25-35

Now great multitudes were going with him. He turned and said to them,

"If anyone comes to me, and doesn't disregard his own father, mother, wife, children, brothers, and sisters, yes, and his own life also, he can't be my disciple. Whoever doesn't bear his own cross, and come after me, can't be my disciple.

For which of you, desiring to build a tower, doesn't first sit down and count the cost, to see if he has enough to complete it? Or perhaps, when he has laid a foundation, and is not able to finish, everyone who sees begins to mock him, saying, this man began to build, and wasn't able to finish.'

Or what king, as he goes to encounter another king in war, will not sit down first and consider whether he is able with ten thousand to meet him who comes against him with twenty thousand? Or else, while the other is yet a great way off, he sends an envoy and asks for conditions of peace.

So therefore, whoever of you who doesn't renounce all that he has, he can't be my disciple. Salt is good, but if the salt becomes flat and tasteless, with what do you season it? It is fit neither for the soil nor for the manure pile. It is thrown out. He who has ears to hear, let him hear."

The Parable of the Wandering Sheep
Lk 15:1-7 / Mt 18:10-14

Now all the tax collectors and sinners were coming close to him to hear him.

The Pharisees and the scribes murmured, saying, "This man welcomes sinners, and eats with them."

He told them this parable. "See that you don't despise one of these little ones, for I tell you that in heaven their angels always see the face of my Father who is in heaven. For the Son of Man came to save that which was lost. "What do you think? If a man has one hundred sheep, and one of them goes astray, doesn't he leave the ninety-nine, go to the mountains, and seek that which has gone astray?

If he finds it, most certainly I tell you, he rejoices over it more than over the ninety-nine which have not gone astray. When he comes home, he calls together his friends and his neighbors, saying to them, rejoice with me, for I have found my sheep which was lost!'

I tell you that even so there will be more joy in heaven over one sinner who repents, than over ninety-nine righteous people who need no repentance. Even so it is not the will of your Father who is in heaven that one of these little ones should perish.

The Parable of the Lost Coin
Lk 15:8-10

Or what woman, if she had ten drachma coins, if she lost one drachma coin, wouldn't light a lamp, sweep the house, and seek diligently until she found it?

When she has found it, she calls together her friends and neighbors, saying, rejoice with me, for I have found the drachma which I had lost.'

Even so, I tell you, there is joy in the presence of the angels of God over one sinner repenting."

The Parable of the Lost Son
Lk 15:11-32

He said, "A certain man had two sons. The younger of them said to his father, Father, give me my share of your property.' He divided his livelihood between them. Not many days after, the younger son gathered all this together and traveled into a far country. There he wasted his property with riotous living. When he had spent all of it, there arose a severe famine in that country, and he began to be in need.

He went and joined himself to one of the citizens of that country, and he sent him into his fields to feed pigs. He wanted to fill his belly with the husks that the pigs ate, but no one gave him any. But when he came to himself, he said, how many hired servants of my father have bread enough to spare, and I'm dying with hunger! I will get up and go to my father, and will tell him, "Father, I have sinned against heaven, and in your sight. I am no more worthy to be called your son. Make me as one of your hired servants."'

"He arose and came to his father. But while he was still far off, his father saw him, and was moved with compassion, and ran, and fell on his neck, and kissed him. The son said to him, Father, I have sinned against heaven, and in your sight. I am no longer worthy to be called your son.'

"But the father said to his servants, bring out the best robe, and put it on him. Put a ring on his hand, and shoes on his feet. Bring the fattened calf, kill it, and let us eat, and celebrate.

For this, my son, was dead, and is alive again. He was lost, and is found.' They began to celebrate.

"Now his elder son was in the field. As he came near to the house, he heard music and dancing. He called one of the servants to him, and asked what was going on.

He said to him, Your brother has come, and your father has killed the fattened calf, because he has received him back safe and healthy.'

But he was angry, and would not go in.

Therefore his father came out, and begged him.

But he answered his father, Behold, these many years I have served you, and I never disobeyed a commandment of yours, but you never gave me a goat, that I might celebrate with my friends. But when this, your son, came, who has devoured your living with prostitutes, you killed the fattened calf for him.'

"He said to him, Son, you are always with me, and all that is mine is yours. But it was appropriate to celebrate and be glad, for this, your brother, was dead, and is alive again. He was lost, and is found.'"

The Parable of the Shrewd Manager
Lk 16:1-14

He also said to his disciples, "There was a certain rich man who had a manager. An accusation was made to him that this man was wasting his possessions. He called him, and said to him, What is this that I hear about you? Give an accounting of your management, for you can no longer be

manager.'
"The manager said within himself, What will I do, seeing that my lord is taking away the management position from me? I don't have strength to dig. I am ashamed to beg.

I know what I will do, so that when I am removed from management, they may receive me into their houses.' Calling each one of his lord's debtors to him, he said to the first, How much do you owe to my lord?'

He said, A hundred batos of oil.'

He said to him, Take your bill, and sit down quickly and write fifty.'

Then he said to another, How much do you owe?'

He said, A hundred cors of wheat.'

He said to him, Take your bill, and write eighty.' "His lord commended the dishonest manager because he had done wisely, for the children of this world are, in their own generation, wiser than the children of the light.

I tell you, make for yourselves friends by means of unrighteous mammon, so that when you fail, they may receive you into the eternal tents. He who is faithful in a very little is faithful also in much. He who is dishonest in a very little is also dishonest in much.

If therefore you have not been faithful in the unrighteous mammon, who will commit to your trust the true riches? If you have not been faithful in that which is another's, who will give you that which is your own? No servant can serve two masters, for either he will hate the one, and love the other; or else he will hold to one, and despise the other. You aren't able to serve God and Mammon."

The Pharisees, who were lovers of money, also heard all these things, and they scoffed at him.

Chapter Eleven:
The Requirements of the kingdom of God

Additional Teachings
Lk 16:15-18

He said to them, "You are those who justify yourselves in the sight of men, but God knows your hearts. For that which is exalted among men is an abomination in the sight of God. The law and the prophets were until John. From that time the Good News of the Kingdom of God is preached, and everyone is forcing his way into it. But it is easier for heaven and earth to pass away, than for one tiny stroke of a pen in the law to fall.

Everyone who divorces his wife, and marries another, commits adultery. He who marries one who is divorced from a husband commits adultery.

The Rich Man and Lazarus
Lk 16:19-31

"Now there was a certain rich man, and he was clothed in purple and fine linen, living in luxury every day. A certain beggar, named Lazarus, was laid at his gate, full of sores, and desiring to be fed with the crumbs that fell from the rich man's table. Yes, even the dogs came and licked his sores.

It happened that the beggar died, and that he was carried away by the angels to Abraham's bosom. The rich man also died and was buried. In Hades, he lifted up his eyes, being in torment, and saw Abraham far off, and Lazarus at his bosom.

He cried and said, Father Abraham, have mercy on me, and send Lazarus, that he may dip the tip of his finger in water, and cool my tongue! For I am in anguish in this flame.' "But Abraham said, Son, remember that you, in your lifetime, received your good things, and Lazarus, in the same way, bad things. But now here he is comforted, and you are in anguish.

Besides all this, between us and you there is a great gulf fixed, that those who want to pass from here to you are not able, and that no one may cross over from there to us.'

"He said, I ask you therefore, father, that you would send him to my father's house; for I have five brothers, that he may testify to them, so they won't also come into this place of torment.'

"But Abraham said to him, they have Moses and the prophets. Let them listen to them.'

"He said, 'No, Father Abraham, but if one goes to them from the dead, they will repent.'

"He said to him, if they don't listen to Moses and the prophets, neither will they be persuaded if one rises from the dead.'"

Sin, Faith, Duty
Lk 17:1-10

He said to the disciples, "It is impossible that no occasions of stumbling should come, but woe to him through whom they come! It would be better for him if a millstone were hung around his neck, and he were thrown into the sea, rather than that he should cause one of these little ones to stumble.

Be careful. If your brother sins against you, rebuke him. If he repents, forgive him.

If he sins against you seven times in the day, and seven times returns, saying, I repent,' you shall forgive him." The apostles said to the Lord, "Increase our faith." The Lord said, "If you had faith like a grain of mustard seed, you would tell this sycamore tree, Be uprooted, and be planted in the sea,' and it would obey you. But who is there among you, having a servant plowing or keeping sheep, that will say, when he comes in from the field, come immediately and sit down at the table,' and will not rather tell him, prepare my supper, clothe yourself properly, and serve me, while I eat and drink. Afterward you shall eat and drink'? Does he thank that servant because he did the things that were commanded? I think not. Even so you also, when you have done all the things that are commanded you, say, we are unworthy servants. We have done our duty.'"

Jesus Heals Ten Men with Leprosy
Lk 17:11-19

It happened as he was on his way to Jerusalem, that he was passing along the borders of Samaria and Galilee. As he entered into a certain village, ten men who were lepers met him, who stood at a distance.

They lifted up their voices, saying, "Jesus, Master, have mercy on us!"

When he saw them, he said to them, "Go and show yourselves to the priests."

It happened that as they went, they were cleansed.

One of them, when he saw that he was healed, turned back, glorifying God with a loud voice. He fell on his face at Jesus' feet, giving him thanks; and he was a Samaritan. Jesus answered, "Weren't the ten cleansed? But where are the nine? Were there none found who returned to give glory to God, except this stranger?"

Then he said to him, "Get up, and go your way. Your faith has healed you."

The Coming of the Kingdom of God
Lk 17:20-37

Being asked by the Pharisees when the Kingdom of God would come, he answered them, "The Kingdom of God doesn't come with observation; neither will they say, Look, here!' or, Look, there!' for behold, the Kingdom of God is within you."

He said to the disciples, "The days will come, when you will desire to see one of the days of the Son of Man, and you will not see it. They will tell you, Look, here!' or Look, there!' Don't go away, nor follow after them, for as the lightning, when it flashes out of the one part under the sky, shines to the other part under the sky; so will the Son of Man be in his day. But first, he must suffer many things and be rejected by this generation.

As it happened in the days of Noah, even so will it be also in the days of the Son of Man. They ate, they drank, they were married, they were given in marriage, until the day that Noah entered into the ship, and the flood came, and destroyed them all. Likewise, even as it happened in the days of Lot: they ate, they drank, they bought, they sold, they planted, they built; but in the day that Lot went out from Sodom, it rained fire and sulfur from the sky and destroyed them all. It will be the same way in the day that the Son of Man is revealed.

In that day, he who will be on the housetop, and his goods in the house, let him not go down to take them away. Let him who is in the field likewise not turn back.

Remember Lot's wife! Whoever seeks to save his life loses it, but whoever loses his life preserves it. I tell you, in that night there will be two people in one bed. The one will be taken, and the other will be left. There will be two grinding grain together. One will be taken, and the other will be left."

They, answering, asked him, "Where, Lord?" He said to them, "Where the body is, there will the vultures also be gathered together."

The Parable of the Persistent Widow
Lk 18:1-8

He also spoke a parable to them that they must always pray, and not give up, saying, "There was a judge in a certain city who didn't fear God, and didn't respect man.

A widow was in that city, and she often came to him, saying, Defend me from my adversary!'

He wouldn't for a while, but afterward he said to himself, Though I neither fear God, nor respect man, yet because this widow bothers me, I will defend her, or else she will wear me out by her continual coming.'"

The Lord said, "Listen to what the unrighteous judge says. Won't God avenge his chosen ones, who are crying out to him day and night, and yet he exercises patience with them?

I tell you that he will avenge them quickly. Nevertheless, when the Son of Man comes, will he find faith on the earth?"

The Parable of the Pharisee and the Tax Collector Lk 18:9-14

He spoke also this parable to certain people who were convinced of their own righteousness, and who despised all others.

"Two men went up into the temple to pray; one was a Pharisee, and the other was a tax collector. The Pharisee stood and prayed to himself like this: God, I thank you, that I am not like the rest of men, extortionists, unrighteous, adulterers, or even like this tax collector.

I fast twice a week. I give tithes of all that I get.' But the tax collector, standing far away, wouldn't even lift up his eyes to heaven, but beat his breast, saying, God, be merciful to me, a sinner!'

I tell you, this man went down to his house justified rather than the other; for everyone who exalts himself will be humbled, but he who humbles himself will be exalted."

Question about Divorce
Mk 10:1-12 / Mt 19:1-12

Jesus then left that place and went into the region of Judea and across the Jordan. He arose from there and came into the borders of Judea and beyond the Jordan. Multitudes came together to him again. As he usually did, he was again teaching them.

Pharisees came to him testing him, and asked him, "Is it lawful for a man to divorce his wife?"

He answered, "What did Moses command you?"

They said, "Moses allowed a certificate of divorce to be written, and to divorce her."

But Jesus said to them, "For your hardness of heart, he wrote you this commandment.

But from the beginning of the creation, God made them male and female. For this cause a man will leave his father and mother, and will join to his wife, and the two will become one flesh, so that they are no longer two, but one flesh. What therefore God has joined together, let no man separate."

In the house, his disciples asked him again about the same matter.

He said to them, "Whoever divorces his wife, and marries another, commits adultery against her. If a woman herself divorces her husband, and marries another, she commits adultery."

They asked him, "Why then did Moses command us to give her a bill of divorce, and divorce her?"

He said to them, "Moses, because of the hardness of your hearts, allowed you to divorce your wives, but from the beginning it has not been so. I tell you that whoever divorces his wife, except for sexual immorality, and marries another, commits adultery; and he who marries her when she is divorced commits adultery."

His disciples said to him, "If this is the case of the man with his wife, it is not expedient to marry."

But he said to them, "Not all men can receive this saying, but those to whom it is given. For there are eunuchs who were born that way from their mother's womb, and there are eunuchs who were made eunuchs by men; and there are eunuchs who made themselves eunuchs for the Kingdom of Heaven's sake. He who is able to receive it, let him receive it."

The Little Children and Jesus
Mk 10:13-16 / Mt 19:13-15 / Lk 18:15-17

They were bringing to him little children, that he should touch them, but the disciples rebuked those who were bringing them. But when Jesus saw it, he was moved with indignation, and said to them, "Allow the little children to come to me! Don't forbid them, for the Kingdom of God belongs to such as these. Most certainly I tell you, whoever will not receive the Kingdom of God like a little child, he will in no way enter into it."

He took them in his arms, and blessed them, laying his hands on them.

The Rich and the Kingdom of God
Mt 19:16-30 / Mk 10:17-31 / Lk 18:18-30

Behold, one came to him and said, "Good teacher, what good thing shall I do, that I may have eternal life?"

He said to him, "Why do you call me good? No one is good but one, that is, God. But if you want to enter into life, keep the commandments."

He said to him, "Which ones?"

Jesus said, "You shall not murder.' You shall not commit adultery.' You shall not steal.' You shall not offer false testimony.' Honor your father and mother.' And, You shall love your neighbor as yourself.'"

The young man said to him, "All these things I have observed from my youth. What do I still lack?"

Jesus said to him, "If you want to be perfect, go, sell what you have, and give to the poor, and you will have treasure in heaven; and come, follow me."

But when the young man heard the saying, he went away sad, for he was one who had great possessions.

Jesus said to his disciples, "Most certainly I say to you, a rich man will enter into the Kingdom of Heaven with difficulty. Again I tell you, it is easier for a camel to go through a needle's eye, than for a rich man to enter into the Kingdom of God."

When the disciples heard it, they were exceedingly astonished, saying, "Who then can be saved?"

Looking at them, Jesus said, "With men this is impossible, but with God all things are possible."

Then Peter answered, "Behold, we have left everything, and followed you. What then will we have?"

Jesus said to them, "Most certainly I tell you that you who have followed me, in the regeneration when the Son of Man will sit on the throne of his glory, you also will sit on twelve thrones, judging the twelve tribes of Israel. Everyone who has left houses, or brothers, or sisters, or father, or mother, or wife, or children, or lands, for my name's sake, will receive one hundred times, and will inherit eternal life. But many will be last who are first; and first who are last.

The Parable of the Workers in the Vineyard
Mt 20:1-16

"For the Kingdom of Heaven is like a man who was the master of a household, who went out early in the morning to hire laborers for his vineyard. When he had agreed with the laborers for a denarius a day, he sent them into his vineyard. He went out about the third hour, and saw others standing idle in the marketplace.

To them he said, You also go into the vineyard, and whatever is right I will give you.' So they went their way.

Again he went out about the sixth and the ninth hour and did likewise. About the eleventh hour he went out and found others standing idle. He said to them, why do you stand here all day idle?'

"They said to him, Because no one has hired us.'

"He said to them, you also go into the vineyard, and you will receive whatever is right.

When evening had come, the lord of the vineyard said to his manager, Call the laborers and pay them their wages, beginning from the last to the first.'

"When those who were hired at about the eleventh hour came, they each received a denarius.

When the first came, they supposed that they would receive more; and they likewise each received a denarius. When they received it, they murmured against the master of the household, saying, these last have spent one hour, and you have made them equal to us, who have borne the burden of the day and the scorching heat!'

"But he answered one of them, Friend, I am doing you no wrong. Didn't you agree with me for a denarius?

Take that which is yours and go your way. It is my desire to give to this last just as much as to you. Isn't it lawful for me to do what I want to with what I own? Or is your eye evil, because I am good?'

So, the last will be first, and the first last. For many are called, but few are chosen."

Jesus Predicts His Death a Third Time
Lk 18:31-34 / Mt 20:17-19 / Mk 10:32-34

He took the twelve aside, and said to them, "Behold, we are going up to Jerusalem, and all the things that are written through the prophets concerning the Son of Man will be completed. For he will be delivered up to the Gentiles, will be mocked, treated shamefully, and spit on. They will scourge and kill him. On the third day, he will rise again."

They understood none of these things. This saying was hidden from them, and they didn't understand the things that were said.

The Request of James and John
Mt 20:20-28 / Mk 10:35-45

Then the mother of the sons of Zebedee came to him with her sons, kneeling and asking a certain thing of him. He said to her, "What do you want?"

She said to him, "Command that these, my two sons, may sit, one on your right hand, and one on your left hand, in your Kingdom."

But Jesus answered, "You don't know what you are asking. Are you able to drink the cup that I am about to drink, and be baptized with the baptism that I am baptized with?"

They said to him, "We are able."

He said to them, "You will indeed drink my cup, and be baptized with the baptism that I am baptized with, but to sit on my right hand and on my left hand is not mine to give; but it is for whom it has been prepared by my Father."

When the ten heard it, they were indignant with the two brothers.

But Jesus summoned them, and said, "You know that the rulers of the nations lord it over them, and their great ones exercise authority over them. It shall not be so among you, but whoever desires to become great among you shall be your servant. Whoever desires to be first among you shall be your bondservant, even as the Son of Man came not to be served, but to serve, and to give his life as a ransom for many."

Chapter Twelve:
The Spiritual Blindness

A Blind Beggar Receives His Sight
Lk 18:35-43 / Mk 10:46-52 / (Mt 20:29-34)

It happened, as he came near Jericho, a certain blind man sat by the road, begging.

Hearing a multitude going by, he asked what this meant. They told him that Jesus of Nazareth was passing by. He cried out, "Jesus, you son of David, have mercy on me!"

Those who led the way rebuked him, that he should be quiet; but he cried out all the more, "You son of David, have mercy on me!"

Jesus stood still, and said, "Call him."

They called the blind man, saying to him, "Cheer up! Get up. He is calling you!"

He, casting away his cloak, sprang up, and came to Jesus.

> Editor Footnote: If the blind man ran to Jesus by himself, he may go the wrong direction.

Standing still, Jesus commanded him to be brought to him. When he had come near, he asked him,

"What do you want me to do?"

He said, "Lord, that I may see again."

Jesus said to him, "Receive your sight. Your faith has healed you."

Immediately he received his sight, and followed him, glorifying God. All the people, when they saw it, praised God.

Jesus met Zacchaeus
Lk 19:1-10

He entered and was passing through Jericho. There was a man named Zacchaeus. He was a chief tax collector, and he was rich. He was trying to see who Jesus was, and couldn't because of the crowd, because he was short. He ran ahead and climbed up into a sycamore tree to see him, for he was to pass that way.

When Jesus came to the place, he looked up and saw him, and said to him, "Zacchaeus, hurry and come down, for today I must stay at your house."

He hurried, came down, and received him joyfully. When they saw it, they all murmured, saying, "He has gone in to lodge with a man who is a sinner."

Zacchaeus stood and said to the Lord, "Behold, Lord, half of my goods I give to the poor. If I have wrongfully exacted anything of anyone, I restore four times as much."

Jesus said to him, "Today, salvation has come to this house, because he also is a son of Abraham.

For the Son of Man came to seek and to save that which was lost."

Jesus healed another two Blind Men
Mt 20:29-34 / (Lk 18:35-43 / Mk 10:46-52)

As they went out from Jericho, a great multitude followed him.

Behold, two blind men sitting by the road, when they heard that Jesus was passing by, cried out, "Lord, have mercy on us, you son of David!"

The multitude rebuked them, telling them that they should be quiet, but they cried out even more, "Lord, have mercy on us, you son of David!"

Jesus stood still, and called them, and asked, "What do you want me to do for you?"

They told him, "Lord, that our eyes may be opened." Jesus, being moved with compassion, touched their eyes; and immediately their eyes received their sight, and they followed him.

Jesus Heals a Man Born Blind
Jn 9:1-12

As he passed by, he saw a man blind from birth.

His disciples asked him, "Rabbi, who sinned, this man or his parents, that he was born blind?"

Jesus answered, "Neither did this man sin, nor his parents; but, that the works of God might be revealed in him.

I must work the works of him who sent me, while it is day. The night is coming, when no one can work. While I am in the world, I am the light of the world."

When he had said this, he spat on the ground, made mud with the saliva, anointed the blind man's eyes with the mud, and said to him, "Go, wash in the pool of Siloam" (which means "Sent").

So he went away, washed, and came back seeing. The neighbors therefore, and those who saw that he was blind before, said, "Isn't this he who sat and begged?"

Others were saying, "It is he."

Still others were saying, "He looks like him."

He said, "I am he."

They therefore were asking him, "How were your eyes opened?"

He answered, "A man called Jesus made mud, anointed my eyes, and said to me, Go to the pool of Siloam, and wash.' So I went away and washed, and I received sight."

Then they asked him, "Where is he?"

He said, "I don't know."

The Pharisees Investigate the Healing
Jn 9:13-34

They brought him who had been blind to the Pharisees. It was a Sabbath when Jesus made the mud and opened his eyes. Again therefore the Pharisees also asked him how he received his sight. He said to them, "He put mud on my eyes, I washed, and I see."

Some therefore of the Pharisees said, "This man is not from God, because he doesn't keep the Sabbath."

Others said, "How can a man who is a sinner do such signs?"

There was division among them. Therefore they asked the blind man again, "What do you say about him, because he opened your eyes?"

He said, "He is a prophet."

The Jews therefore did not believe concerning him, that he had been blind, and had received his sight, until they called the parents of him who had received his sight, and asked them, "Is this your son, whom you say was born blind? How then does he now see?"

His parents answered them, "We know that this is our son, and that he was born blind;

but how he now sees, we don't know; or who opened his eyes, we don't know. He is of age. Ask him. He will speak for himself."

His parents said these things because they feared the Jews; for the Jews had already agreed that if any man would confess him as Christ, he would be put out of the synagogue.

Therefore his parents said, "He is of age. Ask him."

So they called the man who was blind a second time, and said to him, "Give glory to God. We know that this man is a sinner."

He therefore answered, "I don't know if he is a sinner. One thing I do know: that though I was blind, now I see."

They said to him again, "What did he do to you? How did he open your eyes?"

He answered them, "I told you already, and you didn't listen. Why do you want to hear it again? You don't also want to become his disciples, do you?"

They insulted him and said, "You are his disciple, but we are disciples of Moses. We know that God has spoken to Moses. But as for this man, we don't know where he comes from."

The man answered them, "How amazing! You don't know where he comes from, yet he opened my eyes. We know that God doesn't listen to sinners, but if anyone is a worshiper of God, and does his will, he listens to him. Since the world began it has never been heard of that anyone opened the eyes of someone born blind. If this man were not from God, he could do nothing."

They answered him, "You were altogether born in sins, and do you teach us?"

They threw him out.

Spiritual Blindness
Jn 9:35-41

Jesus heard that they had thrown him out, and finding him, he said, "Do you believe in the Son of God?"

He answered, "Who is he, Lord, that I may believe in him?"

Jesus said to him, "You have both seen him, and it is he who speaks with you."

He said, "Lord, I believe!" and he worshiped him.

Jesus said, "I came into this world for judgment, that those who don't see may see; and that those who see may become blind."

Those of the Pharisees who were with him heard these things, and said to him, "Are we also blind?"

Jesus said to them, "If you were blind, you would have no sin; but now you say, We see.' Therefore your sin remains.

The Good Shepherd and His Sheep
Jn 10:1-21

"Most certainly, I tell you, one who doesn't enter by the door into the sheep fold, but climbs up some other way, the same is a thief and a robber. But one who enters in by the door is the shepherd of the sheep. The gatekeeper opens the gate for him, and the sheep listen to his voice. He calls his own sheep by name, and leads them out. Whenever he brings out his own sheep, he goes before them, and the sheep follow him, for they know his voice. They will by no means follow a stranger, but will flee from him; for they don't know the voice of strangers."

Jesus spoke this parable to them, but they didn't understand what he was telling them.

Jesus therefore said to them again, "Most certainly, I tell you, I am the sheep's door. All who came before me are thieves and robbers, but the sheep didn't listen to them.

I am the door. If anyone enters in by me, he will be saved, and will go in and go out, and will find pasture. The thief only comes to steal, kill, and destroy. I came that they may have life, and may have it abundantly. I am the good shepherd. The good shepherd lays down his life for the sheep. He who is a hired hand, and not a shepherd, who doesn't own the sheep, sees the wolf coming, leaves the sheep, and flees. The wolf snatches the sheep, and scatters them. The hired hand flees because he is a hired hand, and doesn't care for the sheep. I am the good shepherd. I know my own, and I'm known by my own; even as the Father knows me, and I know the Father. I lay down my life for the sheep.

I have other sheep, which are not of this fold. I must bring them also, and they will hear my voice. They will become one flock with one shepherd. Therefore, the Father loves me, because I lay down my life, that I may take it again. No one takes it away from me, but I lay it down by myself. I have the power to lay it down, and I have the power to take it again. I received this commandment from my Father."

Therefore, a division arose again among the Jews because of these words. Many of them said, "He has a demon, and is insane! Why do you listen to him?"

Others said, "These are not the sayings of one possessed by a demon. It isn't possible for a demon to open the eyes of the blind, is it?"

Further Conflict Over Jesus' Claims
Jn 10:22-42

It was the Feast of the Dedication at Jerusalem. It was winter, and Jesus was walking in the temple, in Solomon's porch.

The Jews therefore came around him and said to him, "How long will you hold us in suspense? If you are the Christ, tell us plainly."

Jesus answered them, "I told you, and you don't believe. The works that I do in my Father's name, these testify about me. But you don't believe, because you are not of my sheep, as I told you. My sheep hear my voice, and I know them, and they follow me. I give eternal life to them. They will never perish, and no one will snatch them out of my hand. My Father, who has given them to me, is greater than all. No one is able to snatch them out of my Father's hand. I and the Father are one."

Therefore, Jews took up stones again to stone him.

Jesus answered them, "I have shown you many good works from my Father. For which of those works do you stone me?"

The Jews answered him, "We don't stone you for a good work, but for blasphemy: because you, being a man, make yourself God."

Jesus answered them, "Isn't it written in your law, I said, you are gods?'

If he called them gods, to whom the word of God came (and the Scripture can't be broken), do you say of him whom the Father sanctified and sent into the world, You blaspheme,' because I said, I am the Son of God?' If I don't do the works of my Father, don't believe me.

But if I do them, though you don't believe me, believe the works; that you may know and believe that the Father is in me, and I in the Father."

They sought again to seize him, and he went out of their hand. He went away again beyond the Jordan into the place where John was baptizing at first, and there he stayed.

Many came to him. They said, "John indeed did no sign, but everything that John said about this man is true."

Many believed in him there.

The Death of Lazarus
Jn 11:1-16

Now a certain man was sick, Lazarus from Bethany, of the village of Mary and her sister, Martha. It was that Mary who had anointed the Lord with ointment, and wiped his feet with her hair, whose brother, Lazarus, was sick.

The sisters therefore sent to him, saying, "Lord, behold, he for whom you have great affection is sick."

But when Jesus heard it, he said, "This sickness is not to death, but for the glory of God, that God's Son may be glorified by it."

Now Jesus loved Martha, and her sister, and Lazarus. When therefore he heard that he was sick, he stayed two days in the place where he was. Then after this he said to the disciples, "Let's go into Judea again."

The disciples told him, "Rabbi, the Jews were just trying to stone you, and are you going there again?"

Jesus answered, "Aren't there twelve hours of daylight? If a man walks in the day, he doesn't stumble, because he sees the light of this world. But if a man walks in the night, he stumbles, because the light isn't in him."

He said these things, and after that, he said to them, "Our friend, Lazarus, has fallen asleep, but I am going so that I may awake him out of sleep."

The disciples therefore said, "Lord, if he has fallen asleep, he will recover."

Now Jesus had spoken of his death, but they thought that he spoke of taking rest in sleep.

So Jesus said to them plainly then, "Lazarus is dead. I am glad for your sakes that I was not there, so that you may believe. Nevertheless, let's go to him."

Thomas therefore, who is called Didymus, said to his fellow disciples, "Let's go also, that we may die with him."

Jesus Comforts the Sisters of Lazarus
Jn 11:17-37

So when Jesus came, he found that he had been in the tomb four days already.

Now Bethany was near Jerusalem, about fifteen stadia away. Many of the Jews had joined the women around Martha and Mary, to console them concerning their brother. Then when Martha heard that Jesus was coming, she went and met him, but Mary stayed in the house.

Therefore, Martha said to Jesus, "Lord, if you would have been here, my brother wouldn't have died. Even now I know that, whatever you ask of God, God will give you."

Jesus said to her, "Your brother will rise again."

Martha said to him, "I know that he will rise again in the resurrection at the last day."

Jesus said to her, "I am the resurrection and the life. He who believes in me will still live, even if he dies. Whoever lives and believes in me will never die. Do you believe this?"

She said to him, "Yes, Lord. I have come to believe that you are the Christ, God's Son, he who comes into the world."

When she had said this, she went away, and called Mary, her sister, secretly, saying, "The Teacher is here, and is calling you."

When she heard this, she arose quickly, and went to him. Now Jesus had not yet come into the village, but was in the place where Martha met him. Then the Jews who were with her in the house, and were consoling her, when they saw Mary, that she rose up quickly and went out, followed her, saying, "She is going to the tomb to weep there."

Therefore when Mary came to where Jesus was, and saw him, she fell down at his feet, saying to him, "Lord, if you would have been here, my brother wouldn't have died."

When Jesus therefore saw her weeping, and the Jews weeping who came with her, he groaned in the spirit, and was troubled, and said, "Where have you laid him?"

They told him, "Lord, come and see."

Jesus wept.

The Jews therefore said, "See how much affection he had for him!"

Some of them said, "Couldn't this man, who opened the eyes of him who was blind, have also kept this man from dying?"

Jesus Raises Lazarus from the Dead
Jn 11:38-44

Jesus therefore, again groaning in himself, came to the tomb. Now it was a cave, and a stone lay against it.

"Jesus said, "Take away the stone."

Martha, the sister of him who was dead, said to him, "Lord, by this time there is a stench, for he has been dead four days."

Jesus said to her, "Didn't I tell you that if you believed, you would see God's glory?"

So they took away the stone from the place where the dead man was lying. Jesus lifted up his eyes, and said, "Father, I thank you that you listened to me. I know that you always listen to me, but because of the multitude that stands around I said this, that they may believe that you sent me."

When he had said this, he cried with a loud voice, "Lazarus, come out!"

He who was dead came out, bound hand and foot with wrappings, and his face was wrapped around with a cloth.

Jesus said to them, "Free him, and let him go."

The Plot to Kill Jesus
Jn 11:45-57

Therefore many of the Jews, who came to Mary and saw what Jesus did, believed in him. But some of them went away to the Pharisees, and told them the things which Jesus had done.

The chief priests therefore and the Pharisees gathered a council, and said, "What are we doing? For this man does many signs. If we leave him alone like this, everyone will believe in him, and the Romans will come and take away both our place and our nation."

But a certain one of them, Caiaphas, being high priest that year, said to them, "You know nothing at all, nor do you consider that it is advantageous for us that one man should die for the people, and that the whole nation not perish." Now he didn't say this of himself, but being high priest that year, he prophesied that Jesus would die for the nation, and not for the nation only, but that he might also gather together into one the children of God who are scattered abroad. So from that day forward they took counsel that they might put him to death.

Jesus therefore walked no more openly among the Jews, but departed from there into the country near the wilderness, to a city called Ephraim. He stayed there with his disciples.

Now the Passover of the Jews was at hand. Many went up from the country to Jerusalem before the Passover, to purify themselves.

Then they sought for Jesus and spoke one with another, as they stood in the temple, "What do you think that he isn't coming to the feast at all?"

Now the chief priests and the Pharisees had commanded that if anyone knew where he was, he should report it, that they might seize him.

Jesus Anointed at Bethany
Jn 12:1-11 / Mt 26:6-12 / Mk 14:3-9

Then six days before the Passover, Jesus came to Bethany, where Lazarus was, who had been dead, whom he raised from the dead. So they made him a supper there. Martha served, but Lazarus was one of those who sat at the table with him.

Mary, therefore, took a pound of ointment of pure nard, very precious, and anointed the feet of Jesus, and wiped his feet with her hair. The house was filled with the fragrance of the ointment.

Then Judas Iscariot, Simon's son, one of his disciples, who would betray him, said,

"Why wasn't this ointment sold for three hundred denarii, and given to the poor?"

Now he said this, not because he cared for the poor, but because he was a thief, and having the money box, used to steal what was put into it.

But Jesus said, "Leave her alone. She has kept this for the day of my burial. For you always have the poor with you, but you don't always have me.

Most certainly I tell you, wherever this Good News is preached in the whole world, what this woman has done will also be spoken of as a memorial of her."

A large crowd therefore of the Jews learned that he was there, and they came, not for Jesus' sake only, but that they might see Lazarus also, whom he had raised from the dead.

But the chief priests conspired to put Lazarus to death also, because on account of him many of the Jews went away and believed in Jesus.

Chapter Thirteen:
Jesus entered Jerusalem in Triumphant

Jesus Comes to Jerusalem as King
Lk 19:28-44 / Jn 12:12-19 / Mk 11:1-11
/ Mt 21:1-11

Having said these things, he went on ahead, going up to Jerusalem.

It happened, when he drew near to Bethsphage and Bethany, at the mountain that is called Olivet, he sent two of his disciples, saying, "Go your way into the village on the other side, in which, as you enter, you will find a colt tied, whereon no man ever yet sat. Untie it and bring it. If anyone asks you, why are you untying it?' say to him: The Lord needs it.'"

Those who were sent went away and found things just as he had told them.

As they were untying the colt, its owners said to them, "Why are you untying the colt?"

They said, "The Lord needs it."

They brought it to Jesus. They threw their cloaks on the colt, and set Jesus on them.

Jesus, having found a young donkey, sat on it. As it is written,

"Don't be afraid, daughter of Zion.

Behold, your King comes, sitting on a donkey's colt."

His disciples didn't understand these things at first, but when Jesus was glorified, then they remembered that these things were written about him, and that they had done these things to him.

The multitude therefore that was with him when he called Lazarus out of the tomb, and raised him from the dead, was testifying about it. For this cause also the multitude went and met him, because they heard that he had done this sign.

As he went, they spread their cloaks on the road. As he was now getting near, at the descent of the Mount of Olives, the whole multitude of the disciples began to rejoice and praise God with a loud voice for all the mighty works which they had seen, saying, "Blessed is the King who comes in the name of the Lord!"

Many spread their garments on the way, and others were cutting down branches from the trees, and spreading them on the road.

Those who went in front, and those who followed, cried out, "Hosanna! Blessed is he who comes in the name of the Lord! Blessed is the kingdom of our father David that is coming in the name of the Lord! Hosanna in the highest!"

The Pharisees therefore said among themselves, "See how you accomplish nothing. Behold, the world has gone after him."

Some of the Pharisees from the multitude said to him, "Teacher, rebuke your disciples!"

He answered them, "I tell you that if these were silent, the stones would cry out."

When he drew near, he saw the city and wept over it, saying, "If you, even you, had known today the things which belong to your peace! But now, they are hidden from your eyes. For the days will come on you, when your enemies will throw up a barricade against you, surround you, hem you in on every side, and will dash you and your children within you to the ground. They will not leave in you one stone on another, because you didn't know the time of your visitation."

When he had come into Jerusalem, all the city was stirred up, saying, "Who is this?"

The multitudes said, "This is the prophet, Jesus, from Nazareth of Galilee."

Jesus entered into the temple in Jerusalem. When he had looked around at everything, it being now evening, he went out to Bethany with the twelve.

Jesus Predicts His Death
Jn 12:20-36

Now there were certain Greeks among those that went up to worship at the feast. These, therefore, came to Philip, who was from Bethsaida of Galilee, and asked him, saying, "Sir, we want to see Jesus."

Philip came and told Andrew, and in turn, Andrew came with Philip, and they told Jesus.

Jesus answered them, "The time has come for the Son of Man to be glorified. Most certainly I tell you, unless a grain of wheat falls into the earth and dies, it remains by itself alone. But if it dies, it bears much fruit. He who loves his life will lose it. He who hates his life in this world will keep it to eternal life. If anyone serves me, let him follow me. Where I am, there will my servant also be. If anyone serves me, the Father will honor him.

"Now my soul is troubled. What shall I say? Father, save me from this time?' But for this cause I came to this time. Father, glorify your name!"

Then there came a voice out of the sky, saying, "I have both glorified it, and will glorify it again."

The multitude therefore, who stood by and heard it, said that it had thundered. Others said, "An angel has spoken to him."

Jesus answered, "This voice hasn't come for my sake, but for your sakes. Now is the judgment of this world. Now the prince of this world will be cast out. And I, if I am lifted up from the earth, will draw all people to myself."

But he said this, signifying by what kind of death he should die.

The multitude answered him, "We have heard out of the law that the Christ remains forever. How do you say, The Son of Man must be lifted up?' Who is this Son of Man?"

Jesus therefore said to them, "Yet a little while the light is with you. Walk while you have the light, that darkness doesn't overtake you. He who walks in the darkness doesn't know where he is going. While you have the light, believe in the light, that you may become children of light."

Jesus said these things, and he departed and hid himself from them.

Belief and Unbelief Among the Jews
Jn 12:37-50

But though he had done so many signs before them, yet they didn't believe in him, that the word of Isaiah the prophet might be fulfilled, which he spoke,

"Lord, who has believed our report?

To whom has the arm of the Lord been revealed?"

For this cause they couldn't believe, for Isaiah said again,
"He has blinded their eyes and he hardened their heart,

lest they should see with their eyes,

and perceive with their heart,

and would turn, and I would heal them."

Isaiah said these things when he saw his glory, and spoke of him.

Nevertheless even of the rulers many believed in him, but because of the Pharisees they didn't confess it, so that they wouldn't be put out of the synagogue, for they loved men's praise more than God's praise.

Jesus cried out and said, "Whoever believes in me, believes not in me, but in him who sent me. He who sees me sees him who sent me. I have come as a light into the world, that whoever believes in me may not remain in the darkness. If anyone listens to my sayings, and doesn't believe, I don't judge him. For I came not to judge the world, but to save the world. He who rejects me, and doesn't receive my sayings, has one who judges him. The word that I spoke, the same will judge him in the last day. For I spoke not from myself, but the Father who sent me, he gave me a commandment, what I should say, and what I should speak. I know that his commandment is eternal life. The things therefore which I speak, even as the Father has said to me, so I speak."

Jesus Curses a Fig Tree
Mk 11:12-14 / Mt 21:18-19

The next day, when they had come out from Bethany, he was hungry. Seeing a fig tree afar off having leaves, he came to see if perhaps he might find anything on it. When he came to it, he found nothing but leaves, for it was not the season for figs.

Jesus told it, "May no one ever eat fruit from you again!" and his disciples heard it.

Jesus drove out the Temple the Second Time
Mk 11:15-18 / Mt 21:12-17 / Lk 19:45-48
/ (Jn 2:13-17)

They came to Jerusalem, and Jesus entered into the temple, and began to throw out those who sold and those who bought in the temple, and overthrew the tables of the money changers, and the seats of those who sold the doves. He would not allow anyone to carry a container through the temple.

He taught, saying to them, "Isn't it written, My house will be called a house of prayer for all the nations?' But you have made it a den of robbers!"

The chief priests and the scribes heard it, and sought how they might destroy him. For they feared him, because all the multitude was astonished at his teaching.

The blind and the lame came to him in the temple, and he healed them. But when the chief priests and the scribes saw the wonderful things that he did, and the children who were crying in the temple and saying, "Hosanna to the son of David!"

They were indignant, and said to him, "Do you hear what these are saying?"

Jesus said to them, "Yes, did you never read, Out of the mouth of babes and nursing babies you have perfected praise?'"

He left them, and went out of the city to Bethany, and lodged there.

The fig tree withered
Mk 11:19-26 / Mt 21:20-22

When evening came, he went out of the city. As they passed by in the morning, they saw the fig tree withered away from the roots.

Peter, remembering, said to him, "Rabbi, look! The fig tree which you cursed has withered away."

Jesus answered them, "Have faith in God. For most certainly I tell you, whoever may tell this mountain, Be taken up and cast into the sea,' and doesn't doubt in his heart, but believes that what he says is happening; he shall have whatever he says. Therefore I tell you, all things whatever you pray and ask for, believe that you have received them, and you shall have them. Whenever you stand praying, forgive, if you have anything against anyone; so that your Father, who is in heaven, may also forgive you your transgressions. But if you do not forgive, neither will your Father in heaven forgive your transgressions."

The Authority of Jesus Questioned
Mt 21:23-27 / Mk 11:27-33 / Lk 20:1-8

When he had come into the temple, the chief priests and the elders of the people came to him as he was teaching, and said, "By what authority do you do these things? Who gave you this authority?"

Jesus answered them, "I also will ask you one question, which if you tell me, I likewise will tell you by what authority I do these things. The baptism of John, where was it from? From heaven or from men?"

They reasoned with themselves, saying, "If we say, From heaven,' he will ask us, why then did you not believe him?' But if we say, From men,' we fear the multitude, for all hold John as a prophet."

They answered Jesus, and said, "We don't know."

He also said to them, "Neither will I tell you by what authority I do these things.

The Parable of the Two Sons
Mt 21:28-32

But what do you think? A man had two sons, and he came to the first, and said, Son, go work today in my vineyard.'

He answered, 'I will not,' but afterward he changed his mind, and went.

He came to the second, and said the same thing. He answered, 'I go, sir,' but he didn't go.

Which of the two did the will of his father?"

They said to him, "The first."

Jesus said to them, "Most certainly I tell you that the tax collectors and the prostitutes are entering into the Kingdom of God before you. For John came to you in the way of righteousness, and you didn't believe him, but the tax collectors and the prostitutes believed him. When you saw it, you didn't even repent afterward, that you might believe him,

The Parable of the Tenants
Mk 12:1-12 / Mt 21:33-46 / Lk 20:9-19

He began to speak to them in parables. "A man planted a vineyard, put a hedge around it, dug a pit for the wine press, built a tower, rented it out to a farmer, and went into another country. When it was time, he sent a servant to the farmer to get from the farmer his share of the fruit of the vineyard. They took him, beat him, and sent him away empty.

Again, he sent another servant to them; and they threw stones at him, wounded him in the head, and sent him away shamefully treated. Again, he sent another; and they killed him; and many others, beating some, and killing some. Therefore, still having one, his beloved son, he sent him last to them, saying, They will respect my son.'

But those farmers said among themselves, this is the heir. Come, let's kill him, and the inheritance will be ours.'

They took him, killed him, and cast him out of the vineyard.
What therefore will the lord of the vineyard do? He will come and destroy the farmers and will give the vineyard to others.

Jesus said to them, "Did you never read in the Scriptures,

The stone which the builders rejected,

the same was made the head of the corner.

This was from the Lord.

It is marvelous in our eyes?'

"Therefore, I tell you, the Kingdom of God will be taken away from you and will be given to a nation producing its fruit. He who falls on this stone will be broken to pieces, but on whomever it will fall, it will scatter him as dust."

When the chief priests and the Pharisees heard his parables, they perceived that he spoke about them. When they sought to seize him, they feared the multitudes, because they considered him to be a prophet.

Paying Taxes to Caesar
Lk 20:20-26 / Mt 22:15-22 / Mk 12:13-17

They watched him, and sent out spies, who pretended to be righteous, that they might trap him in something he said, so as to deliver him up to the power and authority of the governor.

They asked him, "Teacher, we know that you say and teach what is right, and aren't partial to anyone, but truly teach the way of God. Is it lawful for us to pay taxes to Caesar, or not?"

But he perceived their craftiness, and said to them, "Why do you test me? Show me a denarius. Whose image and inscription are on it?"

They answered, "Caesar's."

He said to them, "Then give to Caesar the things that are Caesar's, and to God the things that are God's."

They weren't able to trap him in his words before the people. They marveled at his answer and were silent.

The Resurrection and Marriage
Lk 20:27-40 / Mt 22:23-33 / Mk 12:18-27

Some of the Sadducees came to him, those who deny that there is a resurrection.

They asked him, "Teacher, Moses wrote to us that if a man's brother dies having a wife, and he is childless, his brother should take the wife and raise children for his brother. There were therefore seven brothers. The first took a wife and died childless.

The second took her as wife, and he died childless.

The third took her, and likewise the seven all left no children, and died.

Afterward the woman also died.

Therefore in the resurrection whose wife of them will she be? For the seven had her as a wife."

Jesus said to them, "The children of this age marry, and are given in marriage. But those who are considered worthy to attain to that age and the resurrection from the dead, neither marry, nor are given in marriage. For they can't die any more, for they are like the angels, and are children of God, being children of the resurrection. But that the dead are raised, even Moses showed at the bush, when he called the Lord The God of Abraham, the God of Isaac, and the God of Jacob.' Now he is not the God of the dead, but of the living, for all are alive to him."

Some of the scribes answered, "Teacher, you speak well."

They didn't dare to ask him any more questions.

The Greatest Commandment
Mt 22:34-40 / Mk 12:28-34

But the Pharisees, when they heard that he had silenced the Sadducees, gathered themselves together. One of the scribes came, and heard them questioning together. Knowing that he had answered them well, asked him, "Which commandment is the greatest of all?"

Jesus answered, "The greatest is, Hear, Israel, the Lord our God, the Lord is one: you shall love the Lord your God with all your heart, and with all your soul, and with all your mind, and with all your strength. 'This is the first commandment.

The second is like this, You shall love your neighbor as yourself. 'There is no other commandment greater than these."
The scribe said to him, "Truly, teacher, you have said well that he is one, and there is none other but he, and to love him with all the heart, and with all the understanding, with all the soul, and with all the strength, and to love his neighbor as himself, is more important than all whole burnt offerings and sacrifices."

When Jesus saw that he answered wisely, he said to him, "You are not far from the Kingdom of God."

No one dared ask him any question after that.

Whose Son Is the Christ?
Mt 22:41-46 / Lk 20:41-44 / Mk 12:35-37

Now while the Pharisees were gathered together, Jesus asked them a question, saying, "What do you think of the Christ? Whose son is he?"

They said to him, "Of David."

He said to them, "How then does David in the Spirit call him Lord, saying, The Lord said to my Lord, sit on my right hand, until I make your enemies a footstool for your feet?' "If then David calls him Lord, how is he his son?"

No one was able to answer him a word, neither did any man dare ask him any more questions from that day forward.

A Warning Against Hypocrisy
Mt 23"1-12 / Lk 20:45-47 / Mk 12:38-40

Then Jesus spoke to the multitudes and to his disciples, saying, "The scribes and the Pharisees sat on Moses' seat. All things therefore whatever they tell you to observe, observe and do, but don't do their works; for they say, and don't do. For they bind heavy burdens that are grievous to be borne, and lay them on men's shoulders; but they themselves will not lift a finger to help them. But all their works they do to be seen by men. They make their phylacteries broad, enlarge the fringes of their garments, and love the place of honor at feasts, the best seats in the synagogues, the salutations in the marketplaces, and to be called Rabbi, Rabbi' by men. who devour widows' houses, and for a pretense make long prayers: these will receive greater condemnation."

But don't you be called Rabbi,' for one is your teacher, the Christ, and all of you are brothers. Call no man on the earth your father, for one is your Father, he who is in heaven.

Neither be called masters, for one is your master, the Christ. But he who is greatest among you will be your servant. Whoever exalts himself will be humbled, and whoever humbles himself will be exalted.

Seven Woes on the Teachers of the Law and the Pharisees
Mt 23:13-39

"Woe to you, scribes and Pharisees, hypocrites! For you devour widows' houses, and as a pretense you make long prayers. Therefore you will receive greater condemnation.

"But woe to you, scribes and Pharisees, hypocrites! Because you shut up the Kingdom of Heaven against men; for you don't enter in yourselves, neither do you allow those who are entering in to enter.

Woe to you, scribes and Pharisees, hypocrites! For you travel around by sea and land to make one proselyte; and when he becomes one, you make him twice as much of a son of Gehenna as yourselves.

"Woe to you, you blind guides, who say, Whoever swears by the temple, it is nothing; but whoever swears by the gold of the temple, he is obligated.'

You blind fools! For which is greater, the gold, or the temple that sanctifies the gold?

Whoever swears by the altar, it is nothing; but whoever swears by the gift that is on it, he is obligated?' You blind fools! For which is greater, the gift, or the altar that sanctifies the gift?

He therefore swears by the altar, swears by it, and by everything on it. He who swears by the temple, swears by it, and by him who was living in it. He who swears by heaven, swears by the throne of God, and by him who sits on it.

"Woe to you, scribes and Pharisees, hypocrites! For you tithe mint, dill, and cumin, and have left undone the weightier matters of the law: justice, mercy, and faith. But you ought to have done these, and not to have left the other undone. You blind guides, who strain out a gnat, and swallow a camel!

"Woe to you, scribes and Pharisees, hypocrites! For you clean the outside of the cup and of the platter, but within they are full of extortion and unrighteousness. You blind Pharisee, first clean the inside of the cup and of the platter, that its outside may become clean also.

"Woe to you, scribes and Pharisees, hypocrites! For you are like whitened tombs, which outwardly appear beautiful, but inwardly are full of dead men's bones, and of all uncleanness. Even so you also outwardly appear righteous to men, but inwardly you are full of hypocrisy and iniquity. "Woe to you, scribes and Pharisees, hypocrites! For you build the tombs of the prophets, and decorate the tombs of the righteous, and say, if we had lived in the days of our fathers, we wouldn't have been partakers with them in the blood of the prophets.'

Therefore, you testify to yourselves that you are children of those who killed the prophets.

Fill up, then, the measure of your fathers. You serpents, you offspring of vipers, how will you escape the judgment of Gehenna? Therefore behold, I send to you prophets, wise men, and scribes. Some of them you will kill and crucify; and some of them you will scourge in your synagogues, and persecute from city to city; that on you may come all the righteous blood shed on the earth, from the blood of righteous Abel to the blood of Zachariah son of Barachiah, whom you killed between the sanctuary and the altar.

Most certainly I tell you, all these things will come upon this generation.

"Jerusalem, Jerusalem, who kills the prophets, and stones those who are sent to her! How often I would have gathered your children together, even as a hen gathers her chicks under her wings, and you would not! Behold, your house is left to you desolate.

For I tell you, you will not see me from now on, until you say, Blessed is he who comes in the name of the Lord!'"

The Widow's Offering
Mk 12:41-44 / Lk 21:1-4

Jesus sat down opposite the treasury, and saw how the multitude cast money into the treasury. Many who were rich cast in much. A poor widow came, and she cast in two small brass coins, which equal a quadrans coin.

He called his disciples to himself, and said to them, "Most certainly I tell you, this poor widow gave more than all those who are giving into the treasury, for they all gave

out of their abundance, but she, out of her poverty, gave all
that she had to live on."

Chapter Fourteen:
The End Time Prophecy

The Destruction of the Temple and Signs of the End Times
Mt 24:1-35 / Lk 21:5-28 & Lk 21:29-36 / Mk 13:1-31

Jesus went out from the temple and was going on his way. His disciples came to him to show him the buildings of the temple. As some were talking about the temple and how it was decorated with beautiful stones and gifts, he said,

"As for these things which you see, the days will come, in which there will not be left here one stone on another that will not be thrown down."

As he sat on the Mount of Olives, the disciples came to him privately, saying, "Tell us, when will these things be? What is the sign of your coming, and of the end of the age?" Jesus answered them, "Be careful that no one leads you astray. For many will come in my name, saying, I am the Christ,' and will lead many astray. You will hear of wars and rumors of wars. See that you aren't troubled, for all this must happen, but the end is not yet. For nation will rise against nation, and kingdom against kingdom; and there will be famines, plagues, and earthquakes in various places. But all these things are the beginning of birth pains. Then they will deliver you up to oppression and will kill you. You will be hated by all of the nations for my name's sake.

Then many will stumble, and will deliver up one another, and will hate one another. Many false prophets will arise and will lead many astray. Because iniquity will be multiplied, the love of many will grow cold. But he who endures to the end, the same will be saved.

This Good News of the Kingdom will be preached in the whole world for a testimony to all the nations, and then the end will come.

There will be great earthquakes, famines, and plagues in various places. There will be terrors and great signs from heaven. But before all these things, they will lay their hands on you and will persecute you, delivering you up to synagogues and prisons, bringing you before kings and governors for my name's sake. It will turn out as a testimony for you.

Settle it therefore in your hearts not to meditate beforehand on how to answer, for I will give you a mouth and wisdom which all your adversaries will not be able to withstand or to contradict. You will be handed over even by parents, brothers, relatives, and friends. They will cause some of you to be put to death. You will be hated by all men for my name's sake.

And not a hair of your head will perish. "By your endurance you will win your lives.

"But when you see Jerusalem surrounded by armies, then know that it's when, therefore, you see the abomination of desolation, which was spoken of through Daniel the prophet, standing in the holy place (let the reader understand), then let those who are in Judea flee to the mountains.

Let him who is on the housetop not go down to take out things that are in his house. Let him who is in the field not return back to get his clothes. But woe to those who are with child and to nursing mothers in those days! Pray that your flight will not be in the winter, nor on a Sabbath, for then there will be great oppression, such as has not been from the beginning of the world until now, no, nor ever will be. Unless those days had been shortened, no flesh would have been saved. But for the sake of the chosen ones, those days will be shortened.

"Then if any man tells you, Behold, here is the Christ,' or there,' don't believe it.

For there will arise false christs, and false prophets, and they will show great signs and wonders, so as to lead astray, if possible, even the chosen ones.

"Behold, I have told you beforehand. If therefore they tell you, Behold, he is in the wilderness,' don't go out; Behold, he is in the inner rooms,' don't believe it. For as the lightning flashes from the east, and is seen even to the west, so will be the coming of the Son of Man.

There will be signs in the sun, moon, and stars; and on the earth anxiety of nations, in perplexity for the roaring of the sea and the waves; men fainting for fear, and for expectation of the things which are coming on the world: for the powers of the heavens will be shaken. Then they will see the Son of Man coming in a cloud with power and great glory.

But when these things begin to happen, look up, and lift up your head, because your redemption is near."

For wherever the carcass is, there is where the vultures gather. But immediately after the oppression of those days, the sun will be darkened, the moon will not give its light, the stars will fall from the sky, and the powers of the heavens will be shaken; and then the sign of the Son of Man will appear in the sky. Then all the tribes of the earth will mourn, and they will see the Son of Man coming on the clouds of the sky with power and great glory. He will send out his angels with the great sound of a trumpet, and they will gather together his chosen ones from the four winds, from one end of the sky to the other.

He told them a parable. "See the fig tree, and all the trees. When they are already budding, you see it and know by yourself that the summer is already near. Even so you also, when you see these things happening, know that the Kingdom of God is near. Most certainly I tell you, this generation will not pass away until all things are accomplished.

Heaven and earth will pass away, but my words will by no means pass away.

"So be careful, or your heart will be loaded down with carousing, drunkenness, and cares of this life, and that day will come on you suddenly. For it will come like a snare on all those who dwell on the surface of all the earth. Therefore, be watchful all the time, praying that you may be counted worthy to escape all these things that will happen, and to stand before the Son of Man."

The Day and Hour Unknown
Mt 24:36-51 / Mk 13:32-36 / (Lk 12:35-48)

But no one knows of that day and hour, not even the angels of heaven, but my Father only. "As the days of Noah were, so will be the coming of the Son of Man. For as in those days which were before the flood they were eating and drinking, marrying and giving in marriage, until the day that Noah entered into the ship, and they didn't know until the flood came, and took them all away, so will be the coming of the Son of Man. Then two men will be in the field: one will be taken and one will be left; two women grinding at the mill, one will be taken and one will be left. Watch therefore, for you don't know in what hour your Lord will come. But know this, that if the master of the house had known in what watch of the night the thief was coming, he would have watched, and would not have allowed his house to be broken into. Therefore, also be ready, for in an hour that you don't expect, the Son of Man will come.

"Who then is the faithful and wise servant, whom his lord has set over his household, to give them their food in due season? Blessed is that servant whom his lord finds doing so when he comes. Most certainly I tell you that he will set him over all that he has.

But if that evil servant should say in his heart, My lord is delaying his coming,' and begins to beat his fellow servants, and eat and drink with the drunkards, the lord of that servant will come in a day when he doesn't expect it, and in an hour when he doesn't know it, and will cut him in pieces, and appoint his portion with the hypocrites. There is where the weeping and grinding of teeth will be.

The Parable of the Ten Virgins
Mt 25:1-13

"Then the Kingdom of Heaven will be like ten virgins, who took their lamps, and went out to meet the bridegroom. Five of them were foolish, and five were wise. Those who were foolish when they took their lamps, took no oil with them, but the wise took oil in their vessels with their lamps. Now while the bridegroom delayed, they all slumbered and slept.

But at midnight there was a cry, Behold! The bridegroom is coming! Come out to meet him!'

Then all those virgins arose and trimmed their lamps.

The foolish said to the wise, give us some of your oil, for our lamps are going out.'

But the wise answered, saying, what if there isn't enough for us and you? You go rather to those who sell and buy for yourselves.'

While they went away to buy, the bridegroom came, and those who were ready went in with him to the marriage feast, and the door was shut.

Afterward the other virgins also came, saying, Lord, Lord, open to us.'

But he answered, most certainly I tell you, I don't know you.'

Watch therefore, for you don't know the day nor the hour in which the Son of Man is coming.

The Parable of the Bags of Gold
Mt 25:14-30 / Lk 19:11-27

"For it is like a man, going into another country, who called his own servants, and entrusted his goods to them. To one he gave five talents, to another two, to another one; to each according to his own ability. Then he went on his journey. Immediately he who received the five talents went and traded with them, and made another five talents.

In the same way, he also who got the two gained another two. But he who received the one went away and dug in the earth, and hid his lord's money.

"Now after a long time the lord of those servants came, and reconciled accounts with them.

He who received the five talents came and brought another five talents, saying, Lord, you delivered to me five talents. Behold, I have gained another five talents besides them.'
"His lord said to him, well done, good and faithful servant. You have been faithful over a few things; I will set you over many things. Enter into the joy of your lord.'

"He also who got the two talents came and said, Lord, you delivered to me two talents. Behold, I have gained another two talents besides them.'

"His lord said to him, well done, good and faithful servant. You have been faithful over a few things, I will set you over many things. Enter into the joy of your lord.' "He also who had received the one talent came and said, Lord, I knew you that you are a hard man, reaping where you did not sow, and gathering where you did not scatter.

I was afraid, and went away and hid your talent in the earth. Behold, you have what is yours.'

"But his lord answered him, You wicked and slothful servant. You knew that I reap where I didn't sow and gather where I didn't scatter. You ought therefore to have deposited my money with the bankers, and in my coming I should have received back my own with interest.

Take away therefore the talent from him and give it to him who has the ten talents. For to everyone who has will be given, and he will have abundance, but from him who doesn't have, even that which he has will be taken away. Throw out the unprofitable servant into the outer darkness, where there will be weeping and gnashing of teeth.'

The Sheep and the Goats
Mt 25:31-46

"But when the Son of Man comes in his glory, and all the holy angels with him, then he will sit on the throne of his glory. Before him all the nations will be gathered, and he will separate them one from another, as a shepherd separates the sheep from the goats. He will set the sheep on his right hand, but the goats on the left.

Then the King will tell those on his right hand, Come, blessed of my Father, inherit the Kingdom prepared for you from the foundation of the world; for I was hungry, and you gave me food to eat. I was thirsty, and you gave me drink. I was a stranger, and you took me in.

I was naked, and you clothed me. I was sick, and you visited me. I was in prison, and you came to me.' "Then the righteous will answer him, saying, Lord, when did we see you hungry, and feed you; or thirsty, and give you a drink? When did we see you as a stranger, and take you in; or naked, and clothe you? When did we see you sick, or in prison, and come to you?'

"The King will answer them, most certainly I tell you, because you did it to one of the least of these my brothers, you did it to me.'

Then he will say also to those on the left hand, Depart from me, you cursed, into the eternal fire which is prepared for the devil and his angels; for I was hungry, and you didn't give me food to eat; I was thirsty, and you gave me no drink; I was a stranger, and you didn't take me in; naked, and you didn't clothe me; sick, and in prison, and you didn't visit me.' "Then they will also answer, saying, Lord, when did we see you hungry, or thirsty, or a stranger, or naked, or sick, or in prison, and didn't help you?'

"Then he will answer them, saying, Most certainly I tell you, because you didn't do it to one of the least of these, you didn't do it to me.'

These will go away into eternal punishment, but the righteous into eternal life."

Chapter Fifteen:
The Last Super

The Plot Against Jesus
Mt 26:1-5 / Mk 14:1-2 / Lk 21:37-38

It happened, when Jesus had finished all these words, that he said to his disciples, "You know that after two days the Passover is coming, and the Son of Man will be delivered up to be crucified."

Every day Jesus was teaching in the temple, and every night he would go out and spend the night on the mountain that is called Olivet. All the people came early in the morning to him in the temple to hear him.

Then the chief priests, the scribes, and the elders of the people were gathered in the court of the high priest, who was called Caiaphas. They took counsel together that they might take Jesus by deceit and kill him.

But they said, "Not during the feast, lest a riot occur among the people."

Every day Jesus was teaching in the temple, and every night he would go out and spend the night on the mountain that is called Olivet. All the people came early in the morning to him in the temple to hear him.

Judas Agrees to Betray Jesus
Lk 22:1-6 / Mk 14:10-11 / Mt 26:14-16

Now the feast of unleavened bread, which is called the Passover, drew near.

The chief priests and the scribes sought how they might put him to death, for they feared the people. Satan entered into Judas, who was also called Iscariot, who was numbered with the twelve. He went away and talked with the chief priests and captains about how he might deliver him to them. And said, "What are you willing to give me, that I should deliver him to you?"

They weighed out for him thirty pieces of silver.

He consented and sought an opportunity to deliver him to them in the absence of the multitude.

Preparation for the Last Supper
Lk 22:7-13 / Mk 14:12-16 / Mt 26:17-19

The day of unleavened bread came on which the Passover must be sacrificed.

He sent Peter and John, saying, "Go and prepare the Passover for us, that we may eat."

They said to him, "Where do you want us to prepare?"

He said to them, "Behold, when you have entered into the city, a man carrying a pitcher of water will meet you. Follow him into the house which he enters. Tell the master of the house, The Teacher says to you, "Where is the guest room, where I may eat the Passover with my disciples?"'

He will show you a large, furnished upper room. Make preparations there."

They went, found things as he had told them, and they prepared the Passover.

Jesus Washes His Disciples' Feet
Jn 13:1-17

Now before the feast of the Passover, Jesus, knowing that his time had come that he would depart from this world to the Father, having loved his own who were in the world, he loved them to the end. During supper, the devil having already put into the heart of Judas Iscariot, Simon's son, to betray him, Jesus, knowing that the Father had given all things into his hands, and that he came from God, and was going to God, arose from supper, and laid aside his outer garments. He took a towel and wrapped a towel around his waist.

Then he poured water into the basin, and began to wash the disciples' feet, and to wipe them with the towel that was wrapped around him.

Then he came to Simon Peter. He said to him, "Lord, do you wash my feet?"

Jesus answered him, "You don't know what I am doing now, but you will understand later."

Peter said to him, "You will never wash my feet!"

Jesus answered him, "If I don't wash you, you have no part with me."

Simon Peter said to him, "Lord, not my feet only, but also my hands and my head!"

Jesus said to him, "Someone who has bathed only needs to have his feet washed but is completely clean. You are clean, but not all of you."

For he knew who would betray him, therefore he said, "You are not all clean."

So, when he had washed their feet, put his outer garment back on, and sat down again, he said to them, "Do you know what I have done to you? You call me, Teacher' and Lord.' You say so correctly, for so I am. If I then, the Lord and the Teacher, have washed your feet, you also ought to wash one another's feet. For I have given you an example, that you also should do as I have done to you. Most certainly I tell you, a servant is not greater than his lord, neither one who is sent greater than he who sent him. If you know these things, blessed are you if you do them."

The Last Super
Lk 22:14-20 / Mk 14:22-25
/ Mt 26:20 & Mt 26:26-29

When the hour had come, he sat down with the twelve apostles.

He said to them, "I have earnestly desired to eat this Passover with you before I suffer, for I tell you, I will no longer by any means eat of it until it is fulfilled in the Kingdom of God."

He received a cup, and when he had given thanks, he said, "Take this, and share it among yourselves, for I tell you, I will not drink at all again from the fruit of the vine, until the Kingdom of God comes."

He took bread, and when he had given thanks, he broke it, and gave to them, saying, "This is my body which is given for you. Do this in memory of me."

Likewise, he took the cup after supper, saying, "This cup is the new covenant in my blood, which is poured out for you. But I tell you that I will not drink this fruit of the vine from now on, until that day when I drink it anew with you in my Father's Kingdom."

Jesus Predicts His Betrayal
Jn 13:18-30 / Mt 26:21-25 / Lk 22:21-23
/ Mk 14:17-21

"I don't speak concerning all of you. I know whom I have chosen. But that the Scripture may be fulfilled, He who eats bread with me has lifted up his heel against me.' From now on, I tell you before it happens, that when it happens, you may believe that I am him. Most certainly I tell you, he who receives whomever I send, receives me; and he who receives me, receives him who sent me."

As they were eating, he said, "Most certainly I tell you that one of you will betray me."

They were exceedingly sorrowful, and each began to ask him, "It isn't me, is it, Lord?"

He answered, "He who dipped his hand with me in the dish, the same will betray me.

The Son of Man goes, even as it is written of him, but woe to that man through whom the Son of Man is betrayed! It would be better for that man if he had not been born."

Judas, who betrayed him, answered, "It isn't me, is it, Rabbi?"

He said to him, "You said it."

One of his disciples, whom Jesus loved, was at the table, leaning against Jesus' breast.

Simon Peter therefore beckoned to him, and said to him, "Tell us who it is of whom he speaks."

He, leaning back, as he was, on Jesus' breast, asked him, "Lord, who is it?"

Jesus therefore answered, "It is he to whom I will give this piece of bread when I have dipped it."

So when he had dipped the piece of bread, he gave it to Judas, the son of Simon Iscariot.

After the piece of bread, then Satan entered into him.

Then Jesus said to him, "What you do, do quickly."

Now no man at the table knew why he said this to him. For some thought, because Judas had the money box, that Jesus said to him, "Buy what things we need for the feast," or that he should give something to the poor. Therefore, having received that morsel, he went out immediately. It was night.

About Who is Greater
Lk 22:24-30

There arose also a contention among them, which of them was considered to be greatest.

He said to them, "The kings of the nations lord it over them, and those who have authority over them are called benefactors.' But not so with you. But one who is the greater among you, let him become as the younger, and one who is governing, as one who serves. For who is greater, one who sits at the table, or one who serves? Isn't he who sits at the table? But I am in your midst as one who serves. But you are those who have continued with me in my trials. I confer on you a kingdom, even as my Father conferred on me, that you may eat and drink at my table in my Kingdom. You will sit on thrones, judging the twelve tribes of Israel."

Jesus Predicts Peter's Denial
Jn 13:31-38 / Lk 22:31-38 / Mt 26:31-35
/ Mk 14:27-31

When he had gone out, Jesus said, "Now the Son of Man has been glorified, and God has been glorified in him. If God has been glorified in him, God will also glorify him in himself, and he will glorify him immediately. Little children, I will be with you a little while longer. You will seek me, and as I said to the Jews, Where I am going, you can't come,' so now I tell you. A new commandment I give to you, that you love one another, just like I have loved you; that you also love one another. By this everyone will know that you are my disciples, if you have love for one another."

Simon Peter said to him, "Lord, where are you going?"

Jesus answered, "Where I am going, you can't follow now, but you will follow afterwards."

Peter said to him, "Lord, why can't I follow you now? I will lay down my life for you."

The Lord said, "Simon, Simon, behold, Satan asked to have you, that he might sift you as wheat, but I prayed for you, that your faith wouldn't fail. You, when you have turned again, establish your brothers."

He said to him, "Lord, I am ready to go with you both to prison and to death!"

Then Jesus said to them, "All of you will be made to stumble because of me tonight, for it is written, I will strike the shepherd, and the sheep of the flock will be scattered.'

But after I am raised up, I will go before you into Galilee."

But Peter answered him, "Even if all will be made to stumble because of you, I will never be made to stumble."

Jesus said to him, "Most certainly I tell you that tonight, before the rooster crows, you will deny me three times."

Peter said to him, "Even if I must die with you, I will not deny you."

All of the disciples also said likewise.

He said to them, "When I sent you out without purse, and wallet, and shoes, did you lack anything?"

They said, "Nothing."

Then he said to them, "But now, whoever has a purse, let him take it, and likewise a wallet. Whoever has none, let him sell his cloak, and buy a sword. For I tell you that this which is written must still be fulfilled in me: He was counted with transgressors.' For that which concerns me has an end."

They said, "Lord, behold, here are two swords."

He said to them, "That is enough."

Jesus Comforts His Disciples
Jn 14:1-4

"Don't let your heart be troubled. Believe in God. Believe also in me. In my Father's house are many homes. If it weren't so, I would have told you. I am going to prepare a place for you. If I go and prepare a place for you, I will come again, and will receive you to myself; that where I am, you may be there also. Where I go, you know, and you know the way."

Jesus the Way to the Father
Jn 14:5-14

Thomas said to him, "Lord, we don't know where you are going. How can we know the way?"

Jesus said to him, "I am the way, the truth, and the life. No one comes to the Father, except through me. If you had known me, you would have known my Father also. From now on, you know him, and have seen him."

Philip said to him, "Lord, show us the Father, and that will be enough for us."

Jesus said to him, "Have I been with you such a long time, and do you not know me, Philip? He who has seen me has seen the Father. How do you say, Show us the Father?' Don't you believe that I am in the Father, and the Father in me? The words that I tell you, I speak not from myself; but the Father who lives in me does his works. Believe me that I am in the Father, and the Father in me; or else believe me for the very works' sake. Most certainly I tell you, he who believes in me, the works that I do, he will do also; and he will do greater works than these, because I am going to my Father. Whatever you will ask in my name, that will I do, that the Father may be glorified in the Son. If you will ask anything in my name, I will do it."

Jesus Promises the Holy Spirit
Jn 14:15-31

"If you love me, keep my commandments. I will pray to the Father, and he will give you another Counselor, that he may be with you forever, the Spirit of truth, whom the world can't receive; for it doesn't see him, neither knows him. You know him, for he lives with you, and will be in you. I will not leave you orphans. I will come to you. Yet a little while, and the world will see me no more; but you will see me. Because I live, you will live also. In that day you will know that I am in my Father, and you in me, and I in you. One who has my commandments, and keeps them, that person is one who loves me. One who loves me will be loved by my Father, and I will love him, and will reveal myself to him."

Judas (not Iscariot) said to him, "Lord, what has happened that you are about to reveal yourself to us, and not to the world?"

Jesus answered him, "If a man loves me, he will keep my word. My Father will love him, and we will come to him, and make our home with him. He who doesn't love me doesn't keep my words. The word which you hear isn't mine, but the Father's who sent me. I have said these things to you, while still living with you. But the Counselor, the Holy Spirit, whom the Father will send in my name, he will teach you all things, and will remind you of all that I said to you. Peace I leave with you. My peace I give to you; not as the world gives, give I to you. Don't let your heart be troubled, neither let it be fearful. You heard how I told you, I go away, and I come to you.' If you loved me, you would have rejoiced, because I said I am going to my Father;' for the Father is greater than I. Now I have told you before it happens so that, when it happens, you may believe. I will no more speak much with you, for the prince of the world comes, and he has nothing in me. But that the world may know that I love the Father, and as the Father commanded me, even so I do. Arise, let us go from here."

The Parable of the True Vine and Branches
Jn 15:1-17

"I am the true vine, and my Father is the farmer. Every branch in me that doesn't bear fruit, he takes away. Every branch that bears fruit, he prunes, that it may bear more fruit. You are already pruned clean because of the word which I have spoken to you. Remain in me, and I in you. As the branch can't bear fruit by itself, unless it remains in the vine, so neither can you, unless you remain in me. I am the vine. You are the branches. He who remains in me, and I in him, the same bears much fruit, for apart from me you can do nothing. If a man doesn't remain in me, he is thrown out as a branch, and is withered; and they gather them, throw them into the fire, and they are burned. If you remain in me, and my words remain in you, you will ask whatever you desire, and it will be done for you.

"In this is my Father glorified, that you bear much fruit; and so you will be my disciples. Even as the Father has loved me, I also have loved you. Remain in my love. If you keep my commandments, you will remain in my love; even as I have kept my Father's commandments and remain in his love. I have spoken these things to you, that my joy may remain in you, and that your joy may be made full.

"This is my commandment, that you love one another, even as I have loved you. Greater love has no one than this, that someone lay down his life for his friends. You are my friends, if you do whatever I command you. No longer do I call you servants, for the servant doesn't know what his lord does. But I have called you friends, for everything that I heard from my Father, I have made known to you. You didn't choose me, but I chose you, and appointed you, that you should go and bear fruit, and that your fruit should remain; that whatever you will ask of the Father in my name, he may give it to you. I command these things to you, that you may love one another."

The World Hates the Disciples
Jn 15:18-25

"If the world hates you, you know that it has hated me before it hated you. If you were of the world, the world would love its own. But because you are not of the world, since I chose you out of the world, therefore the world hates you. Remember the word that I said to you: A servant is not greater than his lord.

'If they persecuted me, they will also persecute you. If they kept my word, they will keep yours also. But all these things will they do to you for my name's sake, because they don't know him who sent me.

If I had not come and spoken to them, they would not have had sin; but now they have no excuse for their sin. He who hates me, hates my Father also. If I hadn't done among them the works which no one else did, they wouldn't have had sin. But now have they seen and also hated both me and my Father. But this happened so that the word may be fulfilled which was written in their law, They hated me without a cause."

Jesus goes and sends the Holy Spirit
Jn 15:26-27 & Jn 16:1-15

"When the Counselor has come, whom I will send to you from the Father, the Spirit of truth, who proceeds from the Father, he will testify about me. You will also testify, because you have been with me from the beginning.

"These things have I spoken to you, so that you wouldn't be caused to stumble. They will put you out of the synagogues. Yes, the time comes that whoever kills you will think that he offers service to God. They will do these things because they have not known the Father, nor me. But I have told you these things, so that when the time comes, you may remember that I told you about them. I didn't tell you these things from the beginning, because I was with you. But now I am going to him who sent me, and none of you asks me, where are you going?' But because I have told you these things, sorrow has filled your heart.

Nevertheless, I tell you the truth: It is to your advantage that I go away, for if I don't go away, the Counselor won't come to you. But if I go, I will send him to you. When he comes, he will convict the world about sin, about righteousness, and about judgment; about sin, because they don't believe in me; about righteousness, because I am going to my Father, and you won't see me anymore; about judgment, because the prince of this world has been judged.

"I have yet many things to tell you, but you can't bear them now. However, when he, the Spirit of truth, has come, he will guide you into all truth, for he will not speak from himself; but whatever he hears, he will speak. He will declare to you things that are coming.

He will glorify me, for he will take from what is mine, and will declare it to you. All things whatever the Father has are mine; therefore, I said that he takes of mine, and will declare it to you.

The Disciples' Grief Will Turn to Joy
Jn 16:16-33 & Jn 17:1-5

"A little while, and you will not see me. Again, a little while, and you will see me."

Some of his disciples therefore said to one another, "What is this that he says to us, A little while, and you won't see me, and again a little while, and you will see me;' and, Because I go to the Father?'"

They said therefore, "What is this that he says, A little while?' We don't know what he is saying."

Therefore, Jesus perceived that they wanted to ask him, and he said to them, "Do you inquire among yourselves concerning this, that I said, A little while, and you won't see me, and again a little while, and you will see me?' Most certainly I tell you, that you will weep and lament, but the world will rejoice. You will be sorrowful, but your sorrow will be turned into joy. A woman, when she gives birth, has sorrow, because her time has come. But when she has delivered the child, she doesn't remember the anguish anymore, for the joy that a human being is born into the world. Therefore, you now have sorrow, but I will see you again, and your heart will rejoice, and no one will take your joy away from you.

"In that day you will ask me no questions. Most certainly I tell you, whatever you may ask of the Father in my name, he will give it to you. Until now, you have asked nothing in my name. Ask, and you will receive that your joy may be made full. I have spoken these things to you in figures of speech. But the time is coming when I will no longer speak to you in figures of speech but will tell you plainly about the Father.

In that day you will ask in my name; and I don't say to you, that I will pray to the Father for you, for the Father himself loves you, because you have loved me, and have believed that I came from God. I came from the Father and have come into the world. Again, I leave the world and go to the Father."

His disciples said to him, "Behold, now you speak plainly, and speak no figures of speech.

Now we know that you know all things, and don't need anyone to question you. By this we believe that you came from God."

Jesus answered them, "Do you now believe? Behold, the time is coming, yes, and has now come, that you will be scattered, everyone to his own place, and you will leave me alone. Yet I am not alone, because the Father is with me. I have told you these things, that in me you may have peace. In the world you have oppression; but cheer up! I have overcome the world."

Jesus said these things, and lifting up his eyes to heaven, he said, "Father, the time has come. Glorify your Son, that your Son may also glorify you; even as you gave him authority over all flesh, he will give eternal life to all whom you have given him. This is eternal life, that they should know you, the only true God, and him whom you sent, Jesus Christ.

I glorified you on the earth. I have accomplished the work which you have given me to do.

Now, Father, glorify me with your own self with the glory which I had with you before the world existed.

Jesus Prays for His Disciples
Jn 17:6-19

"I have revealed you to those whom you gave me out of the world. They were yours; I revealed your name to the people whom you have given me out of the world. They were yours, and you gave them to me. They have kept your word. Now they have known that all the things you have given me are from you, for the words which you have given me I have given to them, and they received them, and knew for sure that I came from you, and they have believed that you sent me.

I pray for them. I don't pray for the world, but for those whom you have given me, for they are yours. All things that are mine are yours, and yours are mine, and I am glorified in them.

I am no longer in the world, but these are in the world, and I am coming to you. Holy Father, keep them through your name which you have given me, that they may be one, even as we are. While I was with them in the world, I kept them in your name. Those whom you gave me I have kept. None of them is lost, except the son of destruction, that the Scripture might be fulfilled.

But now I come to you, and I say these things in the world, that they may have my joy made full in themselves.

I have given them your word. The world hated them, because they are not of the world, even as I am not of the world. I pray not that you will take them from the world, but that you would keep them from the evil one. They are not of the world even as I am not of the world. Sanctify them in your truth. Your word is truth. As you sent me into the world, even so I have sent them into the world. For their sakes I sanctify myself, that they themselves also may be sanctified in truth.

Jesus Prays for All Believers
Jn 17:20-26 / Mk 14:26 / Mt 26:30

Not for these only do I pray, but for those also who believe in me through their word,

that they may all be one; even as you, Father, are in me, and I in you, that they also may be one in us; that the world may believe that you sent me. The glory which you have given me, I have given to them; that they may be one, even as we are one; I in them, and you in me, that they may be perfected into one; that the world may know that you sent me, and loved them, even as you loved me. Father, I desire that they also whom you have given me be with me where I am, that they may see my glory, which you have given me, for you loved me before the foundation of the world. Righteous Father, the world hasn't known you, but I knew you; and these knew that you sent me. I made known to them your name, and will make it known; that the love with which you loved me may be in them, and I in them."

When they had sung a hymn, they went out to the Mount of Olives.

Chapter Sixteen:
Jesus's Arrest and Trials

Jesus Pray at Gethsemane
Mk 14:32-42 / Jn 18:1-2 / Lk 22:39-46
/ Mt 26:36-46

They came to a place which was named Gethsemane. He said to his disciples, "Sit here, while I pray."

He took with him Peter, James, and John, and began to be greatly troubled and distressed.

He said to them, "My soul is exceedingly sorrowful, even to death. Stay here, and watch."

He went forward a little, and fell on the ground, and prayed that, if it were possible, the hour might pass away from him.

He said, "Abba, Father, all things are possible to you. Please remove this cup from me. However, not what I desire, but what you desire."

He came and found them sleeping, and said to Peter, "Simon, are you sleeping? Couldn't you watch one hour? Watch and pray, that you may not enter into temptation. The spirit indeed is willing, but the flesh is weak."

Again he went away, and prayed, saying the same words. Again he returned, and found them sleeping, for their eyes were very heavy, and they didn't know what to answer him.

He came the third time, and said to them, "Sleep on now, and take your rest. It is enough. The hour has come. Behold, the Son of Man is betrayed into the hands of sinners. Arise, let us be going. Behold, he who betrays me is at hand."

Now Judas, who betrayed him, also knew the place, for Jesus often met there with his disciples.

Jesus Arrested
Lk 22:47-53 / Jn 18:3-14 / Mk 14:44-52
/ Mt 26:47-56

While he was still speaking, behold, a multitude, and he who was called Judas, one of the twelve, was leading them. He came near to Jesus to kiss him. Judas then, having taken a detachment of soldiers and officers from the chief priests and the Pharisees, came there with lanterns, torches, and weapons.

Jesus therefore, knowing all the things that were happening to him, went out, and said to them, "Who are you looking for?"

They answered him, "Jesus of Nazareth."

Jesus said to them, "I am he."

Judas also, who betrayed him, was standing with them.

When therefore he said to them, "I am he," they went backward, and fell to the ground.

Again therefore he asked them, "Who are you looking for?"

They said, "Jesus of Nazareth."

Jesus answered, "I told you that I am he. If therefore you seek me, let these go their way," that the word might be fulfilled which he spoke, "Of those whom you have given me, I have lost none."

But Jesus said to him, "Judas, do you betray the Son of Man with a kiss?"

Now he who betrayed him had given them a sign, saying, "Whomever I will kiss, that is he. Seize him, and lead him away safely."

When he had come, immediately he came to him, and said, "Rabbi! Rabbi!" and kissed him.

They laid their hands on him, and seized him.

When those who were around him saw what was about to happen, they said to him, "Lord, shall we strike with the sword?"

Simon Peter, therefore, having a sword, drew it, and struck the high priest's servant, and cut off his right ear. The servant's name was Malchus.

Jesus therefore said to Peter, "Put the sword into its sheath. The cup which the Father has given me, shall I not surely drink it?"

But Jesus answered, "Let me at least do this" and he touched his ear and healed him.

Then Jesus said to him, "Put your sword back into its place, for all those who take the sword will die by the sword. Or do you think that I couldn't ask my Father, and he would even now send me more than twelve legions of angels? How then would the Scriptures be fulfilled that it must be so?"

Jesus said to the chief priests, captains of the temple, and elders, who had come against him, "Have you come out as against a robber, with swords and clubs? When I was with you in the temple daily, you didn't stretch out your hands against me. But this is your hour, and the power of darkness."

But all this has happened, so that the Scriptures of the prophets might be fulfilled."

Then all the disciples left him and fled. So, the detachment, the commanding officer, and the officers of the Jews, seized Jesus and bound him, and led him to Annas first, for he was father-in-law to Caiaphas, who was high priest that year. Now it was Caiaphas who advised the Jews that it was expedient that one man should perish for the people.

A certain young man followed him, having a linen cloth thrown around himself, over his naked body. The young men grabbed him, but he left the linen cloth and fled from them naked.

Jesus Before the Sanhedrin
Mk14:52-65 / Jn 18:15-24 / Mt 26:57-68

They led Jesus away to the high priest. All the chief priests, the elders, and the scribes came together with him.

Simon Peter followed Jesus, as did another disciple. Now that disciple was known to the high priest, and entered in with Jesus into the court of the high priest; but Peter was standing at the door outside. So, the other disciple, who was known to the high priest, went out and spoke to her who kept the door, and brought in Peter.

Then the maid who kept the door said to Peter, "Are you also one of this man's disciples?" He said, "I am not." Now the servants and the officers were standing there, having made a fire of coals, for it was cold. They were warming themselves. Peter was with them, standing and warming himself.

The high priest therefore asked Jesus about his disciples, and about his teaching.

Jesus answered him, "I spoke openly to the world. I always taught in synagogues, and in the temple, where the Jews always meet. I said nothing in secret. Why do you ask me? Ask those who have heard me what I said to them. Behold, these know the things which I said."

When he had said this, one of the officers standing by slapped Jesus with his hand, saying, "Do you answer the high priest like that?"

Jesus answered him, "If I have spoken evil, testify of the evil; but if well, why do you beat me?"

Annas sent him bound to Caiaphas, the high priest. Now the chief priests and the whole council sought witnesses against Jesus to put him to death and found none. For many gave false testimony against him, and their testimony didn't agree with each other.

Some stood up, and gave false testimony against him, saying, "We heard him say, I will destroy this temple that is made with hands, and in three days I will build another made without hands.'"

Even so, their testimony did not agree. The high priest stood up in the midst, and asked Jesus, "Have you no answer? What is it which these testify against you?"

But he stayed quiet and answered nothing.

Again, the high priest asked him, "Are you the Christ, the Son of the Blessed?"

Jesus said, "I am. You will see the Son of Man sitting at the right hand of Power and coming with the clouds of the sky."

The high priest tore his clothes, and said, "What further need have we of witnesses? You have heard the blasphemy! What do you think?"

They all condemned him to be worthy of death. Some began to spit on him, and to cover his face, and to beat him with fists, and to tell him, "Prophesy!"

The officers struck him with the palms of their hands.

Peter Disowns Jesus
Lk 22:54-62 / Jn 18:25-27 / Mk14:66-72
/ Mt 26:69-75

They seized him, and led him away, and brought him into the high priest's house. But Peter followed from a distance. When they had kindled a fire in the middle of the courtyard, and had sat down together, Peter sat among them.

A certain servant girl saw him as he sat in the light, and looking intently at him, said, "This man also was with him."

He denied Jesus, saying, "Woman, I don't know him."

After about one hour passed, another confidently affirmed, saying, "Truly this man also was with him, for he is a Galilean!"

One of the servants of the high priest, being a relative of him whose ear Peter had cut off, said, "Didn't I see you in the garden with him?"

But Peter said, "Man, I don't know what you are talking about!"

Immediately, while he was still speaking, a rooster crowed.

The Lord turned, and looked at Peter. Then Peter remembered the Lord's word, how he said to him, "Before the rooster crows you will deny me three times."

He went out, and wept bitterly.

The Guards Mock Jesus
Lk 22:63-65

The men who held Jesus mocked him and beat him. Having blindfolded him, they struck him on the face and asked him, "Prophesy! Who is the one who struck you?"

They spoke many other things against him, insulting him.

Jesus Before the Chief Priest
Lk 22:66-71

As soon as it was day, the assembly of the elders of the people was gathered, both chief priests and scribes, and they led him away into their council, saying,

"If you are the Christ, tell us."

But he said to them, "If I tell you, you won't believe, and if I ask, you will in no way answer me or let me go. From now on, the Son of Man will be seated at the right hand of the power of God."

They all said, "Are you then the Son of God?"

He said to them, "You say it, because I am."

They said, "Why do we need any more witness? For we ourselves have heard from his own mouth!"

Judas Hangs Himself
Mt 27:1-10

Now when morning had come, all the chief priests and the elders of the people took counsel against Jesus to put him to death: and they bound him, and led him away, and delivered him up to Pontius Pilate, the governor.

Then Judas, who betrayed him, when he saw that Jesus was condemned, felt remorse, and brought back the thirty pieces of silver to the chief priests and elders, saying, "I have sinned in that I betrayed innocent blood."

But they said, "What is that to us? You see to it."

He threw down the pieces of silver in the sanctuary and departed. He went away and hanged himself.

The chief priests took the pieces of silver, and said, "It's not lawful to put them into the treasury, since it is the price of blood."

They took counsel, and bought the potter's field with them, to bury strangers in. Therefore, that field was called "The Field of Blood" to this day. Then that which was spoken through Jeremiah the prophet was fulfilled, saying,

"They took the thirty pieces of silver,

the price of him upon whom a price had been set,

whom some of the children of Israel priced,

and they gave them for the potter's field,

as the Lord commanded me."

Jesus Before the Pilate
Jn 18:28-40 / Lk 23:1-7 / Mt 27:11-14 / Mk 15:1-2

They led Jesus therefore from Caiaphas into the Praetorium. It was early, and they themselves didn't enter into the Praetorium, that they might not be defiled, but might eat the Passover. The whole company of them rose up and brought him before Pilate.

They began to accuse him, saying, "We found this man perverting the nation, forbidding paying taxes to Caesar, and saying that he himself is Christ, a king."

Pilate therefore went out to them, and said, "What accusation do you bring against this man?"

They answered him, "If this man weren't an evildoer, we wouldn't have delivered him up to you."

Pilate therefore said to them, "Take him yourselves, and judge him according to your law."

Therefore, the Jews said to him, "It is not lawful for us to put anyone to death,"

That the word of Jesus might be fulfilled, which he spoke, signifying by what kind of death he should die.

Pilate therefore entered again into the Praetorium, called Jesus, and said to him, "Are you the King of the Jews?"

Jesus answered him, "Do you say this by yourself, or did others tell you about me?"

Pilate answered, "I'm not a Jew, am I? Your own nation and the chief priests delivered you to me. What have you done?"

Jesus answered, "My Kingdom is not of this world. If my Kingdom were of this world, then my servants would fight, that I wouldn't be delivered to the Jews. But now my Kingdom is not from here."

Pilate therefore said to him, "Are you a king then?"

Jesus answered, "You say that I am a king. For this reason I have been born, and for this reason I have come into the world, that I should testify to the truth. Everyone who is of the truth listens to my voice."

Pilate said to him, "What is truth?"

When he had said this, he went out again to the Jews, and said to them, "I find no basis for a charge against him.

But they insisted, saying, "He stirs up the people, teaching throughout all Judea, beginning from Galilee even to this place."

But when Pilate heard Galilee mentioned, he asked if the man was a Galilean. When he found out that he was in Herod's jurisdiction, he sent him to Herod, who was also in Jerusalem during those days.

Jesus Before Herod
Lk 23:8-12

Now when Herod saw Jesus, he was exceedingly glad, for he had wanted to see him for a long time, because he had heard many things about him. He hoped to see some miracle done by him. He questioned him with many words, but he gave no answers.

The chief priests and the scribes stood, vehemently accusing him. Herod with his soldiers humiliated him and mocked him. Dressing him in luxurious clothing, they sent him back to Pilate. Herod and Pilate became friends with each other that very day, for before that they were enemies with each other.

Jesus Before the Pilate again
Lk 23:13-17

Pilate called together the chief priests and the rulers and the people, and said to them, "You brought this man to me as one that perverts the people, and see, I have examined him before you and found no basis for a charge against this man concerning those things of which you accuse him. Neither has Herod, for I sent you to him, and see, nothing worthy of death has been done by him. I will therefore chastise him and release him."

The Soldiers Mock Jesus
Jn 19:1-3

So Pilate then took Jesus, and flogged him. The soldiers twisted thorns into a crown, and put it on his head, and dressed him in a purple garment.

They kept saying, "Hail, King of the Jews!" and they kept slapping him.

Jesus Handed to Cruxifiction
Jn 19:4-16 / Mt 27:15-31 / Lk 23:17-25
/ Mk 15:3-20

Then Pilate went out again, and said to them, "Behold, I bring him out to you, that you may know that I find no basis for a charge against him."

Jesus therefore came out, wearing the crown of thorns and the purple garment.

Pilate said to them, "Behold, the man!"

When therefore the chief priests and the officers saw him, they shouted, saying, "Crucify! Crucify!"

The chief priests accused him of many things.

Pilate again asked him, "Have you no answer? See how many things they testify against you!"

But Jesus made no further answer, so that Pilate marveled.

Now at the feast the governor was accustomed to release to the multitude one prisoner, whom they desired. They had then a notable prisoner, called Barabbas.

When therefore they were gathered together, Pilate said to them, "Whom do you want me to release to you? Barabbas, or Jesus, who is called Christ?"

For he knew that because of envy they had delivered him up.

While he was sitting on the judgment seat, his wife sent to him, saying, "Have nothing to do with that righteous man, for I have suffered many things this day in a dream because of him."

Now the chief priests and the elders persuaded the multitudes to ask for Barabbas, and destroy Jesus.

But the governor answered them, "Which of the two do you want me to release to you?"

They said, "Barabbas!"

Pilate said to them, "What then shall I do to Jesus, who is called Christ?"

They all said to him, "Let him be crucified!"

Pilate said to them, "Take him yourselves, and crucify him, for I find no basis for a charge against him."

But they all cried out together, saying, "Away with this man! Release to us Barabbas!"

One who was thrown into prison for a certain revolt in the city, and for murder. Then Pilate spoke to them again, wanting to release Jesus, but they shouted, saying, "Crucify! Crucify him!"

He said to them the third time, "Why? What evil has this man done? I have found no capital crime in him. I will therefore chastise him and release him."

But they were urgent with loud voices, asking that he might be crucified. Their voices and the voices of the chief priests prevailed. The Jews answered him, "We have a law, and by our law he ought to die, because he made himself the Son of God."

When therefore Pilate heard this saying, he was more afraid. He entered into the Praetorium again, and said to Jesus, "Where are you from?"

But Jesus gave him no answer.

Pilate therefore said to him, "Aren't you speaking to me? Don't you know that I have power to release you, and have power to crucify you?"

Jesus answered, "You would have no power at all against me, unless it were given to you from above. Therefore, he who delivered me to you has greater sin."

At this, Pilate was seeking to release him, but the Jews cried out, saying, "If you release this man, you aren't Caesar's friend! Everyone who makes himself a king speaks against Caesar!"

When Pilate therefore heard these words, he brought Jesus out, and sat down on the judgment seat at a place called "The Pavement," but in Hebrew, "Gabbatha."

Now it was the Preparation Day of the Passover, at about the sixth hour. He said to the Jews, "Behold, your King!"

They cried out, "Away with him! Away with him! Crucify him!"

Pilate said to them, "Shall I crucify your King?"

The chief priests answered, "We have no king but Caesar!"

So, when Pilate saw that nothing was being gained, but rather that a disturbance was starting, he took water, and washed his hands before the multitude, saying, "I am innocent of the blood of this righteous person. You see to it."

All the people answered, "May his blood be on us, and on our children!"

Pilate decreed that what they asked for should be done. He released him who had been thrown into prison for insurrection and murder, for whom they asked, but he delivered Jesus up to their will. So then he delivered him to them to be crucified. So they took Jesus and led him away.

Then the governor's soldiers took Jesus into the Praetorium, and gathered the whole garrison together against him. They stripped him, and put a scarlet robe on him.

They braided a crown of thorns and put it on his head, and a reed in his right hand; and they kneeled down before him, and mocked him, saying, "Hail, King of the Jews!"

They spat on him, and took the reed and struck him on the head. When they had mocked him, they took the robe off of him, and put his clothes on him, and led him away to crucify him.

Chapter Seventeen:
Jesus's Death and Resurrection

The Crucifixion of Jesus
Lk 23:26-31 / Mk 15:21-22 / Mt 27:32-33
/ Jn 19:17-18

When they led him away, they grabbed one Simon of Cyrene, coming from the country, and laid on him the cross, to carry it after Jesus. They brought him to the place called Golgotha, which is, being interpreted, "The place of a skull."

A great multitude of the people followed him, including women who also mourned and lamented him.

But Jesus, turning to them, said,

"Daughters of Jerusalem, don't weep for me,

but weep for yourselves and for your children.

For behold, the days are coming

in which they will say,

Blessed are the barren, the wombs that never bore,

and the breasts that never nursed.'

Then they will begin to tell the mountains,

Fall on us!' and tell the hills, Cover us.'

For if they do these things in the green tree,

what will be done in the dry?"

Jesus's First Word while on the Cross
Mk 15:23-25 / Jn 19:23-24 / Lk 23:34-37
/ Mt 27:34-36

It was the third hour, and they crucified him. Then the soldiers, when they had crucified Jesus, took his garments and made four parts, to every soldier a part; and also the coat. Now the coat was without seam, woven from the top throughout.

"Then they said to one another, "Let's not tear it, but cast lots for it to decide whose it will be,"

that the Scripture might be fulfilled, which says,

"They parted my garments among them. For my cloak they cast lots."

Therefore the soldiers did these things.

Jesus said, "Father, forgive them, for they don't know what they are doing."

Dividing his garments among them, they cast lots. The people stood watching.

The rulers with them also scoffed at him, saying, "He saved others. Let him save himself, if this is the Christ of God, his chosen one!"

The soldiers also mocked him, coming to him and offering him vinegar, and saying, "If you are the King of the Jews, save yourself!"

The Title on the Cross and the Insulted by Others
Jn 19:18-22 / Lk 23:32-33 & Lk 23:38
/ Mt 27:37-43 / Mk 15:26-32

Pilate wrote a title also, and put it on the cross. There was written, "JESUS OF NAZARETH, THE KING OF THE JEWS." Therefore, many of the Jews read this title, for the place where Jesus was crucified was near the city; and it was written in Hebrew, in Latin, and in Greek.

The chief priests of the Jews therefore said to Pilate, "Don't write, The King of the Jews,' but, he said, I am King of the Jews.'"

Pilate answered, "What I have written, I have written."

There were also others, two criminals, led with him to be put to death. When they came to the place that is called The Skull, they crucified him there with the criminals, one on the right and the other on the left. The Scripture was fulfilled, which says, "He was numbered with transgressors."

Those who passed by blasphemed him, wagging their heads, and saying, "Ha! You who destroy the temple, and build it in three days, save yourself, and come down from the cross!"

Likewise, also the chief priests mocking among themselves with the scribes said, "He saved others. He can't save himself. Let the Christ, the King of Israel, now come down from the cross, that we may see and believe him."

Those who were crucified with him insulted him.

Jesus's Second Word while on the Cross
Jn 19:25-27

But there were standing by the cross of Jesus his mother, and his mother's sister, Mary the wife of Clopas, and Mary Magdalene. Therefore, when Jesus saw his mother, and the disciple whom he loved standing there,

he said to his mother, "Woman, behold your son!"

Then he said to the disciple, "Behold, your mother!"

From that hour, the disciple took her to his own home.

Jesus's Third Word while on the Cross
Lk 23:39-44 / Mt 27:44

One of the criminals who was hanged insulted him, saying, "If you are the Christ, save yourself and us!"

But the other answered, and rebuking him said, "Don't you even fear God, seeing you are under the same condemnation? And we indeed justly, for we receive the due reward for our deeds, but this man has done nothing wrong."

He said to Jesus, "Lord, remember me when you come into your Kingdom."

Jesus said to him, "Assuredly I tell you, today you will be with me in Paradise."

Jesus's Fourth Word while on the Cross
Mk 15:33-36 / Mt 27:45-49

When the sixth hour had come, there was darkness over the whole land until the ninth hour. At the ninth hour Jesus cried with a loud voice, saying, "Eloi, Eloi, lama sabachthani?" which is, being interpreted, "My God, my God, why have you forsaken me?"

Some of those who stood by, when they heard it, said, "Behold, he is calling Elijah."

One ran, and filling a sponge full of vinegar, put it on a reed, and gave it to him to drink, saying, "Let him be. Let's see whether Elijah comes to take him down."

Jesus's Fifth, Sixth, and Seventh Word
while on the Cross
Jn 19:28-30 / Mk 15:37 / Lk 23:45-46 / Mt 27:50

After this, Jesus, seeing that all things were now finished, that the Scripture might be fulfilled, said, "I am thirsty."

Now a vessel full of vinegar was set there; so they put a sponge full of the vinegar on hyssop, and held it at his mouth. When Jesus therefore had received the vinegar, he said, "It is finished."

He bowed his head, and gave up his spirit. Jesus, crying with a loud voice, said, "Father, into your hands I commit my spirit!"

Having said this, he breathed his last.

The Earthquake and the Curtain torn in Two
Mt 27:51-56 / Lk 23:47-49 / Mk 15:38-41

Behold, the veil of the temple was torn in two from the top to the bottom. The earth quaked and the rocks were split. The tombs were opened, and many bodies of the saints who had fallen asleep were raised; and coming out of the tombs after his resurrection, they entered into the holy city and appeared to many.

Now the centurion, and those who were with him watching Jesus, when they saw the earthquake, and the things that were done, feared exceedingly, saying, "Truly this was the Son of God."

Many women were there watching from afar, who had followed Jesus from Galilee, serving him. Among them were Mary Magdalene, Mary the mother of James and Joses, and the mother of the sons of Zebedee.

All the multitudes that came together to see this, when they saw the things that were done, returned home beating their breasts. All his acquaintances, and the women who followed with him from Galilee, stood at a distance, watching these things.

The Burial of Jesus
Jn 19:31-42 / Lk 23:50-56 / Mk 15:42-43
& Mk 15:46-47 / Mt 27:57-61

Therefore, the Jews, because it was the Preparation Day, so that the bodies wouldn't remain on the cross on the

Sabbath (for that Sabbath was a special one), asked of Pilate that their legs might be broken, and that they might be taken away. Therefore, the soldiers came, and broke the legs of the first, and of the other who was crucified with him; but when they came to Jesus, and saw that he was already dead, they didn't break his legs.

However, one of the soldiers pierced his side with a spear, and immediately blood and water came out.

He who has seen has testified, and his testimony is true. He knows that he tells the truth, that you may believe. For these things happened, that the Scripture might be fulfilled, "A bone of him will not be broken."

Again, another Scripture says, "They will look on him whom they pierced."

Behold, a man named Joseph, who was a member of the council, a good and righteous man (he had not consented to their counsel and deed), from Arimathaea, a city of the Jews, who was also waiting for the Kingdom of God: this man went to Pilate and asked for Jesus' body.

Pilate marveled if he were already dead; and summoning the centurion, he asked him whether he had been dead long. When he found out from the centurion, he granted the body to Joseph.

Nicodemus, who at first came to Jesus by night, also came bringing a mixture of myrrh and aloes, about a hundred Roman pounds. So, they took Jesus' body, and bound it in linen cloths with the spices, as the custom of the Jews is to bury. Now in the place where he was crucified there was a garden. In the garden was a new tomb in which no man had ever yet been laid.

Then because of the Jews' Preparation Day (for the tomb was near at hand) they laid Jesus there. Joseph took the body, and wrapped it in a clean linen cloth, and laid it in his own new tomb, which he had cut out in the rock, and he rolled a great stone to the door of the tomb and departed.

The women, who had come with him out of Galilee, followed after, and saw the tomb, and how his body was laid. They returned, and prepared spices and ointments. On the Sabbath they rested according to the commandment.

The Guard at the Tomb
Mt 27:62-66

Now on the next day, which was the day after the Preparation Day, the chief priests and the Pharisees were gathered together to Pilate, saying, "Sir, we remember what that deceiver said while he was still alive: After three days I will rise again.' Command therefore that the tomb be made secure until the third day, lest perhaps his disciples come at night and steal him away, and tell the people, He is risen from the dead;' and the last deception will be worse than the first."

Pilate said to them, "You have a guard. Go, make it as secure as you can."

So they went with the guard and made the tomb secure, sealing the stone.

Jesus Has Risen
Mk 16:1-3 / Mt 25:1-8 / Lk 24:3-11 / Jn 20:1-10

When the Sabbath was past, Mary Magdalene, and Mary the mother of James, and Salome, bought spices, that they might come and anoint him. Very early on the first day of the week, they came to the tomb when the sun had risen.

They were saying among themselves, "Who will roll away the stone from the door of the tomb for us?"

Behold, there was a great earthquake, for an angel of the Lord descended from the sky and came and rolled away the stone from the door and sat on it. His appearance was like lightning, and his clothing white as snow. For fear of him, the guards shook and became like dead men.

The angel answered the women, "Don't be afraid, for I know that you seek Jesus, who has been crucified. He is not here, for he has risen, just like he said. Come, see the place where the Lord was lying."

They entered in, and didn't find the Lord Jesus' body. It happened, while they were greatly perplexed about this, behold, two men stood by them in dazzling clothing. Becoming terrified, they bowed their faces down to the earth.

They said to them, "Why do you seek the living among the dead? He isn't here but is risen. Remember what he told you when he was still in Galilee, saying that the Son of Man must be delivered up into the hands of sinful men, and be crucified, and the third day rise again?"

They remembered his words,

"Go quickly and tell his disciples, He has risen from the dead, and behold, he goes before you into Galilee; there you will see him.' Behold, I have told you."

They departed quickly from the tomb with fear and great joy and ran to bring his disciples word.

Returned from the tomb, and told all these things to the eleven, and to all the rest. Now they were Mary Magdalene, Joanna, and Mary the mother of James. The other women with them told these things to the apostles.

These words seemed to them to be nonsense, and they didn't believe them. Therefore, she ran and came to Simon Peter, and to the other disciple whom Jesus loved, and said to them, "They have taken away the Lord out of the tomb, and we don't know where they have laid him!"

Therefore, Peter and the other disciple went out, and they went toward the tomb. They both ran together. The other disciple outran Peter and came to the tomb first. Stooping and looking in, he saw the linen clothes lying, yet he didn't enter in. Then Simon Peter came, following him, and entered into the tomb. He saw the linen cloths lying, and the cloth that had been on his head, not lying with the linen cloths, but rolled up in a place by itself.

So, then the other disciple who came first to the tomb also entered in, and he saw and believed.

For as yet they didn't know the Scripture, that he must rise from the dead. So, the disciples went away again to their own homes.

Jesus Appears to Mary Magdalene
Jn 20:11-18 / Mt 28:9-11 / Mk 16:4-11

But Mary was standing outside at the tomb weeping. So, as she wept, she stooped and looked into the tomb, and she saw two angels in white sitting, one at the head, and one at the feet, where the body of Jesus had lain.

They told her, "Woman, why are you weeping?"

She said to them, "Because they have taken away my Lord, and I don't know where they have laid him."

When she had said this, she turned around and saw Jesus standing, and didn't know that it was Jesus.

Jesus said to her, "Woman, why are you weeping? Who are you looking for?"

She, supposing him to be the gardener, said to him, "Sir, if you have carried him away, tell me where you have laid him, and I will take him away."

Jesus said to her, "Mary."

She turned and said to him, "Rabboni!" which is to say, "Teacher!"

Jesus said to her, "Don't hold me, for I haven't yet ascended to my Father; but go to my brothers, and tell them, I am ascending to my Father and your Father, to my God and your God.'"

Then Jesus said to them, "Don't be afraid. Go tell my brothers that they should go into Galilee, and there they will see me."

Mary Magdalene came and told the disciples that she had seen the Lord, and that he had said these things to her. She went and told those who had been with him, as they mourned and wept. When they heard that he was alive, and had been seen by her, they disbelieved.

The Guards' Report
Mt 28:11-15

Now while they were going, behold, some of the guards came into the city, and told the chief priests all the things that had happened. When they were assembled with the elders, and had taken counsel, they gave a large amount of silver to the soldiers, saying, "Say that his disciples came by night, and stole him away while we slept. If this comes to the governor's ears, we will persuade him and make you free of worry."

So they took the money and did as they were told. This saying was spread abroad among the Jews and continues until this day.

On the Road to Emmaus
Lk 24:13-32 / Mk 16:12

Behold, two of them were going that very day to a village named Emmaus, which was sixty stadia from Jerusalem. They talked with each other about all of these things which had happened. It happened, while they talked and questioned together, that Jesus himself came near, and went with them. But their eyes were kept from recognizing him.

He said to them, "What are you talking about as you walk, and are sad?"

One of them, named Cleopas, answered him, "Are you the only stranger in Jerusalem who doesn't know the things which have happened there in these days?"

He said to them, "What things?"

They said to him, "The things concerning Jesus, the Nazarene, who was a prophet mighty in deed and word before God and all the people; and how the chief priests and our rulers delivered him up to be condemned to death and crucified him. But we were hoping that it was he who would redeem Israel. Yes, and besides all this, it is now the third day since these things happened. Also, certain women of our company amazed us, having arrived early at the tomb; and when they didn't find his body, they came saying that they had also seen a vision of angels, who said that he was alive. Some of us went to the tomb, and found it just like the women had said, but they didn't see him."

He said to them, "Foolish men, and slow of heart to believe in all that the prophets have spoken! Didn't the Christ have to suffer these things and to enter into his glory?"

Beginning from Moses and from all the prophets, he explained to them in all the Scriptures the things concerning himself. They drew near to the village, where they were going, and he acted like he would go further.

They urged him, saying, "Stay with us, for it is almost evening, and the day is almost over." He went in to stay with them. It happened, that when he had sat down at the table with them, he took the bread and gave thanks. Breaking it, he gave to them. Their eyes were opened, and they recognized him, and he vanished out of their sight.

They said one to another, "Weren't our hearts burning within us, while he spoke to us along the way, and while he opened the Scriptures to us?"

Simon returned to tell the Disciples about Jesus
Lk 24:33-35

They rose up that very hour, returned to Jerusalem, and found the eleven gathered together, and those who were with them, saying, "The Lord is risen indeed, and has appeared to Simon!"

They related the things that happened along the way, and how he was recognized by them in the breaking of the bread.

Jesus Appears to the Disciples
Lk 24:36-43 / Jn 20:19-23 / Mk 16:13-14

As they said these things, Jesus himself stood among them, and said to them, "Peace be to you."

But they were terrified and filled with fear and supposed that they had seen a spirit.

He said to them, "Why are you troubled? Why do doubts arise in your hearts? See my hands and my feet, that it is truly me. Touch me and see, for a spirit doesn't have flesh and bones, as you see that I have."

When he had said this, he showed them his hands and his feet.

Jesus therefore said to them again, "Peace be to you. As the Father has sent me, even so I send you."

When he had said this, he breathed on them, and said to them, "Receive the Holy Spirit!

If you forgive anyone's sins, they have been forgiven them. If you retain anyone's sins, they have been retained."

While they still didn't believe for joy, and wondered, he said to them, "Do you have anything here to eat?"

They gave him a piece of a broiled fish and some honeycomb. He took them and ate in front of them.

Jesus Appears to Thomas
Jn 20:24-29

But Thomas, one of the twelve, called Didymus, wasn't with them when Jesus came.

The other disciples therefore said to him, "We have seen the Lord!" But he said to them, "Unless I see in his hands the print of the nails, and put my hand into his side, I will not believe it."

After eight days again his disciples were inside, and Thomas was with them. Jesus came, the doors being locked, and stood in the midst, and said, "Peace be to you."

Then he said to Thomas, "Reach here your finger, and see my hands. Reach here your hand and put it into my side. Don't be unbelieving but believing."

Thomas answered him, "My Lord and my God!"

Jesus said to him, "Because you have seen me, you have believed. Blessed are those who have not seen and have believed."

Jesus and the Miraculous Catch of Fish
Jn 21:1-14

After these things, Jesus revealed himself again to the disciples at the sea of Tiberias. He revealed himself this way. Simon Peter, Thomas called Didymus, Nathanael of Cana in Galilee, and the sons of Zebedee, and two others of his disciples were together.

Simon Peter said to them, "I'm going fishing."

They told him, "We are also coming with you."

They immediately went out and entered into the boat. That night, they caught nothing. But when day had already come, Jesus stood on the beach, yet the disciples didn't know that it was Jesus.

Jesus therefore said to them, "Children, have you anything to eat?"

They answered him, "No."

He said to them, "Cast the net on the right side of the boat, and you will find some."

They cast it therefore, and now they weren't able to draw it in for the multitude of fish. That disciple therefore whom Jesus loved said to Peter, "It's the Lord!"

So when Simon Peter heard that it was the Lord, he wrapped his coat around him (for he was naked), and threw himself into the sea. But the other disciples came in the little boat (for they were not far from the land, but about two hundred cubits away), dragging the net full of fish. So when they got out on the land, they saw a fire of coals there, and fish laid on it, and bread.

Jesus said to them, "Bring some of the fish which you have just caught."

Simon Peter went up, and drew the net to land, full of great fish, one hundred fifty-three; and even though there were so many, the net wasn't torn.

Jesus said to them, "Come and eat breakfast."

None of the disciples dared inquire of him, "Who are you?" knowing that it was the Lord.

Then Jesus came and took the bread, gave it to them, and the fish likewise.

This is now the third time that Jesus was revealed to his disciples, after he had risen from the dead.

Jesus Reinstates Peter
Jn 21:15-23 / Lk 24:44-48 / Mk 16:15-18

So when they had eaten their breakfast, Jesus said to Simon Peter,

"Simon, son of Jonah, do you love me more than these?

He said to Him, "Yes, Lord, you know that I have affection for you."

He said to him, :Feed my lambs"

He said to him again a second time, "Simon, son of Jonah, do you love me?"

He said to him, "Yes, Lord; you know that I have affection for you."

He said to him, "Tend my sheep."

He said to him the third time, "Simon, son of Jonah, do you have affection for me?"

Peter was grieved because he asked him the third time, "Do you have affection for me?"

He said to him, "Lord, you know everything. You know that I have affection for you."

Jesus said to him, "Feed my sheep. Most certainly I tell you, when you were young, you dressed yourself, and walked where you wanted to. But when you are old, you will stretch out your hands, and another will dress you, and carry you where you don't want to go."

Now he said this, signifying by what kind of death he would glorify God. When he had said this, he said to him, "Follow me."

Then Peter, turning around, saw a disciple following. This was the disciple whom Jesus sincerely loved, the one who had also leaned on Jesus' breast at the supper and asked, "Lord, who is going to betray You?"

Peter seeing him, said to Jesus, "Lord, what about this man?"

Jesus said to him, "If I desire that he stay until I come, what is that to you? You follow me."

This saying therefore went out among the brothers, that this disciple wouldn't die. Yet Jesus didn't say to him that he wouldn't die, but, "If I desire that he stay until I come, what is that to you?"

He said to them, "This is what I told you, while I was still with you, that all things which are written in the law of Moses, the prophets, and the psalms, concerning me must be fulfilled."

Then he opened their minds, that they might understand the Scriptures.

He said to them, "Thus it is written, and thus it was necessary for the Christ to suffer and to rise from the dead the third day, and that repentance and remission of sins should be preached in his name to all the nations, beginning at Jerusalem.   You are witnesses of these things."

He said to them, "Go into all the world, and preach the Good News to the whole creation.

He who believes and is baptized will be saved; but he who disbelieves will be condemned.

These signs will accompany those who believe: in my name they will cast out demons; they will speak with new languages; they will take up serpents; and if they drink any deadly thing, it will in no way hurt them; they will lay hands on the sick, and they will recover."

The Great Commission
Mt 28:16-20

But the eleven disciples went into Galilee, to the mountain where Jesus had sent them. When they saw him, they bowed down to him, but some doubted.

Jesus came to them and spoke to them, saying, "All authority has been given to me in heaven and on earth. Go, and make disciples of all nations, baptizing them in the name of the Father and of the Son and of the Holy Spirit, teaching them to observe all things that I commanded you. Behold, I am with you always, even to the end of the age." Amen.

The Ascension of Jesus
Lk 24:49-53 / Mk 16:19-20 / Jn 21:24-25
& Jn 20:30-31

Behold, I send out the promise of my Father on you. But wait in the city of Jerusalem until you are clothed with power from on high."

He led them out as far as Bethany, and he lifted up his hands, and blessed them.

So then the Lord, after he had spoken to them, was received up into heaven, and sat down at the right hand of God. They worshiped him, and returned to Jerusalem with great joy, and were continually in the temple, praising and blessing God. Amen.

They went out, and preached everywhere, the Lord working with them, and confirming the word by the signs that followed. Amen.

This is the disciple who testifies about these things and wrote these things. We know that his witness is true. Therefore, Jesus did many other signs in the presence of his disciples, which are not written in this book; but these are written, that you may believe that Jesus is the Christ, the Son of God, and that believing you may have life in his name.

Reference
Gospel Harmony

The Beginning of the Good News
Mk 1: 1 / Luke 1:1-4 / Jn 1:1-14

(Mark 1 : 1) The beginning of the Good News of Jesus Christ, the Son of God.

(Luke 1 : 1) Since many have undertaken to set in order a narrative concerning those matters which have been fulfilled among us,

(Luke 1 : 2) even as those who from the beginning were eyewitnesses and servants of the word delivered them to us,

(Luke 1 : 2) it seemed good to me also, having traced the course of all things accurately from the first, to write to you in order, most excellent Theophilus;

(John 1 : 1) In the beginning was the Word, and the Word was with God, and the Word was God.

(John 1 : 2) The same was in the beginning with God.

(John 1 : 3) All things were made through him. Without him was not anything made that has been made.

(John 1 : 4) In him was life, and the life was the light of men.

(John 1 : 5) The light shines in the darkness, and the darkness hasn't overcome it.

(John 1 : 6) There came a man, sent from God, whose name was John.

(John 1 : 7) The same came as a witness, that he might testify about the light, that all might believe through him.

(John 1 : 8) He was not the light, but was sent that he might testify about the light.

(John 1 : 9) The true light that enlightens everyone was coming into the world.

(John 1 : 10) He was in the world, and the world was made through him, and the world didn't recognize him.

(John 1 : 11) He came to his own, and those who were his own didn't receive him.

(John 1 : 12) But as many as received him, to them he gave the right to become God's children, to those who believe in his name:

(John 1 : 13) who were born not of blood, nor of the will of the flesh, nor of the will of man, but of God.

(John 1 : 14) The Word became flesh, and lived among us. We saw his glory, such glory as of the one and only Son of the Father, full of grace and truth.

The Birth of John the Baptist
Lk 1:5-25

(Luke 1 : 5) There was in the days of Herod, the king of Judea, a certain priest named Zacharias, of the priestly division of Abijah. He had a wife of the daughters of Aaron, and her name was Elizabeth.

(Luke 1 : 6) They were both righteous before God, walking blamelessly in all the commandments and ordinances of the Lord.

(Luke 1 : 7) But they had no child, because Elizabeth was barren, and they both were well advanced in years.

(Luke 1 : 8) Now it happened, while he executed the priest's office before God in the order of his division,

(Luke 1 : 9) according to the custom of the priest's office, his lot was to enter into the temple of the Lord and burn incense.

(Luke 1 : 10) The whole multitude of the people were praying outside at the hour of incense.

(Luke 1 : 11) An angel of the Lord appeared to him, standing on the right side of the altar of incense.

(Luke 1 : 12) Zacharias was troubled when he saw him, and fear fell upon him.

(Luke 1 : 13) But the angel said to him, "Don't be afraid, Zacharias, because your request has been heard, and your wife, Elizabeth, will bear you a son, and you shall call his name John.

(Luke 1 : 14) You will have joy and gladness; and many will rejoice at his birth.

(Luke 1 : 15) For he will be great in the sight of the Lord, and he will drink no wine nor strong drink. He will be filled with the Holy Spirit, even from his mother's womb.

(Luke 1 : 16) He will turn many of the children of Israel to the Lord, their God.

(Luke 1 : 17) He will go before him in the spirit and power of Elijah, to turn the hearts of the fathers to the children,' and the disobedient to the wisdom of the just; to prepare a people prepared for the Lord."

(Luke 1 : 18) Zacharias said to the angel, "How can I be sure of this? For I am an old man, and my wife is well advanced in years."

(Luke 1 : 19) The angel answered him, "I am Gabriel, who stands in the presence of God. I was sent to speak to you, and to bring you this good news.

(Luke 1 : 20) Behold, you will be silent and not able to speak, until the day that these things will happen, because you didn't believe my words, which will be fulfilled in their proper time."

(Luke 1 : 21) The people were waiting for Zacharias, and they marveled that he delayed in the temple.

(Luke 1 : 22) When he came out, he could not speak to them, and they perceived that he had seen a vision in the temple. He continued making signs to them, and remained mute.

(Luke 1 : 23) It happened, when the days of his service were fulfilled, he departed to his house.

(Luke 1 : 24) After these days Elizabeth, his wife, conceived, and she hid herself five months, saying,

(Luke 1 : 25) "Thus has the Lord done to me in the days in which he looked at me, to take away my reproach among men."

The Birth of Jesus
Mt 1:18

(Matthew 1 : 18) Now the birth of Jesus Christ was like this; for after his mother, Mary, was engaged to Joseph, before they came together, she was found pregnant by the Holy Spirit.

The Genealogy of Mary, Wife of Joseph.
Lk 3:24-38

> (Editor Footnote)   Mary is the daughter of Heli. Joseph is the son of Jacob, the son in law of Heli.

(Luke 3 : 24) the son of Heli, the son of Matthat, the son of Levi, the son of Melchi, the son of Jannai, the son of Joseph,

(Luke 3 : 25) the son of Mattathias, the son of Amos, the son of Nahum, the son of Esli, the son of Naggai,

(Luke 3 : 26) the son of Maath, the son of Mattathias, the son of Semein, the son of Joseph, the son of Judah,

(Luke 3 : 27) the son of Joanan, the son of Rhesa, the son of Zerubbabel, the son of Shealtiel, the son of Neri,

(Luke 3 : 28) the son of Melchi, the son of Addi, the son of Cosam, the son of Elmodam, the son of Er,

(Luke 3 : 29) the son of Joshua, the son of Eliezer, the son of Jorim, the son of Matthat, the son of Levi,

(Luke 3 : 30) the son of Simeon, the son of Judah, the son of Joseph, the son of Jonan, the son of Eliakim,

(Luke 3 : 31) the son of Melea, the son of Menan, the son of Mattatha, the son of Nathan, the son of David,

(Luke 3 : 32) the son of Jesse, the son of Obed, the son of Boaz, the son of Salmon, the son of Nahshon,

(Luke 3 : 33) the son of Amminadab, the son of Aram, the son of Hezron, the son of Perez, the son of Judah,

(Luke 3 : 34) the son of Jacob, the son of Isaac, the son of Abraham, the son of Terah, the son of Nahor,

(Luke 3 : 35) the son of Serug, the son of Reu, the son of Peleg, the son of Eber, the son of Shelah,

(Luke 3 : 36) the son of Cainan, the son of Arphaxad, the son of Shem, the son of Noah, the son of Lamech,

(Luke 3 : 37) the son of Methuselah, the son of Enoch, the son of Jared, the son of Mahalaleel, the son of Cainan,

(Luke 3 : 38) the son of Enos, the son of Seth, the son of Adam, the son of God.

The Genealogy of Joseph, husband of Mary.
Mt 1:1-17

(Matthew 1 : 1) The book of the genealogy of Jesus Christ, the son of David, the son of Abraham:

(Matthew 1 : 2) Abraham became the father of Isaac. Isaac became the father of Jacob. Jacob became the father of Judah and his brothers.

(Matthew 1 : 3) Judah became the father of Perez and Zerah by Tamar. Perez became the father of Hezron. Hezron became the father of Ram.

(Matthew 1 : 4) Ram became the father of Amminadab. Amminadab became the father of Nahshon. Nahshon became the father of Salmon.

(Matthew 1 : 5) Salmon became the father of Boaz by Rahab. Boaz became the father of Obed by Ruth. Obed became the father of Jesse.

(Matthew 1 : 6) Jesse became the father of King David. David became the father of Solomon by her who had been the wife of Uriah.

(Matthew 1 : 7) Solomon became the father of Rehoboam. Rehoboam became the father of Abijah. Abijah became the father of Asa.

(Matthew 1 : 8) Asa became the father of Jehoshaphat. Jehoshaphat became the father of Joram. Joram became the father of Uzziah.

(Matthew 1 : 9) Uzziah became the father of Jotham. Jotham became the father of Ahaz. Ahaz became the father of Hezekiah.

(Matthew 1 : 10) Hezekiah became the father of Manasseh. Manasseh became the father of Amon. Amon became the father of Josiah.

(Matthew 1 : 11) Josiah became the father of Jechoniah and his brothers, at the time of the exile to Babylon.

(Matthew 1 : 12) After the exile to Babylon, Jechoniah became the father of Shealtiel. Shealtiel became the father of Zerubbabel.

(Matthew 1 : 13) Zerubbabel became thc father of Abiud. Abiud became the father of Eliakim. Eliakim became the father of Azor.

(Matthew 1 : 14) Azor became the father of Zadok. Zadok became the father of Achim. Achim became the father of Eliud.

(Matthew 1 : 15) Eliud became the father of Eleazar. Eleazar became the father of Matthan. Matthan became the father of Jacob.

(Matthew 1 : 16) Jacob became the father of Joseph, the husband of Mary, from whom was born Jesus, who is called Christ.

(Matthew 1 : 17) So all the generations from Abraham to David are fourteen generations; from David to the exile to Babylon fourteen generations; and from the carrying away to Babylon to the Christ, fourteen generations.

The Birth of Jesus
Lk 1:26-38

(Luke 1 : 26) Now in the sixth month the angel Gabriel was sent from God to a city in Galilee named Nazareth,

(Luke 1 : 27) to a virgin pledged to be married to a man whose name was Joseph, of the house of David. The virgin's name was Mary.

> (Editor Footnote) Joseph is the son of Jacob, and son in law of Heli. Mary's husband Joseph was the descendant of King David, from the line of Solomon. Mary is the daughter of Heli. Heli is the descendant of king David but from the line of Nathan, who was one of the sons of King David and could be the prophet Nathan who talked with King David when he sinned.
>
> The angel Gabriel appeared to Mary outside of her house.

(Luke 1 : 28) Having come in, the angel said to her, "Rejoice, you highly favored one! The Lord is with you. Blessed are you among women!"

(Luke 1 : 29) But when she saw him, she was greatly troubled at the saying, and considered what kind of salutation this might be.

(Luke 1 : 30) The angel said to her, "Don't be afraid, Mary, for you have found favor with God.

(Luke 1 : 31) Behold, you will conceive in your womb, and give birth to a son, and will call his name Jesus.'

(Luke 1 : 32) He will be great, and will be called the Son of the Most High. The Lord God will give him the throne of his father, David,

(Luke 1 : 33) and he will reign over the house of Jacob forever. There will be no end to his Kingdom."

(Luke 1 : 34) Mary said to the angel, "How can this be, seeing I am a virgin?"

(Luke 1 : 35) The angel answered her, "The Holy Spirit will come on you, and the power of the Most High will overshadow you. Therefore also the holy one who is born from you will be called the Son of God.

(Luke 1 : 36) Behold, Elizabeth, your relative, also has conceived a son in her old age; and this is the sixth month with her who was called barren.

(Luke 1 : 37) For everything spoken by God is possible."

(Luke 1 : 38) Mary said, "Behold, the handmaid of the Lord; be it to me according to your word." The angel departed from her.

Mary went to meet Elizabeth
Lk 1:39-80

(Luke 1 : 39) Mary arose in those days and went into the hill country with haste, into a city of Judah,

(Luke 1 : 40) and entered into the house of Zacharias and greeted Elizabeth.

(Luke 1 : 41) It happened, when Elizabeth heard Mary's greeting, that the baby leaped in her womb, and Elizabeth was filled with the Holy Spirit.

(Luke 1 : 42) She called out with a loud voice, and said, "Blessed are you among women, and blessed is the fruit of your womb!

(Luke 1 : 43) Why am I so favored, that the mother of my Lord should come to me?

(Luke 1 : 44) For behold, when the voice of your greeting came into my ears, the baby leaped in my womb for joy!

(Luke 1 : 45) Blessed is she who believed, for there will be a fulfillment of the things which have been spoken to her from the Lord!"

(Luke 1 : 46) Mary said, "My soul magnifies the Lord.

(Luke 1 : 47) My spirit has rejoiced in God my Savior,

(Luke 1 : 48) for he has looked at the humble state of his handmaid. For behold, from now on, all generations will call me blessed.

(Luke 1 : 49) For he who is mighty has done great things for me. Holy is his name.

(Luke 1 : 50) His mercy is for generations of generations on those who fear him.

(Luke 1 : 51) He has shown strength with his arm. He has scattered the proud in the imagination of their hearts.

(Luke 1 : 52) He has put down princes from their thrones. And has exalted the lowly.

(Luke 1 : 53) He has filled the hungry with good things. He has sent the rich away empty.

(Luke 1 : 54) He has given help to Israel, his servant, that he might remember mercy,

(Luke 1 : 55) As he spoke to our fathers, to Abraham and his seed forever."

(Luke 1 : 56) Mary stayed with her about three months, and then returned to her house.

(Luke 1 : 57) Now the time that Elizabeth should give birth was fulfilled, and she gave birth to a son.

(Luke 1 : 58) Her neighbors and her relatives heard that the Lord had magnified his mercy towards her, and they rejoiced with her.

(Luke 1 : 59) It happened on the eighth day, that they came to circumcise the child; and they would have called him Zacharias, after the name of the father.

(Luke 1 : 60) His mother answered, "Not so; but he will be called John."

(Luke 1 : 61) They said to her, "There is no one among your relatives who is called by this name."

(Luke 1 : 62) They made signs to his father, what he would have him called.

(Luke 1 : 63) He asked for a writing tablet, and wrote, "His name is John." They all marveled.

(Luke 1 : 64) His mouth was opened immediately, and his tongue freed, and he spoke, blessing God.

(Luke 1 : 65) Fear came on all who lived around them, and all these sayings were talked about throughout all the hill country of Judea.

(Luke 1 : 66) All who heard them laid them up in their heart, saying, "What then will this child be?" The hand of the Lord was with him.

(Luke 1 : 67) His father, Zacharias, was filled with the Holy Spirit, and prophesied, saying,

(Luke 1 : 68) "Blessed be the Lord, the God of Israel, for he has visited and worked redemption for his people;

(Luke 1 : 69) and has raised up a horn of salvation for us in the house of his servant David

(Luke 1 : 70) (as he spoke by the mouth of his holy prophets who have been from of old),

(Luke 1 : 71) salvation from our enemies, and from the hand of all who hate us;

(Luke 1 : 72) to show mercy towards our fathers, to remember his holy covenant,

(Luke 1 : 73) the oath which he spoke to Abraham, our father,

(Luke 1 : 74) to grant to us that we, being delivered out of the hand of our enemies, should serve him without fear,

(Luke 1 : 75) In holiness and righteousness before him all the days of our life.

(Luke 1 : 76) And you, child, will be called a prophet of the Most High, for you will go before the face of the Lord to prepare his ways,

(Luke 1 : 77) to give knowledge of salvation to his people by the remission of their sins,

(Luke 1 : 78) because of the tender mercy of our God, whereby the dawn from on high will visit us,

(Luke 1 : 79) to shine on those who sit in darkness and the shadow of death; to guide our feet into the way of peace."

(Luke 1 : 80) The child was growing, and becoming strong in spirit, and was in the desert until the day of his public appearance to Israel.

(Editor Footnote)   Joseph found out Mary was pregnant by the Holy Spirit.

God told Joseph to accept Mary who was Pregnant by the Holy Spirit
Mt 1: 19-25

(Matthew 1 : 19)   Joseph, her husband, being a righteous man, and not willing to make her a public example, intended to put her away secretly.

(Matthew 1 : 20)   But when he thought about these things, behold, an angel of the Lord appeared to him in a dream, saying, "Joseph, son of David, don't be afraid to take to yourself Mary, your wife, for that which is conceived in her is of the Holy Spirit.

(Matthew 1 : 21)   She shall give birth to a son. You shall call his name Jesus, for it is he who shall save his people from their sins."

(Matthew 1 : 22)   Now all this has happened, that it might be fulfilled which was spoken by the Lord through the prophet, saying,

(Matthew 1 : 23)   "Behold, the virgin shall be with child, and shall give birth to a son. They shall call his name Immanuel"; which is, being interpreted, "God with us."

(Matthew 1 : 24) Joseph arose from his sleep, and did as the angel of the Lord commanded him, and took his wife to himself;

(Matthew 1 : 25) and didn't know her sexually until she had given birth to her firstborn son. He named him Jesus.

Jesus was Born in Bethlehem
Lk 2:1-39

(Luke 2 : 1) Now it happened in those days, that a decree went out from Caesar Augustus that all the world should be enrolled.

(Luke 2 : 2) This was the first enrollment made when Quirinius was governor of Syria.

(Luke 2 : 3) All went to enroll themselves, everyone to his own city.

(Luke 2 : 4) Joseph also went up from Galilee, out of the city of Nazareth, into Judea, to the city of David, which is called Bethlehem, because he was of the house and family of David;

(Luke 2 : 5) to enroll himself with Mary, who was pledged to be married to him as wife, being pregnant.

(Luke 2 : 6) It happened, while they were there, that the day had come that she should give birth.

(Luke 2 : 7) She gave birth to her firstborn son. She wrapped him in bands of cloth, and laid him in a feeding trough, because there was no room for them in the inn.

(Luke 2 : 8) There were shepherds in the same country staying in the field, and keeping watch by night over their flock.

(Luke 2 : 9) Behold, an angel of the Lord stood by them, and the glory of the Lord shone around them, and they were terrified.

(Luke 2 : 10) The angel said to them, "Don't be afraid, for behold, I bring you good news of great joy which will be to all the people.

(Luke 2 : 11) For there is born to you, this day, in the city of David, a Savior, who is Christ the Lord.

(Luke 2 : 12) This is the sign to you: you will find a baby wrapped in strips of cloth, lying in a feeding trough."

(Luke 2 : 13) Suddenly, there was with the angel a multitude of the heavenly army praising God, and saying,

(Luke 2 : 14) "Glory to God in the highest, on earth peace, good will toward men."

(Luke 2 : 15) It happened, when the angels went away from them into the sky, that the shepherds said one to another, "Let's go to Bethlehem, now, and see this thing that has happened, which the Lord has made known to us."

(Luke 2 : 16) They came with haste, and found both Mary and Joseph, and the baby was lying in the feeding trough.

(Luke 2 : 17) When they saw it, they publicized widely the saying which was spoken to them about this child.

(Luke 2 : 18) All who heard it wondered at the things which were spoken to them by the shepherds.

(Luke 2 : 19) But Mary kept all these sayings, pondering them in her heart.

(Luke 2 : 20) The shepherds returned, glorifying and praising God for all the things that they had heard and seen, just as it was told them.

(Luke 2 : 21) When eight days were fulfilled for the circumcision of the child, his name was called Jesus, which was given by the angel before he was conceived in the womb.

(Luke 2 : 22) When the days of their purification according to the law of Moses were fulfilled, they brought him up to Jerusalem, to present him to the Lord

(Luke 2 : 23) (as it is written in the law of the Lord, "Every male who opens the womb shall be called holy to the Lord"),

(Luke 2 : 24) and to offer a sacrifice according to that which is said in the law of the Lord, "A pair of turtledoves, or two young pigeons."

(Luke 2 : 25) Behold, there was a man in Jerusalem whose name was Simeon. This man was righteous and devout, looking for the consolation of Israel, and the Holy Spirit was on him.

(Luke 2 : 26) It had been revealed to him by the Holy Spirit that he should not see death before he had seen the Lord's Christ.

(Luke 2 : 27) He came in the Spirit into the temple. When the parents brought in the child, Jesus, that they might do concerning him according to the custom of the law,

(Luke 2 : 28) then he received him into his arms, and blessed God, and said,

(Luke 2 : 29) "Now you are releasing your servant, Master, according to your word, in peace;

(Luke 2 : 30) for my eyes have seen your salvation,

(Luke 2 : 31) which you have prepared before the face of all peoples;

(Luke 2 : 32) a light for revelation to the nations, and the glory of your people Israel."

(Luke 2 : 33) Joseph and his mother were marveling at the things which were spoken concerning him,

(Luke 2 : 34) and Simeon blessed them, and said to Mary, his mother, "Behold, this child is set for the falling and the rising of many in Israel, and for a sign which is spoken against.

(Luke 2 : 35) Yes, a sword will pierce through your own soul, that the thoughts of many hearts may be revealed."

(Luke 2 : 36) There was one Anna, a prophetess, the daughter of Phanuel, of the tribe of Asher (she was of a great age, having lived with a husband seven years from her virginity,

(Luke 2 : 37) and she had been a widow for about eighty-four years), who didn't depart from the temple, worshiping with fasting and petitions night and day.

(Luke 2 : 38) Coming up at that very hour, she gave thanks to the Lord and spoke of him to all those who were looking for redemption in Jerusalem.

(Luke 2 : 39) When they had accomplished all things that were according to the law of the Lord, they returned into Galilee, to their own city, Nazareth.

The Wise Men came to see Jesus
Mt 2:1-14

(Matthew 2 : 1)   Now when Jesus was born in Bethlehem of Judea in the days of King Herod, behold, wise men from the east came to Jerusalem, saying,

(Matthew 2 : 2)   "Where is he who is born King of the Jews? For we saw his star in the east, and have come to worship him."

(Matthew 2 : 3)   When King Herod heard it, he was troubled, and all Jerusalem with him.

(Matthew 2 : 4)   Gathering together all the chief priests and scribes of the people, he asked them where the Christ would be born.

(Matthew 2 : 5)   They said to him, "In Bethlehem of Judea, for this is written through the prophet,

(Matthew 2 : 6)   You Bethlehem, land of Judah, are in no way least among the princes of Judah: for out of you shall come a governor, who shall shepherd my people, Israel.'"

(Matthew 2 : 7)   Then Herod secretly called the wise men, and learned from them exactly what time the star appeared.

(Matthew 2 : 8)   He sent them to Bethlehem, and said, "Go and search diligently for the young child. When you have found him, bring me word, so that I also may come and worship him."

(Matthew 2 : 9)   They, having heard the king, went their way; and behold, the star, which they saw in the east, went before them, until it came and stood over where the young child was.

(Matthew 2 : 10) When they saw the star, they rejoiced with exceedingly great joy.

(Matthew 2 : 11) They came into the house and saw the young child with Mary, his mother, and they fell down and worshiped him. Opening their treasures, they offered to him gifts: gold, frankincense, and myrrh.

(Matthew 2 : 12) Being warned in a dream that they shouldn't return to Herod, they went back to their own country another way.

(Matthew 2 : 13) Now when they had departed, behold, an angel of the Lord appeared to Joseph in a dream, saying, "Arise and take the young child and his mother, and flee into Egypt, and stay there until I tell you, for Herod will seek the young child to destroy him."

(Matthew 2 : 14) He arose and took the young child and his mother by night, and departed into Egypt,

King Herod Ordered to kill the Children
Mt 2:15-18

(Matthew 2 : 15)   and was there until the death of Herod; that it might be fulfilled which was spoken by the Lord through the prophet, saying, "Out of Egypt I called my son."

(Matthew 2 : 16) Then Herod, when he saw that he was mocked by the wise men, was exceedingly angry, and sent out, and killed all the male children who were in Bethlehem and in all the surrounding countryside, from two years old and under, according to the exact time which he had learned from the wise men.

(Matthew 2 : 17)   Then that which was spoken by Jeremiah the prophet was fulfilled, saying,

(Matthew 2 : 18)   "A voice was heard in Ramah, lamentation, weeping and great mourning, Rachel weeping for her children; she wouldn't be comforted, because they are no more."

Joseph returned to Galilee
Mt 2:19-22

(Matthew 2 : 19)   But when Herod was dead, behold, an angel of the Lord appeared in a dream to Joseph in Egypt, saying,

(Matthew 2 : 20)   "Arise and take the young child and his mother, and go into the land of Israel, for those who sought the young child's life are dead."

(Matthew 2 : 21)   He arose and took the young child and his mother, and came into the land of Israel.

(Matthew 2 : 22)   But when he heard that Archelaus was reigning over Judea in the place of his father, Herod, he was afraid to go there. Being warned in a dream, he withdrew into the region of Galilee,

The Boy Jesus
Lk 2:40-52 / Mt 2:23

(Luke 2 : 40)   The child was growing, and was becoming strong in spirit, being filled with wisdom, and the grace of God was upon him.

(Luke 2 : 41) His parents went every year to Jerusalem at the feast of the Passover.

(Luke 2 : 42) When he was twelve years old, they went up to Jerusalem according to the custom of the feast,

(Luke 2 : 43) and when they had fulfilled the days, as they were returning, the boy Jesus stayed behind in Jerusalem. Joseph and his mother didn't know it,

(Luke 2 : 44) but supposing him to be in the company, they went a day's journey, and they looked for him among their relatives and acquaintances.

(Luke 2 : 45) When they didn't find him, they returned to Jerusalem, looking for him.

(Luke 2 : 46) It happened after three days they found him in the temple, sitting in the midst of the teachers, both listening to them, and asking them questions.

(Luke 2 : 47) All who heard him were amazed at his understanding and his answers.

(Luke 2 : 48) When they saw him, they were astonished, and his mother said to him, "Son, why have you treated us this way? Behold, your father and I were anxiously looking for you."

(Luke 2 : 49) He said to them, "Why were you looking for me? Didn't you know that I must be in my Father's house?"

(Luke 2 : 50) They didn't understand the saying which he spoke to them.

(Luke 2 : 51) And he went down with them, and came to Nazareth. He was subject to them, and his mother kept all these sayings in her heart.

(Luke 2 : 52) And Jesus increased in wisdom and stature, and in favor with God and men.

(Matthew 2 : 23)   and came and lived in a city called Nazareth; that it might be fulfilled which was spoken through the prophets: "He will be called a Nazarene."

The Beginning of John the Baptist Ministry
Lk 3:1-18/ Mk 1:2-18/ Mt 3:1-12

(Luke 3 : 1) Now in the fifteenth year of the reign of Tiberius Caesar, Pontius Pilate being governor of Judea, and Herod being tetrarch of Galilee, and his brother Philip tetrarch of the region of Ituraea and Trachonitis, and Lysanias tetrarch of Abilene,

(Luke 3 : 2) in the high priesthood of Annas and Caiaphas, the word of God came to John, the son of Zacharias, in the wilderness.

(Mark 1 : 2) As it is written in the prophets, "Behold, I send my messenger before your face, who will prepare your way before you.

(Mark 1 : 3) The voice of one crying in the wilderness, Make ready the way of the Lord! Make his paths straight!'"

(Mark 1 : 4) John came baptizing in the wilderness and preaching the baptism of repentance for forgiveness of sins.

(Mark 1 : 5) All the country of Judea and all those of Jerusalem went out to him. They were baptized by him in the Jordan river, confessing their sins.

(Matthew 3 : 1)   In those days, John the Baptizer came, preaching in the wilderness of Judea, saying,

(Matthew 3 : 2)   "Repent, for the Kingdom of Heaven is at hand!"

(Luke 3 : 3) He came into all the region around the Jordan, preaching the baptism of repentance for remission of sins.

(Matthew 3 : 3)   For this is he who was spoken of by Isaiah the prophet, saying, "The voice of one crying in the wilderness, make ready the way of the Lord. Make his paths straight."

(Luke 3 : 4) As it is written in the book of the words of Isaiah the prophet,

"The voice of one crying in the wilderness,

Make ready the way of the Lord.

Make his paths straight.

(Luke 3 : 5) Every valley will be filled.

Every mountain and hill will be brought low.

The crooked will become straight,

and the rough ways smooth.

(Luke 3 : 6) All flesh will see God's salvation.'"

(Matthew 3 : 4) Now John himself wore clothing made of camel's hair, with a leather belt around his waist. His food was locusts and wild honey.

(Matthew 3 : 5) Then people from Jerusalem, all of Judea, and all the region around the Jordan went out to him.

(Matthew 3 : 6) They were baptized by him in the Jordan, confessing their sins.

(Matthew 3 : 7) But when he saw many of the Pharisees and Sadducees coming for his baptism, he said to them, "You offspring of vipers, who warned you to flee from the wrath to come?

(Matthew 3 : 8) Therefore produce fruit worthy of repentance!

(Matthew 3 : 9 Don't think to yourselves, We have Abraham for our father,' for I tell you that God is able to raise up children to Abraham from these stones.

(Matthew 3 : 10) "Even now the ax lies at the root of the trees. Therefore every tree that doesn't produce good fruit is cut down, and cast into the fire.

(Luke 3 : 7) He said therefore to the multitudes who went out to be baptized by him, "You offspring of vipers, who warned you to flee from the wrath to come?

(Luke 3 : 8) Therefore produce fruits worthy of repentance, and don't begin to say among yourselves, We have Abraham for our father;' for I tell you that God is able to raise up children to Abraham from these stones!

(Luke 3 : 9) Even now the ax also lies at the root of the trees. Every tree therefore that doesn't produce good fruit is cut down, and thrown into the fire."

(Luke 3 : 10) The multitudes asked him, "What then must we do?"

(Luke 3 : 11) He answered them, "He who has two coats, let him give to him who has none. He who has food, let him do likewise."

(Luke 3 : 12) Tax collectors also came to be baptized, and they said to him, "Teacher, what must we do?"

(Luke 3 : 13) He said to them, "Collect no more than that which is appointed to you."

(Luke 3 : 14) Soldiers also asked him, saying, "What about us? What must we do?" He said to them, "Extort from no one by violence, neither accuse anyone wrongfully. Be content with your wages."

> (Mark 1 : 6) John was clothed with camel's hair and a leather belt around his waist. He ate locusts and wild honey.

(Luke 3 : 15) As the people were in expectation, and all men reasoned in their hearts concerning John, whether perhaps he was the Christ,

(Luke 3 : 16) John answered them all, "I indeed baptize you with water, but he comes who is mightier than I, the strap of whose sandals I am not worthy to loosen. He will baptize you in the Holy Spirit and fire,

(Luke 3 : 17) whose fan is in his hand, and he will thoroughly cleanse his threshing floor, and will gather the wheat into his barn; but he will burn up the chaff with unquenchable fire."

(Luke 3 : 18) Then with many other exhortations he preached good news to the people,

> (Mark 1 : 7) He preached, saying, "After me comes he who is mightier than I, the thong of whose sandals I am not worthy to stoop down and loosen.
>
> (Mark 1 : 8) I baptized you in water, but he will baptize you in the Holy Spirit."

(Matthew 3 : 11)   I indeed baptize you in water for repentance, but he who comes after me is mightier than I, whose shoes I am not worthy to carry. He will baptize you in the Holy Spirit.

(Matthew 3 : 12)   His winnowing fork is in his hand, and he will thoroughly cleanse his threshing floor. He will gather his wheat into the barn, but the chaff, he will burn up with unquenchable fire."

Jesus got Baptized by John the Baptist
Mt 3:13-17 / Mk 1:9-11/Lk 3:21-22

(Matthew 3 : 13)   Then Jesus came from Galilee to the Jordan to John, to be baptized by him.

(Matthew 3 : 14)   But John would have hindered him, saying, "I need to be baptized by you, and you come to me?"

(Matthew 3 : 15)   But Jesus, answering, said to him, "Allow it now, for this is the fitting way for us to fulfill all righteousness." Then he allowed him.

(Mark 1 : 9) It happened in those days, that Jesus came from Nazareth of Galilee, and was baptized by John in the Jordan.

(Mark 1 : 10) Immediately coming up from the water, he saw the heavens parting, and the Spirit descending on him like a dove.

(Mark 1 : 11) A voice came out of the sky, "You are my beloved Son, in whom I am well pleased."

(Matthew 3 : 16)   Jesus, when he was baptized, went up directly from the water: and behold, the heavens were opened to him. He saw the Spirit of God descending as a dove, and coming on him.

(Matthew 3 : 17)   Behold, a voice out of the heavens said, "This is my beloved Son, with whom I am well pleased."

(Luke 3 : 21)   Now it happened, when all the people were baptized, Jesus also had been baptized, and was praying. The sky was opened,

(Luke 3 : 22)   and the Holy Spirit descended in a bodily form as a dove on him; and a voice came out of the sky, saying "You are my beloved Son. In you I am well pleased."

John the Baptist Testified about Jesus
Jn 1:15-28

(John 1 : 15)   John testified about him. He cried out, saying, "This was he of whom I said, He who comes after me has surpassed me, for he was before me.'"

(John 1 : 16)   From his fullness we all received grace upon grace.

(John 1 : 17)   For the law was given through Moses. Grace and truth were realized through Jesus Christ.

(John 1 : 18) No one has seen God at any time. The one and only Son, who is in the bosom of the Father, he has declared him.

John the Baptist Denies Being the Christ
Jn 1:19-28

(John 1 : 19) This is John's testimony, when the Jews sent priests and Levites from Jerusalem to ask him, "Who are you?"

(John 1 : 20) He declared, and didn't deny, but he declared, "I am not the Christ."

(John 1 : 21) They asked him, "What then? Are you Elijah?"

He said, "I am not."

"Are you the prophet?"

He answered, "No."

(John 1 : 22) They said therefore to him, "Who are you? Give us an answer to take back to those who sent us. What do you say about yourself?"

(John 1 : 23) He said, "I am the voice of one crying in the wilderness, Make straight the way of the Lord,' as Isaiah the prophet said."

(John 1 : 24) The ones who had been sent were from the Pharisees.

(John 1 : 25) They asked him, "Why then do you baptize, if you are not the Christ, nor Elijah, nor the prophet?"

(John 1 : 26) John answered them, "I baptize in water, but among you stands one whom you don't know.

(John 1 : 27) He is the one who comes after me, who is preferred before me, whose sandal strap I'm not worthy to loosen."
(John 1 : 28) These things were done in Bethany beyond the Jordan, where John was baptizing.

The Beginning of Jesus's Ministry
Lk 3:23 / John 1:29-36

(Luke 3 : 23) Jesus himself, when he began to teach, was about thirty years old, being the son (as was supposed) of Joseph, the son of Heli,

(John 1 : 29) The next day, he saw Jesus coming to him, and said, "Behold, the Lamb of God, who takes away the sin of the world!

(John 1 : 30) This is he of whom I said, After me comes a man who is preferred before me, for he was before me.'

(John 1 : 31) I didn't know him, but for this reason I came baptizing in water: that he would be revealed to Israel."

(John 1 : 32) John testified, saying, "I have seen the Spirit descending like a dove out of heaven, and it remained on him.

(John 1 : 33) I didn't recognize him, but he who sent me to baptize in water, he said to me, â˜On whomever you will see the Spirit descending, and remaining on him, the same is he who baptizes in the Holy Spirit.'

(John 1 : 34) I have seen, and have testified that this is the Son of God."

(John 1 : 35) Again, the next day, John was standing with two of his disciples,

(John 1 : 36) and he looked at Jesus as he walked, and said, "Behold, the Lamb of God!"

Two Disciples of John the Baptist followed Jesus Jn 1:37-42

(John 1 : 37) The two disciples heard him speak, and they followed Jesus.

(John 1 : 38) Jesus turned, and saw them following, and said to them, "What are you looking for?" They said to him, "Rabbi" (which is to say, being interpreted, Teacher), "where are you staying?"

(John 1 : 39) He said to them, "Come, and see." They came and saw where he was staying, and they stayed with him that day. It was about the tenth hour.

(John 1 : 40) One of the two who heard John, and followed him, was Andrew, Simon Peter's brother.

(John 1 : 41) He first found his own brother, Simon, and said to him, "We have found the Messiah!" (which is, being interpreted, Christ).

(John 1 : 42) He brought him to Jesus. Jesus looked at him, and said, "You are Simon the son of Jonah. You shall be called Cephas" (which is by interpretation, Peter).

Jesus called Philip
Jn 1:43-44

(John 1 : 43) On the next day, he was determined to go out into Galilee, and he found Philip. Jesus said to him, "Follow me."

(John 1 : 44) Now Philip was from Bethsaida, of the city of Andrew and Peter.

Jesus met Nathanel
Jn 1:45-51

(John 1 : 45) Philip found Nathanael, and said to him, "We have found him, of whom Moses in the law, and the prophets, wrote: Jesus of Nazareth, the son of Joseph."

(John 1 : 46) Nathanael said to him, "Can any good thing come out of Nazareth?" Philip said to him, "Come and see."

(John 1 : 47) Jesus saw Nathanael coming to him, and said about him, "Behold, an Israelite indeed, in whom is no deceit!"

(John 1 : 48) Nathanael said to him, "How do you know me?" Jesus answered him, "Before Philip called you, when you were under the fig tree, I saw you."

(John 1 : 49) Nathanael answered him, "Rabbi, you are the Son of God! You are King of Israel!"

(John 1 : 50) Jesus answered him, "Because I told you, I saw you underneath the fig tree,' do you believe? You will see greater things than these!"

(John 1 : 51) He said to him, "Most certainly, I tell you, hereafter you will see heaven opened, and the angels of God ascending and descending on the Son of Man."

Jesus turn Water into Wine
Jn 2:1-12

(John 2 : 1) The third day, there was a marriage in Cana of Galilee. Jesus' mother was there.

(John 2 : 2) Jesus also was invited, with his disciples, to the marriage.

(John 2 : 3) When the wine ran out, Jesus' mother said to him, "They have no wine."

(John 2 : 4) Jesus said to her, "Woman, what does that have to do with you and me? My hour has not yet come." (John 2 : 5) His mother said to the servants, "Whatever he says to you, do it."

(John 2 : 6) Now there were six water pots of stone set there after the Jews' way of purifying, containing two or three metretes apiece.

(John 2 : 7) Jesus said to them, "Fill the water pots with water." They filled them up to the brim.

(John 2 : 8) He said to them, "Now draw some out, and take it to the ruler of the feast." So they took it.

(John 2 : 9) When the ruler of the feast tasted the water now become wine, and didn't know where it came from (but the servants who had drawn the water knew), the ruler of the feast called the bridegroom,

(John 2 : 10) and said to him, "Everyone serves the good wine first, and when the guests have drunk freely, then that which is worse. You have kept the good wine until now!"

(John 2 : 11) This beginning of his signs Jesus did in Cana of Galilee, and revealed his glory; and his disciples believed in him.

(John 2 : 12) After this, he went down to Capernaum, he, and his mother, his brothers, and his disciples; and they stayed there a few days.

Jesus cleaned out the Temple Court in Jerusalem the first time
Jn 2:13-25

(John 2 : 13) The Passover of the Jews was at hand, and Jesus went up to Jerusalem.

(John 2 : 14) He found in the temple those who sold oxen, sheep, and doves, and the changers of money sitting.

(John 2 : 15) He made a whip of cords, and threw all out of the temple, both the sheep and the oxen; and he poured out the changers' money, and overthrew their tables.

(John 2 : 16) To those who sold the doves, he said, "Take these things out of here! Don't make my Father's house a marketplace!"

(John 2 : 17) His disciples remembered that it was written, "Zeal for your house will eat me up."

(John 2 : 18) The Jews therefore answered him, "What sign do you show us, seeing that you do these things?"

(John 2 : 19) Jesus answered them, "Destroy this temple, and in three days I will raise it up."

(John 2 : 20) The Jews therefore said, "It took forty-six years to build this temple! Will you raise it up in three days?"

(John 2 : 21) But he spoke of the temple of his body.

(John 2 : 22) When therefore he was raised from the dead, his disciples remembered that he said this, and they believed the Scripture, and the word which Jesus had said.

(John 2 : 23) Now when he was in Jerusalem at the Passover, during the feast, many believed in his name, observing his signs which he did.

(John 2 : 24) But Jesus didn't trust himself to them, because he knew everyone,

(John 2 : 25) and because he didn't need for anyone to testify concerning man; for he himself knew what was in man.

Jesus met and talked with Nicodemus
Jn 3:1-21

(John 3 : 1) Now there was a man of the Pharisees named Nicodemus, a ruler of the Jews.

(John 3 : 2) The same came to him by night, and said to him, "Rabbi, we know that you are a teacher come from God, for no one can do these signs that you do, unless God is with him."

(John 3 : 3) Jesus answered him, "Most certainly, I tell you, unless one is born anew, he can't see the Kingdom of God."

(John 3 : 4) Nicodemus said to him, "How can a man be born when he is old? Can he enter a second time into his mother's womb, and be born?"

(John 3 : 5) Jesus answered, "Most certainly I tell you, unless one is born of water and spirit, he can't enter into the Kingdom of God!

(John 3 : 6) That which is born of the flesh is flesh. That which is born of the Spirit is spirit.

(John 3 : 7) Don't marvel that I said to you, You must be born anew.'

(John 3 : 8) The windblows where it wants to, and you hear its sound, but don't know where it comes from and where it is going. So is everyone who is born of the Spirit."

(John 3 : 9) Nicodemus answered him, "How can these things be?"

(John 3 : 10) Jesus answered him, "Are you the teacher of Israel, and don't understand these things?

(John 3 : 11) Most certainly I tell you, we speak that which we know, and testify of that which we have seen, and you don't receive our witness.

(John 3 : 12) If I told you earthly things and you don't believe, how will you believe if I tell you heavenly things?

(John 3 : 13) No one has ascended into heaven, but he who descended out of heaven, the Son of Man, who is in heaven.

(John 3 : 14) As Moses lifted up the serpent in the wilderness, even so must the Son of Man be lifted up,

(John 3 : 15) that whoever believes in him should not perish but have eternal life.

(John 3 : 16) For God so loved the world, that he gave his one and only Son, that whoever believes in him should not perish, but have eternal life.

(John 3 : 17) For God didn't send his Son into the world to judge the world, but that the world should be saved through him.

(John 3 : 18) He who believes in him is not judged. He who doesn't believe has been judged already, because he has not believed in the name of the one and only Son of God.

(John 3 : 19) This is the judgment, that the light has come into the world, and men loved the darkness rather than the light; for their works were evil.

(John 3 : 20) For everyone who does evil hates the light, and doesn't come to the light, lest his works would be exposed.

(John 3 : 21) But he who does the truth comes to the light, that his works may be revealed, that they have been done in God."

The Disciples of Jesus did Baptize for Others
Jn 3:22-36

(John 3 : 22) After these things, Jesus came with his disciples into the land of Judea. He stayed there with them, and baptized.

(John 3 : 23) John also was baptizing in Enon near Salim, because there was much water there. They came, and were baptized.

(John 3 : 24) For John was not yet thrown into prison.

(John 3 : 25) There arose therefore a questioning on the part of John's disciples with some Jews about purification.

(John 3 : 26) They came to John, and said to him, "Rabbi, he who was with you beyond the Jordan, to whom you have testified, behold, the same baptizes, and everyone is coming to him."

(John 3 : 27) John answered, "A man can receive nothing, unless it has been given him from heaven.

(John 3 : 28) You yourselves testify that I said, I am not the Christ,' but, I have been sent before him.'

(John 3 : 29) He who has the bride is the bridegroom; but the friend of the bridegroom, who stands and hears him, rejoices greatly because of the bridegroom's voice. This, my joy, therefore is made full.

(John 3 : 30) He must increase, but I must decrease.

(John 3 : 31) He who comes from above is above all. He who is from the earth belongs to the earth, and speaks of the earth. He who comes from heaven is above all.

(John 3 : 32) What he has seen and heard, of that he testifies; and no one receives his witness.

(John 3 : 33) He who has received his witness has set his seal to this, that God is true.

(John 3 : 34) For he whom God has sent speaks the words of God; for God gives the Spirit without measure.

(John 3 : 35) The Father loves the Son, and has given all things into his hand.

(John 3 : 36) One who believes in the Son has eternal life, but one who disobeys the Son won't see life, but the wrath of God remains on him."

Jesus met and talked with the Samaritan woman Jn 4:1-42

(John 4 : 1) Therefore when the Lord knew that the Pharisees had heard that Jesus was making and baptizing more disciples than John

(John 4 : 2) (although Jesus himself didn't baptize, but his disciples),

(John 4 : 3) he left Judea, and departed into Galilee. (John 4 : 4) He needed to pass through Samaria.

(John 4 : 5) So he came to a city of Samaria, called Sychar, near the parcel of ground that Jacob gave to his son, Joseph.

(John 4 : 6) Jacob's well was there. Jesus therefore, being tired from his journey, sat down by the well. It was about the sixth hour.

(John 4 : 7) A woman of Samaria came to draw water. Jesus said to her, "Give me a drink."

(John 4 : 8) For his disciples had gone away into the city to buy food.

(John 4 : 9) The Samaritan woman therefore said to him, "How is it that you, being a Jew, ask for a drink from me, a Samaritan woman?" (For Jews have no dealings with Samaritans.)

(John 4 : 10) Jesus answered her, "If you knew the gift of God, and who it is who says to you, Give me a drink,' you would have asked him, and he would have given you living water."

(John 4 : 11) The woman said to him, "Sir, you have nothing to draw with, and the well is deep. From where then have you that living water?

(John 4 : 12) Are you greater than our father, Jacob, who gave us the well, and drank of it himself, as did his children, and his livestock?"

(John 4 : 13) Jesus answered her, "Everyone who drinks of this water will thirst again,

(John 4 : 14) but whoever drinks of the water that I will give him will never thirst again; but the water that I will give him will become in him a well of water springing up to eternal life."

(John 4 : 15) The woman said to him, "Sir, give me this water, so that I don't get thirsty, neither come all the way here to draw."

(John 4 : 16) Jesus said to her, "Go, call your husband, and come here."

(John 4 : 17)   The woman answered, "I have no husband." Jesus said to her, "You said well, I have no husband,'

(John 4 : 18) for you have had five husbands; and he whom you now have is not your husband. This you have said truly."
(John 4 : 19) The woman said to him, "Sir, I perceive that you are a prophet.

(John 4 : 20) Our fathers worshiped in this mountain, and you Jews say that in Jerusalem is the place where people ought to worship."

(John 4 : 21) Jesus said to her, "Woman, believe me, the hour comes, when neither in this mountain, nor in Jerusalem, will you worship the Father.

(John 4 : 22) You worship that which you don't know. We worship that which we know; for salvation is from the Jews.

(John 4 : 23) But the hour comes, and now is, when the true worshipers will worship the Father in spirit and truth, for the Father seeks such to be his worshipers.

(John 4 : 24) God is spirit, and those who worship him must worship in spirit and truth."

(John 4 : 25) The woman said to him, "I know that Messiah comes," (he who is called Christ). "When he has come, he will declare to us all things."

(John 4 : 26) Jesus said to her, "I am he, the one who speaks to you."

(John 4 : 27) At this, his disciples came. They marveled that he was speaking with a woman; yet no one said, "What are you looking for?" or, "Why do you speak with her?"

(John 4 : 28) So the woman left her water pot, and went away into the city, and said to the people,

(John 4 : 29) "Come, see a man who told me everything that I did. Can this be the Christ?"

(John 4 : 30) They went out of the city, and were coming to him.

(John 4 : 31) In the meanwhile, the disciples urged him, saying, "Rabbi, eat."

(John 4 : 32) But he said to them, "I have food to eat that you don't know about."

(John 4 : 33) The disciples therefore said one to another, "Has anyone brought him something to eat?"

(John 4 : 34) Jesus said to them, "My food is to do the will of him who sent me, and to accomplish his work.

(John 4 : 35) Don't you say, There are yet four months until the harvest?' Behold, I tell you, lift up your eyes, and look at the fields, that they are white for harvest already.

(John 4 : 36) He who reaps receives wages, and gathers fruit to eternal life; that both he who sows and he who reaps may rejoice together.

(John 4 : 37) For in this the saying is true, One sows, and another reaps.'

(John 4 : 38) I sent you to reap that for which you haven't labored. Others have labored, and you have entered into their labor."

(John 4 : 39) From that city many of the Samaritans believed in him because of the word of the woman, who testified, "He told me everything that I did."

(John 4 : 40) So when the Samaritans came to him, they begged him to stay with them. He stayed there two days.

(John 4 : 41) Many more believed because of his word. (John 4 : 42) They said to the woman, "Now we believe, not because of your speaking; for we have heard for ourselves, and know that this is indeed the Christ, the Savior of the world."

Jesus' Second Miracle: Healing the Son of a Nobleman
Jn 4:43-54

(John 4 : 43) After the two days he went out from there and went into Galilee.

(John 4 : 44) For Jesus himself testified that a prophet has no honor in his own country.

(John 4 : 45) So when he came into Galilee, the Galileans received him, having seen all the things that he did in Jerusalem at the feast, for they also went to the feast.

(John 4 : 46) Jesus came therefore again to Cana of Galilee, where he made the water into wine. There was a certain nobleman whose son was sick at Capernaum.

(John 4 : 47) When he heard that Jesus had come out of Judea into Galilee, he went to him, and begged him that he would come down and heal his son, for he was at the point of death.

(John 4 : 48) Jesus therefore said to him, "Unless you see signs and wonders, you will in no way believe."

(John 4 : 49) The nobleman said to him, "Sir, come down before my child dies."

(John 4 : 50) Jesus said to him, "Go your way. Your son lives." The man believed the word that Jesus spoke to him, and he went his way.

(John 4 : 51) As he was now going down, his servants met him and reported, saying "Your child lives!"

(John 4 : 52) So he inquired of them the hour when he began to get better. They said therefore to him, "Yesterday at the seventh hour, the fever left him."

(John 4 : 53) So the father knew that it was at that hour in which Jesus said to him, "Your son lives." He believed, as did his whole house.

(John 4 : 54) This is again the second sign that Jesus did, having come out of Judea into Galilee.

The Healing at the Pool
Jn 5:1-15

(John 5 : 1) After these things, there was a feast of the Jews, and Jesus went up to Jerusalem.

(John 5 : 2) Now in Jerusalem by the sheep gate, there is a pool, which is called in Hebrew, "Bethesda," having five porches.

(John 5 : 3) In these lay a great multitude of those who were sick, blind, lame, or paralyzed, waiting for the moving of the water;

(John 5 : 4) for an angel went down at certain times into the pool, and stirred up the water. Whoever stepped in first after the stirring of the water was healed of whatever disease he had.

(John 5 : 5) A certain man was there, who had been sick for thirty-eight years.

(John 5 : 6) When Jesus saw him lying there, and knew that he had been sick for a long time, he asked him, "Do you want to be made well?"

(John 5 : 7) The sick man answered him, "Sir, I have no one to put me into the pool when the water is stirred up, but while I'm coming, another steps down before me." (John 5 : 8) Jesus said to him, "Arise, take up your mat, and walk."

(John 5 : 9) Immediately, the man was made well and took up his mat and walked. Now it was the Sabbath on that day.

(John 5 : 10) So the Jews said to him who was cured, "It is the Sabbath. It is not lawful for you to carry the mat." (John 5 : 11) He answered them, "He who made me well, the same said to me, Take up your mat, and walk.'"

(John 5 : 12)   Then they asked him, "Who is the man who said to you, Take up your mat, and walk'?" (John 5 : 13)   But he who was healed didn't know who it was, for Jesus had withdrawn, a crowd being in the place. (John 5 : 14)   Afterward Jesus found him in the temple, and said to him, "Behold, you are made well. Sin no more, so that nothing worse happens to you."

(John 5 : 15)   The man went away and told the Jews that it was Jesus who had made him well.

The Authority of the Son
Jn 5: 16-30

(John 5 : 16)   For this cause the Jews persecuted Jesus, and sought to kill him, because he did these things on the Sabbath.

(John 5 : 17)   But Jesus answered them, "My Father is still working, so I am working, too."

(John 5 : 18)   For this cause therefore the Jews sought all the more to kill him, because he not only broke the Sabbath, but also called God his own Father, making himself equal with God.

(John 5 : 19)   Jesus therefore answered them, "Most certainly, I tell you, the Son can do nothing of himself, but what he sees the Father doing. For whatever things he does, these the Son also does likewise.

(John 5 : 20)   For the Father has affection for the Son, and shows him all things that he himself does. He will show him greater works than these, that you may marvel.

(John 5 : 21) For as the Father raises the dead and gives them life, even so the Son also gives life to whom he desires.

(John 5 : 22) For the Father judges no one, but he has given all judgment to the Son,

(John 5 : 23) that all may honor the Son, even as they honor the Father. He who doesn't honor the Son doesn't honor the Father who sent him.

(John 5 : 24) "Most certainly I tell you, he who hears my word, and believes him who sent me, has eternal life, and doesn't come into judgment, but has passed out of death into life. (John 5 : 25) Most certainly, I tell you, the hour comes, and now is, when the dead will hear the Son of God's voice; and those who hear will live.

(John 5 : 26) For as the Father has life in himself, even so he gave to the Son also to have life in himself.

(John 5 : 27) He also gave him authority to execute judgment, because he is a son of man.

(John 5 : 28) Don't marvel at this, for the hour comes, in which all that are in the tombs will hear his voice,

(John 5 : 29) and will come out; those who have done good, to the resurrection of life; and those who have done evil, to the resurrection of judgment.

(John 5 : 30) I can of myself do nothing. As I hear, I judge, and my judgment is righteous; because I don't seek my own will, but the will of my Father who sent me.

Testimonies About Jesus
Jn 5:31-47

(John 5 : 31)   "If I testify about myself, my witness is not valid.

(John 5 : 32)   It is another who testifies about me. I know that the testimony which he testifies about me is true. (John 5 : 33)   You have sent to John, and he has testified to the truth.

(John 5 : 34)   But the testimony which I receive is not from man. However, I say these things that you may be saved.

(John 5 : 35)   He was the burning and shining lamp, and you were willing to rejoice for a while in his light.

(John 5 : 36)   But the testimony which I have is greater than that of John, for the works which the Father gave me to accomplish, the very works that I do, testify about me, that the Father has sent me.

(John 5 : 37)   The Father himself, who sent me, has testified about me. You have neither heard his voice at any time, nor seen his form.

(John 5 : 38)   You don't have his word living in you; because you don't believe him whom he sent.

(John 5 : 39)   "You search the Scriptures, because you think that in them you have eternal life; and these are they which testify about me.

(John 5 : 40)   Yet you will not come to me, that you may have life.

(John 5 : 41)   I don't receive glory from men.

(John 5 : 42)   But I know you, that you don't have God's love in yourselves.

(John 5 : 43)   I have come in my Father's name, and you don't receive me. If another comes in his own name, you will receive him.

(John 5 : 44)   How can you believe, who receive glory from one another, and you don't seek the glory that comes from the only God?

(John 5 : 45)   "Don't think that I will accuse you to the Father. There is one who accuses you, even Moses, on whom you have set your hope.

(John 5 : 46)   For if you believed Moses, you would believe me; for he wrote about me.

(John 5 : 47)   But if you don't believe his writings, how will you believe my words?"

Jesus was Tempted by the Devil
Mt 4:1-11 / Mk 1:12-13 / Lk 4:1-13

(Matthew 4 : 1)   Then Jesus was led up by the Spirit into the wilderness to be tempted by the devil.

(Matthew 4 : 2)   When he had fasted forty days and forty nights, he was hungry afterward.

(Matthew 4 : 3)   The tempter came and said to him, "If you are the Son of God, command that these stones become bread."

(Matthew 4 : 4)   But he answered, "It is written, Man shall not live by bread alone, but by every word that proceeds out of the mouth of God.'"

(Matthew 4 : 5)   Then the devil took him into the holy city. He set him on the pinnacle of the temple,

(Matthew 4 : 6)   and said to him, "If you are the Son of God, throw yourself down, for it is written, He will put his angels in charge of you.' And On their hands they will bear you up, so that you don't dash your foot against a stone.'" (Matthew 4 : 7)   Jesus said to him, "Again, it is written, You shall not test the Lord, your God.'"

(Matthew 4 : 8)   Again, the devil took him to an exceedingly high mountain, and showed him all the kingdoms of the world, and their glory.

(Matthew 4 : 9)   He said to him, "I will give you all of these things, if you will fall down and worship me." (Matthew 4 : 10)   Then Jesus said to him, "Get behind me,Satan! For it is written, You shall worship the Lord your God, and you shall serve him only.'"

(Matthew 4 : 11)   Then the devil left him, and behold, angels came and served him.

(Mark 1 : 12)   Immediately the Spirit drove him out into the wilderness.

(Mark 1 : 13)   He was there in the wilderness forty days tempted by Satan. He was with the wild animals; and the angels were serving him.

(Luke 4 : 1)   Jesus, full of the Holy Spirit, returned from the Jordan, and was led by the Spirit into the wilderness

(Luke 4 : 2)   for forty days, being tempted by the devil. He ate nothing in those days. Afterward, when they were completed, he was hungry.

(Luke 4 : 3)   The devil said to him, "If you are the Son of God, command this stone to become bread."

(Luke 4 : 4)   Jesus answered him, saying, "It is written, Man shall not live by bread alone, but by every word of God.'"

(Luke 4 : 5)   The devil, leading him up on a high mountain, showed him all the kingdoms of the world in a moment of time.

(Luke 4 :6)   The devil said to him, "I will give you all this authority, and their glory, for it has been delivered to me; and I give it to whomever I want.

(Luke 4 : 7) If you therefore will worship before me, it will all be yours."

(Luke 4 : 8)   Jesus answered him, "Get behind me Satan! For it is written, You shall worship the Lord your God, and you shall serve him only.'"

(Luke 4 : 9)   He led him to Jerusalem, and set him on the pinnacle of the temple, and said to him, "If you are the Son of God, cast yourself down from here,

(Luke 4 : 10) for it is written, He will put his angels in charge of you, to guard you;'

(Luke 4 : 11) and, On their hands they will bear you up,

lest perhaps you dash your foot against a stone.'" (Luke 4 : 12) Jesus answering, said to him, "It has been said, You shall not tempt the Lord your God.'" (Luke 4 : 13) When the devil had completed every temptation, he departed from him until another time.

(Editor Footnote): The disciples went back to their home after Jesus went to the wilderness.

Jesus was teaching in the synagogues
Lk 4:14-30

(Luke 4 : 14) Jesus returned in the power of the Spirit into Galilee, and news about him spread through all the surrounding area.

(Luke 4 : 15) He taught in their synagogues, being glorified by all.

(Luke 4 : 16) He came to Nazareth, where he had been brought up. He entered, as was his custom, into the synagogue on the Sabbath day, and stood up to read.

(Luke 4 : 17) The book of the prophet Isaiah was handed to him. He opened the book, and found the place where it was written,

(Luke 4 : 18)   "The Spirit of the Lord is on me,

because he has anointed me to preach good news to the poor.

IIe has sent me to heal the broken hearted,

to proclaim release to the captives,

recovering of sight to the blind,

to deliver those who are crushed,

(Luke 4 : 19)   and to proclaim the acceptable year of the   Lord."
(Luke 4 : 20)   He closed the book, gave it back to the attendant, and sat down. The eyes of all in the synagogue were fastened on him.

(Luke 4 : 21)   He began to tell them, "Today, this Scripture has been fulfilled in your hearing."

(Luke 4 : 22)   All testified about him, and wondered at the gracious words which proceeded out of his mouth, and they said, "Isn't this Joseph's son?"

(Luke 4 : 23)   He said to them, "Doubtless you will tell me this parable, Physician, heal yourself! Whatever we have heard done at Capernaum, do also here in your hometown.'"

(Luke 4 : 24)   He said, "Most certainly I tell you, no prophet is acceptable in his hometown.

(Luke 4 : 25)   But truly I tell you, there were many widows in Israel in the days of Elijah, when the sky was shut up three years and six months, when a great famine came over all the land.

(Luke 4 : 26)   Elijah was sent to none of them, except to Zarephath, in the land of Sidon, to a woman who was a widow.

(Luke 4 : 27)   There were many lepers in Israel in the time of Elisha the prophet, yet not one of them was cleansed, except Naaman, the Syrian."

(Luke 4 : 28)   They were all filled with wrath in the synagogue, as they heard these things.

(Luke 4 : 29)   They rose up, threw him out of the city, and led him to the brow of the hill that their city was built on, that they might throw him off the cliff.

(Luke 4 : 30) But he, passing through their midst, went his way.

Jesus ordered the impure spirit to come out
Lk 4:31-37

(Luke 4 : 31)   He came down to Capernaum, a city of Galilee. He was teaching them on the Sabbath day,

(Luke 4 : 32)   and they were astonished at his teaching, for his word was with authority.

(Luke 4 : 33)   In the synagogue there was a man who had a spirit of an unclean demon, and he cried out with a loud voice,

(Luke 4 : 34)   saying, "Ah! what have we to do with you, Jesus of Nazareth? Have you come to destroy us? I know you who you are: the Holy One of God!"

(Luke 4 : 35)   Jesus rebuked him, saying, "Be silent, and come out of him!" When the demon had thrown him down in their midst, he came out of him, having done him no harm.

(Luke 4 : 36)   Amazement came on all, and they spoke together, one with another, saying, "What is this word? For with authority and power he commands the unclean spirits, and they come out!"

(Luke 4 : 37)   News about him went out into every place of the surrounding region.

John the Baptist was put in Prison by Herod
Lk 3:19-20

(Luke 3 : 19) but Herod the tetrarch, being reproved by him for Herodias, his brother's wife, and for all the evil things which Herod had done,

(Luke 3 : 20) added this also to them all, that he shut up John in prison.

Jesus went to Galilee
Mt 4:12-17 / Mk 1:14-15

(Matthew 4 : 12)   Now when Jesus heard that John was delivered up, he withdrew into Galilee.

(Matthew 4 : 13)   Leaving Nazareth, he came and lived in Capernaum, which is by the sea, in the region of Zebulun and Naphtali,

(Matthew 4 : 14)   that it might be fulfilled which was spoken through Isaiah the prophet, saying,

(Matthew 4 : 15)   "The land of Zebulun and the land of Naphtali,

toward the sea, beyond the Jordan,

Galilee of the Gentiles,

(Matthew 4 : 16)   the people who sat in darkness saw a great light,

to those who sat in the region and shadow of death,

to them light has dawned."

(Matthew 4 : 17)   From that time, Jesus began to preach, and to say, "Repent! For the Kingdom of Heaven is at hand."

(Mark 1 : 14) Now after John was taken into custody, Jesus came into Galilee, preaching the Good News of the Kingdom of God,

(Mark 1 : 15) and saying, "The time is fulfilled, and the Kingdom of God is at hand! Repent, and believe in the Good News."

Jesus called Peter, Andrew, James and John
Lk 5:1-11 / Mt 4:18-22 / Mk 1:16-20

(Luke 5 : 1)   Now it happened, while the multitude pressed on him and heard the word of God, that he was standing by the lake of Gennesaret.

(Luke 5 : 2)   He saw two boats standing by the lake, but the fishermen had gone out of them, and were washing their nets.

(Luke 5 : 3)   He entered into one of the boats, which was Simon's, and asked him to put out a little from the land. He sat down and taught the multitudes from the boat.

(Luke 5 : 4)   When he had finished speaking, he said to Simon, "Put out into the deep, and let down your nets for a catch."

(Luke 5 : 5) Simon answered him, "Master, we worked all night, and took nothing; but at your word I will let down the net."

(Luke 5 : 6)   When they had done this, they caught a great multitude of fish, and their net was breaking.

(Luke 5 : 7)   They beckoned to their partners in the other boat, that they should come and help them. They came, and filled both boats, so that they began to sink. (Luke 5 : 8) But Simon Peter, when he saw it, fell down at Jesus' knees, saying, "Depart from me, for I am a sinful man, Lord."

(Luke 5 : 9) For he was amazed, and all who were with him, at the catch of fish which they had caught;

(Luke 5 : 10)   and so also were James and John, sons of Zebedee, who were partners with Simon. Jesus said to Simon, "Don't be afraid. From now on you will be catching people alive."

(Luke 5 : 11)   When they had brought their boats to land, they left everything, and followed him.

(Matthew 4 : 18)   Walking by the sea of Galilee, he saw two brothers: Simon, who is called Peter, and Andrew, his brother, casting a net into the sea; for they were fishermen.

(Matthew 4 : 19)   He said to them, "Come after me, and I will make you fishers for men."

(Matthew 4 : 20)   They immediately left their nets and followed him.

(Matthew 4 : 21)   Going on from there, he saw two other brothers, James the son of Zebedee, and John his brother, in the boat with Zebedee their father, mending their nets. He called them.

(Matthew 4 : 22)   They immediately left the boat and their father, and followed him.

(Mark 1 : 16) Passing along by the sea of Galilee, he saw Simon and Andrew the brother of Simon casting a net into the sea, for they were fishermen.

(Mark 1 : 17) Jesus said to them, "Come after me, and I will make you into fishers for men."

(Mark 1 : 18) Immediately they left their nets, and followed   him.
(Mark 1 : 19) Going on a little further from there, he saw James the son of Zebedee, and John, his brother, who were also in the boat mending the nets.

(Mark 1 : 20) Immediately he called them, and they left their father, Zebedee, in the boat with the hired servants, and went after him.

Jesus casted out the Demon Processed Man Mk 1:21-27

(Mark 1 : 21) They went into Capernaum, and immediately on the Sabbath day he entered into the synagogue and taught.

(Mark 1 : 22) They were astonished at his teaching, for he taught them as having authority, and not as the scribes.

(Mark 1 : 23) Immediately there was in their synagogue a man with an unclean spirit, and he cried out,

(Mark 1 : 24) saying, "Ha! What do we have to do with you, Jesus, you Nazarene? Have you come to destroy us? I know you who you are: the Holy One of God!"

(Mark 1 : 25) Jesus rebuked him, saying, "Be quiet, and come out of him!"

(Mark 1 : 26) The unclean spirit, convulsing him and crying with a loud voice, came out of him.

(Mark 1 : 27) They were all amazed, so that they questioned among themselves, saying, "What is this? A new teaching? For with authority he commands even the unclean spirits, and they obey him!"

Jesus healed Peter's Mother-in-Law
Mk 1:28-31 / Mt 8"14-15 / Lk 4:38-39

(Mark 1 : 28) The report of him went out immediately everywhere into all the region of Galilee and its surrounding area.

(Mark 1 : 29) Immediately, when they had come out of the synagogue, they came into the house of Simon and Andrew, with James and John.

(Mark 1 : 30) Now Simon's wife's mother lay sick with a fever, and immediately they told him about her.

(Mark 1 : 31) He came and took her by the hand, and raised her up. The fever left her, and she served them.

(Matthew 8 : 14)   When Jesus came into Peter's house, he saw his wife's mother lying sick with a fever.

(Matthew 8 : 15) He touched her hand, and the fever left her. She got up and served him.

> (Luke 4 : 38)   He rose up from the synagogue, and entered into Simon's house. Simon's mother-in-law was afflicted with a great fever, and they begged him for her.
>
> (Luke 4 : 39)   He stood over her, and rebuked the fever; and it left her. Immediately she rose up and served them.

Jesus healed People and Drove out Demons and healed the Sicks
Mk 1:32-34 / Mt 8:16-17 / Mt 4:23-25 / Lk 4:40-44

(Mark 1 : 32) At evening, when the sun had set, they brought to him all who were sick, and those who were possessed by demons.

(Mark 1 : 33) All the city was gathered together at the door.

(Mark 1 : 34) He healed many who were sick with various diseases, and cast out many demons. He didn't allow the demons to speak, because they knew him.

> (Matthew 8 : 16)   When evening came, they brought to him many possessed with demons. He cast out the spirits with a word, and healed all who were sick;

(Matthew 8 : 17)   that it might be fulfilled which was spoken through Isaiah the prophet, saying: "He took our infirmities, and bore our diseases."

(Matthew 4 : 23)   Jesus went about in all Galilee, teaching in their synagogues, preaching the Good News of the Kingdom, and healing every disease and every sickness among the people.

(Matthew 4 : 24)   The report about him went out into all Syria. They brought to him all who were sick, afflicted with various diseases and torments, possessed with demons, epileptics, and paralytics; and he healed them.

(Matthew 4 : 25)   Great multitudes from Galilee, Decapolis, Jerusalem, Judea and from beyond the Jordan followed him.

(Luke 4 : 40)   When the sun was setting, all those who had any sick with various diseases brought them to him; and he laid his hands on every one of them, and healed them.

(Luke 4 : 41)   Demons also came out of many, crying out, and saying, "You are the Christ, the Son of God!" Rebuking them, he didn't allow them to speak, because they knew that he was the Christ.

(Luke 4 : 42)   When it was day, he departed and went into an uninhabited place, and the multitudes looked for him, and came to him, and held on to him, so that he wouldn't go away from them.

(Luke 4 : 43)   But he said to them, "I must preach the good news of the Kingdom of God to the other cities also. For this reason I have been sent."

(Luke 4 : 44)   He was preaching in the synagogues of Galilee.

Jesus went to Pray Alone
Mk 1:35-39

(Mark 1 : 35) Early in the morning, while it was still dark, he rose up and went out, and departed into a deserted place, and prayed there.

(Mark 1 : 36) Simon and those who were with him followed after him;

(Mark 1 : 37) and they found him, and told him, "Everyone is looking for you."

(Mark 1 : 38) He said to them, "Let's go elsewhere into the next towns, that I may preach there also, because I came out for this reason."

(Mark 1 : 39) He went into their synagogues throughout all Galilee, preaching and casting out demons.

Jesus healed a Leprosy Man
Mk 1:40-45 / Lk 5:12-16 / Mt 8:1-4

(Mark 1 : 40) A leper came to him, begging him, kneeling down to him, and saying to him, "If you want to, you can make me clean."

(Mark 1 : 41) Being moved with compassion, he stretched out his hand, and touched him, and said to him, "I want to. Be made clean."

(Mark 1 : 42) When he had said this, immediately the leprosy departed from him, and he was made clean.

(Mark 1 : 43) He strictly warned him, and immediately sent him out,

(Mark 1 : 44) and said to him, "See you say nothing to anybody, but go show yourself to the priest, and offer for your cleansing the things which Moses commanded, for a testimony to them.

(Mark 1 : 45) But he went out, and began to proclaim it much, and to spread about the matter, so that Jesus could no more openly enter into a city but was outside in desert places: and they came to him from everywhere.

(Luke 5 : 12)   It happened, while he was in one of the cities, behold, there was a man full of leprosy. When he saw Jesus, he fell on his face, and begged him, saying, "Lord, if you want to, you can make me clean."

(Luke 5 : 13)   He stretched out his hand, and touched him, saying, "I want to. Be made clean." Immediately the leprosy left him.

(Luke 5 : 14)   He commanded him to tell no one, "But go your way, and show yourself to the priest, and offer for your cleansing according to what Moses commanded, for a testimony to them."

(Luke 5 : 15)   But the report concerning him spread much more, and great multitudes came together to hear, and to be healed by him of their infirmities.

> (Luke 5 : 16)   But he withdrew himself into the desert, and prayed.

(Matthew 8 : 1)   When he came down from the mountain, great multitudes followed him.

(Matthew 8 : 2)   Behold, a leper came to him and worshiped him, saying, "Lord, if you want to, you can make me clean."

(Matthew 8 : 3)   Jesus stretched out his hand, and touched him, saying, "I want to. Be made clean." Immediately his leprosy was cleansed.

(Matthew 8 : 4)   Jesus said to him, "See that you tell nobody, but go, show yourself to the priest, and offer the gift that Moses commanded, as a testimony to them."

Jesus healed the Paralyzed Man
Mk 2:1-12 / Lk 5:17-26 / Mt 9:1-8

(Mark 2 : 1) When he entered again into Capernaum after some days, it was heard that he was in the house.

(Mark 2 : 2) Immediately many were gathered together, so that there was no more room, not even around the door; and he spoke the word to them.

(Mark 2 : 3) Four people came, carrying a paralytic to him.

(Mark 2 : 4)   When they could not come near to him for the crowd, they removed the roof where he was. When they had broken it up, they let down the mat that the paralytic was lying on.

(Mark 2 : 5) Jesus, seeing their faith, said to the paralytic, "Son, your sins are forgiven you."

(Mark 2 : 6)   But there were some of the scribes sitting there, and reasoning in their hearts,

(Mark 2 : 7) "Why does this man speak blasphemies like that? Who can forgive sins but God alone?"

(Mark 2 : 8)   Immediately Jesus, perceiving in his spirit that they so reasoned within themselves, said to them, "Why do you reason these things in your hearts?

(Mark 2 : 9)   Which is easier, to tell the paralytic, Your sins are forgiven;' or to say, Arise, and take up your bed, and walk?'

(Mark 2 : 10 But that you may know that the Son of Man has authority on earth to forgive sins" he said to the paralytic

(Mark 2 : 11) "I tell you, arise, take up your mat, and go to your house."

(Mark 2 : 12) He arose, and immediately took up the mat, and went out in front of them all; so that they were all amazed, and glorified God, saying, "We never saw anything like this!"

(Luke 5 : 17)   It happened on one of those days, that he was teaching; and there were Pharisees and teachers of the law sitting by, who had come out of every village of

Galilee, Judea, and Jerusalem. The power of the Lord was with him to heal them.

(Luke 5 : 18) Behold, men brought a paralyzed man on a cot, and they sought to bring him in to lay before Jesus.

(Luke 5 : 19) Not finding a way to bring him in because of the multitude, they went up to the housetop, and let him down through the tiles with his cot into the midst before Jesus.

(Luke 5 : 20) Seeing their faith, he said to him, "Man, your sins are forgiven you."

(Luke 5 : 21) The scribes and the Pharisees began to reason, saying, "Who is this that speaks blasphemies? Who can forgive sins, but God alone?"

(Luke 5 : 22) But Jesus, perceiving their thoughts, answered them, "Why are you reasoning so in your hearts?

(Luke 5 : 23) Which is easier to say, Your sins are forgiven you;' or to say, Arise and walk?'

(Luke 5 : 24) But that you may know that the Son of Man has authority on earth to forgive sins" (he said to the paralyzed man), "I tell you, arise, and take up your cot, and go to your house."

(Luke 5 : 25) Immediately he rose up before them, and took up that which he was laying on, and departed to his house, glorifying God.

(Luke 5 : 26)   Amazement took hold on all, and they glorified God. They were filled with fear, saying, "We have seen strange things today."

(Matthew 9 : 1)   He entered into a boat, and crossed over, and came into his own city.

(Matthew 9 : 2)   Behold, they brought to him a man who was paralyzed, lying on a bed. Jesus, seeing their faith, said to the paralytic, "Son, cheer up! Your sins are forgiven you."

(Matthew 9 : 3)   Behold, some of the scribes said to themselves, "This man blasphemes."

(Matthew 9 : 4)   Jesus, knowing their thoughts, said, "Why do you think evil in your hearts?

(Matthew 9 : 5)   For which is easier, to say, Your sins are forgiven;' or to say, Get up, and walk?'

(Matthew 9 : 6)   But that you may know that the Son of Man has authority on earth to forgive sins..." (then he said to the paralytic), "Get up, and take up your mat, and go up to your house."

(Matthew 9 : 7)   He arose and departed to his house.

(Matthew 9 : 8)   But when the multitudes saw it, they marveled and glorified God, who had given such authority to men.

Jesus called Levi, the Tax Collector
Mk 2:13-17 / Lk 5:27-32 / Mt 9:9-13

(Mark 2 : 13)   He went out again by the seaside. All the multitude came to him, and he taught them.

(Mark 2 : 14)   As he passed by, he saw Levi, the son of Alphaeus, sitting at the tax office, and he said to him, "Follow me." And he arose and followed him.

(Mark 2 : 15)   It happened, that he was reclining at the table in his house, and many tax collectors and sinners sat down with Jesus and his disciples, for there were many, and they followed him.

(Mark 2 : 16)   The scribes and the Pharisees, when they saw that he was eating with the sinners and tax collectors, said to his disciples, "Why is it that he eats and drinks with tax collectors and sinners?"

(Mark 2 : 17)   When Jesus heard it, he said to them, "Those who are healthy have no need for a physician, but those who are sick. I came not to call the righteous, but sinners to repentance."

(Luke 5 : 27)   After these things he went out, and saw a tax collector named Levi sitting at the tax office, and said to him, "Follow me!"

(Luke 5 : 28)   He left everything, and rose up and followed him.

(Luke 5 : 29) Levi made a great feast for him in his house. There was a great crowd of tax collectors and others who were reclining with them.

(Luke 5 : 30) Their scribes and the Pharisees murmured against his disciples, saying, "Why do you eat and drink with the tax collectors and sinners?"

(Luke 5 : 31) Jesus answered them, "Those who are healthy have no need for a physician, but those who are sick do.

(Luke 5 : 32) I have not come to call the righteous, but sinners to repentance."

(Matthew 9 : 9) As Jesus passed by from there, he saw a man called Matthew sitting at the tax collection office. He said to him, "Follow me." He got up and followed him.

(Matthew 9 : 10) It happened as he sat in the house, behold, many tax collectors and sinners came and sat down with Jesus and his disciples.

(Matthew 9 : 11) When the Pharisees saw it, they said to his disciples, "Why does your teacher eat with tax collectors and sinners?"

(Matthew 9 : 12) When Jesus heard it, he said to them, "Those who are healthy have no need for a physician, but those who are sick do.

(Matthew 9 : 13)   But you go and learn what this means: I desire mercy, and not sacrifice,' for I came not to call the righteous, but sinners to repentance."

Question about Fasting
Lk 5:33-39 / Mk 2:18-22 / Mt 9:14-17

(Luke 5 : 33)   They said to him, "Why do John's disciples often fast and pray, likewise also the disciples of the Pharisees, but yours eat and drink?"

(Luke 5 : 34)   He said to them, "Can you make the friends of the bridegroom fast, while the bridegroom is with them?

(Luke 5 : 35)   But the days will come when the bridegroom will be taken away from them. Then they will fast in those days."

(Luke 5 : 36)   He also told a parable to them. "No one puts a piece from a new garment on an old garment, or else he will tear the new, and also the piece from the new will not match the old.

(Luke 5 : 37)   No one puts new wine into old wineskins, or else the new wine will burst the skins, and it will be spilled, and the skins will be destroyed.

(Luke 5 : 38)   But new wine must be put into fresh wineskins, and both are preserved.

(Luke 5 : 39)   No man having drunk old wine immediately desires new, for he says, The old is better.'"

(Mark 2 : 18)   John's disciples and the Pharisees were fasting, and they came and asked him, "Why do John's disciples and the disciples of the Pharisees fast, but your disciples don't fast?"

(Mark 2 : 19)   Jesus said to them, "Can the groomsmen fast while the bridegroom is with them? As long as they have the bridegroom with them, they can't fast.

(Mark 2 : 20)   But the days will come when the bridegroom will be taken away from them, and then will they fast in that day.

(Mark 2 : 21)   No one sews a piece of unshrunk cloth on an old garment, or else the patch shrinks and the new tears away from the old, and a worse hole is made.

(Mark 2 : 22)   No one puts new wine into old wineskins, or else the new wine will burst the skins, and the wine pours out, and the skins will be destroyed; but they put new wine into fresh wineskins."

(Matthew 9 : 14)   Then John's disciples came to him, saying, "Why do we and the Pharisees fast often, but your disciples don't fast?"

(Matthew 9 : 15)   Jesus said to them, "Can the friends of the bridegroom mourn, as long as the bridegroom is with them? But the days will come when the bridegroom will be taken away from them, and then they will fast.

> (Matthew 9 : 16)   No one puts a piece of unshrunk cloth on an old garment; for the patch would tear away from the garment, and a worse hole is made.
>
> (Matthew 9 : 17)   Neither do people put new wine into old wineskins, or else the skins would burst, and the wine be spilled, and the skins ruined. No, they put new wine into fresh wineskins, and both are preserved."

Jesus Is Lord of the Sabbath
Mt 12:1-14 / Mk 2:23-28 & Mk 3:1-6 / Lk 6:1-12

(Matthew 12 : 1)   At that time, Jesus went on the Sabbath day through the grain fields. His disciples were hungry and began to pluck heads of grain and to eat.

(Matthew 12 : 2)   But the Pharisees, when they saw it, said to him, "Behold, your disciples do what is not lawful to do on the Sabbath."

(Matthew 12 : 3)   But he said to them, "Haven't you read what David did, when he was hungry, and those who were with him;

(Matthew 12 : 4)   how he entered into God's house, and ate the show bread, which was not lawful for him to eat, neither for those who were with him, but only for the priests?

(Matthew 12 : 5)   Or have you not read in the law, that on the Sabbath day, the priests in the temple profane the Sabbath, and are guiltless?

(Matthew 12 : 6)   But I tell you that one greater than the temple is here.

(Matthew 12 : 7)   But if you had known what this means, I desire mercy, and not sacrifice,' you would not have condemned the guiltless.

(Matthew 12 : 8)   For the Son of Man is Lord of the Sabbath."
(Matthew 12 : 9)   He departed there, and went into their synagogue.

(Matthew 12 : 10)   And behold there was a man with a withered hand. They asked him, "Is it lawful to heal on the Sabbath   day?"   that   they   might   accuse   him.
(Matthew 12 : 11)   He said to them, "What man is there among you, who has one sheep, and if this one falls into a pit on the Sabbath day, won't he grab on to it, and lift it out?

(Matthew 12 : 12)   Of how much more value then is a man than a sheep! Therefore it is lawful to do good on the Sabbath day."

(Matthew 12 : 13)   Then he told the man, "Stretch out your hand." He stretched it out; and it was restored whole, just like the other.

(Matthew 12 : 14)   But the Pharisees went out, and conspired against him, how they might destroy him.

(Mark 2 : 23)   It happened that he was going on the Sabbath day through the grain fields, and his disciples began, as they went, to pluck the ears of grain.

(Mark 2 : 24)   The Pharisees said to him, "Behold, why do they do that which is not lawful on the Sabbath day?"

(Mark 2 : 25)   He said to them, "Did you never read what David did, when he had need, and was hungry, he, and those who were with him?

(Mark 2 : 26)   How he entered into God's house when Abiathar was high priest, and ate the show bread, which is not lawful to eat except for the priests, and gave also to those who were with him?"

(Mark 2 : 27)   He said to them, "The Sabbath was made for man, not man for the Sabbath.

(Mark 2 : 28)   Therefore the Son of Man is lord even of the Sabbath."

(Mark 3 : 1)   He entered again into the synagogue, and there was a man there who had his hand withered.

(Mark 3 : 2)   They watched him, whether he would heal him on the Sabbath day, that they might accuse him.

(Mark 3 : 3)   He said to the man who had his hand withered, "Stand up."

(Mark 3 : 4)   He said to them, "Is it lawful on the Sabbath day to do good, or to do harm? To save a life, or to kill?" But they were silent.

(Mark 3 : 5)   When he had looked around at them with anger, being grieved at the hardening of their hearts, he said to the man, "Stretch out your hand." He stretched it out, and his hand was restored as healthy as the other.

(Mark 3 : 6)The Pharisees went out, and immediately conspired with the Herodians against him, how they might destroy him.

(Luke 6 : 1) Now it happened on the second Sabbath after the first, that he was going through the grain fields. His disciples plucked the heads of grain, and ate, rubbing them in their hands.

(Luke 6 : 2) But some of the Pharisees said to them, "Why do you do that which is not lawful to do on the Sabbath day?"

(Luke 6 : 3) Jesus, answering them, said, "Haven't you read what David did when he was hungry, he, and those who were with him;

(Luke 6 : 4) how he entered into God's house, and took and ate the show bread, and gave also to those who were with him, which is not lawful to eat except for the priests alone?"

(Luke 6 : 5) He said to them, "The Son of Man is lord of the Sabbath."

(Luke 6 : 6) It also happened on another Sabbath that he entered into the synagogue and taught. There was a man there, and his right hand was withered.

(Luke 6 : 7)   The scribes and the Pharisees watched him, to see whether he would heal on the Sabbath, that they might find an accusation against him.

(Luke 6 : 8)   But he knew their thoughts; and he said to the man who had the withered hand, "Rise up, and stand in the middle." He arose and stood.

(Luke 6 : 9)   Then Jesus said to them, "I will ask you something: Is it lawful on the Sabbath to do good, or to do harm? To save a life, or to kill?"

(Luke 6 : 10)   He looked around at them all, and said to the man, "Stretch out your hand." He did, and his hand was restored as sound as the other.

(Luke 6 : 11) But they were filled with rage, and talked with one another about what they might do to Jesus. (Luke 6 : 12)   It happened in these days, that he went out to the mountain to pray, and he continued all night in prayer to God.

Jesus taught People and drove out Demon
Mk 3:7-12 / Lk 6:17-19

(Mark 3 : 7)   Jesus withdrew to the sea with his disciples, and a great multitude followed him from Galilee, from Judea,

(Mark 3 : 8)   from Jerusalem, from Idumaea, beyond the Jordan, and those from around Tyre and Sidon. A great multitude, hearing what great things he did, came to him.

(Mark 3 : 9) He spoke to his disciples that a little boat should stay near him because of the crowd, so that they wouldn't press on him.

(Mark 3 : 10) For he had healed many, so that as many as had diseases pressed on him that they might touch him.

(Mark 3 : 11) The unclean spirits, whenever they saw him, fell down before him, and cried, "You are the Son of God!"

(Mark 3 : 12) He sternly warned them that they should not make him known.

(Luke 6 : 17) He came down with them, and stood on a level place, with a crowd of his disciples, and a great number of the people from all Judea and Jerusalem, and the sea coast of Tyre and Sidon, who came to hear him and to be healed of their diseases;

(Luke 6 : 18) as well as those who were troubled by unclean spirits, and they were being healed.

(Luke 6 : 19) All the multitude sought to touch him, for power came out of him and healed them all.

The Twelve Disciples of Jesus
Mk 3:13-19 / Lk 6:13-16

(Mark 3 : 13) He went up into the mountain, and called to himself those whom he wanted, and they went to him.

(Mark 3 : 14)   He appointed twelve, that they might be with him, and that he might send them out to preach,

(Mark 3 : 15)   and to have authority to heal sicknesses and to cast out demons:

(Mark 3 : 16)   Simon, to whom he gave the name Peter;

(Mark 3 : 17)   James the son of Zebedee; John, the brother of James, and he called them Boanerges, which means, Sons of Thunder;

(Mark 3 : 18)   Andrew; Philip; Bartholomew; Matthew; Thomas; James, the son of Alphaeus; Thaddaeus; Simon the Zealot;

(Mark 3 : 19)   and Judas Iscariot, who also betrayed him. He came into a house.

(Luke 6 : 13)   When it was day, he called his disciples, and from them he chose twelve, whom he also named apostles:

(Luke 6 : 14)   Simon, whom he also named Peter; Andrew, his brother; James; John; Philip; Bartholomew;

(Luke 6 : 15)   Matthew; Thomas; James, the son of Alphaeus; Simon, who was called the Zealot;

(Luke 6 : 16)   Judas the son of James; and Judas Iscariot, who also became a traitor.

The Beatitudes
Mt 5:1-12 / Lk 6:20-26

(Matthew 5 : 1) Seeing the multitudes, he went up onto the mountain. When he had sat down, his disciples came to him.

(Matthew 5 : 2) He opened his mouth and taught them, saying,

(Matthew 5 : 3) "Blessed are the poor in spirit, for theirs is the Kingdom of Heaven.

(Matthew 5 : 4) Blessed are those who mourn, for they shall be comforted.

(Matthew 5 : 5) Blessed are the gentle, for they shall inherit the earth.

(Matthew 5 : 6) Blessed are those who hunger and thirst after righteousness, for they shall be filled.

(Matthew 5 : 7) Blessed are the merciful, for they shall obtain mercy.

(Matthew 5 : 8) Blessed are the pure in heart, for they shall see God.

(Matthew 5 : 9) Blessed are the peacemakers, for they shall be called children of God.

(Matthew 5 : 10) Blessed are those who have been persecuted for righteousness' sake, for theirs is the Kingdom of Heaven.

(Matthew 5 : 11) "Blessed are you when people reproach you, persecute you, and say all kinds of evil against you falsely, for my sake.

(Matthew 5 : 12) Rejoice, and be exceedingly glad, for great is your reward in heaven. For that is how they persecuted the prophets who were before you.

(Luke 6 : 20)   He lifted up his eyes to his disciples, and said, "Blessed are you who are poor, for yours is the Kingdom of God.

(Luke 6 : 21)   Blessed are you who hunger now, for you will be filled. Blessed are you who weep now, for you will laugh.

(Luke 6 : 22)   Blessed are you when men shall hate you, and when they shall exclude and mock you, and throw out your name as evil, for the Son of Man's sake.

(Luke 6 : 23)   Rejoice in that day, and leap for joy, for behold, your reward is great in heaven, for their fathers did the same thing to the prophets.

(Luke 6 : 24)   "But woe to you who are rich! For you have received your consolation.

(Luke 6 : 25)   Woe to you, you who are full now, for you will be hungry. Woe to you who laugh now, for you will mourn and weep.

(Luke 6 : 26)   Woe, when men speak well of you, for their fathers did the same thing to the false prophets.

Salt and Light
Mt 5:13-16

(Matthew 5 : 13)   "You are the salt of the earth, but if the salt has lost its flavor, with what will it be salted? It is then good for nothing, but to be cast out and trodden under the feet of men.

(Matthew 5 : 14)   You are the light of the world. A city located on a hill can't be hidden.

(Matthew 5 : 15)   Neither do you light a lamp, and put it under a measuring basket, but on a stand; and it shines to all who are in the house.

(Matthew 5 : 16)   Even so, let your light shine before men; that they may see your good works, and glorify your Father who is in heaven.

(Mark 4 : 21)   He said to them, "Is the lamp brought to be put under a basket or under a bed? Isn't it put on a stand?

(Mark 4 : 22)   For there is nothing hidden, except that it should be made known; neither was anything made secret, but that it should come to light.

(Mark 4 : 23)   If any man has ears to hear, let him hear."

(Mark 4 : 24)   He said to them, "Take heed what you hear. With whatever measure you measure, it will be measured to you, and more will be given to you who hear.

(Mark 4 : 25)   For whoever has, to him will more be given, and he who doesn't have, even that which he has will be taken away from him."

The Fulfillment of the Law
Mt 5:17-20

(Matthew 5 : 17)   "Don't think that I came to destroy the law or the prophets. I didn't come to destroy, but to fulfill.

(Matthew 5 : 18)   For most certainly, I tell you, until heaven and earth pass away, not even one smallest letter or one tiny pen stroke shall in any way pass away from the law, until all things are accomplished.

(Matthew 5 : 19)   Whoever, therefore, shall break one of these least commandments, and teach others to do so, shall be called least in the Kingdom of Heaven; but whoever shall do and teach them shall be called great in the Kingdom of Heaven.

(Matthew 5 : 20)   For I tell you that unless your righteousness exceeds that of the scribes and Pharisees, there is no way you will enter into the Kingdom of Heaven.

Murder
Mt 5:21-26

(Matthew 5 : 21)   "You have heard that it was said to the ancient ones, You shall not murder;' and Whoever shall murder shall be in danger of the judgment.'

(Matthew 5 : 22)   But I tell you, that everyone who is angry with his brother without a cause shall be in danger of the judgment; and whoever shall say to his brother, Raca!' shall be in danger of the council; and whoever shall say, You fool!' shall be in danger of the fire of Gehenna.

(Matthew 5 : 23)   "If therefore you are offering your gift at the altar, and there remember that your brother has anything against you,

(Matthew 5 : 24)   leave your gift there before the altar, and go your way. First be reconciled to your brother, and then come and offer your gift.

(Matthew 5 : 25)   Agree with your adversary quickly, while you are with him on the way; lest perhaps the prosecutor deliver you to the judge, and the judge deliver you to the officer, and you be cast into prison.

(Matthew 5 : 26)   Most certainly I tell you, you shall by no means get out of there, until you have paid the last penny.

Adultery
Mt 5:27-30

(Matthew 5 : 27)   "You have heard that it was said, You shall not commit adultery;'

(Matthew 5 : 28) but I tell you that everyone who gazes at a woman to lust after her has committed adultery with her already in his heart.

(Matthew 5 : 29)   If your right eye causes you to stumble, pluck it out and throw it away from you. For it is more profitable for you that one of your members should perish, than for your whole body to be cast into Gehenna.

(Matthew 5 : 30)   If your right hand causes you to stumble, cut it off, and throw it away from you. For it is more profitable for you that one of your members should perish, than for your whole body to be cast into Gehenna.

Divorce
Mt 5:31-32

(Matthew 5 : 31)   "It was also said, Whoever shall put away his wife, let him give her a writing of divorce,'

(Matthew 5 : 32)   but I tell you that whoever puts away his wife, except for the cause of sexual immorality, makes her an adulteress; and whoever marries her when she is put away commits adultery.

Oaths
Mt 5:33-37

(Matthew 5 : 33)   "Again you have heard that it was said to them of old time, You shall not make false vows, but shall perform to the Lord your vows,'

(Matthew 5 : 34)   but I tell you, don't swear at all: neither by heaven, for it is the throne of God;

(Matthew 5 : 35) nor by the earth, for it is the footstool of his feet; nor by Jerusalem, for it is the city of the great King.

(Matthew 5 : 36) Neither shall you swear by your head, for you can't make one hair white or black.

(Matthew 5 : 37) But let your Yes' be Yes' and your No' be No.' Whatever is more than these is of the evil one.

Love for Enemies
Mt 5:38-48 / Lk 6:27-36

(Matthew 5 : 38) "You have heard that it was said, An eye for an eye, and a tooth for a tooth.'

(Matthew 5 : 39) But I tell you, don't resist him who is evil; but whoever strikes you on your right cheek, turn to him the other also.

(Matthew 5 : 40) If anyone sues you to take away your coat, let him have your cloak also.

(Matthew 5 : 41) Whoever compels you to go one mile, go with him two.

(Matthew 5 : 42) Give to him who asks you, and don't turn away him who desires to borrow from you.

(Luke 6 : 27) "But I tell you who hear: love your enemies, do good to those who hate you,

(Luke 6 : 28) bless those who curse you, and pray for those who mistreat you.

(Luke 6 : 29)   To him who strikes you on the cheek, offer also the other; and from him who takes away your cloak, don't withhold your coat also.

(Luke 6 : 30)   Give to everyone who asks you, and don't ask him who takes away your goods to give them back again.

(Luke 6 : 31)   "As you would like people to do to you, do exactly so to them.

(Luke 6 : 32)   If you love those who love you, what credit is that to you? For even sinners love those who love them.

(Luke 6 : 33)   If you do good to those who do good to you, what credit is that to you? For even sinners do the same.

(Luke 6 : 34)   If you lend to those from whom you hope to receive, what credit is that to you? Even sinners lend to sinners, to receive back as much.

(Luke 6 : 35)   But love your enemies, and do good, and lend, expecting nothing back; and your reward will be great, and you will be children of the Most High; for he is kind toward the unthankful and evil.

(Luke 6 : 36)   "Therefore be merciful, even as your Father is also merciful.

(Matthew 5 : 43)   "You have heard that it was said, You shall love your neighbor, and hate your enemy.'

(Matthew 5 : 44)   But I tell you, love your enemies, bless those who curse you, do good to those who hate you, and pray for those who mistreat you and persecute you,

(Matthew 5 : 45)   that you may be children of your Father who is in heaven. For he makes his sun to rise on the evil and the good, and sends rain on the just and the unjust.

(Matthew 5 : 46)   For if you love those who love you, what reward do you have? Don't even the tax collectors do the same?

(Matthew 5 : 47) If you only greet your friends, what more do you do than others? Don't even the tax collectors do the same?

(Matthew 5 : 48)   Therefore you shall be perfect, just as your Father in heaven is perfect.

Giving to the Needy
Mt 6:1-4

(Matthew 6 : 1)   "Be careful that you don't do your charitable giving before men, to be seen by them, or else you have no reward from your Father who is in heaven. (Matthew 6 : 2)   Therefore when you do merciful deeds, don't sound a trumpet before yourself, as the hypocrites do in the synagogues and in the streets, that they may get glory from men. Most certainly I tell you, they have received their reward.

(Matthew 6 : 3) But when you do merciful deeds, don't let your left hand know what your right hand does,

(Matthew 6 : 4) so that your merciful deeds may be in secret, then your Father who sees in secret will reward you openly.

Prayer
Mt 6:5-15 / Lk 11:1-4

(Matthew 6 : 5) "When you pray, you shall not be as the hypocrites, for they love to stand and pray in the synagogues and in the corners of the streets, that they may be seen by men. Most certainly, I tell you, they have received their reward.

(Matthew 6 : 6) But you, when you pray, enter into your inner room, and having shut your door, pray to your Father who is in secret, and your Father who sees in secret will reward you openly.

(Matthew 6 : 7) In praying, don't use vain repetitions, as the Gentiles do; for they think that they will be heard for their much speaking.

(Matthew 6 :8) Therefore don't be like them, for your Father knows what things you need, before you ask him.

(Matthew 6 : 9) Pray like this: Our Father in heaven, may your name be kept holy.

(Matthew 6 : 10) Let your Kingdom come. Let your will be done, as in heaven, so on earth.

(Matthew 6 : 11) Give us today our daily bread.

(Matthew 6 : 12) Forgive us our debts, as we also forgive our debtors.

(Matthew 6 : 13) Bring us not into temptation, but deliver us from the evil one. For yours is the Kingdom, the power, and the glory forever. Amen.

(Matthew 6 : 14) "For if you forgive men their trespasses, your heavenly Father will also forgive you.

(Matthew 6 : 15)   But if you don't forgive men their trespasses, neither will your Father forgive your trespasses.

(Luke 11 : 1)   It happened, that when he finished praying in a certain place, one of his disciples said to him, "Lord, teach us to pray, just as John also taught his disciples."
(Luke 11 : 2)   He said to them, "When you pray, say, Our Father in heaven, may your name be kept holy. May your Kingdom come. May your will be done on earth, as it is in heaven.
(Luke 11 : 3)   Give us day by day our daily bread.
(Luke 11 : 4)   Forgive us our sins, for we ourselves also forgive everyone who is indebted to us. Bring us not into temptation, but deliver us from the evil one.'"

Fasting
Mt 6:16-18

(Matthew 6 : 16)   "Moreover when you fast, don't be like the hypocrites, with sad faces. For they disfigure their faces, that they may be seen by men to be fasting. Most certainly I tell you, they have received their reward.

(Matthew 6 : 17)   But you, when you fast, anoint your head, and wash your face;

(Matthew 6 : 18)   so that you are not seen by men to be fasting, but by your Father who is in secret, and your Father, who sees in secret, will reward you.

Treasures in Heaven and the lamp of the Body Mt 6:19-24 / Lk 11: 33-36

(Matthew 6 : 19)   "Don't lay up treasures for yourselves on the earth, where moth and rust consume, and where thieves break through and steal;

(Matthew 6 : 20)   but lay up for yourselves treasures in heaven, where neither moth nor rust consume, and where thieves don't break through and steal;

(Matthew 6 : 21)   for where your treasure is, there your heart will be also.

(Matthew 6 : 22) "The lamp of the body is the eye. If therefore your eye is sound, your whole body will be full of light.

(Matthew 6 : 23) But if your eye is evil, your whole body will be full of darkness. If therefore the light that is in you is darkness, how great is the darkness!

(Matthew 6 : 24)   "No one can serve two masters, for either he will hate the one and love the other; or else he will be devoted to one and despise the other. You can't serve both God and Mammon.

(Luke 11 : 33) "No one, when he has lit a lamp, puts it in a cellar or under a basket, but on a stand, that those who come in may see the light.

(Luke 11 : 34)   The lamp of the body is the eye. Therefore when your eye is good, your whole body is also full of light; but when it is evil, your body also is full of darkness.

(Luke 11 : 35)   Therefore see whether the light that is in you isn't darkness.

(Luke 11 : 36)   If therefore your whole body is full of light, having no part dark, it will be wholly full of light, as when the lamp with its bright shining gives you light."

Do Not Worry
Mt 6:25-34 / Lk 12:22-34

(Luke 12 : 22)   He said to his disciples, "Therefore I tell you, don't be anxious for your life, what you will eat, nor yet for your body, what you will wear.

(Luke 12 : 23)   Life is more than food, and the body is more than clothing.

(Luke 12 : 24)   Consider the ravens: they don't sow, they don't reap, they have no warehouse or barn, and God feeds them. How much more valuable are you than birds!

(Matthew 6 : 25)   Therefore I tell you, don't be anxious for your life: what you will eat, or what you will drink; nor yet for your body, what you will wear. Isn't life more than food, and the body more than clothing?

(Matthew 6 : 26)   See the birds of the sky, that they don't sow, neither do they reap, nor gather into barns. Your heavenly Father feeds them. Aren't you of much more value than they?

(Luke 12 : 25)   Which of you by being anxious can add a cubit to his height?

(Matthew 6 : 27)   "Which of you, by being anxious, can add one moment to his lifespan?

(Luke 12 : 26)   If then you aren't able to do even the least things, why are you anxious about the rest?

(Matthew 6 : 28)   Why are you anxious about clothing? Consider the lilies of the field, how they grow. They don't toil, neither do they spin,

(Matthew 6 : 29)   yet I tell you that even Solomon in all his glory was not dressed like one of these.

(Matthew 6 : 30)   But if God so clothes the grass of the field, which today exists, and tomorrow is thrown into the oven, won't he much more clothe you, you of little faith?

(Matthew 6 : 31)   "Therefore don't be anxious, saying, What will we eat?', What will we drink?' or, With what will we be clothed?'

(Luke 12 : 27)   Consider the lilies, how they grow. They don't toil, neither do they spin; yet I tell you, even Solomon in all his glory was not arrayed like one of these.

(Luke 12 : 28)   But if this is how God clothes the grass in the field, which today exists, and tomorrow is cast into the oven, how much more will he clothe you, O you of little faith?

(Luke 12 : 29)   Don't seek what you will eat or what you will drink; neither be anxious.

(Luke 12 : 30)   For the nations of the world seek after all of these things, but your Father knows that you need these things.

(Luke 12 : 31)   But seek God's Kingdom, and all these things will be added to you.

(Matthew 6 : 32)   For the Gentiles seek after all these things; for your heavenly Father knows that you need all these things.

(Matthew 6 : 33)   But seek first God's Kingdom, and his righteousness; and all these things will be given to you as well.

(Matthew 6 : 34)   Therefore don't be anxious for tomorrow, for tomorrow will be anxious for itself. Each day's own evil is sufficient.

(Luke 12 : 32) Don't be afraid, little flock, for it is your Father's good pleasure to give you the Kingdom.

(Luke 12 : 33) Sell that which you have, and give gifts to the needy. Make for yourselves purses which don't grow old, a treasure in the heavens that doesn't fail, where no thief approaches, neither moth destroys.

(Luke 12 :34)   For where your treasure is, there will your heart be also.

Do not Judge
Lk 6:37-47 / Mt 7:1-6

(Luke 6 : 37)   Don't judge, and you won't be judged. Don't condemn, and you won't be condemned. Set free, and you will be set free.

(Luke 6 : 38)   "Give, and it will be given to you: good measure, pressed down, shaken together, and running over, will be given to you. For with the same measure you measure it will be measured back to you."

(Luke 6 : 39)   He spoke a parable to them. "Can the blind guide the blind? Won't they both fall into a pit?

(Luke 6 : 40)   A disciple is not above his teacher, but everyone when he is fully trained will be like his teacher. (Luke 6 : 41)   Why do you see the speck of chaff that is in your brother's eye, but don't consider the beam that is in your own eye?

(Luke 6 : 42)   Or how can you tell your brother, Brother, let me remove the speck of chaff that is in your eye,' when you yourself don't see the beam that is in your own eye? You hypocrite! First remove the beam from your own eye, and then you can see clearly to remove the speck of chaff that is in your brother's eye.

(Luke 6 : 43)   For there is no good tree that produces rotten fruit; nor again a rotten tree that produces good fruit.

(Luke 6 : 44)   For each tree is known by its own fruit. For people don't gather figs from thorns, nor do they gather grapes from a bramble bush.

(Luke 6 : 45)   The good man out of the good treasure of his heart brings out that which is good, and the evil man out of the evil treasure of his heart brings out that which is evil, for out of the abundance of the heart, his mouth speaks.

(Matthew 7 : 1)   "Don't judge, so that you won't be judged.

(Matthew 7 : 2)   For with whatever judgment you judge, you will be judged; and with whatever measure you measure, it will be measured to you.

> (Matthew 7 : 3) Why do you see the speck that is in your brother's eye, but don't consider the beam that is in your own eye?
>
> (Matthew 7 : 4) Or how will you tell your brother, Let me remove the speck from your eye;' and behold, the beam is in your own eye?
>
> (Matthew 7 : 5) You hypocrite! First remove the beam out of your own eye, and then you can see clearly to remove the speck out of your brother's eye.

(Matthew 7 : 6) "Don't give that which is holy to the dogs, neither throw your pearls before the pigs, lest perhaps they trample them under their feet, and turn and tear you to pieces.

(Luke 6 : 46) "Why do you call me, Lord, Lord,' and don't do the things which I say?

(Luke 6 : 47) Everyone who comes to me, and hears my words, and does them, I will show you who he is like.

Ask, Seek, Knock
Lk 11:5-13 / Mt 7:7-12

(Luke 11 : 5) He said to them, "Which of you, if you go to a friend at midnight, and tell him, Friend, lend me three loaves of bread,

(Luke 11 : 6) for a friend of mine has come to me from a journey, and I have nothing to set before him,'

(Luke 11 : 7) and he from within will answer and say, Don't bother me. The door is now shut, and my children are with me in bed. I can't get up and give it to you'?

(Luke 11 : 8) I tell you, although he will not rise and give it to him because he is his friend, yet because of his persistence, he will get up and give him as many as he needs.

(Matthew 7 : 7) "Ask, and it will be given you. Seek, and you will find. Knock, and it will be opened for you.

(Matthew 7 : 8) For everyone who asks receives. He who seeks finds. To him who knocks it will be opened. (Matthew 7 : 9) Or who is there among you, who, if his son asks him for bread, will give him a stone?

(Matthew 7 : 10) Or if he asks for a fish, who will give him a serpent?

(Matthew 7 : 11) If you then, being evil, know how to give good gifts to your children, how much more will your Father who is in heaven give good things to those who ask him!

(Matthew 7 : 12) Therefore whatever you desire for men to do to you, you shall also do to them; for this is the law and the prophets.

(Luke 11 : 9) "I tell you, keep asking, and it will be given you. Keep seeking, and you will find. Keep knocking, and it will be opened to you.

(Luke 11 : 10)   For everyone who asks receives. He who seeks finds. To him who knocks it will be opened. (Luke 11 : 11)   "Which of you fathers, if your son asks for bread, will give him a stone? Or if he asks for a fish, he won't give him a snake instead of a fish, will he?

(Luke 11 : 12)   Or if he asks for an egg, he won't give him a scorpion, will he?

(Luke 11 : 13)   If you then, being evil, know how to give good gifts to your children, how much more will your heavenly Father give the Holy Spirit to those who ask him?"

The Narrow and Wide Gates
Mt 7: 13-14 / (Lk 13:22-35)

(Matthew 7 : 13)   "Enter in by the narrow gate; for wide is the gate and broad is the way that leads to destruction, and many are those who enter in by it.

(Matthew 7 : 14)   How narrow is the gate, and restricted is the way that leads to life! Few are those who find it.

True and False Prophets
Mt 7:15-20

(Matthew 7 : 15)   "Beware of false prophets, who come to you in sheep's clothing, but inwardly are ravening wolves.

(Matthew 7 : 16)   By their fruits you will know them. Do you gather grapes from thorns, or figs from thistles?

(Matthew 7 : 17)   Even so, every good tree produces good fruit; but the corrupt tree produces evil fruit.

(Matthew 7 : 18)   A good tree can't produce evil fruit, neither can a corrupt tree produce good fruit.

(Matthew 7 : 19)   Every tree that doesn't grow good fruit is cut down, and thrown into the fire.

(Matthew 7 : 20)   Therefore by their fruits you will know them.

True and False Disciples
Mt 7:21-23

(Matthew 7 : 21)   Not everyone who says to me, Lord, Lord,' will enter into the Kingdom of Heaven; but he who does the will of my Father who is in heaven.

(Matthew 7 : 22)   Many will tell me in that day, Lord, Lord, didn't we prophesy in your name, in your name cast out demons, and in your name do many mighty works?'

(Matthew 7 : 23)   Then I will tell them, I never knew you. Depart from me, you who work iniquity.'

The Wise and Foolish Builders
Mt 7:24-29 / Lk 6:48-49

(Matthew 7 : 24)   "Everyone therefore who hears these words of mine, and does them, I will liken him to a wise man, who built his house on a rock.

(Matthew 7 : 25)   The rain came down, the floods came, and the winds blew, and beat on that house; and it didn't fall, for it was founded on the rock.

(Matthew 7 : 26)   Everyone who hears these words of mine, and doesn't do them will be like a foolish man, who built his house on the sand.

(Matthew 7 : 27)   The rain came down, the floods came, and the winds blew, and beat on that house; and it fell and great was its fall."

(Matthew 7 : 28)   It happened, when Jesus had finished saying these things, that the multitudes were astonished at his teaching,

(Matthew 7 : 29)   for he taught them with authority, and not like the scribes.

(Luke 6 : 48)   He is like a man building a house, who dug and went deep, and laid a foundation on the rock. When a flood arose, the stream broke against that house, and could not shake it, because it was founded on the rock.

(Luke 6 : 49)   But he who hears, and doesn't do, is like a man who built a house on the earth without a foundation, against which the stream broke, and immediately it fell, and the ruin of that house was great."

Jesus healed the Servant of the Centurion
Lk 7: 1-10 / Mt 8:5-13

(Luke 7 : 1)   After he had finished speaking in the hearing of the people, he entered into Capernaum.

(Luke 7 : 2)   A certain centurion's servant, who was dear to him, was sick and at the point of death.

(Luke 7 : 3) When he heard about Jesus, he sent to him elders of the Jews, asking him to come and save his servant.

(Luke 7 : 4) When they came to Jesus, they begged him earnestly, saying, "He is worthy for you to do this for him,

(Luke 7 : 5) for he loves our nation, and he built our synagogue for us."

(Luke 7 : 6) Jesus went with them. When he was now not far from the house, the centurion sent friends to him, saying to him, "Lord, don't trouble yourself, for I am not worthy for you to come under my roof.

(Luke 7 : 7) Therefore I didn't even think myself worthy to come to you; but say the word, and my servant will be healed.

(Luke 7 : 8) For I also am a man placed under authority, having under myself soldiers. I tell this one, Go!' and he goes; and to another, Come!' and he comes; and to my servant, Do this,' and he does it."

(Luke 7 : 9) When Jesus heard these things, he marveled at him, and turned and said to the multitude who followed him, "I tell you, I have not found such great faith, no, not in Israel."

(Luke 7 : 10) Those who were sent, returning to the house, found that the servant who had been sick was well.

(Matthew 8 : 5)   When he came into Capernaum, a centurion came to him, asking him,

(Matthew 8 : 6)   and saying, "Lord, my servant lies in the house paralyzed, grievously tormented."

(Matthew 8 : 7)   Jesus said to him, "I will come and heal him."

(Matthew 8 : 8)   The centurion answered, "Lord, I'm not worthy for you to come under my roof. Just say the word, and my servant will be healed.

(Matthew 8 : 9)   For I am also a man under authority, having under myself soldiers. I tell this one, Go,' and he goes; and tell another, Come,' and he comes; and tell my servant, Do this,' and he does it."

(Matthew 8 : 10)   When Jesus heard it, he marveled, and said to those who followed,

(Matthew 8 : 11)   I tell you that many will come from the east and the west, and will sit down with Abraham, Isaac, and Jacob in the Kingdom of Heaven,

(Matthew 8 : 12)   but the children of the Kingdom will be thrown out into the outer darkness. There will be weeping and gnashing of teeth."

(Matthew 8 : 13)   Jesus said to the centurion, "Go your way. Let it be done for you as you have believed." His servant was healed in that hour.

Jesus Raises a Widow's Son
Lk 7:11-17

(Luke 7 : 11) It happened soon afterwards, that he went to a city called Nain. Many of his disciples, along with a great multitude, went with him.

(Luke 7 : 12) Now when he drew near to the gate of the city, behold, one who was dead was carried out, the only son of his mother, and she was a widow. Many people of the city were with her.

(Luke 7 : 13) When the Lord saw her, he had compassion on her, and said to her,

(Luke 7 : 14) He came near and touched the coffin, and the bearers stood still. He said, "Young man, I tell you, arise!"

(Luke 7 : 15) He who was dead sat up, and began to speak. And he gave him to his mother.

(Luke 7 : 16) Fear took hold of all, and they glorified God, saying, "A great prophet has arisen among us!" and, "God has visited his people!"

(Luke 7 : 17) This report went out concerning him in the whole of Judea, and in all the surrounding region.

Jesus and John the Baptist
Mt 11:1-19 / Lk 7:18-35

(Matthew 11 : 1) It happened that when Jesus had finished directing his twelve disciples, he departed from there to teach and preach in their cities.

(Matthew 11 : 2)   Now when John heard in the prison the works of Christ, he sent two of his disciples

(Matthew 11 : 3)   and said to him, "Are you he who comes, or should we look for another?"

(Matthew 11 : 4)   Jesus answered them, "Go and tell John the things which you hear and see:

(Matthew 11 : 5)   the blind receive their sight, the lame walk, the lepers are cleansed, the deaf hear,the dead are raised up, and the poor have good news preached to them.

(Matthew 11 : 6)   Blessed is he who finds no occasion for stumbling in me."

(Matthew 11 : 7)   As these went their way, Jesus began to say to the multitudes concerning John, "What did you go out into the wilderness to see? A reed shaken by the wind?

(Matthew 11 : 8)   But what did you go out to see? A man in soft clothing? Behold, those who wear soft clothing are in king's houses.

(Matthew 11 : 9)   But why did you go out? To see a prophet? Yes, I tell you, and much more than a prophet.

(Matthew 11 : 10)   For this is he, of whom it is written, Behold, I send my messenger before your face, who will prepare your way before you.'

(Matthew 11 : 11)   Most certainly I tell you, among those who are born of women there has not arisen anyone greater than John the Baptizer; yet he who is least in the Kingdom of Heaven is greater than he.

(Matthew 11 : 12) From the days of John the Baptizer until now, the Kingdom of Heaven suffers violence, and the violent take it by force.

(Matthew 11 : 13)   For all the prophets and the law prophesied until John.

(Matthew 11 : 14)   If you are willing to receive it, this is Elijah, who is to come.

(Matthew 11 : 15)   He who has ears to hear, let him hear.

(Matthew 11 : 16)   "But to what shall I compare this generation? It is like children sitting in the marketplaces, who call to their companions

(Matthew 11 : 17)   and say, We played the flute for you, and you didn't dance. We mourned for you, and you didn't lament.'

(Matthew 11 : 18)   For John came neither eating nor drinking, and they say, He has a demon.'

(Matthew 11 : 19)   The Son of Man came eating and drinking, and they say, Behold, a gluttonous man and a drunkard, a friend of tax collectors and sinners!' But wisdom is justified by her children."

(Luke 7 : 18)   The disciples of John told him about all these things.

(Luke 7 : 19)   John, calling to himself two of his disciples, sent them to Jesus, saying, "Are you the one who is coming, or should we look for another?"

(Luke 7 : 20)   When the men had come to him, they said, "John the Baptizer has sent us to you, saying, Are you he who comes, or should we look for another?'"

(Luke 7 : 21)   In that hour he cured many of diseases and plagues and evil spirits; and to many who were blind he gave sight.

(Luke 7 : 22)   Jesus answered them, "Go and tell John the things which you have seen and heard: that the blind receive their sight, the lame walk, the lepers are cleansed, the deaf hear, the dead are raised up, and the poor have good news preached to them.

(Luke 7 : 23)   Blessed is he who finds no occasion for stumbling in me."

(Luke 7 : 24)   When John's messengers had departed, he began to tell the multitudes about John, "What did you go out into the wilderness to see? A reed shaken by the wind?

(Luke 7 : 25)   But what did you go out to see? A man clothed in soft clothing? Behold, those who are gorgeously dressed, and live delicately, are in kings' courts.

(Luke 7 : 26)   But what did you go out to see? A prophet? Yes, I tell you, and much more than a prophet.

(Luke 7 : 27)   This is he of whom it is written, Behold, I send my messenger before your face, who will prepare your way before you.'

(Luke 7 : 28)   "For I tell you, among those who are born of women there is not a greater prophet than John the

Baptizer, yet he who is least in the Kingdom of God is greater than he."

(Luke 7 : 29)   When all the people and the tax collectors heard this, they declared God to be just, having been baptized with John's baptism.

(Luke 7 : 30)   But the Pharisees and the lawyers rejected the counsel of God, not being baptized by him themselves.

(Luke 7 : 31)   "To what then will I liken the people of this generation? What are they like?

(Luke 7 :32)   They are like children who sit in the marketplace, and call one to another, saying, We piped to you, and you didn't dance. We mourned, and you didn't weep.'

(Luke 7 : 33)   For John the Baptizer came neither eating bread nor drinking wine, and you say, He has a demon.'

(Luke 7 : 34)   The Son of Man has come eating and drinking, and you say, Behold, a gluttonous man, and a drunkard; a friend of tax collectors and sinners!'

(Luke 7 : 35)   Wisdom is justified by all her children."

Jesus Anointed by a Sinful Woman
Lk 7:36-50

(Luke 7 : 36)   One of the Pharisees invited him to eat with him. He entered into the Pharisee's house, and sat at the table.

(Luke 7 : 37)   Behold, a woman in the city who was a sinner, when she knew that he was reclining in the Pharisee's house, she brought an alabaster jar of ointment.

(Luke 7 : 38)   Standing behind at his feet weeping, she began to wet his feet with her tears, and she wiped them with the hair of her head, kissed his feet, and anointed them with the ointment.

(Luke 7 : 39)   Now when the Pharisee who had invited him saw it, he said to himself, "This man, if he were a prophet, would have perceived who and what kind of woman this is who touches him, that she is a sinner."

(Luke 7 : 40)   Jesus answered him, "Simon, I have something to tell you." He said, "Teacher, say on."

(Luke 7 : 41)   "A certain lender had two debtors. The one owed five hundred denarii, and the other fifty.

(Luke 7 : 42)   When they couldn't pay, he forgave them both. Which of them therefore will love him most?" (Luke 7 : 43)   Simon answered, "He, I suppose, to whom he forgave the most." He said to him, "You have judged correctly."

(Luke 7 : 44)   Turning to the woman, he said to Simon, "Do you see this woman? I entered into your house, and you gave me no water for my feet, but she has wet my feet with her tears, and wiped them with the hair of her head.

(Luke 7 : 45)   You gave me no kiss, but she, since the time I came in, has not ceased to kiss my feet.

(Luke 7 : 46)   You didn't anoint my head with oil, but she has anointed my feet with ointment.

(Luke 7 : 47)   Therefore I tell you, her sins, which are many, are forgiven, for she loved much. But to whom little is forgiven, the same loves little."

(Luke 7 : 48)   He said to her, "Your sins are forgiven."

(Luke 7 : 49)   Those who sat at the table with him began to say to themselves, "Who is this who even forgives sins?"

(Luke 7 : 50)   He said to the woman, "Your faith has saved you. Go in peace."

Women who followed Jesus

Lk 8 :1-3

(Luke 8 : 1)   It happened soon afterwards, that he went about through cities and villages, preaching and bringing the good news of the Kingdom of God. With him were the twelve,

(Luke 8 : 2)   and certain women who had been healed of evil spirits and infirmities: Mary who was called Magdalene, from whom seven demons had gone out;

(Luke 8 : 3)   and Joanna, the wife of Chuzas, Herod's steward; Susanna; and many others; who served them from their possessions.

The Parable of the Growing Seed
Mk 4:26-29 / Lk 8:16-18

(Mark 4 : 26)   He said, "The Kingdom of God is as if a man should cast seed on the earth,

(Mark 4 : 27)   and should sleep and rise night and day, and the seed should spring up and grow, he doesn't know how.

(Mark 4 : 28)   For the earth bears fruit: first the blade, then the ear, then the full grain in the ear.

(Mark 4 : 29)   But when the fruit is ripe, immediately he puts in the sickle, because the harvest has come."

(Luke 8 : 16)   "No one, when he has lit a lamp, covers it with a container, or puts it under a bed; but puts it on a stand, that those who enter in may see the light.

(Luke 8 : 17)   For nothing is hidden, that will not be revealed; nor anything secret, that will not be known and come to light.

(Luke 8 : 18)   Be careful therefore how you hear. For whoever has, to him will be given; and whoever doesn't have, from him will be taken away even that which he thinks he has."

Mother and Brothers of Jesus
Mk 3:31-35 / Mt 12:46-50 / Lk 8:19-21

(Mark 3 : 31)   His mother and his brothers came, and standing outside, they sent to him, calling him.

(Mark 3 : 32)   A multitude was sitting around him, and they told him, "Behold, your mother, your brothers, and your sisters are outside looking for you."

(Mark 3 : 33) He answered them, "Who are my mother and my brothers?"

(Mark 3 : 34) Looking around at those who sat around him, he said, "Behold, my mother and my brothers!

(Mark 3 : 35) For whoever does the will of God, the same is my brother, and my sister, and mother."

(Matthew 12 : 46) While he was yet speaking to the multitudes, behold, his mother and his brothers stood outside, seeking to speak to him.

(Matthew 12 : 47) One said to him, "Behold, your mother and your brothers stand outside, seeking to speak to you."

(Matthew 12 : 48) But he answered him who spoke to him, "Who is my mother? Who are my brothers?"

(Matthew 12 : 49) He stretched out his hand towards his disciples, and said, "Behold, my mother and my brothers!

(Matthew 12 : 50) For whoever does the will of my Father who is in heaven, he is my brother, and sister, and mother."

(Luke 8 : 19) His mother and brothers came to him, and they could not come near him for the crowd.

(Luke 8 : 20) It was told him by some saying, "Your mother and your brothers stand outside, desiring to see you."

(Luke 8 : 21) But he answered them, "My mother and my brothers are these who hear the word of God, and do it."

Jesus Calms the Storm
Mk 4:35-41 / Lk 8:22-25 / Mt 8:23-27

(Mark 4 : 35)   On that day, when evening had come, he said to them, "Let's go over to the other side."

(Mark 4 : 36)   Leaving the multitude, they took him with them, even as he was, in the boat. Other small boats were also with him.

(Mark 4 : 37)   A big wind storm arose, and the waves beat into the boat, so much that the boat was already filled.

(Mark 4 : 38)   He himself was in the stern, asleep on the cushion, and they woke him up, and told him, "Teacher, don't you care that we are dying?"

(Mark 4 : 39)   He awoke, and rebuked the wind, and said to the sea, "Peace! Be still!" The wind ceased, and there was a great calm.

(Mark 4 : 40)   He said to them, "Why are you so afraid? How is it that you have no faith?"

(Mark 4 : 41)   They were greatly afraid, and said to one another, "Who then is this, that even the wind and the sea obey him?"

(Luke 8 : 22) Now it happened on one of those days, that he entered into a boat, himself and his disciples, and he said to them, "Let's go over to the other side of the lake." So they launched out.

(Luke 8 : 23) But as they sailed, he fell asleep. A wind storm came down on the lake, and they were taking on dangerous amounts of water.

(Luke 8 : 24) They came to him, and awoke him, saying, "Master, master, we are dying!" He awoke, and rebuked the wind and the raging of the water, and they ceased, and it was calm.

(Luke 8 : 25) He said to them, "Where is your faith?" Being afraid they marveled, saying one to another, "Who is this, then, that he commands even the winds and the water, and they obey him?"

(Matthew 8 : 23) When he got into a boat, his disciples followed him.

(Matthew 8 : 24) Behold, a violent storm came up on the sea, so much that the boat was covered with the waves, but he was asleep.

(Matthew 8 : 25) They came to him, and woke him up, saying, "Save us, Lord! We are dying!"

(Matthew 8 : 26)   He said to them, "Why are you fearful, O you of little faith?" Then he got up, rebuked the wind and the sea, and there was a great calm.

(Matthew 8 : 27)   The men marveled, saying, "What kind of man is this, that even the wind and the sea obey him?"

Jesus Restores a Demon-Possessed Man
Lk 8:26-39 / Mk 5:1-20 / Mt 8:28-34

(Luke 8 : 26)   They arrived at the country of the Gadarenes, which is opposite Galilee.

(Luke 8 : 27)   When Jesus stepped ashore, a certain man out of the city who had demons for a long time met him. He wore no clothes, and didn't live in a house, but in the tombs.

(Luke 8 : 28)   When he saw Jesus, he cried out, and fell down before him, and with a loud voice said, "What do I have to do with you, Jesus, you Son of the Most High God? I beg you, don't torment me!"

(Luke 8 : 29)   For Jesus was commanding the unclean spirit to come out of the man. For the unclean spirit had often seized the man. He was kept under guard, and bound with chains and fetters. Breaking the bands apart, he was driven by the demon into the desert.

(Luke 8 : 30)   Jesus asked him, "What is your name?" He said, "Legion," for many demons had entered into him.

(Luke 8 : 31)   They begged him that he would not command them to go into the abyss.

(Luke 8 : 32) Now there was there a herd of many pigs feeding on the mountain, and they begged him that he would allow them to enter into those. He allowed them.

(Luke 8 : 33) The demons came out of the man, and entered into the pigs, and the herd rushed down the steep bank into the lake, and were drowned.

(Luke 8 : 34) When those who fed them saw what had happened, they fled, and told it in the city and in the country.

(Luke 8 : 35) People went out to see what had happened. They came to Jesus, and found the man from whom the demons had gone out, sitting at Jesus' feet, clothed and in his right mind; and they were afraid.

(Luke 8 : 36) Those who saw it told them how he who had been possessed by demons was healed.

(Luke 8 : 37) All the people of the surrounding country of the Gadarenes asked him to depart from them, for they were very much afraid. He entered into the boat, and returned.

(Luke 8 : 38) But the man from whom the demons had gone out begged him that he might go with him, but Jesus sent him away, saying,

(Luke 8 : 39) "Return to your house, and declare what great things God has done for you." He went his way, proclaiming throughout the whole city what great things Jesus had done for him.

(Mark 5 : 1)   They came to the other side of the sea, into the country of the Gadarenes.

(Mark 5 : 2)   When he had come out of the boat, immediately a man with an unclean spirit met him out of the tombs.

(Mark 5 : 3)   He lived in the tombs. Nobody could bind him any more, not even with chains,

(Mark 5 : 4)   because he had been often bound with fetters and chains, and the chains had been torn apart by him, and the fetters broken in pieces. Nobody had the strength to tame him.

(Mark 5 : 5)   Always, night and day, in the tombs and in the mountains, he was crying out, and cutting himself   with   stones.
(Mark 5 : 6)   When he saw Jesus from afar, he ran and bowed down to him,

(Mark 5 : 7)   and crying out with a loud voice, he said, "What have I to do with you, Jesus, you Son of the Most High God? I adjure you by God, don't torment me."

(Mark 5 : 8)   For he said to him, "Come out of the man, you unclean spirit!"

(Mark 5 : 9)   He asked him, "What is your name?" He said to him, "My name is Legion, for we are many."

(Mark 5 : 10)   He begged him much that he would not send them away out of the country.

(Mark 5 : 11) Now on the mountainside there was a great herd of pigs feeding.

(Mark 5 : 12)   All the demons begged him, saying, "Send us into the pigs, that we may enter into them."

(Mark 5 : 13)   At once Jesus gave them permission. The unclean spirits came out and entered into the pigs. The herd of about two thousand rushed down the steep bank into the sea, and they were drowned in the sea.

(Mark 5 : 14)   Those who fed them fled, and told it in the city and in the country. The people came to see what it was that had happened.

(Mark 5 : 15)   They came to Jesus, and saw him who had been possessed by demons sitting, clothed, and in his right mind, even him who had the legion; and they were afraid.

(Mark 5 : 16)   Those who saw it declared to them how it happened to him who was possessed by demons, and about the pigs.

(Mark 5 : 17)   They began to beg him to depart from their region.

(Mark 5 : 18)   As he was entering into the boat, he who had been possessed by demons begged him that he might be with him.

(Mark 5 : 19)   He didn't allow him, but said to him, "Go to your house, to your friends, and tell them what great things the Lord has done for you, and how he had mercy on you."

(Mark 5 : 20)   He went his way, and began to proclaim in Decapolis how Jesus had done great things for him, and everyone marveled.

(Matthew 8 : 28)   When he came to the other side, into the country of the Gergesenes, two people possessed by demons met him there, coming out of the tombs, exceedingly fierce, so that nobody could pass that way.

(Matthew 8 : 29)   Behold, they cried out, saying, "What do we have to do with you, Jesus, Son of God? Have you come here to torment us before the time?"

(Matthew 8 : 30)   Now there was a herd of many pigs feeding far away from them.

(Matthew 8 : 31)   The demons begged him, saying, "If you cast us out, permit us to go away into the herd of pigs."

(Matthew 8 : 32)   He said to them, "Go!" They came out, and went into the herd of pigs: and behold, the whole herd of pigs rushed down the cliff into the sea, and died in the water.

(Matthew 8 : 33)   Those who fed them fled, and went away into the city, and told everything, including what happened to those who were possessed with demons.

(Matthew 8 : 34)   Behold, all the city came out to meet Jesus. When they saw him, they begged that he would depart from their borders.

Jesus Raises a Dead Girl and Heals a Sick Woman
Mk 5:21-43 / Lk 8:40-56 / Mt 9:18-26

(Mark 5 : 21)   When Jesus had crossed back over in the boat to the other side, a great multitude was gathered to him; and he was by the sea.

(Mark 5 : 22)   Behold, one of the rulers of the synagogue, Jairus by name, came; and seeing him, he fell at his feet,

(Mark 5 : 23) and begged him much, saying, "My little daughter is at the point of death. Please come and lay your hands on her, that she may be made healthy, and live."

(Mark 5 : 24)   He went with him, and a great multitude followed him, and they pressed upon him on all sides.

(Mark 5 : 25)   A certain woman, who had an issue of blood for twelve years,

(Mark 5 : 26)   and had suffered many things by many physicians, and had spent all that she had, and was no better, but rather grew worse,

(Mark 5 : 27)   having heard the things concerning Jesus, came up behind him in the crowd, and touched his clothes.

(Mark 5 : 28) For she said, "If I just touch his clothes, I will be made well."

(Mark 5 : 29) Immediately the flow of her blood was dried up, and she felt in her body that she was healed of her affliction.

(Mark 5 : 30) Immediately Jesus, perceiving in himself that the power had gone out from him, turned around in the crowd, and asked, "Who touched my clothes?" (Mark 5 : 31) His disciples said to him, "You see the multitude pressing against you, and you say, Who touched me?'"

(Mark 5 : 32) He looked around to see her who had done this thing.

(Mark 5 : 33) But the woman, fearing and trembling, knowing what had been done to her, came and fell down before him, and told him all the truth.

(Mark 5 : 34) He said to her, "Daughter, your faith has made you well. Go in peace, and be cured of your disease." (Mark 5 : 35) While he was still speaking, people came from the synagogue ruler's house saying, "Your daughter is dead. Why bother the Teacher any more?"

(Mark 5 : 36) But Jesus, when he heard the message spoken, immediately said to the ruler of the synagogue, "Don't be afraid, only believe."

(Mark 5 : 37) He allowed no one to follow him, except Peter, James, and John the brother of James.

(Mark 5 : 38) He came to the synagogue ruler's house, and he saw an uproar, weeping, and great wailing.

(Mark 5 : 39) When he had entered in, he said to them, "Why do you make an uproar and weep? The child is not dead, but is asleep."

(Mark 5 : 40) They ridiculed him. But he, having put them all out, took the father of the child, her mother, and those who were with him, and went in where the child was lying.

(Mark 5 : 41)   Taking the child by the hand, he said to her, "Talitha cumi!" which means, being interpreted, "Girl, I tell you, get up!"

(Mark 5 : 42)   Immediately the girl rose up and walked, for she was twelve years old. They were amazed with great amazement.

(Mark 5 : 43)   He strictly ordered them that no one should know this, and commanded that something should be given to her to eat.

(Luke 8 : 40)   It happened, when Jesus returned, that the multitude welcomed him, for they were all waiting for him.

(Luke 8 : 41)   Behold, there came a man named Jairus, and he was a ruler of the synagogue. He fell down at Jesus' feet, and begged him to come into his house,

(Luke 8 : 42)   for he had an only daughter, about twelve years of age, and she was dying. But as he went, the multitudes pressed against him.

(Luke 8 : 43) A woman who had a flow of blood for twelve years, who had spent all her living on physicians, and could not be healed by any,

(Luke 8 : 44)   came behind him, and touched the fringe of his cloak, and immediately the flow of her blood stopped.

(Luke 8 : 45)   Jesus said, "Who touched me?" When all denied it, Peter and those with him said, "Master, the multitudes press and jostle you, and you say, Who touched me?'"

(Luke 8 : 46)   But Jesus said, "Someone did touch me, for I perceived that power has gone out of me."

(Luke 8 : 47)   When the woman saw that she was not hidden, she came trembling, and falling down before him declared to him in the presence of all the people the reason why she had touched him, and how she was healed immediately.

(Luke 8 : 48)   He said to her, "Daughter, cheer up. Your faith has made you well. Go in peace."

(Luke 8 : 49)   While he still spoke, one from the ruler of the synagogue's house came, saying to him, "Your daughter is dead. Don't trouble the Teacher."

(Luke 8 : 50)   But Jesus hearing it, answered him, "Don't be afraid. Only believe, and she will be healed."

(Luke 8 : 51)   When he came to the house, he didn't allow anyone to enter in, except Peter, John, James, the father of the child, and her mother.

(Luke 8 : 52)   All were weeping and mourning her, but he said, "Don't weep. She isn't dead, but sleeping."

(Luke 8 : 53)   They were ridiculing him, knowing that she was dead.

(Luke 8 : 54)   But he put them all outside, and taking her by the hand, he called, saying, "Child, arise!"

(Luke 8 : 55)   Her spirit returned, and she rose up immediately. He commanded that something be given to her to eat.

(Luke 8 : 56)   Her parents were amazed, but he commanded them to tell no one what had been done.

(Matthew 9 : 18)   While he told these things to them, behold, a ruler came and worshiped him, saying, "My daughter has just died, but come and lay your hand on her, and she will live."

(Matthew 9 : 19)   Jesus got up and followed him, as did his disciples.

(Matthew 9 : 20)   Behold, a woman who had an issue of blood for twelve years came behind him, and touched the fringe of his garment;

(Matthew 9 : 21)   for she said within herself, "If I just touch his garment, I will be made well."

(Matthew 9 : 22)   But Jesus, turning around and seeing her, said, "Daughter, cheer up! Your faith has made you well." And the woman was made well from that hour.

(Matthew 9 : 23)   When Jesus came into the ruler's house, and saw the flute players, and the crowd in noisy disorder,

(Matthew 9 : 24)   he said to them, "Make room, because the girl isn't dead, but sleeping." They were ridiculing him.

> (Matthew 9 : 25)   But when the crowd was put out, he entered in, took her by the hand, and the girl arose.
>
> (Matthew 9 : 26)   The report of this went out into all that land.

Jesus healed the Blind Men and the Mute Person Mt 9:27-34

(Matthew 9 : 27)   As Jesus passed by from there, two blind men followed him, calling out and saying, "Have mercy on us, son of David!"

(Matthew 9 : 28)   When he had come into the house, the blind men came to him. Jesus said to them, "Do you believe that I am able to do this?" They told him, "Yes, Lord."

(Matthew 9 : 29)   Then he touched their eyes, saying, "According to your faith be it done to you."

(Matthew 9 : 30)   Their eyes were opened. Jesus strictly commanded them, saying, "See that no one knows about this."

(Matthew 9 : 31)   But they went out and spread abroad his fame in all that land.

(Matthew 9 : 32)   As they went out, behold, a mute man who was demon possessed was brought to him.

(Matthew 9 : 33)   When the demon was cast out, the mute man spoke. The multitudes marveled, saying, "Nothing like this has ever been seen in Israel!"

(Matthew 9 : 34)   But the Pharisees said, "By the prince of the demons, he casts out demons."

The Harvest is Plentiful, but the Workers are Few
Mt 9:35-38

(Matthew 9 : 35)   Jesus went about all the cities and the villages, teaching in their synagogues, and preaching the Good News of the Kingdom, and healing every disease and every sickness among the people.

(Matthew 9 : 36)   But when he saw the multitudes, he was moved with compassion for them, because they were harassed and scattered, like sheep without a shepherd.

(Matthew 9 : 37)   Then he said to his disciples, "The harvest indeed is plentiful, but the laborers are few.

(Matthew 9 : 38)   Pray therefore that the Lord of the harvest will send out laborers into his harvest."

Jesus Sends Out the Twelve
Mt 10:1-42 / Mk 6:7-13 / Lk 9:1-6

(Matthew 10 : 1)   He called to himself his twelve disciples, and gave them authority over unclean spirits, to cast them out, and to heal every disease and every sickness. (Matthew 10 : 2) Now the names of the twelve apostles are these. The first, Simon, who is called Peter; Andrew, his brother; James the son of Zebedee; John, his brother;

(Matthew 10 : 3)   Philip; Bartholomew; Thomas; Matthew the tax collector; James the son of Alphaeus; Lebbaeus, who was also called Thaddaeus;

(Matthew 10 : 4)   Simon the Canaanite; and Judas Iscariot, who also betrayed him.

(Matthew 10 : 5)   Jesus sent these twelve out, and commanded them, saying, "Don't go among the Gentiles, and don't enter into any city of the Samaritans.

(Matthew 10 : 6)   Rather, go to the lost sheep of the house of Israel.

(Matthew 10 : 7)   As you go, preach, saying, The Kingdom of Heaven is at hand!'

(Matthew 10 : 8)   Heal the sick, cleanse the lepers, and cast out demons. Freely you received, so freely give.

(Matthew 10 : 9)   Don't take any gold, nor silver, nor brass in your money belts.

(Matthew 10 : 10)   Take no bag for your journey, neither two coats, nor shoes, nor staff: for the laborer is worthy of his food.

(Matthew 10 : 11)   Into whatever city or village you enter, find out who in it is worthy; and stay there until you go on.

(Matthew 10 : 12)   As you enter into the household, greet it.

(Matthew 10 : 13)   If the household is worthy, let your peace come on it, but if it isn't worthy, let your peace return to you.

(Matthew 10 : 14)   Whoever doesn't receive you, nor hear your words, as you go out of that house or that city, shake off the dust from your feet.

(Matthew 10 : 15)   Most certainly I tell you, it will be more tolerable for the land of Sodom and Gomorrah in the day of judgment than for that city.

(Matthew 10 : 16)   "Behold, I send you out as sheep in the midst of wolves. Therefore be wise as serpents, and harmless as doves.

(Matthew 10 : 17)   But beware of men: for they will deliver you up to councils, and in their synagogues they will scourge you.

(Matthew 10 : 18)   Yes, and you will be brought before governors and kings for my sake, for a testimony to them and to the nations.

(Matthew 10 : 19)   But when they deliver you up, don't be anxious how or what you will say, for it will be given you in that hour what you will say.

(Matthew 10 : 20)   For it is not you who speak, but the Spirit of your Father who speaks in you.

(Matthew 10 : 21)   "Brother will deliver up brother to death, and the father his child. Children will rise up against parents, and cause them to be put to death.

(Matthew 10 : 22)   You will be hated by all men for my name's sake, but he who endures to the end will be saved.

(Matthew 10 : 23)   But when they persecute you in this city, flee into the next, for most certainly I tell you, you will not have gone through the cities of Israel, until the Son of Man has come.

(Matthew 10 : 24) "A disciple is not above his teacher, nor a servant above his lord.

(Matthew 10 : 25) It is enough for the disciple that he be like his teacher, and the servant like his lord. If they have called the master of the house Beelzebul, how much more those of his household!

(Matthew 10 : 26) Therefore don't be afraid of them, for there is nothing covered that will not be revealed; and hidden that will not be known.

(Matthew 10 : 27) What I tell you in the darkness, speak in the light; and what you hear whispered in the ear, proclaim on the housetops.

(Matthew 10 : 28) Don't be afraid of those who kill the body, but are not able to kill the soul. Rather, fear him who is able to destroy both soul and body in Gehenna.

(Matthew 10 : 29) "Aren't two sparrows sold for an assarion coin? Not one of them falls on the ground apart from your Father's will,

(Matthew 10 : 30) but the very hairs of your head are all numbered.

(Matthew 10 : 31) Therefore don't be afraid. You are of   more   value   than   many   sparrows. (Matthew 10 : 32) Everyone therefore who confesses me before men, him I will also confess before my Father who is in heaven.

(Matthew 10 : 33) But whoever denies me before men, him I will also deny before my Father who is in heaven.

(Matthew 10 : 34) "Don't think that I came to send peace on the earth. I didn't come to send peace, but a sword.

(Matthew 10 : 35) For I came to set a man at odds against his father, and a daughter against her mother, and a daughter-in-law against her mother-in-law.

(Matthew 10 : 36) A man's foes will be those of his own   household.
(Matthew 10 : 37) He who loves father or mother more than me is not worthy of me; and he who loves son or daughter more than me isn't worthy of me.

(Matthew 10 : 38) He who doesn't take his cross and follow after me, isn't worthy of me.

(Matthew 10 : 39) He who seeks his life will lose it; and he who loses his life for my sake will find it.

(Matthew 10 : 40) He who receives you receives me, and he who receives me receives him who sent me.

(Matthew 10 : 41) He who receives a prophet in the name of a prophet will receive a prophet's reward. He who receives a righteous man in the name of a righteous man will receive a righteous man's reward.

(Matthew 10 : 42) Whoever gives one of these little ones just a cup of cold water to drink in the name of a disciple, most certainly I tell you he will in no way lose his reward."

(Mark 6 : 7)   He called to himself the twelve, and began to send them out two by two; and he gave them authority over the unclean spirits.

(Mark 6 : 8)   He commanded them that they should take nothing for their journey, except a staff only: no bread, no wallet, no money in their purse,

(Mark 6 : 9)   but to wear sandals, and not put on two tunics.

(Mark 6 : 10)   He said to them, "Wherever you enter into a house, stay there until you depart from there.

(Mark 6 : 11)   Whoever will not receive you nor hear you, as you depart from there, shake off the dust that is under your feet for a testimony against them. Assuredly, I tell you, it will be more tolerable for Sodom and Gomorrah in the day of judgment than for that city!"

(Mark 6 : 12)   They went out and preached that people should repent.

(Mark 6 : 13)   They cast out many demons, and anointed many with oil who were sick, and healed them.

(Luke 9 : 1)   He called the twelve together, and gave them power and authority over all demons, and to cure diseases.

(Luke 9 : 2)   He sent them out to preach the Kingdom of God, and to heal the sick.

(Luke 9 : 3) He said to them, "Take nothing for your journey neither staffs, nor wallet, nor bread, nor money; neither have two coats apiece.

(Luke 9 : 4) Into whatever house you enter, stay there, and depart from there.

(Luke 9 : 5) As many as don't receive you, when you depart from that city, shake off even the dust from your feet for a testimony against them."

(Luke 9 : 6) They departed, and went throughout the villages, preaching the Good News, and healing everywhere.

Woe on Unrepentant Towns
Mt 11:20-24

(Matthew 11 : 20) Then Jesus began to denounce the towns in which most of his miracles had been performed, because they did not repent.

(Matthew 11 : 21) "Woe to you, Chorazin! Woe to you, Bethsaida! For if the mighty works had been done in Tyre and Sidon which were done in you, they would have repented long ago in sackcloth and ashes.

(Matthew 11 : 22) But I tell you, it will be more tolerable for Tyre and Sidon on the day of judgment than for you.

(Matthew 11 : 23) You, Capernaum, who are exalted to heaven, you will go down to Hades.For if the mighty works had been done in Sodom which were done in you, it would have remained until this day.

(Matthew 11 : 24)   But I tell you that it will be more tolerable for the land of Sodom, on the day of judgment, than for you."

The Father Revealed in the Son
Mt 11:25-30

(Matthew 11 : 25)   At that time, Jesus answered, "I thank you, Father, Lord of heaven and earth, that you hid these things from the wise and understanding, and revealed them to infants.

(Matthew 11 : 26)   Yes, Father, for so it was well-pleasing in your sight.

(Matthew 11 : 27)   All things have been delivered to me by my Father. No one knows the Son, except the Father; neither does anyone know the Father, except the Son, and he to whom the Son desires to reveal him.

(Matthew 11 : 28) "Come to me, all you who labor and are heavily burdened, and I will give you rest.

(Matthew 11 : 29)   Take my yoke upon you, and learn from me, for I am gentle and lowly in heart; and you will find rest for your souls.

(Matthew 11 : 30) For my yoke is easy, and my burden is light."

God's Chosen Servant
Mt 12:15-21

(Matthew 12 : 15)   Jesus, perceiving that, withdrew from there. Great multitudes followed him; and he healed them all,

(Matthew 12 : 16)   and commanded them that they should not make him known:

(Matthew 12 : 17)   that it might be fulfilled which was spoken through Isaiah the prophet, saying,

(Matthew 12 : 18)   "Behold, my servant whom I have chosen;

my beloved in whom my soul is well pleased:

I will put my Spirit on him.

He will proclaim justice to the nations.

(Matthew 12 : 19)   He will not strive, nor shout;

neither will anyone hear his voice in the streets.

(Matthew 12 : 20)   He won't break a bruised reed.

He won't quench a smoking flax,

until he leads justice to victory.

(Matthew 12 : 21)   In his name, the nations will hope."

Jesus and Beelzebul
Mt 12:22-37 / Mk 3:20-30 / Lk 11:14-23
& Lk 11:27-28

(Matthew 12 : 22)   Then one possessed by a demon, blind and mute, was brought to him and he healed him, so that the blind and mute man both spoke and saw.

(Matthew 12 : 23)   All the multitudes were amazed, and said, "Can this be the son of David?"

(Matthew 12 : 24)   But when the Pharisees heard it, they said, "This man does not cast out demons, except by Beelzebul,   the   prince   of   the   demons." (Matthew 12 : 25)   Knowing their thoughts, Jesus said to them, "Every kingdom divided against itself is brought to desolation, and every city or house divided against itself will not stand.

(Matthew 12 : 26)   If Satan casts out Satan, he is divided against himself. How then will his kingdom stand?

(Matthew 12 : 27)   If I by Beelzebul cast out demons, by whom do your children cast them out? Therefore they will be your judges.

(Matthew 12 : 28)   But if I by the Spirit of God cast out demons, then the Kingdom of God has come upon you.

(Matthew 12 : 29)   Or how can one enter into the house of the strong man, and plunder his goods, unless he first bind the strong man? Then he will plunder his house.

(Matthew 12 : 30)   "He who is not with me is against me, and he who doesn't gather with me, scatters.

(Matthew 12 : 31)   Therefore I tell you, every sin and blasphemy will be forgiven men, but the blasphemy against the Spirit will not be forgiven men.

(Matthew 12 : 32)   Whoever speaks a word against the Son of Man, it will be forgiven him; but whoever speaks against the Holy Spirit, it will not be forgiven him, neither in this age, nor in that which is to come.

(Matthew 12 : 33)   "Either make the tree good, and its fruit good, or make the tree corrupt, and its fruit corrupt; for the tree is known by its fruit.

(Matthew 12 : 34)   You offspring of vipers, how can you, being evil, speak good things? For out of the abundance of the heart, the mouth speaks.

(Matthew 12 : 35)   The good man out of his good treasure brings out good things, and the evil man out of his evil treasure brings out evil things.

(Matthew 12 : 36)   I tell you that every idle word that men speak, they will give account of it in the day of judgment.

(Matthew 12 : 37)   For by your words you will be justified, and by your words you will be condemned."

(Mark 3 : 20)   The multitude came together again, so that they could not so much as eat bread.

(Mark 3 : 21)   When his friends heard it, they went out to seize him: for they said, "He is insane."

(Mark 3 : 22)   The scribes who came down from Jerusalem said, "He has Beelzebul," and, "By the prince of the demons he casts out the demons."

(Mark 3 : 23)   He summoned them, and said to them in parables, "How can Satan cast out Satan?

(Mark 3 : 24)   If a kingdom is divided against itself, that kingdom cannot stand.

(Mark 3 : 25)   If a house is divided against itself, that house cannot stand.

(Mark 3 : 26)   If Satan has risen up against himself, and is divided, he can't stand, but has an end.

(Mark 3 : 27)   But no one can enter into the house of the strong man to plunder, unless he first binds the strong man; and then he will plunder his house.

(Mark 3 : 28)   Most certainly I tell you, all sins of the descendants of man will be forgiven, including their blasphemies with which they may blaspheme;

(Mark 3 : 29)   but whoever may blaspheme against the Holy Spirit never has forgiveness, but is subject to eternal   condemnation."
(Mark 3 : 30)   because they said, "He has an unclean spirit."

(Luke 11 : 14)   He was casting out a demon, and it was mute. It happened, when the demon had gone out, the mute man spoke; and the multitudes marveled.

(Luke 11 : 15)   But some of them said, "He casts out demons by Beelzebul, the prince of the demons."

(Luke 11 : 16)   Others, testing him, sought from him a sign from heaven.

(Luke 11 : 17)   But he, knowing their thoughts, said to them, "Every kingdom divided against itself is brought to desolation. A house divided against itself falls.

(Luke 11 : 18)   If Satan also is divided against himself, how will his kingdom stand? For you say that I cast out demons by Beelzebul.

(Luke 11 : 19)   But if I cast out demons by Beelzebul, by whom do your children cast them out? Therefore will they be your judges.

(Luke 11 : 20)   But if I by the finger of God cast out demons, then the Kingdom of God has come to you.

(Luke 11 : 21)   "When the strong man, fully armed, guards his own dwelling, his goods are safe.

(Luke 11 : 22)   But when someone stronger attacks him and overcomes him, he takes from him his whole armor in which he trusted, and divides his plunder.

(Luke 11 : 23)   "He that is not with me is against me. He who doesn't gather with me scatters.

(Luke 11 : 27)   It came to pass, as he said these things, a certain woman out of the multitude lifted up her voice, and said to him, "Blessed is the womb that bore you, and the breasts which nursed you!"

(Luke 11 : 28)   But he said, "On the contrary, blessed are those who hear the word of God, and keep it."

The Sign of Jonah
Mt 12:38-45 / Lk 11:29-32 & Lk 11:24-26
/ (Mt 16:1-4) / (Mk 8:11-13)

(Matthew 12 : 38)   Then certain of the scribes and Pharisees answered, "Teacher, we want to see a sign from you."

(Matthew 12 : 39) But he answered them, "An evil and adulterous generation seeks after a sign, but no sign will be given it but the sign of Jonah the prophet.

(Matthew 12 : 40)   For as Jonah was three days and three nights in the belly of the whale, so will the Son of Man be three days and three nights in the heart of the earth.

(Matthew 12 : 41)   The men of Nineveh will stand up in the judgment with this generation, and will condemn it, for they repented at the preaching of Jonah; and behold, someone greater than Jonah is here.

(Matthew 12 : 42)   The queen of the south will rise up in the judgment with this generation, and will condemn it, for she came from the ends of the earth to hear the wisdom of Solomon; and behold, someone greater than Solomon is here.

(Luke 11 : 29)   When the multitudes were gathering together to him, he began to say, "This is an evil generation. It seeks after a sign. No sign will be given to it but the sign of Jonah, the prophet.

(Luke 11 : 30)   For even as Jonah became a sign to the Ninevites, so will also the Son of Man be to this generation.

(Luke 11 : 31)   The Queen of the South will rise up in the judgment with the men of this generation, and will condemn them: for she came from the ends of the earth to hear the wisdom of Solomon; and behold, one greater than Solomon is here.

(Luke 11 : 32)   The men of Nineveh will stand up in the judgment with this generation, and will condemn it: for they repented at the preaching of Jonah, and behold, one greater than Jonah is here.

Matthew 12 : 43)   But the unclean spirit, when he is gone out of the man, passes through waterless places, seeking rest, and doesn't find it.

(Matthew 12 : 44)   Then he says, I will return into my house from which I came out,' and when he has come back, he finds it empty, swept, and put in order.

(Matthew 12 : 45)   Then he goes, and takes with himself seven other spirits more evil than he is, and they enter in and dwell there. The last state of that man becomes worse than the first. Even so will it be also to this evil generation."

(Luke 11 : 24) The unclean spirit, when he has gone out of the man, passes through dry places, seeking rest, and finding none, he says, I will turn back to my house from which I came out.'

(Luke 11 : 25) When he returns, he finds it swept and put in order.

(Luke 11 : 26) Then he goes, and takes seven other spirits more evil than himself, and they enter in and dwell there. The last state of that man becomes worse than the first."

Parable of Seed Sowing
Mt 13:1-23 / Mk 4:1-20 / Lk 8:4-15

(Matthew 13 : 1) On that day Jesus went out of the house, and sat by the seaside.

(Matthew 13 : 2) Great multitudes gathered to him, so that he entered into a boat, and sat, and all the multitude stood on the beach.

(Matthew 13 : 3) He spoke to them many things in parables, saying, "Behold, a farmer went out to sow.

(Matthew 13 : 4) As he sowed, some seeds fell by the roadside, and the birds came and devoured them.

(Matthew 13 : 5) Others fell on rocky ground, where they didn't have much soil, and immediately they sprang up, because they had no depth of earth.

(Matthew 13 : 6) When the sun had risen, they were scorched. Because they had no root, they withered away.

(Matthew 13 : 7)   Others fell among thorns. The thorns grew up and choked them.

(Matthew 13 : 8)   Others fell on good soil, and yielded fruit: some one hundred times as much, some sixty, and some thirty.

(Matthew 13 : 9)   He who has ears to hear, let him hear."

(Matthew 13 : 10)   The disciples came, and said to him, "Why do you speak to them in parables?"

(Matthew 13 : 11)   He answered them, "To you it is given to know the mysteries of the Kingdom of Heaven, but it is not given to them.

(Matthew 13 : 12)   For whoever has, to him will be given, and he will have abundance, but whoever doesn't have, from him will be taken away even that which he has.

(Matthew 13 : 13)   Therefore I speak to them in parables, because seeing they don't see, and hearing, they don't hear, neither do they understand.

(Matthew 13 : 14)   In them the prophecy of Isaiah is fulfilled, which says,

By hearing you will hear,

and will in no way understand;

Seeing you will see,

and will in no way perceive:

(Matthew 13 : 15)   for this people's heart has grown callous, their ears are dull of hearing,

they have closed their eyes;

or else perhaps they might perceive with their eyes,

hear with their ears, understand with their heart,

and should turn again; and I would heal them.' (Matthew 13 : 16) "But blessed are your eyes, for they see; and your ears, for they hear.

(Matthew 13 : 17) For most certainly I tell you that many prophets and righteous men desired to see the things which you see, and didn't see them; and to hear the things which you hear, and didn't hear them.

(Matthew 13 : 18) "Hear, then, the parable of the farmer.

(Matthew 13 : 19) When anyone hears the word of the Kingdom, and doesn't understand it, the evil one comes, and snatches away that which has been sown in his heart. This is what was sown by the roadside.

(Matthew 13 : 20) What was sown on the rocky places, this is he who hears the word, and immediately with joy receives it;

(Matthew 13 : 21) yet he has no root in himself, but endures for a while. When oppression or persecution arises because of the word, immediately he stumbles.

(Matthew 13 : 22) What was sown among the thorns, this is he who hears the word, but the cares of this age and the deceitfulness of riches choke the word, and he becomes unfruitful.

(Matthew 13 : 23)   What was sown on the good ground, this is he who hears the word, and understands it, who most certainly bears fruit, and produces, some one hundred times as much, some sixty, and some thirty."

(Mark 4 : 1)   Again he began to teach by the seaside. A great multitude was gathered to him, so that he entered into a boat in the sea, and sat down. All the multitude were on the land by the sea.

(Mark 4 : 2)   He taught them many things in parables, and told them in his teaching,

(Mark 4 : 3)   "Listen! Behold, the farmer went out to sow,

(Mark 4 : 4)   and it happened, as he sowed, some seed fell by the road, and the birds came and devoured it.

(Mark 4 : 5)   Others fell on the rocky ground, where it had little soil, and immediately it sprang up, because it had no depth of soil.

(Mark 4 : 6)   When the sun had risen, it was scorched; and because it had no root, it withered away.

(Mark 4 : 7)   Others fell among the thorns, and the thorns grew up, and choked it, and it yielded no fruit.

(Mark 4 : 8)   Others fell into the good ground, and yielded fruit, growing up and increasing. Some produced thirty times, some sixty times, and some one hundred times as much."

(Mark 4 : 9)   He said, "Whoever has ears to hear, let him hear."

(Mark 4 : 10)   When he was alone, those who were around him with the twelve asked him about the parables.

(Mark 4 : 11)   He said to them, "To you is given the mystery of the Kingdom of God, but to those who are outside, all things are done in parables,

(Mark 4 : 12)   that seeing they may see, and not perceive;

and hearing they may hear, and not understand;

lest perhaps they should turn again,

and their sins should be forgiven them.'"

(Mark 4 : 13) He said to them, "Don't you understand this parable? How will you understand all of the parables?

(Mark 4 : 14) The farmer sows the word.

(Mark 4 : 15) The ones by the road are the ones where the word is sown; and when they have heard, immediately Satan comes, and takes away the word which has been sown in them.

(Mark 4 : 16) These in the same way are those who are sown on the rocky places, who, when they have heard the word, immediately receive it with joy.

(Mark 4 : 17) They have no root in themselves, but are short-lived. When oppression or persecution arises because of the word, immediately they stumble.

(Mark 4 : 18) Others are those who are sown among the thorns. These are those who have heard the word,

(Mark 4 : 19) and the cares of this age, and the deceitfulness of riches, and the lusts of other things entering in choke the word, and it becomes unfruitful.

(Mark 4 : 20)   Those which were sown on the good ground are those who hear the word, and accept it, and bear fruit, some thirty times, some sixty times, and some one hundred times."

(Luke 8 : 4)   When a great multitude came together, and people from every city were coming to him, he spoke by a parable.

(Luke 8 : 5) "The farmer went out to sow his seed. As he sowed, some fell along the road, and it was trampled under foot, and the birds of the sky devoured it.

(Luke 8 : 6)   Other seed fell on the rock, and as soon as it grew, it withered away, because it had no moisture.

(Luke 8 : 7) Other fell amid the thorns, and the thorns grew with it, and choked it.

(Luke 8 : 8) Other fell into the good ground, and grew, and produced one hundred times as much fruit." As he said these things, he called out, "He who has ears to hear, let him hear!"

(Luke 8 : 9) Then his disciples asked him, "What does this parable mean?"

(Luke 8 : 10) He said, "To you it is given to know the mysteries of the Kingdom of God, but to the rest in parables; that seeing they may not see, and hearing they may not understand.'

(Luke 8 : 11) Now the parable is this: The seed is the word of God.

(Luke 8 : 12) Those along the road are those who hear, then the devil comes, and takes away the word from their heart, that they may not believe and be saved.

(Luke 8 : 13) Those on the rock are they who, when they hear, receive the word with joy; but these have no root, who believe for a while, then fall away in time of temptation.

(Luke 8 : 14) That which fell among the thorns, these are those who have heard, and as they go on their way they are choked with cares, riches, and pleasures of life, and bring no fruit to maturity.

(Luke 8 : 15) That in the good ground, these are such as in an honest and good heart, having heard the word, hold it tightly, and produces fruit with patience.

The Parable of the Weeds
Mt 13:24-30

(Matthew 13 : 24) He set another parable before them, saying, "The Kingdom of Heaven is like a man who sowed good seed in his field,

(Matthew 13 : 25)   but while people slept, his enemy came and sowed darnel weeds also among the wheat, and went away.

(Matthew 13 : 26)   But when the blade sprang up and produced fruit, then the darnel weeds appeared also.

(Matthew 13 : 27)   The servants of the householder came and said to him, Sir, didn't you sow good seed in your field? Where did this darnel come from?'

(Matthew 13 : 28)   "He said to them, An enemy has done this.'

"The servants asked him, 'Do you want us to go and gather them up?'

(Matthew 13 : 29)   "But he said, No, lest perhaps while you gather up the darnel weeds, you root up the wheat with them.

(Matthew 13 : 30)   Let both grow together until the harvest, and in the harvest time I will tell the reapers, "First, gather up the darnel weeds, and bind them in bundles to burn them; but gather the wheat into my barn."'"

The Parable of the Weeds Explained
Mt 13:36-43

(Matthew 13 : 36)   Then Jesus sent the multitudes away, and went into the house. His disciples came to him, saying, "Explain to us the parable of the darnel weeds of the field."

(Matthew 13 : 37)   He answered them, "He who sows the good seed is the Son of Man,

(Matthew 13 : 38)   the field is the world; and the good seed, these are the children of the Kingdom; and the darnel weeds are the children of the evil one.

(Matthew 13 : 39)   The enemy who sowed them is the devil. The harvest is the end of the age, and the reapers are angels.

(Matthew 13 : 40)   As therefore the darnel weeds are gathered up and burned with fire; so will it be at the end of this age.

(Matthew 13 : 41)   The Son of Man will send out his angels, and they will gather out of his Kingdom all things that cause stumbling, and those who do iniquity,

(Matthew 13 : 42)   and will cast them into the furnace of fire. There will be weeping and the gnashing of teeth.

(Matthew 13 : 43)   Then the righteous will shine like the sun in the Kingdom of their Father. He who has ears to hear, let him hear.

The Parables of the Hidden Treasure and the Pearl
Mt 13:44-46

(Matthew 13 : 44)   "Again, the Kingdom of Heaven is like a treasure hidden in the field, which a man found, and hid. In his joy, he goes and sells all that he has, and buys that field.

(Matthew 13 : 45)   "Again, the Kingdom of Heaven is like a man who is a merchant seeking fine pearls,

(Matthew 13 : 46)   who having found one pearl of great price, he went and sold all that he had, and bought it.

The Parable of the Net
Mt 13:47-52

(Matthew 13 : 47)   "Again, the Kingdom of Heaven is like a dragnet, that was cast into the sea, and gathered some fish of every kind,

(Matthew 13 : 48)   which, when it was filled, they drew up on the beach. They sat down, and gathered the good into containers, but the bad they threw away.

(Matthew 13 : 49)   So will it be in the end of the world. The angels will come and separate the wicked from among the righteous,

(Matthew 13 : 50)   and will cast them into the furnace of fire. There will be the weeping and the gnashing of teeth."

(Matthew 13 : 51)   Jesus said to them, "Have you understood all these things?" They answered him, "Yes, Lord."
(Matthew 13 : 52)   He said to them, "Therefore every scribe who has been made a disciple in the Kingdom of Heaven is like a man who is a householder, who brings out of his treasure new and old things."

A Prophet Without Honor
Mt 13:53-58 / Mk 6:1-6

(Matthew 13 : 53)   It happened that when Jesus had finished these parables, he departed from there.

(Matthew 13 : 54)   Coming into his own country, he taught them in their synagogue, so that they were astonished, and said, "Where did this man get this wisdom, and these mighty works?

(Matthew 13 : 55)   Isn't this the carpenter's son? Isn't his mother called Mary, and his brothers, James, Joses, Simon, and Judas?

(Matthew 13 : 56)   Aren't all of his sisters with us? Where then did this man get all of these things?"

(Matthew 13 : 57)   They were offended by him. But Jesus said to them, "A prophet is not without honor, except in his own country, and in his own house."

(Matthew 13 : 58)   He didn't do many mighty works there because of their unbelief.

(Mark 6 : 1)   He went out from there. He came into his own country, and his disciples followed him.

(Mark 6 : 2)   When the Sabbath had come, he began to teach in the synagogue, and many hearing him were astonished, saying, "Where did this man get these things?" and, "What is the wisdom that is given to this man, that such mighty works come about by his hands?

(Mark 6 : 3)   Isn't this the carpenter, the son of Mary, and brother of James, Joses, Judah, and Simon? Aren't his sisters here with us?" They were offended at him.

> (Mark 6 : 4)   Jesus said to them, "A prophet is not without honor, except in his own country, and among his own relatives, and in his own house."

(Mark 6 : 5)   He could do no mighty work there, except that he laid his hands on a few sick people and healed them.

(Mark 6 : 6)   He marveled because of their unbelief. He went around the villages teaching.

John the Baptist Beheaded
Mk 6:14-29 / Lk 9:7-9 / Mt 14:1-12

(Mark 6 : 14)   King Herod heard this, for his name had become known, and he said, "John the Baptizer has risen from the dead, and therefore these powers are at work in him."

(Mark 6 : 15)   But others said, "He is Elijah."

Others said, "He is a prophet, or like one of the prophets."

(Mark 6 : 16)   But Herod, when he heard this, said, "This is John, whom I beheaded. He has risen from the dead."

(Mark 6 : 17)   For Herod himself had sent out and arrested John, and bound him in prison for the sake of Herodias, his brother Philip's wife, for he had married her.

(Mark 6 : 18)   For John said to Herod, "It is not lawful for you to have your brother's wife."

(Mark 6 : 19)   Herodias set herself against him, and desired to kill him, but she couldn't,

(Mark 6 : 20)   for Herod feared John, knowing that he was a righteous and holy man, and kept him safe. When he heard him, he did many things, and he heard him gladly.

(Mark 6 : 21)   Then a convenient day came, that Herod on his birthday made a supper for his nobles, the high officers, and the chief men of Galilee.

(Mark 6 : 22)   When the daughter of Herodias herself came in and danced, she pleased Herod and those sitting with him. The king said to the young lady, "Ask me whatever you want, and I will give it to you."

(Mark 6 : 23)   He swore to her, "Whatever you shall ask of me, I will give you, up to half of my kingdom."

(Mark 6 : 24)   She went out, and said to her mother, "What shall I ask?" She said, "The head of John the Baptizer."
(Mark 6 : 25)   She came in immediately with haste to the king, and asked, "I want you to give me right now the head of John the Baptizer on a platter."

(Mark 6 : 26)   The king was exceedingly sorry, but for the sake of his oaths, and of his dinner guests, he didn't wish to refuse her.

(Mark 6 : 27)   Immediately the king sent out a soldier of his guard, and commanded to bring John's head, and he went and beheaded him in the prison,

(Mark 6 : 28)   and brought his head on a platter, and gave it to the young lady; and the young lady gave it to her mother.

(Mark 6 : 29) When his disciples heard this, they came and took up his corpse, and laid it in a tomb.

(Luke 9 : 7) Now Herod the tetrarch heard of all that was done by him; and he was very perplexed, because it was said by some that John had risen from the dead,

(Luke 9 : 8)   and by some that Elijah had appeared, and by others that one of the old prophets had risen again.

(Luke 9 : 9)   Herod said, "John I beheaded, but who is this, about whom I hear such things?" He sought to see him.

(Matthew 14 : 1)   At that time, Herod the tetrarch heard the report concerning Jesus,

(Matthew 14 : 2)   and said to his servants, "This is John the Baptizer. He is risen from the dead. That is why these powers work in him."

(Matthew 14 : 3)   For Herod had laid hold of John, and bound him, and put him in prison for the sake of Herodias, his brother Philip's wife.

(Matthew 14 : 4)   For John said to him, "It is not lawful for you to have her."

(Matthew 14 : 5)   When he would have put him to death, he feared the multitude, because they counted him as a prophet.

(Matthew 14 : 6)   But when Herod's birthday came, the daughter of Herodias danced among them and pleased Herod.

(Matthew 14 : 7)   Whereupon he promised with an oath to give her whatever she should ask.

(Matthew 14 : 8)   She, being prompted by her mother, said, "Give me here on a platter the head of John the Baptizer."

(Matthew 14 : 9)   The king was grieved, but for the sake of his oaths, and of those who sat at the table with him, he commanded it to be given,

(Matthew 14 : 10)   and he sent and beheaded John in the prison.

(Matthew 14 : 11) His head was brought on a platter, and given to the young lady: and she brought it to her mother.

(Matthew 14 : 12)   His disciples came, and took the body, and buried it; and they went and told Jesus.

Jesus Feeds the Five Thousand
Mk 6:30-44 / Jn 6:1-15 / Mt 14:13-21 / Lk 9:10-17

(Mark 6 : 30)   The apostles gathered themselves together to Jesus, and they told him all things, whatever they had done, and whatever they had taught.

(Mark 6 : 31)   He said to them, "You come apart into a deserted place, and rest awhile." For there were many coming and going, and they had no leisure so much as to eat.

(Mark 6 : 32)   They went away in the boat to a deserted place by themselves.

(Mark 6 : 33)   They saw them going, and many recognized him and ran there on foot from all the cities. They arrived before them and came together to him.

(Mark 6 : 34)   Jesus came out, saw a great multitude, and he had compassion on them, because they were like sheep without a shepherd, and he began to teach them many things.

(John 6 : 1) After these things, Jesus went away to the other side of the sea of Galilee, which is also called the Sea of Tiberias.

(John 6 : 2) A great multitude followed him, because they saw his signs which he did on those who were sick.

(John 6 : 3) Jesus went up into the mountain, and he sat there with his disciples.

(John 6 : 4) Now the Passover, the feast of the Jews, was at hand.

(Mark 6 : 35)   When it was late in the day, his disciples came to him, and said, "This place is deserted, and it is late in the day.

(John 6 : 5) Jesus therefore lifting up his eyes, and seeing that a great multitude was coming to him, said to Philip, "Where are we to buy bread, that these may eat?"

(John 6 : 6) This he said to test him, for he himself knew what he would do.

(John 6 : 7) Philip answered him, "Two hundred denarii worth of bread is not sufficient for them, that everyone of them may receive a little."

(Mark 6 : 36)   Send them away, that they may go into the surrounding country and villages, and buy themselves bread, for they have nothing to eat."

(Mark 6 : 37)   But he answered them, "You give them something to eat."

They asked him, "Shall we go and buy two hundred denarii worth of bread, and give them something to eat?"

(John 6 : 8) One of his disciples, Andrew, Simon Peter's brother, said to him,

(John 6 : 9) "There is a boy here who has five barley loaves and two fish, but what are these among so many?" (John 6 : 10) Jesus said, "Have the people sit down." Now there was much grass in that place. So the men sat down, in number about five thousand.

(Mark 6 : 39)   He commanded them that everyone should sit down in groups on the green grass.

(Mark 6 : 40)   They sat down in ranks, by hundreds and by fifties.

(Mark 6 : 41) He took the five loaves and the two fish, and looking up to heaven, he blessed and broke the loaves, and he gave to his disciples to set before them, and he divided the two fish among them all.

(John 6 : 11) Jesus took the loaves; and having given thanks, he distributed to the disciples, and the disciples to those who were sitting down; likewise also of the fish as much as they desired.

(John 6 : 12) When they were filled, he said to his disciples, "Gather up the broken pieces which are left over, that nothing be lost."

(John 6 : 13) So they gathered them up and filled twelve baskets with broken pieces from the five barley loaves, which were left over by those who had eaten. (John 6 : 14) When therefore the people saw the sign which Jesus did, they said, "This is truly the prophet who comes into the world."

(John 6 : 15) Jesus therefore, perceiving that they were about to come and take him by force, to make him king, withdrew again to the mountain by himself.

(Mark 6 : 38)   He said to them, "How many loaves do you have? Go see." When they knew, they said, "Five, and two fish."

(Mark 6 : 42)   They all ate, and were filled.

(Mark 6 : 43)   They took up twelve baskets full of broken pieces and also of the fish.

(Mark 6 : 44)   Those who ate the loaves were five thousand men.

(Matthew 14 : 13)   Now when Jesus heard this, he withdrew from there in a boat, to a deserted place apart. When the multitudes heard it, they followed him on foot from the cities.

(Matthew 14 : 14)   Jesus went out, and he saw a great multitude. He had compassion on them, and healed their sick.

(Matthew 14 : 15)   When evening had come, his disciples came to him, saying, "This place is deserted, and the hour is already late. Send the multitudes away, that they may go into the villages, and buy themselves food." (Matthew 14 : 16)   But Jesus said to them, "They don't need to go away. You give them something to eat."

(Matthew 14 : 17)   They told him, "We only have here five loaves and two fish."

(Matthew 14 : 18)   He said, "Bring them here to me."

(Matthew 14 : 19)   He commanded the multitudes to sit down on the grass; and he took the five loaves and the two fish, and looking up to heaven, he blessed, broke and gave the loaves to the disciples, and the disciples gave to the multitudes.

(Matthew 14 : 20)   They all ate, and were filled. They took up twelve baskets full of that which remained left over from the broken pieces.

(Matthew 14 : 21)   Those who ate were about five thousand men, besides women and children.

(Luke 9 : 10)   The apostles, when they had returned, told him what things they had done. He took them, and withdrew apart to a deserted place of a city called Bethsaida.

(Luke 9 : 11)   But the multitudes, perceiving it, followed him. He welcomed them, and spoke to them of the Kingdom of God, and he cured those who needed healing.

(Luke 9 : 12)   The day began to wear away; and the twelve came, and said to him, "Send the multitude away, that they may go into the surrounding villages and farms, and lodge, and get food, for we are here in a deserted place."

(Luke 9 : 13)   But he said to them, "You give them something to eat."

They said, "We have no more than five loaves and two fish, unless we should go and buy food for all these people."

(Luke 9 : 14)   For they were about five thousand men. He said to his disciples, "Make them sit down in groups of about fifty each."

(Luke 9 : 15)   They did so, and made them all sit down.

(Luke 9 : 16)   He took the five loaves and the two fish, and looking up to the sky, he blessed them, and broke them, and gave them to the disciples to set before the multitude.

(Luke 9 : 17)   They ate, and were all filled. They gathered up twelve baskets of broken pieces that were left over.

Jesus Walks on the Water
Mt 14:22-36 / Jn 6:16-24 / Mk 6:45-56

(Matthew 14 : 22)   Immediately Jesus made the disciples get into the boat, and to go ahead of him to the other side, while he sent the multitudes away.

(Matthew 14 : 23)   After he had sent the multitudes away, he went up into the mountain by himself to pray. When evening had come, he was there alone.

(Matthew 14 : 24)   But the boat was now in the middle of the sea, distressed by the waves, for the wind was contrary.
(Matthew 14 : 25)   In the fourth watch of the night, Jesus came to them, walking on the sea.

(Matthew 14 : 26)   When the disciples saw him walking on the sea, they were troubled, saying, "It's a ghost!" and they cried out for fear.

(Matthew 14 : 27)   But immediately Jesus spoke to them, saying "Cheer up! It is I! Don't be afraid."

(Matthew 14 : 28)   Peter answered him and said, "Lord, if it is you, command me to come to you on the waters."

(Matthew 14 : 29)   He said, "Come!"

Peter stepped down from the boat, and walked on the waters to come to Jesus.

(Matthew 14 : 30)   But when he saw that the wind was strong, he was afraid, and beginning to sink, he cried out, saying, "Lord, save me!"

(Matthew 14 : 31)   Immediately Jesus stretched out his hand, took hold of him, and said to him, "You of little faith, why did you doubt?"

(Matthew 14 : 32)   When they got up into the boat, the wind ceased.

(Matthew 14 : 33)   Those who were in the boat came and worshiped him, saying, "You are truly the Son of God!"

(Matthew 14 : 34)   When they had crossed over, they came to the land of Gennesaret.

(John 6 : 21) They were willing therefore to receive him into the boat. Immediately the boat was at the land where they were going.

(John 6 : 22) On the next day, the multitude that stood on the other side of the sea saw that there was no other boat there, except the one in which his disciples had embarked, and that Jesus hadn't entered with his disciples into the boat, but his disciples had gone away alone.

(John 6 : 23) However boats from Tiberias came near to the place where they ate the bread after the Lord had given thanks.

(John 6 : 24) When the multitude therefore saw that Jesus wasn't there, nor his disciples, they themselves got into the boats, and came to Capernaum, seeking Jesus.

(Matthew 14 : 35) When the people of that place recognized him, they sent into all that surrounding region, and brought to him all who were sick,

(Matthew 14 : 36) and they begged him that they might just touch the fringe of his garment. As many as touched it were made whole.

(Mark 6 : 45) Immediately he made his disciples get into the boat, and to go ahead to the other side, to Bethsaida, while he himself sent the multitude away.

(Mark 6 : 46)   After he had taken leave of them, he went up the mountain to pray.

(Mark 6 : 47)   When evening had come, the boat was in the midst of the sea, and he was alone on the land.

(Mark 6 : 48)   Seeing them distressed in rowing, for the wind was contrary to them, about the fourth watch of the night he came to them, walking on the sea,

(Mark 6 : 49)   but they, when they saw him walking on the sea, supposed that it was a ghost, and cried out;

(Mark 6 : 50)   for they all saw him, and were troubled. But he immediately spoke with them, and said to them, "Cheer up! It is I!

(Mark 6 : 51)   He got into the boat with them; and the wind ceased, and they were very amazed among themselves, and marveled;

(Mark 6 : 52)   for they hadn't understood about the loaves, but their hearts were hardened.

(Mark 6 : 53)   When they had crossed over, they came to land at Gennesaret, and moored to the shore.

(Mark 6 : 54)   When they had come out of the boat, immediately the people recognized him,

(Mark 6 : 55)   and ran around that whole region, and began to bring those who were sick, on their mats, to where they heard he was.

(Mark 6 : 56)   Wherever he entered, into villages, or into cities, or into the country, they laid the sick in the marketplaces, and begged him that they might touch just the fringe of his garment; and as many as touched him were made well.

(John 6 : 16) When evening came, his disciples went down to the sea,

(John 6 : 17) and they entered into the boat, and were going over the sea to Capernaum. It was now dark, and Jesus had not come to them.

(John 6 : 18) The sea was tossed by a great wind blowing.

(John 6 : 19) When therefore they had rowed about twenty-five or thirty stadia, they saw Jesus walking on the sea, and drawing near to the boat; and they were afraid.

(John 6 : 20) But he said to them, "It is I. Don't be afraid."

Jesus the Bread of Life
Jn 6:25-59

(John 6 : 25) When they found him on the other side of the sea, they asked him, "Rabbi, when did you come here?"

(John 6 : 26) Jesus answered them, "Most certainly I tell you, you seek me, not because you saw signs, but because you ate of the loaves, and were filled.

(John 6 : 27) Don't work for the food which perishes, but for the food which remains to eternal life, which the Son of Man will give to you. For God the Father has sealed him."

(John 6 : 28) They said therefore to him, "What must we do, that we may work the works of God?" (John 6 : 29) Jesus answered them, "This is the work of God, that you believe in him whom he has sent." (John 6 : 30) They said therefore to him, "What then do you do for a sign, that we may see, and believe you? What work do you do?

(John 6 : 31) Our fathers ate the manna in the wilderness. As it is written, He gave them bread out of heaven to eat.'" (John 6 : 32) Jesus therefore said to them, "Most certainly, I tell you, it wasn't Moses who gave you the bread out of heaven, but my Father gives you the true bread out of heaven.

(John 6 : 33) For the bread of God is that which comes down out of heaven, and gives life to the world."

(John 6 : 34) They said therefore to him, "Lord, always give us this bread."

(John 6 : 35) Jesus said to them, "I am the bread of life. He who comes to me will not be hungry, and he who believes in me will never be thirsty.

(John 6 : 36) But I told you that you have seen me, and yet you don't believe.

(John 6 : 37) All those whom the Father gives me will come to me. He who comes to me I will in no way throw out.

(John 6 : 38) For I have come down from heaven, not to do my own will, but the will of him who sent me.

(John 6 : 39) This is the will of my Father who sent me, that of all he has given to me I should lose nothing, but should raise him up at the last day.

(John 6 : 40) This is the will of the one who sent me, that everyone who sees the Son, and believes in him, should have eternal life; and I will raise him up at the last day."

(John 6 : 41) The Jews therefore murmured concerning him, because he said, "I am the bread which came down out of heaven."

(John 6 : 42) They said, "Isn't this Jesus, the son of Joseph, whose father and mother we know? How then does he say, I have come down out of heaven?'"

(John 6 : 43) Therefore Jesus answered them, "Don't murmur among yourselves.

(John 6 : 44) No one can come to me unless the Father who sent me draws him, and I will raise him up in the last day.

(John 6 : 45) It is written in the prophets, They will all be taught by God.' Therefore everyone who hears from the Father, and has learned, comes to me.

(John 6 : 46) Not that anyone has seen the Father, except he who is from God. He has seen the Father.

(John 6 : 47) Most certainly, I tell you, he who believes in me has eternal life.

(John 6 : 48) I am the bread of life.

(John 6 : 49) Your fathers ate the manna in the wilderness, and they died.

(John 6 : 50) This is the bread which comes down out of heaven, that anyone may eat of it and not die.

(John 6 : 51) I am the living bread which came down out of heaven. If anyone eats of this bread, he will live forever. Yes, the bread which I will give for the life of the world is my flesh."

(John 6 : 52) The Jews therefore contended with one another, saying, "How can this man give us his flesh to eat?"

(John 6 : 53) Jesus therefore said to them, "Most certainly I tell you, unless you eat the flesh of the Son of Man and drink his blood, you don't have life in yourselves.

(John 6 : 54) He who eats my flesh and drinks my blood has eternal life, and I will raise him up at the last day.

(John 6 : 55) For my flesh is food indeed, and my blood is drink indeed.

(John 6 : 56) He who eats my flesh and drinks my blood lives in me, and I in him.

(John 6 : 57) As the living Father sent me, and I live because of the Father; so he who feeds on me, he will also live because of me.

(John 6 : 58) This is the bread which came down out of heaven not as our fathers ate the manna, and died. He who eats this bread will live forever."

(John 6 : 59) He said these things in the synagogue, as he taught in Capernaum.

Many Disciples Desert Jesus
Jn 6:60-71

(John 6 : 60) Therefore many of his disciples, when they heard this, said, "This is a hard saying! Who can listen to it?"

(John 6 : 61) But Jesus knowing in himself that his disciples murmured at this, said to them, "Does this cause you to stumble?

(John 6 : 62) Then what if you would see the Son of Man ascending to where he was before?

(John 6 : 63) It is the spirit who gives life. The flesh profits nothing. The words that I speak to you are spirit, and are life.

(John 6 : 64) But there are some of you who don't believe." For Jesus knew from the beginning who they were who didn't believe, and who it was who would betray him.

(John 6 : 65) He said, "For this cause have I said to you that no one can come to me, unless it is given to him by my Father."

(John 6 : 66) At this, many of his disciples went back, and walked no more with him.

(John 6 : 67) Jesus said therefore to the twelve, "You don't also want to go away, do you?"

(John 6 : 68) Simon Peter answered him, "Lord, to whom would we go? You have the words of eternal life.

(John 6 : 69) We have come to believe and know that you are the Christ, the Son of the living God."

(John 6 : 70) Jesus answered them, "Didn't I choose you, the twelve, and one of you is a devil?"

(John 6 : 71) Now he spoke of Judas, the son of Simon Iscariot, for it was he who would betray him, being one of the twelve.

Jesus Goes to the Festival of Tabernacles
Jn 7:1-13

(John 7 : 1)   After these things, Jesus was walking in Galilee, for he wouldn't walk in Judea, because the Jews sought to kill him.

(John 7 : 2)   Now the feast of the Jews, the Feast of Booths, was at hand.

(John 7 : 3) His brothers therefore said to him, "Depart from here, and go into Judea, that your disciples also may see your works which you do.

(John 7 : 4)   For no one does anything in secret, and himself seeks to be known openly. If you do these things, reveal yourself to the world."

(John 7 : 5) For even his brothers didn't believe in him. (John 7 : 6) Jesus therefore said to them, "My time has not yet come, but your time is always ready.

(John 7 : 7) The world can't hate you, but it hates me, because I testify about it, that its works are evil.

(John 7 : 8) You go up to the feast. I am not yet going up to this feast, because my time is not yet fulfilled."

(John 7 : 9) Having said these things to them, he stayed in Galilee.

(John 7 : 10) But when his brothers had gone up to the feast, then he also went up, not publicly, but as it were in secret.

(John 7 : 11) The Jews therefore sought him at the feast, and said, "Where is he?"

(John 7 : 12) There was much murmuring among the multitudes concerning him. Some said, "He is a good man."

Others said, "Not so, but he leads the multitude astray."

(John 7 : 13) Yet no one spoke openly of him for fear of the Jews.

Jesus Teaches at the Festival
Jn 7:14-24

(John 7 : 14) But when it was now the midst of the feast, Jesus went up into the temple and taught.

(John 7 : 15) The Jews therefore marveled, saying, "How does this man know letters, having never been educated?"

(John 7 : 16) Jesus therefore answered them, "My teaching is not mine, but his who sent me.

(John 7 : 17) If anyone desires to do his will, he will know about the teaching, whether it is from God, or if I am speaking from myself.

(John 7 : 18)   He who speaks from himself seeks his own glory, but he who seeks the glory of him who sent him is true, and no unrighteousness is in him.

(John 7 : 19)   Didn't Moses give you the law, and yet none of you keeps the law? Why do you seek to kill me?"

(John 7 : 20)   The multitude answered, "You have a demon! Who seeks to kill you?"

(John 7 : 21)   Jesus answered them, "I did one work, and you all marvel because of it.

(John 7 : 22)   Moses has given you circumcision (not that it is of Moses, but of the fathers), and on the Sabbath you circumcise a boy.

(John 7 : 23)   If a boy receives circumcision on the Sabbath, that the law of Moses may not be broken, are you angry with me, because I made a man completely healthy on the Sabbath?

(John 7 : 24) Don't judge according to appearance, but judge righteous judgment."

Division Over Who Jesus Is
Jn 7:25-44

(John 7 : 25)   Therefore some of them of Jerusalem said, "Isn't this he whom they seek to kill?

(John 7 : 26)   Behold, he speaks openly, and they say nothing to him. Can it be that the rulers indeed know that this is truly the Christ?

(John 7 : 27) However we know where this man comes from, but when the Christ comes, no one will know where he comes from."

(John 7 : 28) Jesus therefore cried out in the temple, teaching and saying, "You both know me, and know where I am from. I have not come of myself, but he who sent me is true, whom you don't know.

(John 7 : 29) I know him, because I am from him, and he sent me."

(John 7 : 30) They sought therefore to take him; but no one laid a hand on him, because his hour had not yet come.

(John 7 : 31) But of the multitude, many believed in him. They said, "When the Christ comes, he won't do more signs than those which this man has done, will he?" (John 7 : 32) The Pharisees heard the multitude murmuring these things concerning him, and the chief priests and the Pharisees sent officers to arrest him.

(John 7 : 33) Then Jesus said, "I will be with you a little while longer, then I go to him who sent me.

(John 7 : 34) You will seek me, and won't find me; and where I am, you can't come."

(John 7 : 35) The Jews therefore said among themselves, "Where will this man go that we won't find him? Will he go to the Dispersion among the Greeks, and teach the Greeks?

(John 7 : 36)   What is this word that he said, You will seek me, and won't find me; and where I am, you can't come'?"

(John 7 : 37)   Now on the last and greatest day of the feast, Jesus stood and cried out, "If anyone is thirsty, let him come to me and drink!

(John 7 : 38)   He who believes in me, as the Scripture has said, from within him will flow rivers of living water."

(John 7 : 39)   But he said this about the Spirit, which those believing in him were to receive. For the Holy Spirit was not yet given, because Jesus wasn't yet glorified.

(John 7 : 40)   Many of the multitude therefore, when they heard these words, said, "This is truly the prophet."

(John 7 : 41)   Others said, "This is the Christ."

But some said, "What, does the Christ come out of Galilee?

(John 7 : 42)   Hasn't the Scripture said that the Christ comes of the seed of David,

(John 7 : 43)   So there arose a division in the multitude because of him.

(John 7 : 44)   Some of them would have arrested him, but no one laid hands on him.

Unbelief of the Jewish Leaders
Jn 7:45-53

(John 7 : 45)   The officers therefore came to the chief priests and Pharisees, and they said to them, "Why didn't you bring him?"

(John 7 : 46)   The officers answered, "No man ever spoke like this man!"

(John 7 : 47)   The Pharisees therefore answered them, "You aren't also led astray, are you?

(John 7 : 48)   Have any of the rulers believed in him, or of the Pharisees?

(John 7 : 49)   But this multitude that doesn't know the law is accursed."

(John 7 : 50)   Nicodemus (he who came to him by night, being one of them) said to them,

(John 7 : 51)   "Does our law judge a man, unless it first hears from him personally and knows what he does?"

(John 7 : 52)   They answered him, "Are you also from Galilee? Search, and see that no prophet has arisen out of Galilee."

(John 7 : 53)   Everyone went to his own house,

A Woman Caught in Adultery
Jn 8:1-11

(John 8 : 1)   but Jesus went to the Mount of Olives.
(John 8 : 2) Now very early in the morning, he came again

into the temple, and all the people came to him. He sat down, and taught them.

(John 8 : 3)   The scribes and the Pharisees brought a woman taken in adultery. Having set her in the midst,

(John 8 : 4)   they told him, "Teacher, we found this woman in adultery, in the very act.

(John 8 : 5)   Now in our law, Moses commanded us to stone such women. What then do you say about her?"

(John 8 : 6)   They said this testing him, that they might have something to accuse him of. But Jesus stooped down, and wrote on the ground with his finger.

(John 8 : 7)   But when they continued asking him, he looked up and said to them, "He who is without sin among you, let him throw the first stone at her."

(John 8 : 8)   Again he stooped down, and with his finger wrote on the ground.

(John 8 : 9)   They, when they heard it, being convicted by their conscience, went out one by one, beginning from the oldest, even to the last. Jesus was left alone with the woman where she was, in the middle.

(John 8 : 10)   Jesus, standing up, saw her and said, "Woman, where are your accusers? Did no one condemn you?"

(John 8 : 11)   She said, "No one, Lord." Jesus said, "Neither do I condemn you. Go your way. From now on, sin no more."

Dispute Over Jesus' Testimony
Jn 8:12-20

(John 8 : 12)   Again, therefore, Jesus spoke to them, saying, "I am the light of the world.He who follows me will not walk in the darkness, but will have the light of life."

(John 8 : 13) The Pharisees therefore said to him, "You testify about yourself. Your testimony is not valid."

(John 8 : 14)   Jesus answered them, "Even if I testify about myself, my testimony is true, for I know where I came from, and where I am going; but you don't know where I came from, or where I am going.

(John 8 : 15)   You judge according to the flesh. I judge no one.

(John 8 : 16)   Even if I do judge, my judgment is true, for I am not alone, but I am with the Father who sent me.

(John 8 : 17)   It's also written in your law that the testimony of two people is valid.

(John 8 : 18)   I am one who testifies about myself, and the Father who sent me testifies about me."

(John 8 : 19)   They said therefore to him, "Where is your Father?"

Jesus answered, "You know neither me, nor my Father. If you knew me, you would know my Father also."

(John 8 : 20)   Jesus spoke these words in the treasury, as he taught in the temple. Yet no one arrested him, because his hour had not yet come.

Dispute Over Who Jesus Is
Jn 8:21-30

(John 8 : 21)   Jesus said therefore again to them, "I am going away, and you will seek me, and you will die in your sins. Where I go, you can't come."

(John 8 : 22)   The Jews therefore said, "Will he kill himself, that he says, Where I am going, you can't come?'"

(John 8 : 23)   He said to them, "You are from beneath. I am from above. You are of this world. I am not of this world.

(John 8 : 24)   I said therefore to you that you will die in your sins; for unless you believe that I amhe, you will die in your sins."

(John 8 : 25)   They said therefore to him, "Who are you?"

Jesus said to them, "Just what I have been saying to you from the beginning.

(John 8 : 26)   I have many things to speak and to judge concerning you. However he who sent me is true; and the things which I heard from him, these I say to the world."

(John 8 : 27)   They didn't understand that he spoke to them about the Father.

(John 8 : 28)   Jesus therefore said to them, "When you have lifted up the Son of Man, then you will know that I am he, and I do nothing of myself, but as my Father taught me, I say these things.

(John 8 : 29) He who sent me is with me. The Father hasn't left me alone, for I always do the things that are pleasing to him."

(John 8 : 30) As he spoke these things, many believed in him.

Dispute Over Whose Children Jesus' Opponents Are
Jn 8:31-47

(John 8 : 31) Jesus therefore said to those Jews who had believed him, "If you remain in my word, then you are truly my disciples.

(John 8 : 32) You will know the truth, and the truth will make you free."

(John 8 : 33) They answered him, "We are Abraham's seed, and have never been in bondage to anyone. How do you say, You will be made free?'"

(John 8 : 34) Jesus answered them, "Most certainly I tell you, everyone who commits sin is the bondservant of sin.

(John 8 : 35) A bondservant doesn't live in the house forever. A son remains forever.

(John 8 : 36) If therefore the Son makes you free, you will be free indeed.

(John 8 : 37) I know that you are Abraham's seed, yet you seek to kill me, because my word finds no place in you.

(John 8 : 38) I say the things which I have seen with my Father; and you also do the things which you have seen with your father."

(John 8 : 39)   They answered him, "Our father is Abraham." Jesus said to them, "If you were Abraham's children, you would do the works of Abraham.

"If you were Abraham's children," said Jesus, "then you would do what Abraham did.

(John 8 : 40)   But now you seek to kill me, a man who has told you the truth, which I heard from God. Abraham didn't do this.

(John 8 : 41)   You do the works of your father."

They said to him, "We were not born of sexual immorality. We have one Father, God."

(John 8 : 42)   Therefore Jesus said to them, "If God were your father, you would love me, for I came out and have come from God. For I haven't come of myself, but he sent me.

(John 8 : 43)   Why don't you understand my speech? Because you can't hear my word.

(John 8 : 44)   You are of your father, the devil, and you want to do the desires of your father. He was a murderer from the beginning, and doesn't stand in the truth, because there is no truth in him. When he speaks a lie, he speaks on his own; for he is a liar, and its father.

(John 8 : 45)   But because I tell the truth, you don't believe me.

(John 8 : 46)   Which of you convicts me of sin? If I tell the truth, why do you not believe me?

(John 8 : 47)   He who is of God hears the words of God. For this cause you don't hear, because you are not of God."

Jesus' Claims About Himself
Jn 8:48-59

(John 8 : 48)   Then the Jews answered him, "Don't we say well that you are a Samaritan, and have a demon?"

(John 8 : 49)   Jesus answered, "I don't have a demon, but I honor my Father, and you dishonor me.

(John 8 : 50) But I don't seek my own glory. There is one who seeks and judges.

(John 8 : 51)   Most certainly, I tell you, if a person keeps my word, he will never see death."

(John 8 : 52)   Then the Jews said to him, "Now we know that you have a demon. Abraham died, and the prophets; and you say, If a man keeps my word, he will never taste of death.'

(John 8 : 53) Are you greater than our father, Abraham, who died? The prophets died. Who do you make yourself out to be?"

(John 8 : 54)   Jesus answered, "If I glorify myself, my glory is nothing. It is my Father who glorifies me, of whom you say that he is our God.

(John 8 : 55)   You have not known him, but I know him. If I said, I don't know him,' I would be like you, a liar. But I know him, and keep his word.

(John 8 : 56)   Your father Abraham rejoiced to see my day. He saw it, and was glad."

(John 8 : 57)   The Jews therefore said to him, "You are not yet fifty years old, and have you seen Abraham?"

(John 8 : 58)   Jesus said to them, "Most certainly, I tell you, before Abraham came into existence, I AM."

(John 8 : 59)   Therefore they took up stones to throw at him, but Jesus was hidden, and went out of the temple, having gone through their midst, and so passed by.

Eating with Unclean Hands
Mk 7:1-23 / Mt 15:1-20

(Mark 7 : 1)   Then the Pharisees, and some of the scribes gathered together to him, having come from Jerusalem.

(Mark 7 : 2)   Now when they saw some of his disciples eating bread with defiled, that is, unwashed, hands, they found fault.

(Mark 7 : 3)   (For the Pharisees, and all the Jews, don't eat unless they wash their hands and forearms, holding to the tradition of the elders.

(Mark 7 : 4)   They don't eat when they come from the marketplace, unless they bathe themselves, and there are many other things, which they have received to hold to: washings of cups, pitchers, bronze vessels, and couches.

(Mark 7 : 5)   The Pharisees and the scribes asked him, "Why don't your disciples walk according to the tradition of the elders, but eat their bread with unwashed hands?"

(Mark 7 : 6)   He answered them, "Well did Isaiah prophesy of you hypocrites, as it is written,

This people honors me with their lips,

but their heart is far from me.

(Mark 7 : 7)   But in vain do they worship me,

teaching as doctrines the commandments of men.' (Mark 7 : 8)   "For you set aside the commandment of God, and hold tightly to the tradition of men the washing of pitchers and cups, and you do many other such things."

(Mark 7 : 9)   He said to them, "Full well do you reject the commandment of God, that you may keep your tradition.

(Mark 7 : 10)   For Moses said, Honor your father and your mother;' and, He who speaks evil of father or mother, let him be put to death.'

(Mark 7 : 11)   But you say, If a man tells his father or his mother, "Whatever profit you might have received from me is Corban, that is to say, given to God";'

(Mark 7 : 12)   then you no longer allow him to do anything for his father or his mother,

(Mark 7 : 13)   making void the word of God by your tradition, which you have handed down. You do many things like this."

(Mark 7 : 14)   He called all the multitude to himself, and said to them, "Hear me, all of you, and understand.

(Mark 7 : 15)   There is nothing from outside of the man, that going into him can defile him; but the things which proceed out of the man are those that defile the man.

(Mark 7 : 16) If anyone has ears to hear, let him hear!"

(Mark 7 : 17)   When he had entered into a house away from the multitude, his disciples asked him about the parable.

(Mark 7 : 18)   He said to them, "Are you thus without understanding also? Don't you perceive that whatever goes into the man from outside can't defile him,

(Mark 7 : 19)   because it doesn't go into his heart, but into his stomach, then into the latrine, thus purifying all foods?"

(Mark 7 : 20)   He said, "That which proceeds out of the man, that defiles the man.

(Mark 7 : 21)   For from within, out of the hearts of men, proceed evil thoughts, adulteries, sexual sins, murders, thefts,

(Mark 7 : 22)   coveting, wickedness, deceit, lustful desires, an evil eye, blasphemy, pride, and foolishness.

(Mark 7 : 23)   All these evil things come from within, and defile the man."

(Matthew 15 : 1)   Then Pharisees and scribes came to Jesus from Jerusalem, saying,

(Matthew 15 : 2)   "Why do your disciples disobey the tradition of the elders? For they don't wash their hands when they eat bread."

(Matthew 15 : 3)   He answered them, "Why do you also disobey the commandment of God because of your tradition?

(Matthew 15 : 4)   For God commanded, Honor your father and your mother,' and, He who speaks evil of father or mother, let him be put to death.'

(Matthew 15 : 5)   But you say, Whoever may tell his father or his mother, "Whatever help you might otherwise have gotten from me is a gift devoted to God,"

(Matthew 15 : 6)   he shall not honor his father or mother.' You have made the commandment of God void because of your tradition.

(Matthew 15 : 7)   You hypocrites! Well did Isaiah prophesy of you, saying,

(Matthew 15 : 8)   These people draw near to me with their mouth,

and honor me with their lips;

but their heart is far from me.

(Matthew 15 : 9)   And in vain do they worship me,

teaching as doctrine rules made by men.'"

(Matthew 15 : 10) He summoned the multitude, and said to them, "Hear, and understand.

(Matthew 15 : 11)   That which enters into the mouth doesn't defile the man; but that which proceeds out of the mouth, this defiles the man."

(Matthew 15 : 12)   Then the disciples came, and said to him, "Do you know that the Pharisees were offended, when they heard this saying?"

(Matthew 15 : 13)   But he answered, "Every plant which my heavenly Father didn't plant will be uprooted.

(Matthew 15 : 14)   Leave them alone. They are blind guides of the blind. If the blind guide the blind, both will fall into a pit."

(Matthew 15 : 15)   Peter answered him, "Explain the parable to us."

(Matthew 15 : 16)   So Jesus said, "Do you also still not understand?

(Matthew 15 : 17)   Don't you understand that whatever goes into the mouth passes into the belly, and then out of the body?

(Matthew 15 : 18)   But the things which proceed out of the mouth come out of the heart, and they defile the man.

(Matthew 15 : 19)   For out of the heart come evil thoughts, murders, adulteries, sexual sins, thefts, false testimony, and blasphemies.

(Matthew 15 : 20)   These are the things which defile the man; but to eat with unwashed hands doesn't defile the man."

The Faith of a Canaanite Woman
Mt 15:21-28 / Mk 7:24-30

(Matthew 15 : 21)   Jesus went out from there, and withdrew into the region of Tyre and Sidon.

(Matthew 15 : 22)   Behold, a Canaanite woman came out from those borders, and cried, saying, "Have mercy on me, Lord, you son of David! My daughter is severely possessed by a demon!"

(Matthew 15 : 23)   But he answered her not a word. His disciples came and begged him, saying, "Send her away; for she cries after us."

(Matthew 15 : 24)   But he answered, "I wasn't sent to anyone but the lost sheep of the house of Israel."

(Matthew 15 : 25)   But she came and worshiped him, saying, "Lord, help me."

(Matthew 15 : 26)   But he answered, "It is not appropriate to take the children's bread and throw it to the dogs."

(Matthew 15 : 27)   But she said, "Yes, Lord, but even the dogs eat the crumbs which fall from their masters' table."

(Matthew 15 : 28)   Then Jesus answered her, "Woman, great is your faith! Be it done to you even as you desire." And her daughter was healed from that hour.

(Mark 7 : 24)   From there he arose, and went away into the borders of Tyre and Sidon. He entered into a house, and didn't want anyone to know it, but he couldn't escape notice.

(Mark 7 : 25)   For a woman, whose little daughter had an unclean spirit, having heard of him, came and fell down at his feet.

(Mark 7 : 26)   Now the woman was a Greek, a Syrophoenician by race. She begged him that he would cast the demon out of her daughter.

(Mark 7 : 27) But Jesus said to her, "Let the children be filled first, for it is not appropriate to take the children's bread and throw it to the dogs."

(Mark 7 : 28)   But she answered him, "Yes, Lord. Yet even the dogs under the table eat the children's crumbs."

(Mark 7 : 29)   He said to her, "For this saying, go your way. The demon has gone out of your daughter."

(Mark 7 : 30) She went away to her house, and found the child having been laid on the bed, with the demon gone out.

Jesus Heals a Deaf and Mute Man
Mk 7:31-37

(Mark 7 : 31)   Again he departed from the borders of Tyre and Sidon, and came to the sea of Galilee, through the midst of the region of Decapolis.

(Mark 7 : 32) They brought to him one who was deaf and had an impediment in his speech. They begged him to lay his hand on him.

(Mark 7 : 33) He took him aside from the multitude, privately, and put his fingers into his ears, and he spat, and touched his tongue.

(Mark 7 : 34) Looking up to heaven, he sighed, and said to him, "Ephphatha!" that is, "Be opened!"

(Mark 7 : 35) Immediately his ears were opened, and the impediment of his tongue was released, and he spoke clearly.
(Mark 7 : 36) He commanded them that they should tell no one, but the more he commanded them, so much the more widely they proclaimed it.

(Mark 7 : 37) They were astonished beyond measure, saying, "He has done all things well. He makes even the deaf hear, and the mute speak!"

Jesus feed the Four Thousand
Mk 8:1-10 / Mt 15:29-39

(Mark 8 : 1) In those days, when there was a very great multitude, and they had nothing to eat, Jesus called his disciples to himself, and said to them,

(Mark 8 : 2) "I have compassion on the multitude, because they have stayed with me now three days, and have nothing to eat.

(Mark 8 : 3)   If I send them away fasting to their home, they will faint on the way, for some of them have come a long way."

(Mark 8 : 4)   His disciples answered him, "From where could one satisfy these people with bread here in a deserted place?"

(Mark 8 : 5)   He asked them, "How many loaves do you have?" They said, "Seven."

(Mark 8 : 6)   He commanded the multitude to sit down on the ground, and he took the seven loaves. Having given thanks, he broke them, and gave them to his disciples to serve, and they served the multitude.

(Mark 8 : 7)   They had a few small fish. Having blessed them, he said to serve these also.

(Mark 8 : 8)   They ate, and were filled. They took up seven baskets of broken pieces that were left over.

(Mark 8 : 9)   Those who had eaten were about four thousand. Then he sent them away.

(Mark 8 : 10)   Immediately he entered into the boat with his disciples, and came into the region of Dalmanutha.

(Matthew 15 : 29)   Jesus departed there, and came near to the sea of Galilee; and he went up into the mountain, and sat there.

(Matthew 15 : 30)   Great multitudes came to him, having with them the lame, blind, mute, maimed, and many others, and they put them down at his feet. He healed them,

(Matthew 15 : 31)   so that the multitude wondered when they saw the mute speaking, injured whole, lame walking, and blind seeing and they glorified the God of Israel.

(Matthew 15 : 32) Jesus summoned his disciples and said, "I have compassion on the multitude, because they continue with me now three days and have nothing to eat. I don't want to send them away fasting, or they might faint on the way."

(Matthew 15 : 33) The disciples said to him, "Where should we get so many loaves in a deserted place as to satisfy so great a multitude?"

(Matthew 15 : 34)   Jesus said to them, "How many loaves do you have?" They said, "Seven, and a few small fish."

(Matthew 15 : 35)   He commanded the multitude to sit down on the ground;

(Matthew 15 : 36)   and he took the seven loaves and the fish. He gave thanks and broke them, and gave to the disciples, and the disciples to the multitudes.

(Matthew 15 : 37) They all ate, and were filled. They took up seven baskets full of the broken pieces that were left over.

(Matthew 15 : 38)   Those who ate were four thousand men, besides women and children.

> (Matthew 15 : 39) Then he sent away the multitudes, got into the boat, and came into the borders of Magdala.

The Demand for a Sign
Mt 16:1-4 / Mk 8:11-13
/ (Mt 12:38-45) / (Lk 11:29-32 & Lk 11:24-26)

(Matthew 16 : 1) The Pharisees and Sadducees came, and testing him, asked him to show them a sign from heaven.

(Matthew 16 : 2) But he answered them, "When it is evening, you say, It will be fair weather, for the sky is red.'

(Matthew 16 : 3) In the morning, It will be foul weather today, for the sky is red and threatening.' Hypocrites! You know how to discern the appearance of the sky, but you can't discern the signs of the times!

(Matthew 16 : 4) An evil and adulterous generation seeks after a sign, and there will be no sign given to it, except the sign of the prophet Jonah." He left them, and departed.

> (Mark 8 : 11) The Pharisees came out and began to question him, seeking from him a sign from heaven, and testing him.
>
> (Mark 8 : 12) He sighed deeply in his spirit, and said, "Why does this generation seek a sign? Most certainly I tell you, no sign will be given to this generation."

(Mark 8 : 13)   He left them, and again entering into the boat, departed to the other side.

The Yeast of the Pharisees and Herod
Mk 8:14-21

(Mark 8 : 14) They forgot to take bread; and they didn't have more than one loaf in the boat with them.

(Mark 8 : 15) He warned them, saying, "Take heed: beware of the yeast of the Pharisees and the yeast of Herod." (Mark 8 : 16) They reasoned with one another, saying, "It's because we have no bread."

(Mark 8 : 17) Jesus, perceiving it, said to them, "Why do you reason that it's because you have no bread? Don't you perceive yet, neither understand? Is your heart still hardened?

(Mark 8 : 18) Having eyes, don't you see? Having ears, don't you hear? Don't you remember?

(Mark 8 : 19) When I broke the five loaves among the five thousand, how many baskets full of broken pieces did you take up?"

They told him, "Twelve."

(Mark 8 : 20)   "When the seven loaves fed the four thousand, how many baskets full of broken pieces did you take up?"

They told him, "Seven."

(Mark 8 : 21) He asked them, "Don't you understand, yet?"

Jesus Heals a Blind Man at Bethsaida
Mk 8:22-26 / Mt 16:5-12

(Mark 8 : 22)   He came to Bethsaida. They brought a blind man to him, and begged him to touch him.

(Mark 8 : 23)   He took hold of the blind man by the hand, and brought him out of the village. When he had spit on his eyes, and laid his hands on him, he asked him if he saw anything.

(Mark 8 : 24)   He looked up, and said, "I see men; for I see them like trees walking."

(Mark 8 : 25)   Then again he laid his hands on his eyes. He looked intently, and was restored, and saw everyone clearly.

(Mark 8 : 26)   He sent him away to his house, saying, "Don't enter into the village, nor tell anyone in the village."

(Matthew 16 : 5)   The disciples came to the other side and had forgotten to take bread.

(Matthew 16 : 6)   Jesus said to them, "Take heed and beware of the yeast of the Pharisees and Sadducees." (Matthew 16 : 7)   They reasoned among themselves, saying, "We brought no bread."

(Matthew 16 : 8)   Jesus, perceiving it, said, "Why do you reason among yourselves, you of little faith, because you have brought no bread?'

> (Matthew 16 : 9)   Don't you yet perceive, neither remember the five loaves for the five thousand, and how many baskets you took up?
>
> (Matthew 16 : 10)   Nor the seven loaves for the four thousand, and how many baskets you took up?
>
> (Matthew 16 : 11)   How is it that you don't perceive that I didn't speak to you concerning bread? But beware of the yeast of the Pharisees and Sadducees."
>
> (Matthew 16 : 12)   Then they understood that he didn't tell them to beware of the yeast of bread, but of the teaching of the Pharisees and Sadducees.

Peter Declares That Jesus Is Jesus the Christ
Mt 16:13-20 / Mk 8:27-30 / Lk 9:18-20

(Matthew 16 : 13)   Now when Jesus came into the parts of Caesarea Philippi, he asked his disciples, saying, "Who do men say that I, the Son of Man, am?"

(Matthew 16 : 14)   They said, "Some say John the Baptizer, some, Elijah, and others, Jeremiah, or one of the prophets."
(Matthew 16 : 15)   He said to them, "But who do you say that I am?"

(Matthew 16 : 16)   Simon Peter answered, "You are the Christ, the Son of the living God."

(Matthew 16 : 17)   Jesus answered him, "Blessed are you, Simon Bar Jonah, for flesh and blood has not revealed this to you, but my Father who is in heaven.

(Matthew 16 : 18)   I also tell you that you are Peter, and on this rock I will build my assembly, and the gates of Hades will not prevail against it.

(Matthew 16 : 19)   I will give to you the keys of the Kingdom of Heaven, and whatever you bind on earth will have been bound in heaven; and whatever you release on earth will have been released in heaven."

(Matthew 16 : 20)   Then he commanded the disciples that they should tell no one that he was Jesus the Christ.

(Mark 8 : 27)   Jesus went out, with his disciples, into the villages of Caesarea Philippi. On the way he asked his disciples, "Who do men say that I am?"

(Mark 8 : 28)   They told him, "John the Baptizer, and others say Elijah, but others: one of the prophets." (Mark 8 : 29)   He said to them, "But who do you say that I am?" Peter answered, "You are the Christ."

(Mark 8 : 30)   He commanded them that they should tell no one about him.

(Luke 9 : 18)   It happened, as he was praying alone, that the disciples were with him, and he asked them, "Who do the multitudes say that I am?"

(Luke 9 : 19)   They answered, "John the Baptizer,' but others say, Elijah,' and others, that one of the old prophets is risen again."

(Luke 9 : 20)   He said to them, "But who do you say that I am?" Peter answered, "The Christ of God."

Jesus Predicts His Death
Mk 8:31-33 / Mt 16:21-23 / Lk 9:21-22

(Mark 8 : 31)   He began to teach them that the Son of Man must suffer many things, and be rejected by the elders, the chief priests, and the scribes, and be killed, and after three days rise again.

(Mark 8 : 32)   He spoke to them openly. Peter took him, and began to rebuke him.

(Mark 8 : 33)   But he, turning around, and seeing his disciples, rebuked Peter, and said, "Get behind me, Satan! For you have in mind not the things of God, but the things of men."

(Matthew 16 : 21)   From that time, Jesus began to show his disciples that he must go to Jerusalem and suffer many things from the elders, chief priests, and scribes, and be killed, and the third day be raised up.

(Matthew 16 : 22)   Peter took him aside, and began to rebuke him, saying, "Far be it from you, Lord! This will never be done to you."

(Matthew 16 : 23) But he turned, and said to Peter, "Get behind me, Satan! You are a stumbling block to me, for you are not setting your mind on the things of God, but on the things of men."

(Luke 9 : 21)   But he warned them, and commanded them to tell this to no one,

(Luke 9 : 22)   saying, "The Son of Man must suffer many things, and be rejected by the elders, chief priests, and scribes, and be killed, and the third day be raised up."

The Way of the Cross
Mk 8"34-38 & Mk 9:1 / Mt 16:24-28 / Lk 9:23-27

(Mark 8 : 34)   He called the multitude to himself with his disciples, and said to them,

(Mark 8 : 35)   For whoever wants to save his life will lose it; and whoever will lose his life for my sake and the sake of the Good News will save it.

(Mark 8 : 36)   For what does it profit a man, to gain the whole world, and forfeit his life?

(Mark 8 : 37)   For what will a man give in exchange for his life?

(Mark 8 : 38)   For whoever will be ashamed of me and of my words in this adulterous and sinful generation, the Son of Man also will be ashamed of him, when he comes in the glory of his Father with the holy angels."

(Matthew 16 : 24)   Then Jesus said to his disciples, "If anyone desires to come after me, let him deny himself, and take up his cross, and follow me.

(Matthew 16 : 25)   For whoever desires to save his life will lose it, and whoever will lose his life for my sake will find it.

(Matthew 16 : 26)   For what will it profit a man, if he gains the whole world, and forfeits his life? Or what will a man give in exchange for his life?

(Matthew 16 : 27)   For the Son of Man will come in the glory of his Father with his angels, and then he will render to everyone according to his deeds.

(Matthew 16 : 28)   Most certainly I tell you, there are some standing here who will in no way taste of death, until they see the Son of Man coming in his Kingdom."

(Luke 9 : 23)   He said to all, "If anyone desires to come after me, let him deny himself, take up his cross, and follow me.

(Luke 9 : 24)   For whoever desires to save his life will lose it, but whoever will lose his life for my sake, the same will save it.

(Luke 9 : 25)   For what does it profit a man if he gains the whole world, and loses or forfeits his own self?

(Luke 9 : 26)   For whoever will be ashamed of me and of my words, of him will the Son of Man be ashamed, when he comes in his glory, and the glory of the Father, and of the holy angels.

(Luke 9 : 27) But I tell you the truth: There are some of those who stand here, who will in no way taste of death, until they see the Kingdom of God."

(Mark 9 : 1) He said to them, "Most certainly I tell you, there are some standing here who will in no way taste death until they see the Kingdom of God come with power."

The Transfiguration
Mk 9:2-13 / Mt 17:1-13 / Lk 9:28-36

(Mark 9 : 2) After six days Jesus took with him Peter, James, and John, and brought them up onto a high mountain privately by themselves, and he was changed into another form in front of them.

(Mark 9 : 3) His clothing became glistening, exceedingly white, like snow, such as no launderer on earth can whiten them.

(Mark 9 : 4) Elijah and Moses appeared to them, and they were talking with Jesus.

(Mark 9 : 5) Peter answered Jesus, "Rabbi, it is good for us to be here. Let's make three tents: one for you, one for Moses, and one for Elijah."

(Mark 9 : 6) For he didn't know what to say, for they were very afraid.

(Mark 9 : 7)   A cloud came, overshadowing them, and a voice came out of the cloud, "This is my beloved Son. Listen to him."

(Mark 9 : 8)   Suddenly looking around, they saw no one with them any more, except Jesus only.

(Mark 9 : 9)   As they were coming down from the mountain, he commanded them that they should tell no one what things they had seen, until after the Son of Man had risen from the dead.

(Mark 9 : 10)   They kept this saying to themselves, questioning what the "rising from the dead" meant.

(Mark 9 : 11)   They asked him, saying, "Why do the scribes say that Elijah must come first?"

(Mark 9 : 12)   He said to them, "Elijah indeed comes first, and restores all things. How is it written about the Son of Man, that he should suffer many things and be despised?

(Mark 9 : 13)   But I tell you that Elijah has come, and they have also done to him whatever they wanted to, even as it is written about him."

(Matthew 17 : 1)   After six days, Jesus took with him Peter, James, and John his brother, and brought them up into a high mountain by themselves.

(Matthew 17 : 2)   He was transfigured before them. His face shone like the sun, and his garments became as white as the light.

(Matthew 17 : 3)   Behold, Moses and Elijah appeared to them talking with him.

(Matthew 17 : 4)   Peter answered, and said to Jesus, "Lord, it is good for us to be here. If you want, let's make three tents here: one for you, one for Moses, and one for Elijah."

(Matthew 17 : 5)   While he was still speaking, behold, a bright cloud overshadowed them. Behold, a voice came out of the cloud, saying, "This is my beloved Son, in whom I am well pleased. Listen to him."

(Matthew 17 : 6)   When the disciples heard it, they fell on their faces, and were very afraid.

(Matthew 17 : 7)   Jesus came and touched them and said, "Get up, and don't be afraid."

(Matthew 17 : 8)   Lifting up their eyes, they saw no one, except Jesus alone.

(Matthew 17 : 9)   As they were coming down from the mountain, Jesus commanded them, saying,

(Matthew 17 : 10)   His disciples asked him, saying, "Then why do the scribes say that Elijah must come first?"

(Matthew 17 : 11)   Jesus answered them, "Elijah indeed comes first, and will restore all things,

(Matthew 17 : 12)   but I tell you that Elijah has come already, and they didn't recognize him, but did to him whatever they wanted to. Even so the Son of Man will also suffer by them."

(Matthew 17 : 13)   Then the disciples understood that he spoke to them of John the Baptizer.

(Luke 9 : 28)   It happened about eight days after these sayings, that he took with him Peter, John, and James, and went up onto the mountain to pray.

(Luke 9 : 29)   As he was praying, the appearance of his face was altered, and his clothing became white and dazzling.

(Luke 9 : 30)   Behold, two men were talking with him, who were Moses and Elijah,

(Luke 9 : 31)   who appeared in glory, and spoke of his departure, which he was about to accomplish at Jerusalem.

(Luke 9 : 32)   Now Peter and those who were with him were heavy with sleep, but when they were fully awake, they saw his glory, and the two men who stood with him.

(Luke 9 : 33)   It happened, as they were parting from him, that Peter said to Jesus, "Master, it is good for us to be here. Let's make three tents: one for you, and one for Moses, and one for Elijah," not knowing what he said.

(Luke 9 : 34)   While he said these things, a cloud came and overshadowed them, and they were afraid as they entered into the cloud.

(Luke 9 : 35)   A voice came out of the cloud, saying, "This is my beloved Son. Listen to him!"

> (Luke 9 : 36) When the voice came, Jesus was found alone. They were silent, and told no one in those days any of the things which they had seen.

Jesus Heals a Boy Possessed by an Impure Spirit
Mk 9:14-29 / Mt 17:14-21 / Lk 9:37-43

(Mark 9 : 14) Coming to the disciples, he saw a great multitude around them, and scribes questioning them.

(Mark 9 : 15) Immediately all the multitude, when they saw him, were greatly amazed, and running to him greeted him.

(Mark 9 : 16) He asked the scribes, "What are you asking them?"

(Mark 9 : 17) One of the multitude answered, "Teacher, I brought to you my son, who has a mute spirit;

(Mark 9 : 18) and wherever it seizes him, it throws him down, and he foams at the mouth, and grinds his teeth, and wastes away. I asked your disciples to cast it out, and they weren't able."

(Mark 9 : 19) He answered him, "Unbelieving generation, how long shall I be with you? How long shall I bear with you? Bring him to me."

(Mark 9 : 20) They brought him to him, and when he saw him, immediately the spirit convulsed him, and he fell on the ground, wallowing and foaming at the mouth.

(Mark 9 : 21) He asked his father, "How long has it been since this has come to him?" He said, "From childhood.

(Mark 9 : 22)   Often it has cast him both into the fire and into the water, to destroy him. But if you can do anything, have compassion on us, and help us."

(Mark 9 : 23)   Jesus said to him, "If you can believe, all things are possible to him who believes."

(Mark 9 : 24)   Immediately the father of the child cried out with tears, "I believe. Help my unbelief!"

(Mark 9 : 25)   When Jesus saw that a multitude came running together, he rebuked the unclean spirit, saying to him, "You mute and deaf spirit, I command you, come out of him, and never enter him again!"

(Mark 9 : 26)   Having cried out, and convulsed greatly, it came out of him. The boy became like one dead; so much that most of them said, "He is dead."

(Mark 9 : 27)   But Jesus took him by the hand, and raised him up; and he arose.

(Mark 9 : 28)   When he had come into the house, his disciples asked him privately, "Why couldn't we cast it out?"

(Mark 9 : 29)   He said to them, "This kind can come out by nothing, except by prayer and fasting."

(Matthew 17 : 14)   When they came to the multitude, a man came to him, kneeling down to him, saying,

(Matthew 17 : 15)   "Lord, have mercy on my son, for he is epileptic, and suffers grievously; for he often falls into the fire, and often into the water.

(Matthew 17 : 16)   So I brought him to your disciples, and they could not cure him."

(Matthew 17 : 17)   Jesus answered, "Faithless and perverse generation! How long will I be with you? How long will I bear with you? Bring him here to me."

(Matthew 17 : 18)   Jesus rebuked him, the demon went out of him, and the boy was cured from that hour.

(Matthew 17 : 19)   Then the disciples came to Jesus privately, and said, "Why weren't we able to cast it out?"

(Matthew 17 : 20)   He said to them, "Because of your unbelief. For most certainly I tell you, if you have faith as a grain of mustard seed, you will tell this mountain, Move from here to there,' and it will move; and nothing will be impossible for you.

(Matthew 17 : 21)   But this kind doesn't go out except by prayer and fasting."

(Luke 9 : 37)   It happened on the next day, when they had come down from the mountain, that a great multitude met him.

(Luke 9 : 38)   Behold, a man from the crowd called out, saying, "Teacher, I beg you to look at my son, for he is my only child.

(Luke 9 : 39) Behold, a spirit takes him, he suddenly cries out, and it convulses him so that he foams, and it hardly departs from him, bruising him severely.

(Luke 9 : 40)   I begged your disciples to cast it out, and they couldn't."

(Luke 9 : 41)   Jesus answered, "Faithless and perverse generation, how long shall I bc with you and bear with you? Bring your son here."

(Luke 9 : 42)   While he was still coming, the demon threw him down and convulsed him violently. But Jesus rebuked the unclean spirit, and healed the boy, and gave him back to his father.

(Luke 9 : 43)   They were all astonished at the majesty of God. But while all were marveling at all the things which Jesus did, he said to his disciples,

Jesus Predicts His Death a Second Time
Mk 9:30-32 / Mt 17:22-23 / Lk 9:44-45

(Mark 9 : 30)   They went out from there, and passed through Galilee. He didn't want anyone to know it.

(Mark 9 : 31)   For he was teaching his disciples, and said to them, "The Son of Man is being handed over to the hands of men, and they will kill him; and when he is killed, on the third day he will rise again."

(Mark 9 : 32)   But they didn't understand the saying, and were afraid to ask him.

(Matthew 17 : 22) While they were staying in Galilee, Jesus said to them, "The Son of Man is about to be delivered up into the hands of men,

(Matthew 17 : 23)   and they will kill him, and the third day he will be raised up." They were exceedingly sorry.

(Luke 9 : 44)   "Let these words sink into your ears, for the Son of Man will be delivered up into the hands of men."

(Luke 9 : 45)   But they didn't understand this saying. It was concealed from them, that they should not perceive it, and they were afraid to ask him about this saying.

The Temple Tax
Mt 17:24-27

(Matthew 17 : 24) When they had come to Capernaum, those who collected the didrachma coins came to Peter, and said, "Doesn't your teacher pay the didrachma?"

(Matthew 17 : 25)   He said, "Yes." When he came into the house, Jesus anticipated him, saying, "What do you think, Simon? From whom do the kings of the earth receive toll or tribute? From their children, or from strangers?" (Matthew 17 : 26)   Peter said to him, "From strangers." Jesus said to him, "Therefore the children are exempt.

(Matthew 17 : 27)   But, lest we cause them to stumble, go to the sea, cast a hook, and take up the first fish that comes up. When you have opened its mouth, you will find a stater coin.Take that, and give it to them for me and you."

The Greatest in the kingdom of God
Lk 9:46-48 / Mk 9:33-37 / Mt 18:1-5

(Luke 9 : 46)   There arose an argument among them about which of them was the greatest.

(Mark 9 : 33) He came to Capernaum, and when he was in the house he asked them, "What were you arguing among yourselves on the way?"

(Mark 9 : 34) But they were silent, for they had disputed one with another on the way about who was the greatest.

(Mark 9 : 35) He sat down, and called the twelve; and he said to them, "If any man wants to be first, he shall be last of all, and servant of all."

(Matthew 18 : 1)   In that hour the disciples came to Jesus, saying, "Who then is greatest in the Kingdom of Heaven?"

(Matthew 18 : 2)   Jesus called a little child to himself, and set him in their midst,

(Matthew 18 : 3)   and said, "Most certainly I tell you, unless you turn, and become as little children, you will in no way enter into the Kingdom of Heaven.

(Matthew 18 : 4) Whoever therefore humbles himself as this little child, the same is the greatest in the Kingdom of Heaven.

(Matthew 18 : 5)   Whoever receives one such little child in my name receives me,

(Mark 9 : 36)   He took a little child, and set him in their midst. Taking him in his arms, he said to them,

(Mark 9 : 37)   "Whoever receives one such little child in my name, receives me, and whoever receives me, doesn't receive me, but him who sent me."

(Luke 9 : 47)   Jesus, perceiving the reasoning of their hearts, took a little child, and set him by his side,

(Luke 9 : 48)   and said to them, "Whoever receives this little child in my name receives me. Whoever receives me receives him who sent me. For whoever is least among you all, this one will be great."

Whoever Is Not Against Us Is for Us
Mk 9:38-41 / Lk 9:49-50

(Mark 9 : 38)   John said to him, "Teacher, we saw someone who doesn't follow us casting out demons in your name; and we forbade him, because he doesn't follow us."

(Mark 9 : 39)   But Jesus said, "Don't forbid him, for there is no one who will do a mighty work in my name, and be able quickly to speak evil of me.

(Mark 9 : 40)   For whoever is not against us is on our side.

(Mark 9 : 41)   For whoever will give you a cup of water to drink in my name, because you are Christ's, most certainly I tell you, he will in no way lose his reward.

(Luke 9 : 49)   John answered, "Master, we saw someone casting out demons in your name, and we forbade him, because he doesn't follow with us."

(Luke 9 : 50)   Jesus said to him, "Don't forbid him, for he who is not against us is for us."

Causing to Stumble
Mk 9:42-50 / Mt 18:6-9

(Mark 9 : 42)   Whoever will cause one of these little ones who believe in me to stumble, it would be better for him if he were thrown into the sea with a millstone hung around his neck.

(Mark 9 : 43)   If your hand causes you to stumble, cut it off. It is better for you to enter into life maimed, rather than having your two hands to go into Gehenna, into the unquenchable fire,

(Mark 9 : 44)   where their worm doesn't die, and the fire is not quenched.'

(Mark 9 : 45)   If your foot causes you to stumble, cut it off. It is better for you to enter into life lame, rather than having your two feet to be cast into Gehenna, into the fire that will never be quenched

(Mark 9 : 46)   where their worm doesn't die, and the fire is not quenched.'

(Mark 9 : 47)   If your eye causes you to stumble, cast it out. It is better for you to enter into the Kingdom of God with one eye, rather than having two eyes to be cast into the Gehenna

of fire,

(Mark 9 : 48)   where their worm doesn't die, and the fire is not quenched.'

(Mark 9 : 49)   For everyone will be salted with fire, and every sacrifice will be seasoned with salt.

(Mark 9 : 50)   Salt is good, but if the salt has lost its saltiness, with what will you season it? Have salt in yourselves, and be at peace with one another."

(Matthew 18 : 6)   but whoever causes one of these little ones who believe in me to stumble, it would be better for him that a huge millstone should be hung around his neck, and that he should be sunk in the depths of the sea.

(Matthew 18 : 7)   "Woe to the world because of occasions of stumbling! For it must be that the occasions come, but woe to that person through whom the occasion comes!

(Matthew 18 : 8)   If your hand or your foot causes you to stumble, cut it off, and cast it from you. It is better for you to enter into life maimed or crippled, rather than having two hands or two feet to be cast into the eternal fire.

(Matthew 18 : 9) If your eye causes you to stumble, pluck it out, and cast it from you. It is better for you to enter into life with one eye, rather than having two eyes to be cast into the Gehennaof fire.

Dealing With Sin in the Church
Mt 18:15-20

(Matthew 18 : 15) "If your brother sins against you, go, show him his fault between you and him alone. If he listens to you, you have gained back your brother.

(Matthew 18 : 16) But if he doesn't listen, take one or two more with you, that at the mouth of two or three witnesses every word may be established.

(Matthew 18 : 17) If he refuses to listen to them, tell it to the assembly. If he refuses to hear the assembly also, let him be to you as a Gentile or a tax collector.

(Matthew 18 : 18) Most certainly I tell you, whatever things you bind on earth will have been bound in heaven, and whatever things you release on earth will have been released in heaven.

(Matthew 18 : 19) Again, assuredly I tell you, that if two of you will agree on earth concerning anything that they will ask, it will be done for them by my Father who is in heaven.

(Matthew 18 : 20) For where two or three are gathered together in my name, there I am in their midst."

The Parable of the Unmerciful Servant
Mt 18:21-35

(Matthew 18 : 21)   Then Peter came and said to him, "Lord, how often shall my brother sin against me, and I forgive him? Until seven times?"

(Matthew 18 : 22)   Jesus said to him, "I don't tell you until seven times, but, until seventy times seven.

(Matthew 18 : 23)   Therefore the Kingdom of Heaven is like a certain king, who wanted to reconcile accounts with his servants.

(Matthew 18 : 24)   When he had begun to reconcile, one was brought to him who owed him ten thousand talents.

(Matthew 18 : 25)   But because he couldn't pay, his lord commanded him to be sold, with his wife, his children, and all that he had, and payment to be made.

(Matthew 18 : 26) The servant therefore fell down and kneeled before him, saying, Lord, have patience with me, and I will repay you all!'

(Matthew 18 : 27)   The lord of that servant, being moved with compassion, released him, and forgave him the debt.

(Matthew 18 : 28)   "But that servant went out, and found one of his fellow servants, who owed him one hundred denarii, and he grabbed him, and took him by the throat, saying, Pay me what you owe!'

(Matthew 18 : 29)   "So his fellow servant fell down at his feet and begged him, saying, Have patience with me, and I will repay you!'

(Matthew 18 : 30)   He would not, but went and cast him into prison, until he should pay back that which was due.

(Matthew 18 : 31)   So when his fellow servants saw what was done, they were exceedingly sorry, and came and told to their lord all that was done.

(Matthew 18 : 32)   Then his lord called him in, and said to him, You wicked servant! I forgave you all that debt, because you begged me.

(Matthew 18 : 33)   Shouldn't you also have had mercy on your fellow servant, even as I had mercy on you?'

(Matthew 18 : 34)   His lord was angry, and delivered him to the tormentors, until he should pay all that was due to him.

(Matthew 18 : 35)   So my heavenly Father will also do to you, if you don't each forgive your brother from your hearts for his misdeeds."

Samaritan Opposition
Lk 9:51-56

(Luke 9 : 51)   It came to pass, when the days were near that he should be taken up, he intently set his face to go to Jerusalem,

(Luke 9 : 52)   and sent messengers before his face. They went, and entered into a village of the Samaritans, so as to prepare for him.

(Luke 9 : 53) They didn't receive him, because he was traveling with his face set towards Jerusalem.

(Luke 9 : 54) When his disciples, James and John, saw this, they said, "Lord, do you want us to command fire to come down from the sky, and destroy them, just as Elijah did?"

(Luke 9 : 55) But he turned and rebuked them, "You don't know of what kind of spirit you are.

(Luke 9 : 56)   For the Son of Man didn't come to destroy men's lives, but to save them." They went to another village.

The Cost of Following Jesus
Lk 9:57-62 / Mt 8:18-22

(Luke 9 : 57) As they went on the way, a certain man said to him, "I want to follow you wherever you go, Lord."

(Luke 9 : 58) Jesus said to him, "The foxes have holes, and the birds of the sky have nests, but the Son of Man has no place to lay his head."

(Luke 9 : 59) He said to another, "Follow me!"

But he said, "Lord, allow me first to go and bury my father."

(Luke 9 : 60)   But Jesus said to him, "Leave the dead to bury their own dead, but you go and announce the Kingdom of God."

(Luke 9 : 61)   Another also said, "I want to follow you, Lord, but first allow me to say good-bye to those who are at my house."

(Luke 9 : 62)   But Jesus said to him, "No one, having put his hand to the plow, and looking back, is fit for the Kingdom of God."

(Matthew 8 : 18)   Now when Jesus saw great multitudes around him, he gave the order to depart to the other side.

(Matthew 8 : 19)   A scribe came, and said to him, "Teacher, I will follow you wherever you go."

(Matthew 8 : 20)   Jesus said to him, "The foxes have holes, and the birds of the sky have nests, but the Son of Man has nowhere to lay his head."

(Matthew 8 : 21)   Another of his disciples said to him, "Lord, allow me first to go and bury my father." (Matthew 8 : 22)   But Jesus said to him, "Follow me, and leave the dead to bury their own dead."

Jesus sent out Seventy-Two
Lk 10:1-24

(Luke 10 : 1)   Now after these things, the Lord also appointed seventy others, and sent them two by two ahead of him into every city and place, where he was about to come.

(Luke 10 : 2)   Then he said to them, "The harvest is indeed plentiful, but the laborers are few. Pray therefore to the Lord of the harvest, that he may send out laborers into his harvest.

(Luke 10 : 3)   Go your ways. Behold, I send you out as lambs among wolves.

(Luke 10 : 4)   Carry no purse, nor wallet, nor sandals. Greet no one on the way.

(Luke 10 : 5)   Into whatever house you enter, first say, Peace be to this house.'

(Luke 10 : 6)   If a son of peace is there, your peace will rest on him; but if not, it will return to you.

(Luke 10 : 7)   Remain in that same house, eating and drinking the things they give, for the laborer is worthy of his wages. Don't go from house to house.

(Luke 10 : 8)   Into whatever city you enter, and they receive you, eat the things that are set before you.

(Luke 10 : 9)   Heal the sick who are therein, and tell them, The Kingdom of God has come near to you.'

(Luke 10 : 10)   But into whatever city you enter, and they don't receive you, go out into its streets and say,

(Luke 10 : 11)   Even the dust from your city that clings to us, we wipe off against you. Nevertheless know this, that the Kingdom of God has come near to you.'

(Luke 10 : 12)   I tell you, it will be more tolerable in that day for Sodom than for that city.

(Luke 10 : 13)   "Woe to you, Chorazin! Woe to you, Bethsaida! For if the mighty works had been done in Tyre and Sidon which were done in you, they would have repented long ago, sitting in sackcloth and ashes.

(Luke 10 : 14)   But it will be more tolerable for Tyre and Sidon in the judgment than for you.

(Luke 10 : 15)   You, Capernaum, who are exalted to heaven, will be brought down to Hades.

(Luke 10 : 16)   Whoever listens to you listens to me, and whoever rejects you rejects me. Whoever rejects me rejects him who sent me."

(Luke 10 : 17)   The seventy returned with joy, saying, "Lord, even the demons are subject to us in your name!" (Luke 10 : 18)   He said to them, "I saw Satan having fallen like lightning from heaven.

(Luke 10 : 19)   Behold, I give you authority to tread on serpents and scorpions, and over all the power of the enemy. Nothing will in any way hurt you.

(Luke 10 : 20)   Nevertheless, don't rejoice in this, that the spirits are subject to you, but rejoice that your names are written in heaven."

(Luke 10 : 21)   In that same hour Jesus rejoiced in the Holy Spirit, and said, "I thank you, O Father, Lord of heaven and earth, that you have hidden these things from the wise and understanding, and revealed them to little children. Yes, Father, for so it was well-pleasing in your sight."

(Luke 10 : 22)   Turning to the disciples, he said, "All things have been delivered to me by my Father. No one knows who the Son is, except the Father, and who the Father is, except the Son, and he to whomever the Son desires to reveal him."

(Luke 10 : 23)   Turning to the disciples, he said privately, "Blessed are the eyes which see the things that you see,

(Luke 10 : 24)   for I tell you that many prophets and kings desired to see the things which you see, and didn't see them, and to hear the things which you hear, and didn't hear them."

The Parable of the Good Samaritan
Lk 10:25-37

(Luke 10 : 25)   Behold, a certain lawyer stood up and tested him, saying, "Teacher, what shall I do to inherit eternal life?"

(Luke 10 : 26)   He said to him, "What is written in the law? How do you read it?"

(Luke 10 : 27)   He answered, "You shall love the Lord your God with all your heart, with all your soul, with all your strength, and with all your mind; and your neighbor as yourself."

(Luke 10 : 28)   He said to him, "You have answered correctly. Do this, and you will live."

(Luke 10 : 29)   But he, desiring to justify himself, asked Jesus, "Who is my neighbor?"

(Luke 10 : 30)   Jesus answered, "A certain man was going down from Jerusalem to Jericho, and he fell among robbers, who both stripped him and beat him, and departed, leaving him half dead.

(Luke 10 : 31)   By chance a certain priest was going down that way. When he saw him, he passed by on the other side.

(Luke 10 : 32)   In the same way a Levite also, when he came to the place, and saw him, passed by on the other side.

(Luke 10 : 33)   But a certain Samaritan, as he traveled, came where he was. When he saw him, he was moved with compassion,

(Luke 10 : 34)   came to him, and bound up his wounds, pouring on oil and wine. He set him on his own animal, and brought him to an inn, and took care of him.

(Luke 10 : 35)   On the next day, when he departed, he took out two denarii, and gave them to the host, and said to him, Take care of him. Whatever you spend beyond that, I will repay you when I return.'

(Luke 10 : 36)   Now which of these three do you think seemed to be a neighbor to him who fell among the robbers?" (Luke 10 : 37)   He said, "He who showed mercy on him." Then Jesus said to him, "Go and do likewise."

At the Home of Martha and Mary
Lk 10:38-42

(Luke 10 : 38)   It happened as they went on their way, he entered into a certain village, and a certain woman named Martha received him into her house.

(Luke 10 : 39)   She had a sister called Mary, who also sat at Jesus' feet, and heard his word.

(Luke 10 : 40)   But Martha was distracted with much serving, and she came up to him, and said, "Lord, don't you care that my sister left me to serve alone? Ask her therefore to help me."

(Luke 10 : 41)   Jesus answered her, "Martha, Martha, you are anxious and troubled about many things,

(Luke 10 : 42)   but one thing is needed. Mary has chosen the good part, which will not be taken away from her."

Woes on the Pharisees and the Experts in the Law
Lk 11:37-54

(Luke 11 : 37)   Now as he spoke, a certain Pharisee asked him to dine with him. He went in, and sat at the table.

(Luke 11 : 38)   When the Pharisee saw it, he marveled that he had not first washed himself before dinner.

(Luke 11 : 39)   The Lord said to him, "Now you Pharisees cleanse the outside of the cup and of the platter, but your inward part is full of extortion and wickedness.

(Luke 11 : 40)   You foolish ones, didn't he who made the outside make the inside also?

(Luke 11 : 41)   But give for gifts to the needy those things which are within, and behold, all things will be clean to you.

(Luke 11 : 42)   But woe to you Pharisees! For you tithe mint and rue and every herb, but you bypass justice and the love of God. You ought to have done these, and not to have left the other undone.

(Luke 11 : 43)   Woe to you Pharisees! For you love the best seats in the synagogues, and the greetings in the marketplaces.

(Luke 11 : 44)   Woe to you, scribes and Pharisees, hypocrites! For you are like hidden graves, and the men who walk over them don't know it."

(Luke 11 : 45)   One of the lawyers answered him, "Teacher, in saying this you insult us also."

(Luke 11 : 46)   He said, "Woe to you lawyers also! For you load men with burdens that are difficult to carry, and you yourselves won't even lift one finger to help carry those burdens.

(Luke 11 : 47)   Woe to you! For you build the tombs of the prophets, and your fathers killed them.

(Luke 11 : 48)   So you testify and consent to the works of your fathers. For they killed them, and you build their tombs.

(Luke 11 : 49)   Therefore also the wisdom of God said, I will send to them prophets and apostles; and some of them they will kill and persecute,

(Luke 11 : 50)   that the blood of all the prophets, which was shed from the foundation of the world, may be required of this generation;

(Luke 11 : 51)   from the blood of Abel to the blood of Zachariah, who perished between the altar and the sanctuary.' Yes, I tell you, it will be required of this generation.

(Luke 11 : 52)   Woe to you lawyers! For you took away the key of knowledge. You didn't enter in yourselves, and those who were entering in, you hindered."

(Luke 11 : 53)   As he said these things to them, the scribes and the Pharisees began to be terribly angry, and to draw many things out of him;

(Luke 11 : 54)   lying in wait for him, and seeking to catch him in something he might say, that they might accuse him.

Warnings and Encouragements
Lk 12:1-12

(Luke 12 : 1)   Meanwhile, when a multitude of many thousands had gathered together, so much so that they trampled on each other, he began to tell his disciples first of all, "Beware of the yeast of the Pharisees, which is hypocrisy.

(Luke 12 : 2) But there is nothing covered up, that will not be revealed, nor hidden, that will not be known.

(Luke 12 : 3) Therefore whatever you have said in the darkness will be heard in the light. What you have spoken in the ear in the inner rooms will be proclaimed on the housetops.

(Luke 12 : 4) "I tell you, my friends, don't be afraid of those who kill the body, and after that have no more that they can do.

(Luke 12 : 5) But I will warn you whom you should fear. Fear him, who after he has killed, has power to cast into Gehenna. Yes, I tell you, fear him.

(Luke 12 : 6) "Aren't five sparrows sold for two assaria coins? Not one of them is forgotten by God.

(Luke 12 : 7) But the very hairs of your head are all numbered. Therefore, don't be afraid. You are of more value than many sparrows.

(Luke 12 : 8) "I tell you, everyone who confesses me before men, him will the Son of Man also confess before the angels of God;

(Luke 12 : 9) but he who denies me in the presence of men will be denied in the presence of the angels of God.

(Luke 12 : 10) Everyone who speaks a word against the Son of Man will be forgiven, but those who blaspheme against the Holy Spirit will not be forgiven.

(Luke 12 : 11) When they bring you before the synagogues, the rulers, and the authorities, don't be anxious how or what you will answer, or what you will say;

(Luke 12 : 12) for the Holy Spirit will teach you in that same hour what you must say."

The Parable of the Rich Fool
Lk 12:13-21

(Luke 12 : 13)   One of the multitude said to him, "Teacher, tell my brother to divide the inheritance with me."

(Luke 12 : 14)   But he said to him, "Man, who made me a judge or an arbitrator over you?"

(Luke 12 : 15)   He said to them, "Beware! Keep yourselves from covetousness, for a man's life doesn't consist of the abundance of the things which he possesses." (Luke 12 : 16)   He spoke a parable to them, saying, "The ground of a certain rich man produced abundantly.

(Luke 12 : 17)   He reasoned within himself, saying, What will I do, because I don't have room to store my crops?'

(Luke 12 : 18)   He said, This is what I will do. I will pull down my barns, and build bigger ones, and there I will store all my grain and my goods.

(Luke 12 : 19)   I will tell my soul, "Soul, you have many goods laid up for many years. Take your ease, eat, drink, be merry."'

(Luke 12 : 20)   "But God said to him, You foolish one, tonight your soul is required of you. The things which you have prepared whose will they be?'

(Luke 12 : 21)   So is he who lays up treasure for himself, and is not rich toward God."

Watchfulness
Lk 12:35-48 / (Mt 24:36-51 / Mk 13:32-36)

(Luke 12 : 35)   "Let your waist be dressed and your lamps burning.

(Luke 12 : 36)   Be like men watching for their lord, when he returns from the marriage feast; that, when he comes and knocks, they may immediately open to him.

(Luke 12 : 37)   Blessed are those servants, whom the lord will find watching when he comes. Most certainly I tell you, that he will dress himself, and make them recline, and will come and serve them.

(Luke 12 : 38)   They will be blessed if he comes in the second or third watch, and finds them so.

(Luke 12 : 39)   But know this, that if the master of the house had known in what hour the thief was coming, he would have watched, and not allowed his house to be broken into.

(Luke 12 : 40)   Therefore be ready also, for the Son of Man is coming in an hour that you don't expect him."

(Luke 12 : 41)   Peter said to him, "Lord, are you telling this parable to us, or to everybody?"

(Luke 12 : 42)   The Lord said, "Who then is the faithful and wise steward, whom his lord will set over his household, to give them their portion of food at the right times?

(Luke 12 : 43)   Blessed is that servant whom his lord will find doing so when he comes.

(Luke 12 : 44) Truly I tell you, that he will set him over all that he has.

(Luke 12 : 45) But if that servant says in his heart, My lord delays his coming,' and begins to beat the menservants and the maidservants, and to eat and drink, and to be drunken,

(Luke 12 : 46) then the lord of that servant will come in a day when he isn't expecting him, and in an hour that he doesn't know, and will cut him in two, and place his portion with the unfaithful.

(Luke 12 : 47) That servant, who knew his lord's will, and didn't prepare, nor do what he wanted, will be beaten with many stripes,

(Luke 12 : 48) but he who didn't know, and did things worthy of stripes, will be beaten with few stripes. To whomever much is given, of him will much be required; and to whom much was entrusted, of him more will be asked.

Not Peace but Division
Lk 12:49-53 / (Mt 10:34-36)

(Luke 12 : 49) "I came to throw fire on the earth. I wish it were already kindled.

(Luke 12 : 50) But I have a baptism to be baptized with, and how distressed I am until it is accomplished!

(Luke 12 : 51) Do you think that I have come to give peace in the earth? I tell you, no, but rather division.

(Luke 12 : 52)   For from now on, there will be five in one house divided, three against two, and two against three.

(Luke 12 : 53)   They will be divided, father against son, and son against father; mother against daughter, and daughter against her mother; mother-in-law against her daughter-in-law, and daughter-in-law against her mother-in-law."

Interpreting the Times
Lk 12:54-59

(Luke 12 : 54)   He said to the multitudes also, "When you see a cloud rising from the west, immediately you say, A shower is coming,' and so it happens.

(Luke 12 : 55)   When a south wind blows, you say, There will be a scorching heat,' and it happens.

(Luke 12 : 56)   You hypocrites! You know how to interpret the appearance of the earth and the sky, but how is it that you don't interpret this time?

(Luke 12 : 57)   Why don't you judge for yourselves what is right?

(Luke 12 : 58)   For when you are going with your adversary before the magistrate, try diligently on the way to be released from him, lest perhaps he drag you to the judge, and the judge deliver you to the officer, and the officer throw you into prison.

(Luke 12 : 59)   I tell you, you will by no means get out of there, until you have paid the very last penny."

Repent or Perish
Lk 13:1-9

(Luke 13 : 1)   Now there were some present at the same time who told him about the Galileans, whose blood Pilate had mixed with their sacrifices.

(Luke 13 : 2)   Jesus answered them, "Do you think that these Galileans were worse sinners than all the other Galileans, because they suffered such things?

(Luke 13 : 3)   I tell you, no, but unless you repent, you will all perish in the same way.

(Luke 13 : 4)   Or those eighteen, on whom the tower in Siloam fell, and killed them; do you think that they were worse offenders than all the men who dwell in Jerusalem?

(Luke 13 : 5)   I tell you, no, but, unless you repent, you will all perish in the same way."

(Luke 13 : 6)   He spoke this parable. "A certain man had a fig tree planted in his vineyard, and he came seeking fruit on it, and found none.

(Luke 13 : 7)   He said to the vine dresser, Behold, these three years I have come looking for fruit on this fig tree, and found none. Cut it down. Why does it waste the soil?'

(Luke 13 : 8)   He answered, Lord, leave it alone this year also, until I dig around it, and fertilize it.

(Luke 13 : 9)   If it bears fruit, fine; but if not, after that, you can cut it down.'"

Jesus Heals a Crippled Woman on the Sabbath
Lk 13:10-17

(Luke 13 : 10)   He was teaching in one of the synagogues on the Sabbath day.

(Luke 13 : 11)   Behold, there was a woman who had a spirit of infirmity eighteen years, and she was bent over, and could in no way straighten herself up.

(Luke 13 : 12) When Jesus saw her, he called her, and said to her, "Woman, you are freed from your infirmity."

(Luke 13 : 13)   He laid his hands on her, and immediately she stood up straight, and glorified God.

(Luke 13 : 14) The ruler of the synagogue, being indignant because Jesus had healed on the Sabbath, said to the multitude, "There are six days in which men ought to work. Therefore come on those days and be healed, and not on the Sabbath day!"

(Luke 13 : 15) Therefore the Lord answered him, "You hypocrites! Doesn't each one of you free his ox or his donkey from the stall on the Sabbath, and lead him away to water?

(Luke 13 : 16) Ought not this woman, being a daughter of Abraham, whom Satan had bound eighteen long years, be freed from this bondage on the Sabbath day?"

(Luke 13 : 17)   As he said these things, all his adversaries were disappointed, and all the multitude rejoiced for all the glorious things that were done by him.

The Parable of the Mustard Seed
and leavened flour
Mk 4:30-34 / Lk 13:18-21 / Mt 13:31-35

(Mark 4 : 30)   He said, "How will we liken the Kingdom of God? Or with what parable will we illustrate it?

(Mark 4 : 31)   It's like a grain of mustard seed, which, when it is sown in the earth, though it is less than all the seeds that are on the earth,

(Mark 4 : 32)   yet when it is sown, grows up, and becomes greater than all the herbs, and puts out great branches, so that the birds of the sky can lodge under its shadow."

(Mark 4 : 33)   With many such parables he spoke the word to them, as they were able to hear it.

(Mark 4 : 34)   Without a parable he didn't speak to them; but privately to his own disciples he explained everything.

(Matthew 13 : 31)   He set another parable before them, saying, "The Kingdom of Heaven is like a grain of mustard seed, which a man took, and sowed in his field;

(Matthew 13 : 32)   which indeed is smaller than all seeds. But when it is grown, it is greater than the herbs, and becomes a tree, so that the birds of the air come and lodge in its branches."

(Matthew 13 : 33)   He spoke another parable to them. "The Kingdom of Heaven is like yeast, which a

---

woman took, and hid in three measures of meal, until it was all leavened."

(Matthew 13 : 34)   Jesus spoke all these things in parables to the multitudes; and without a parable, he didn't speak to them,

(Matthew 13 : 35)   that it might be fulfilled which was spoken through the prophet, saying, "I will open my mouth in parables; I will utter things hidden from the foundation of the world."

(Luke 13 : 18) He said, "What is the Kingdom of God like? To what shall I compare it?

(Luke 13 : 19)   It is like a grain of mustard seed, which a man took, and put in his own garden. It grew, and became a large tree, and the birds of the sky lodged in its branches."

(Luke 13 : 20)   Again he said, "To what shall I compare the Kingdom of God?

(Luke 13 : 21)   It is like yeast, which a woman took and hid in three measures of flour, until it was all leavened."

The Narrow Door
Lk 13:22-30 / (Mt 7:13-14)

(Luke 13 : 22)   He went on his way through cities and villages, teaching, and traveling on to Jerusalem.

(Luke 13 : 23)   One said to him, "Lord, are they few who are saved?" He said to them,

(Luke 13 : 24)   "Strive to enter in by the narrow door, for many, I tell you, will seek to enter in, and will not be able.

(Luke 13 : 25)   When once the master of the house has risen up, and has shut the door, and you begin to stand outside, and to knock at the door, saying, Lord, Lord, open to us!' then he will answer and tell you, I don't know you or where you come from.'

(Luke 13 : 26)   Then you will begin to say, We ate and drank in your presence, and you taught in our streets.'

(Luke 13 : 27)   He will say, I tell you, I don't know where you come from. Depart from me, all you workers of iniquity.'

(Luke 13 : 28)   There will be weeping and gnashing of teeth, when you see Abraham, Isaac, Jacob, and all the prophets, in the Kingdom of God, and yourselves being thrown outside.

(Luke 13 : 29)   They will come from the east, west, north, and south, and will sit down in the Kingdom of God.

(Luke 13 : 30) Behold, there are some who are last who will be first, and there are some who are first who will be last."

Jesus' Sorrow for Jerusalem
Lk 13:31-35

(Luke 13 : 31) On that same day, some Pharisees came, saying to him, "Get out of here, and go away, for Herod wants to kill you."

(Luke 13 : 32) He said to them, "Go and tell that fox, Behold, I cast out demons and perform cures today and tomorrow, and the third day I complete my mission.

(Luke 13 : 33) Nevertheless I must go on my way today and tomorrow and the next day, for it can't be that a prophet perish outside of Jerusalem.'

(Luke 13 : 34) "Jerusalem, Jerusalem, that kills the prophets, and stones those who are sent to her! How often I wanted to gather your children together, like a hen gathers her own brood under her wings, and you refused!

(Luke 13 : 35) Behold, your house is left to you desolate. I tell you, you will not see me, until you say, Blessed is he who comes in the name of the Lord!'"

Healing on Sabath day
Lk 14:1-6

(Luke 14 : 1) It happened, when he went into the house of one of the rulers of the Pharisees on a Sabbath to eat bread, that they were watching him.

(Luke 14 : 2) Behold, a certain man who had dropsy was in front of him.

(Luke 14 : 3)   Jesus, answering, spoke to the lawyers and Pharisees, saying, "Is it lawful to heal on the Sabbath?"

(Luke 14 : 4)   But they were silent. He took him, and healed him, and let him go.

(Luke 14 : 5)   He answered them, "Which of you, if your son or an ox fell into a well, wouldn't immediately pull him out on a Sabbath day?"

(Luke 14 : 6)   They couldn't answer him regarding these things.

The Parable of being humble in a Banquet
Lk 14:7-14

(Luke 14 : 7)   He spoke a parable to those who were invited, when he noticed how they chose the best seats, and said to them,

(Luke 14 : 8)   "When you are invited by anyone to a marriage feast, don't sit in the best seat, since perhaps someone more honorable than you might be invited by him,

(Luke 14 : 9)   and he who invited both of you would come and tell you, Make room for this person.' Then you would begin, with shame, to take the lowest place.

(Luke 14 : 10)   But when you are invited, go and sit in the lowest place, so that when he who invited you comes, he may tell you, Friend, move up higher.' Then you will be honored in the presence of all who sit at the table with you.

(Luke 14 : 11)   For everyone who exalts himself will be humbled, and whoever humbles himself will be exalted."

(Luke 14 : 12)   He also said to the one who had invited him, "When you make a dinner or a supper, don't call your friends, nor your brothers, nor your kinsmen, nor rich neighbors, or perhaps they might also return the favor, and pay you back.

(Luke 14 : 13)   But when you make a feast, ask the poor, the maimed, the lame, or the blind;

(Luke 14 : 14)   and you will be blessed, because they don't have the resources to repay you. For you will be repaid in the resurrection of the righteous."

The Parable of the Great Banquet
14:16-24Ref — Mt 22:2-14

(Luke 14 : 15)   When one of those who sat at the table with him heard these things, he said to him, "Blessed is he who will feast in the Kingdom of God!"

(Luke 14 : 16)   But he said to him, "A certain man made a great supper, and he invited many people.

(Luke 14 : 17)   He sent out his servant at supper time to tell those who were invited, Come, for everything is ready now.'

(Luke 14 : 18)   They all as one began to make excuses.

"The first said to him, I have bought a field, and I must go and see it. Please have me excused.:

(Luke 14 : 19)   "Another said, I have bought five yokes of oxen, and I must go try them out. Please have me excused.'

(Luke 14 : 20)   "Another said, I have married a wife, and therefore I can't come.'

(Luke 14 : 21)   "That servant came, and told his lord these things. Then the master of the house, being angry, said to his servant, Go out quickly into the streets and lanes of the city, and bring in the poor, maimed, blind, and lame.'

(Luke 14 : 22)   "The servant said, Lord, it is done as you commanded, and there is still room.'

(Luke 14 : 23)   "The lord said to the servant, Go out into the highways and hedges, and compel them to come in, that my house may be filled.

(Luke 14 : 24)   For I tell you that none of those men who were invited will taste of my supper.'"

(Matthew 22 : 1)   Jesus answered and spoke again in parables to them, saying,

(Matthew 22 : 2)   "The Kingdom of Heaven is like a certain king, who made a marriage feast for his son,

(Matthew 22 : 3)   and sent out his servants to call those who were invited to the marriage feast, but they would not come.

(Matthew 22 : 4)   Again he sent out other servants, saying, Tell those who are invited, "Behold, I have prepared my dinner. My cattle and my fatlings are killed, and all things are ready. Come to the marriage feast!"'

(Matthew 22 : 5)   But they made light of it, and went their ways, one to his own farm, another to his merchandise,

(Matthew 22 : 6)   and the rest grabbed his servants, and treated them shamefully, and killed them.

(Matthew 22 : 7)   When the king heard that, he was angry, and sent his armies, destroyed those murderers, and burned their city.

(Matthew 22 : 8)   "Then he said to his servants, The wedding is ready, but those who were invited weren't worthy.

(Matthew 22 : 9)   Go therefore to the intersections of the highways, and as many as you may find, invite to the marriage feast.'

(Matthew 22 : 10)   Those servants went out into the highways, and gathered together as many as they found, both bad and good. The wedding was filled with guests.

(Matthew 22 : 11)   But when the king came in to see the guests, he saw there a man who didn't have on wedding clothing,

(Matthew 22 : 12)   and he said to him, Friend, how did you come in here not wearing wedding clothing?' He was speechless.

(Matthew 22 : 13)   Then the king said to the servants, Bind him hand and foot, take him away, and throw him into the outer darkness; there is where the weeping and grinding of teeth will be.'

(Matthew 22 : 14)   For many are called, but few chosen."

The Cost of Being a Disciple
Lk 14:25-35

(Luke 14 : 25)   Now great multitudes were going with him. He turned and said to them,

(Luke 14 : 26)   "If anyone comes to me, and doesn't disregard his own father, mother, wife, children, brothers, and sisters, yes, and his own life also, he can't be my disciple.

(Luke 14 : 27)   Whoever doesn't bear his own cross, and come after me, can't be my disciple.

(Luke 14 : 28)   For which of you, desiring to build a tower, doesn't first sit down and count the cost, to see if he has enough to complete it?

(Luke 14 : 29)   Or perhaps, when he has laid a foundation, and is not able to finish, everyone who sees begins to mock him,

(Luke 14 : 30)   saying, This man began to build, and wasn't able to finish.'

(Luke 14 : 31)   Or what king, as he goes to encounter another king in war, will not sit down first and consider whether he is able with ten thousand to meet him who comes against him with twenty thousand?

(Luke 14 : 32)   Or else, while the other is yet a great way off, he sends an envoy, and asks for conditions of peace.

(Luke 14 : 33)   So therefore whoever of you who doesn't renounce all that he has, he can't be my disciple. (Luke 14 : 34)   Salt is good, but if the salt becomes flat and tasteless, with what do you season it?

(Luke 14 : 35)   It is fit neither for the soil nor for the manure pile. It is thrown out. He who has ears to hear, let him hear."

The Parable of the Wandering Sheep
Lk 15:1-7 / Mt 18:10-14

(Luke 15 : 1)   Now all the tax collectors and sinners were coming close to him to hear him.

(Luke 15 : 2)   The Pharisees and the scribes murmured, saying, "This man welcomes sinners, and eats with them."

(Luke 15 : 3)   He told them this parable.

(Matthew 18 : 10)   See that you don't despise one of these little ones, for I tell you that in heaven their angels always see the face of my Father who is in heaven.

(Matthew 18 : 11)   For the Son of Man came to save that which was lost.

(Matthew 18 : 12)   "What do you think? If a man has one hundred sheep, and one of them goes astray, doesn't he leave the ninety-nine, go to the mountains, and seek that which has gone astray?

(Matthew 18 : 13)   If he finds it, most certainly I tell you, he rejoices over it more than over the ninety-nine which have not gone astray.

> (Luke 15 : 4)   "Which of you men, if you had one hundred sheep, and lost one of them, wouldn't leave the ninety-nine in the wilderness, and go after the one that was lost, until he found it?
>
> (Luke 15 : 5)   When he has found it, he carries it on his shoulders, rejoicing.

(Luke 15 : 6)   When he comes home, he calls together his friends and his neighbors, saying to them, Rejoice with me, for I have found my sheep which was lost!'

(Luke 15 : 7)   I tell you that even so there will be more joy in heaven over one sinner who repents, than over ninety-nine righteous people who need no repentance.

(Matthew 18 : 14)   Even so it is not the will of your Father who is in heaven that one of these little ones should perish.

The Parable of the Lost Coin
Lk 15:8-10

(Luke 15 : 8)   Or what woman, if she had ten drachma coins, if she lost one drachma coin, wouldn't light a lamp, sweep the house, and seek diligently until she found it?

(Luke 15 : 9)   When she has found it, she calls together her friends and neighbors, saying, Rejoice with me, for I have found the drachma which I had lost.'

(Luke 15 : 10)   Even so, I tell you, there is joy in the presence of the angels of God over one sinner repenting."

The Parable of the Lost Son
Lk 15:11-32

(Luke 15 : 11)   He said, "A certain man had two sons.

(Luke 15 : 12)   The younger of them said to his father, Father, give me my share of your property.' He divided his livelihood between them.

(Luke 15 : 13)   Not many days after, the younger son gathered all of this together and traveled into a far country. There he wasted his property with riotous living.

(Luke 15 : 14)   When he had spent all of it, there arose a severe famine in that country, and he began to be in need.

(Luke 15 : 15)   He went and joined himself to one of the citizens of that country, and he sent him into his fields to feed pigs.

(Luke 15 : 16)   He wanted to fill his belly with the husks that the pigs ate, but no one gave him any. (Luke 15 : 17)   But when he came to himself he said, How many hired servants of my father's have bread enough to spare, and I'm dying with hunger!

(Luke 15 : 18)   I will get up and go to my father, and will tell him, "Father, I have sinned against heaven, and in your sight.

(Luke 15 : 19)   I am no more worthy to be called your son. Make me as one of your hired servants."'

(Luke 15 : 20)   "He arose, and came to his father. But while he was still far off, his father saw him, and was moved with compassion, and ran, and fell on his neck, and kissed him.

(Luke 15 : 21)   The son said to him, Father, I have sinned against heaven, and in your sight. I am no longer worthy to be called your son.'

(Luke 15 : 22)   "But the father said to his servants, Bring out the best robe, and put it on him. Put a ring on his hand, and shoes on his feet.

(Luke 15 : 23)   Bring the fattened calf, kill it, and let us eat, and celebrate;

(Luke 15 : 24)   for this, my son, was dead, and is alive again. He was lost, and is found.' They began to celebrate. (Luke 15 : 25)   "Now his elder son was in the field. As he came near to the house, he heard music and dancing.

(Luke 15 : 26)   He called one of the servants to him, and asked what was going on.

(Luke 15 : 27)   He said to him, Your brother has come, and your father has killed the fattened calf, because he has received him back safe and healthy.'

(Luke 15 : 28)   But he was angry, and would not go in. Therefore his father came out, and begged him.

(Luke 15 : 29)   But he answered his father, Behold, these many years I have served you, and I never disobeyed a commandment of yours, but you never gave me a goat, that I might celebrate with my friends.

(Luke 15 : 30) But when this, your son, came, who has devoured your living with prostitutes, you killed the fattened calf for him.'

(Luke 15 : 31) "He said to him, Son, you are always with me, and all that is mine is yours.

(Luke 15 : 32) But it was appropriate to celebrate and be glad, for this, your brother, was dead, and is alive again. He was lost, and is found.'"

The Parable of the Shrewd Manager
Lk 16:1-14

(Luke 16 : 1) He also said to his disciples, "There was a certain rich man who had a manager. An accusation was made to him that this man was wasting his possessions.

(Luke 16 : 2) He called him, and said to him, What is this that I hear about you? Give an accounting of your management, for you can no longer be manager.'

(Luke 16 : 3) "The manager said within himself, What will I do, seeing that my lord is taking away the management position from me? I don't have strength to dig. I am ashamed to beg.

(Luke 16 : 4) I know what I will do, so that when I am removed from management, they may receive me into their houses.'

(Luke 16 : 5) Calling each one of his lord's debtors to him, he said to the first, How much do you owe to my lord?'

(Luke 16 : 6)   He said, A hundred batos of oil.' He said to him, Take your bill, and sit down quickly and write fifty.'

(Luke 16 : 7)   Then he said to another, How much do you owe?' He said, A hundred cors of wheat.' He said to him, Take your bill, and write eighty.'

(Luke 16 : 8)   "His lord commended the dishonest manager because he had done wisely, for the children of this world are, in their own generation, wiser than the children of the light.

(Luke 16 : 9)   I tell you, make for yourselves friends by means of unrighteous mammon, so that when you fail, they may receive you into the eternal tents.

(Luke 16 : 10)   He who is faithful in a very little is faithful also in much. He who is dishonest in a very little is also dishonest in much.

(Luke 16 : 11)   If therefore you have not been faithful in the unrighteous mammon, who will commit to your trust the true riches?

(Luke 16 : 12)   If you have not been faithful in that which is another's, who will give you that which is your own?

(Luke 16 : 13)   No servant can serve two masters, for either he will hate the one, and love the other; or else he will hold to one, and despise the other. You aren't able to serve God and Mammon."

(Luke 16 : 14)   The Pharisees, who were lovers of money, also heard all these things, and they scoffed at him.

Additional Teachings
Lk 16:15-18

(Luke 16 : 15)   He said to them, "You are those who justify yourselves in the sight of men, but God knows your hearts. For that which is exalted among men is an abomination in the sight of God.

(Luke 16 : 16)   The law and the prophets were until John. From that time the Good News of the Kingdom of God is preached, and everyone is forcing his way into it.

(Luke 16 : 17)   But it is easier for heaven and earth to pass away, than for one tiny stroke of a pen in the law to fall.

(Luke 16 : 18)   Everyone who divorces his wife, and marries another, commits adultery. He who marries one who is divorced from a husband commits adultery.

The Rich Man and Lazarus
Lk 16:19-31

(Luke 16 : 19)   "Now there was a certain rich man, and he was clothed in purple and fine linen, living in luxury every day.

(Luke 16 : 20)   A certain beggar, named Lazarus, was laid at his gate, full of sores,

(Luke 16 : 21)   and desiring to be fed with the crumbs that fell from the rich man's table. Yes, even the dogs came and licked his sores.

(Luke 16 : 22)   It happened that the beggar died, and that he was carried away by the angels to Abraham's bosom. The rich man also died, and was buried.

(Luke 16 : 23)   In Hades, he lifted up his eyes, being in torment, and saw Abraham far off, and Lazarus at his bosom.

(Luke 16 : 24)   He cried and said, Father Abraham, have mercy on me, and send Lazarus, that he may dip the tip of his finger in water, and cool my tongue! For I am in anguish in this flame.'

(Luke 16 : 25) "But Abraham said, Son, remember that you, in your lifetime, received your good things, and Lazarus, in the same way, bad things. But now here he is comforted and you are in anguish.

(Luke 16 : 26)   Besides all this, between us and you there is a great gulf fixed, that those who want to pass from here to you are not able, and that no one may cross over from there to us.'

(Luke 16 : 27)   "He said, I ask you therefore, father, that you would send him to my father's house;

(Luke 16 : 28)   for I have five brothers, that he may testify to them, so they won't also come into this place of torment.'

(Luke 16 : 29)   "But Abraham said to him, They have Moses and the prophets. Let them listen to them.'

(Luke 16 : 30)   "He said, No, father Abraham, but if one goes to them from the dead, they will repent.'
(Luke 16 : 31)   "He said to him, If they don't listen to Moses

and the prophets, neither will they be persuaded if one rises from the dead.'"

Sin, Faith, Duty
Lk 17:1-10

(Luke 17 : 1)   He said to the disciples, "It is impossible that no occasions of stumbling should come, but woe to him through whom they come!

(Luke 17 : 2)   It would be better for him if a millstone were hung around his neck, and he were thrown into the sea, rather than that he should cause one of these little ones to stumble.

(Luke 17 : 3)   Be careful. If your brother sins against you, rebuke him. If he repents, forgive him.

(Luke 17 : 4)   If he sins against you seven times in the day, and seven times returns, saying, I repent,' you shall forgive him."

(Luke 17 : 5)   The apostles said to the Lord, "Increase our faith."

(Luke 17 : 6)   The Lord said, "If you had faith like a grain of mustard seed, you would tell this sycamore tree, Be uprooted, and be planted in the sea,' and it would obey you.

(Luke 17 : 7)   But who is there among you, having a servant plowing or keeping sheep, that will say, when he comes in from the field, Come immediately and sit down at the table,'

(Luke 17 : 8)   and will not rather tell him, Prepare my supper, clothe yourself properly, and serve me, while I eat and drink. Afterward you shall eat and drink'?

(Luke 17 : 9)   Does he thank that servant because he did the things that were commanded? I think not.

(Luke 17 : 10)   Even so you also, when you have done all the things that are commanded you, say, We are unworthy servants. We have done our duty.'"

Jesus Heals Ten Men With Leprosy
Lk 17:11-19

(Luke 17 : 11)   It happened as he was on his way to Jerusalem, that he was passing along the borders of Samaria and Galilee.

(Luke 17 : 12)   As he entered into a certain village, ten men who were lepers met him, who stood at a distance.

(Luke 17 : 13)   They lifted up their voices, saying, "Jesus, Master, have mercy on us!"

(Luke 17 : 14)   When he saw them, he said to them, "Go and show yourselves to the priests." It happened that as they went, they were cleansed.

(Luke 17 : 15)   One of them, when he saw that he was healed, turned back, glorifying God with a loud voice.

(Luke 17 : 16)   He fell on his face at Jesus' feet, giving him thanks; and he was a Samaritan.

(Luke 17 : 17)   Jesus answered, "Weren't the ten cleansed? But where are the nine?

(Luke 17 : 18)   Were there none found who returned to give glory to God, except this stranger?"

(Luke 17 : 19)   Then he said to him, "Get up, and go your way. Your faith has healed you."

The Coming of the Kingdom of God
17:26,27pp — Mt 24:37-39

(Luke 17 : 20)   Being asked by the Pharisees when the Kingdom of God would come, he answered them, "The Kingdom of God doesn't come with observation;

(Luke 17 : 21)   neither will they say, Look, here!' or, Look, there!' for behold, the Kingdom of God is within you."

(Luke 17 : 22)   He said to the disciples, "The days will come, when you will desire to see one of the days of the Son of Man, and you will not see it.

(Luke 17 : 23)   They will tell you, Look, here!' or Look, there!' Don't go away, nor follow after them,

(Luke 17 : 24)   for as the lightning, when it flashes out of the one part under the sky, shines to the other part under the sky; so will the Son of Man be in his day.

(Luke 17 : 25)   But first, he must suffer many things and be rejected by this generation.

(Luke 17 : 26)   As it happened in the days of Noah, even so will it be also in the days of the Son of Man.

(Luke 17 : 27)   They ate, they drank, they married, they were given in marriage, until the day that Noah entered into the ship, and the flood came, and destroyed them all.

(Luke 17 : 28)   Likewise, even as it happened in the days of Lot: they ate, they drank, they bought, they sold, they planted, they built;

(Luke 17 : 29)   but in the day that Lot went out from Sodom, it rained fire and sulfur from the sky, and destroyed them all.

(Luke 17 : 30)   It will be the same way in the day that the Son of Man is revealed.

(Luke 17 : 31)   In that day, he who will be on the housetop, and his goods in the house, let him not go down to take them away. Let him who is in the field likewise not turn back.

(Luke 17 : 32)   Remember Lot's wife!

(Luke 17 : 33)   Whoever seeks to save his life loses it, but whoever loses his life preserves it.

(Luke 17 : 34)   I tell you, in that night there will be two people in one bed. The one will be taken, and the other will be left.

(Luke 17 : 35)   There will be two grinding grain together. One will be taken, and the other will be left."

(Luke 17 : 36)   [36]

(Luke 17 : 37)   They, answering, asked him, "Where, Lord?" He said to them, "Where the body is, there will the vultures also be gathered together."

The Parable of the Persistent Widow
Lk 18:1-8

(Luke 18 : 1)   He also spoke a parable to them that they must always pray, and not give up,

(Luke 18 : 2)   saying, "There was a judge in a certain city who didn't fear God, and didn't respect man.

(Luke 18 : 3)   A widow was in that city, and she often came to him, saying, Defend me from my adversary!' (Luke 18 : 4)   He wouldn't for a while, but afterward he said to himself, Though I neither fear God, nor respect man,

(Luke 18 : 5)   yet because this widow bothers me, I will defend her, or else she will wear me out by her continual coming.'"

(Luke 18 : 6)   The Lord said, "Listen to what the unrighteous judge says.

(Luke 18 : 7)   Won't God avenge his chosen ones, who are crying out to him day and night, and yet he exercises patience with them?

(Luke 18 : 8)   I tell you that he will avenge them quickly. Nevertheless, when the Son of Man comes, will he find faith on the earth?"

The Parable of the Pharisee and the Tax Collector
Lk 18:9-14

(Luke 18 : 9)   He spoke also this parable to certain people who were convinced of their own righteousness, and who despised all others.

(Luke 18 : 10)   "Two men went up into the temple to pray; one was a Pharisee, and the other was a tax collector.

(Luke 18 : 11)   The Pharisee stood and prayed to himself like this: God, I thank you, that I am not like the rest of men, extortionists, unrighteous, adulterers, or even like this tax collector.

(Luke 18 : 12)   I fast twice a week. I give tithes of all that I get.'

(Luke 18 : 13)   But the tax collector, standing far away, wouldn't even lift up his eyes to heaven, but beat his breast, saying, God, be merciful to me, a sinner!'

(Luke 18 : 14)   I tell you, this man went down to his house justified rather than the other; for everyone who exalts himself will be humbled, but he who humbles himself will be exalted."

Question about Divorce
Mk 10: 1 - 12 / Mt 19 : 1 - 12

(Mark 10 : 1)   He arose from there and came into the borders of Judea and beyond the Jordan. Multitudes came together to him again. As he usually did, he was again teaching them.

(Mark 10 : 2)   Pharisees came to him testing him, and asked him, "Is it lawful for a man to divorce his wife?"

(Mark 10 : 3)   He answered, "What did Moses command you?"

(Mark 10 : 4)   They said, "Moses allowed a certificate of divorce to be written, and to divorce her."

(Mark 10 : 5)   But Jesus said to them, "For your hardness of heart, he wrote you this commandment.

(Mark 10 : 6)   But from the beginning of the creation, God made them male and female.

(Mark 10 : 7)   For this cause a man will leave his father and mother, and will join to his wife,

(Mark 10 : 8)   and the two will become one flesh, so that they are no longer two, but one flesh.

(Mark 10 : 9)   What therefore God has joined together, let no man separate."

(Mark 10 : 10)   In the house, his disciples asked him again about the same matter.

(Mark 10 : 11)   He said to them, "Whoever divorces his wife, and marries another, commits adultery against her.

(Mark 10 : 12)   If a woman herself divorces her husband, and marries another, she commits adultery."

(Matthew 19 : 1)   It happened when Jesus had finished these words, he departed from Galilee, and came into the borders of Judea beyond the Jordan.

(Matthew 19 : 2)   Great multitudes followed him, and he healed them there.

(Matthew 19 : 3) Pharisees came to him, testing him, and saying, "Is it lawful for a man to divorce his wife for any reason?"

(Matthew 19 : 4)   He answered, "Haven't you read that he who made them from the beginning made them male and female,

(Matthew 19 : 5)   and said, For this cause a man shall leave his father and mother, and shall join to his wife; and the two shall become one flesh?'

(Matthew 19 : 6)   So that they are no more two, but one flesh. What therefore God has joined together, don't let man tear apart."

(Matthew 19 : 7)   They asked him, "Why then did Moses command us to give her a bill of divorce, and divorce her?"

(Matthew 19 : 8)   He said to them, "Moses, because of the hardness of your hearts, allowed you to divorce your wives, but from the beginning it has not been so.

(Matthew 19 : 9)   I tell you that whoever divorces his wife, except for sexual immorality, and marries another, commits adultery; and he who marries her when she is divorced commits adultery."

(Matthew 19 : 10)   His disciples said to him, "If this is the case of the man with his wife, it is not expedient to marry."

(Matthew 19 : 11)   But he said to them, "Not all men can receive this saying, but those to whom it is given.

(Matthew 19 : 12)   For there are eunuchs who were born that way from their mother's womb, and there are eunuchs who were made eunuchs by men; and there are eunuchs who made themselves eunuchs for the Kingdom of Heaven's sake. He who is able to receive it, let him receive it."

The Little Children and Jesus
Mk 10:13-16 / Mt 19:13-15 / Lk 18:15-17

(Mark 10 : 13)   They were bringing to him little children, that he should touch them, but the disciples rebuked those who were bringing them.

(Mark 10 : 14)   But when Jesus saw it, he was moved with indignation, and said to them, "Allow the little children to come to me! Don't forbid them, for the Kingdom of God belongs to such as these.

(Mark 10 : 15)   Most certainly I tell you, whoever will not receive the Kingdom of God like a little child, he will in no way enter into it."

(Mark 10 : 16)   He took them in his arms, and blessed them, laying his hands on them.

(Matthew 19 : 13)   Then little children were brought to him, that he should lay his hands on them and pray; and the disciples rebuked them.

(Matthew 19 : 14)   But Jesus said, "Allow the little children, and don't forbid them to come to me; for the Kingdom of Heaven belongs to ones like these."

(Matthew 19 : 15)   He laid his hands on them, and departed from there.

(Luke 18 : 15)   They were also bringing their babies to him, that he might touch them. But when the disciples saw it, they rebuked them.

(Luke 18 : 16)   Jesus summoned them, saying, "Allow the little children to come to me, and don't hinder them, for the Kingdom of God belongs to such as these.

(Luke 18 : 17)   Most certainly, I tell you, whoever doesn't receive the Kingdom of God like a little child, he will in no way enter into it."

The Rich and the Kingdom of God
Mt 19:16-30 / Mk 10:17-31 / Lk 18:18-30

(Matthew 19 : 16)   Behold, one came to him and said, "Good teacher, what good thing shall I do, that I may have eternal life?"

(Matthew 19 : 17)   He said to him, "Why do you call me good? No one is good but one, that is, God. But if you want to enter into life, keep the commandments."

(Matthew 19 : 18)   He said to him, "Which ones?" Jesus said, "You shall not murder.' You shall not commit adultery.' You shall not steal.' You shall not offer false testimony.'

(Matthew 19 : 19)   Honor your father and mother.' And, You shall love your neighbor as yourself.'"

(Matthew 19 : 20)   The young man said to him, "All these things I have observed from my youth. What do I still lack?"

(Matthew 19 : 21)   Jesus said to him, "If you want to be perfect, go, sell what you have, and give to the poor, and you will have treasure in heaven; and come, follow me."

(Matthew 19 : 22)   But when the young man heard the saying, he went away sad, for he was one who had great possessions.

(Matthew 19 : 23)   Jesus said to his disciples, "Most certainly I say to you, a rich man will enter into the Kingdom of Heaven with difficulty.

(Matthew 19 : 24)   Again I tell you, it is easier for a camel to go through a needle's eye, than for a rich man to enter into the Kingdom of God."

(Matthew 19 : 25)   When the disciples heard it, they were exceedingly astonished, saying, "Who then can be saved?"

(Matthew 19 : 26)   Looking at them, Jesus said, "With men this is impossible, but with God all things are possible."

(Matthew 19 : 27)   Then Peter answered, "Behold, we have left everything, and followed you. What then will we have?"

(Matthew 19 : 28)   Jesus said to them, "Most certainly I tell you that you who have followed me, in the regeneration when the Son of Man will sit on the throne of his glory, you also will sit on twelve thrones, judging the twelve tribes of Israel.

(Matthew 19 : 29)   Everyone who has left houses, or brothers, or sisters, or father, or mother, or wife, or children, or lands, for my name's sake, will receive one hundred times, and will inherit eternal life.

(Matthew 19 : 30)   But many will be last who are first; and first who are last.

(Mark 10 : 17)   As he was going out into the way, one ran to him, knelt before him, and asked him, "Good Teacher, what shall I do that I may inherit eternal life?"

(Mark 10 : 18)   Jesus said to him, "Why do you call me good? No one is good except one God.

(Mark 10 : 19)   You know the commandments: Do not murder,' Do not commit adultery,' Do not steal,' Do not give false testimony,' Do not defraud,' Honor your father and mother.'"

(Mark 10 : 20)   He said to him, "Teacher, I have observed all these things from my youth."

(Mark 10 : 21)   Jesus looking at him loved him, and said to him, "One thing you lack. Go, sell whatever you have, and give to the poor, and you will have treasure in heaven; and come, follow me, taking up the cross."

(Mark 10 : 22)   But his face fell at that saying, and he went away sorrowful, for he was one who had great possessions.

(Mark 10 : 23)   Jesus looked around, and said to his disciples, "How difficult it is for those who have riches to enter into the Kingdom of God!"

(Mark 10 : 24)   The disciples were amazed at his words. But Jesus answered again, "Children, how hard is it for those who trust in riches to enter into the Kingdom of God!

(Mark 10 : 25)   It is easier for a camel to go through a needle's eye than for a rich man to enter into the Kingdom of God."

(Mark 10 : 26)   They were exceedingly astonished, saying to him, "Then who can be saved?"

(Mark 10 : 27)   Jesus, looking at them, said, "With men it is impossible, but not with God, for all things are possible with God."

(Mark 10 : 28)   Peter began to tell him, "Behold, we have left all, and have followed you."

(Mark 10 : 29)   Jesus said, "Most certainly I tell you, there is no one who has left house, or brothers, or sisters, or father, or mother, or wife, or children, or land, for my sake, and for the sake of the Good News,

(Mark 10 : 30)   but he will receive one hundred times more now in this time, houses, brothers, sisters, mothers, children, and land, with persecutions; and in the age to come eternal life.

(Mark 10 : 31)   But many who are first will be last; and the last first."

(Luke 18 : 18)   A certain ruler asked him, saying, "Good Teacher, what shall I do to inherit eternal life?"

(Luke 18 : 19)   Jesus asked him, "Why do you call me good? No one is good, except one God.

(Luke 18 : 20)   You know the commandments: Don't commit adultery,' Don't murder,' Don't steal,' Don't give false testimony,' Honor your father and your mother.'"

(Luke 18 : 21)   He said, "I have observed all these things from my youth up."

(Luke 18 : 22)   When Jesus heard these things, he said to him, "You still lack one thing. Sell all that you have, and distribute it to the poor. You will have treasure in heaven. Come, follow me."

(Luke 18 : 23)   But when he heard these things, he became very sad, for he was very rich.

(Luke 18 : 24)   Jesus, seeing that he became very sad, said, "How hard it is for those who have riches to enter into the Kingdom of God!

(Luke 18 : 25)   For it is easier for a camel to enter in through a needle's eye, than for a rich man to enter into the Kingdom of God."

(Luke 18 : 26)   Those who heard it said, "Then who can be saved?"

(Luke 18 : 27)   But he said, "The things which are impossible with men are possible with God."

(Luke 18 : 28)   Peter said, "Look, we have left everything, and followed you."

> (Luke 18 : 29)   He said to them, "Most certainly I tell you, there is no one who has left house, or wife, or brothers, or parents, or children, for the Kingdom of God's sake,
>
> (Luke 18 : 30)   who will not receive many times more in this time, and in the world to come, eternal life."

The Parable of the Workers in the Vineyard
Mt 20:1-16

(Matthew 20 : 1)   "For the Kingdom of Heaven is like a man who was the master of a household, who went out early in the morning to hire laborers for his vineyard.

(Matthew 20 : 2)   When he had agreed with the laborers for a denarius a day, he sent them into his vineyard.

(Matthew 20 : 3)   He went out about the third hour, and saw others standing idle in the marketplace.

(Matthew 20 : 4)   To them he said, You also go into the vineyard, and whatever is right I will give you.' So they went their way.

(Matthew 20 : 5)   Again he went out about the sixth and the ninth hour and did likewise.

(Matthew 20 : 6)   About the eleventh hour he went out and found others standing idle. He said to them, why do you stand here all day idle?'

(Matthew 20 : 7)   "They said to him, Because no one has hired us.'

"He said to them, you also go into the vineyard, and you will receive whatever is right.

(Matthew 20 : 8)   When evening had come, the lord of the vineyard said to his manager, Call the laborers and pay them their wages, beginning from the last to the first.'

(Matthew 20 : 9)   "When those who were hired at about the eleventh hour came, they each received a denarius.

(Matthew 20 : 10)   When the first came, they supposed that they would receive more; and they likewise each received a denarius.

(Matthew 20 : 11)   When they received it, they murmured against the master of the household,

(Matthew 20 : 12)   saying, These last have spent one hour, and you have made them equal to us, who have borne the burden of the day and the scorching heat!'

(Matthew 20 : 13)   "But he answered one of them, Friend, I am doing you no wrong. Didn't you agree with me for a denarius?

(Matthew 20 : 14)   Take that which is yours, and go your way. It is my desire to give to this last just as much as to you.

(Matthew 20 : 15)   Isn't it lawful for me to do what I want to with what I own? Or is your eye evil, because I am good?'

(Matthew 20 : 16)   So the last will be first, and the first last. For many are called, but few are chosen."

Jesus Predicts His Death a Third Time
Lk 18:31-34 / Mt 20:17-19 / Mk 10:32-34

(Luke 18 : 31)   He took the twelve aside, and said to them, "Behold, we are going up to Jerusalem, and all the things that are written through the prophets concerning the Son of Man will be completed.

(Luke 18 : 32)   For he will be delivered up to the Gentiles, will be mocked, treated shamefully, and spit on.

(Luke 18 : 33)   They will scourge and kill him. On the third day, he will rise again."

(Luke 18 : 34)   They understood none of these things. This saying was hidden from them, and they didn't understand the things that were said.

(Matthew 20 : 17) As Jesus was going up to Jerusalem, he took the twelve disciples aside, and on the way he said to them,

(Matthew 20 : 18) "Behold, we are going up to Jerusalem, and the Son of Man will be delivered to the chief priests and scribes, and they will condemn him to death,

(Matthew 20 : 19)   and will hand him over to the Gentiles to mock, to scourge, and to crucify; and the third day he will be raised up."

(Mark 10 : 32)   They were on the way, going up to Jerusalem; and Jesus was going in front of them, and they were amazed; and those who followed were afraid. He again took the twelve, and began to tell them the things that were going to happen to him.

(Mark 10 : 33) "Behold, we are going up to Jerusalem. The Son of Man will be delivered to the chief priests and the scribes. They will condemn him to death, and will deliver him to the Gentiles.

(Mark 10 : 34)   They will mock him, spit on him, scourge him, and kill him. On the third day he will rise again."

The Request of James and John
Mt 20:20-28 / Mk 10:35-45

(Matthew 20 : 20)   Then the mother of the sons of Zebedee came to him with her sons, kneeling and asking a certain thing of him.

(Matthew 20 : 21) He said to her, "What do you want?" She said to him, "Command that these, my two sons, may sit, one on your right hand, and one on your left hand, in your Kingdom."

(Matthew 20 : 22)   But Jesus answered, "You don't know what you are asking. Are you able to drink the cup that I am about to drink, and be baptized with the baptism that I am baptized with?" They said to him, "We are able."

(Matthew 20 : 23)   He said to them, "You will indeed drink my cup, and be baptized with the baptism that I am baptized with, but to sit on my right hand and on my left hand is not mine to give; but it is for whom it has been prepared by my Father."

(Matthew 20 : 24)   When the ten heard it, they were indignant with the two brothers.

(Matthew 20 : 25)   But Jesus summoned them, and said, "You know that the rulers of the nations lord it over them, and their great ones exercise authority over them.

(Matthew 20 : 26)   It shall not be so among you, but whoever desires to become great among you shall be your servant.

(Matthew 20 : 27)   Whoever desires to be first among you shall be your bondservant,

(Matthew 20 : 28)   even as the Son of Man came not to be served, but to serve, and to give his life as a ransom for many."

(Mark 10 : 35)   James and John, the sons of Zebedee, came near to him, saying, "Teacher, we want you to do for us whatever we will ask."

(Mark 10 : 36)   He said to them, "What do you want me to do for you?"

(Mark 10 : 37)   They said to him, "Grant to us that we may sit, one at your right hand, and one at your left hand, in your glory."

(Mark 10 : 38)   But Jesus said to them, "You don't know what you are asking. Are you able to drink the cup that I drink, and to be baptized with the baptism that I am baptized with?"

(Mark 10 : 39)   They said to him, "We are able." Jesus said to them, "You shall indeed drink the cup that I drink, and you shall be baptized with the baptism that I am baptized with;

(Mark 10 : 40)   but to sit at my right hand and at my left hand is not mine to give, but for whom it has been prepared."

(Mark 10 : 41)   When the ten heard it, they began to be indignant towards James and John.

(Mark 10 : 42)   Jesus summoned them, and said to them, "You know that they who are recognized as rulers over the nations lord it over them, and their great ones exercise authority over them.

(Mark 10 : 43)   But it shall not be so among you, but whoever wants to become great among you shall be your servant.

(Mark 10 : 44)   Whoever of you wants to become first among you, shall be bondservant of all.

(Mark 10 : 45)   For the Son of Man also came not to be served, but to serve, and to give his life as a ransom for many."

A Blind Beggar Receives His Sight
Lk 18:35-43 / Mk 10:46-52 / (Mt 20:29-34)

(Luke 18 : 35)   It happened, as he came near Jericho, a certain blind man sat by the road, begging.

(Luke 18 : 36)   Hearing a multitude going by, he asked what this meant.

(Luke 18 : 37)   They told him that Jesus of Nazareth was passing by.

(Luke 18 : 38)   He cried out, "Jesus, you son of David, have mercy on me!"

(Luke 18 : 39)   Those who led the way rebuked him, that he should be quiet; but he cried out all the more, "You son of David, have mercy on me!"

(Mark 10 : 46)   They came to Jericho. As he went out from Jericho, with his disciples and a great multitude, the son of Timaeus, Bartimaeus, a blind beggar, was sitting by the road.

(Mark 10 : 47)   When he heard that it was Jesus the Nazarene, he began to cry out, and say, "Jesus, you son of David, have mercy on me!"

(Mark 10 : 48)   Many rebuked him, that he should be quiet, but he cried out much more, "You son of David, have mercy on me!"

(Mark 10 :49)   Jesus stood still, and said, "Call him." They called the blind man, saying to him, "Cheer up! Get up. He is calling you!"

(Mark 10 : 50)   He, casting away his cloak, sprang up, and came to Jesus.

(Mark 10 : 51)   Jesus asked him, "What do you want me to do for you?" The blind man said to him, "Rabboni, that I may see again."

(Mark 10 : 52)   Jesus said to him, "Go your way. Your faith has made you well." Immediately he received his sight, and followed Jesus on the way.

Editor: If the blind man went to the Jesus by himself, he may go the wrong direction.

(Luke 18 : 40)   Standing still, Jesus commanded him to be brought to him. When he had come near, he asked him,

(Luke 18 : 41)   "What do you want me to do?"

He said, "Lord, that I may see again."

(Luke 18 : 42)   Jesus said to him, "Receive your sight. Your faith has healed you."

(Luke 18 : 43)   Immediately he received his sight, and followed him, glorifying God. All the people, when they saw it, praised God.

Jesus met Zacchaeus
Lk 19:1-10

(Luke 19 : 1) He entered and was passing through Jericho.

(Luke 19 : 2)   There was a man named Zacchaeus. He was a chief tax collector, and he was rich.

(Luke 19 : 3)   He was trying to see who Jesus was, and couldn't because of the crowd, because he was short.

(Luke 19 : 4)   He ran on ahead, and climbed up into a sycamore tree to see him, for he was to pass that way. (Luke 19 : 5)

When Jesus came to the place, he looked up and saw him, and said to him, "Zacchaeus, hurry and come down, for today I must stay at your house."

(Luke 19 : 6)   He hurried, came down, and received him joyfully.

(Luke 19 : 7)   When they saw it, they all murmured, saying, "He has gone in to lodge with a man who is a sinner."

(Luke 19 : 8)   Zacchaeus stood and said to the Lord, "Behold, Lord, half of my goods I give to the poor. If I have wrongfully exacted anything of anyone, I restore four times as much."

(Luke 19 : 9)   Jesus said to him, "Today, salvation has come to this house, because he also is a son of Abraham.

(Luke 19 : 10)   For the Son of Man came to seek and to save that which was lost."

Jesus healed the other two blind men
Mt 20:29-34 / (Lk 18:35-43 / Mk 10:46-52)

(Matthew 20 : 29)   As they went out from Jericho, a great multitude followed him.

(Matthew 20 : 30)   Behold, two blind men sitting by the road, when they heard that Jesus was passing by, cried out, "Lord, have mercy on us, you son of David!"

(Matthew 20 : 31)   The multitude rebuked them, telling them that they should be quiet, but they cried out even more, "Lord, have mercy on us, you son of David!"

(Matthew 20 : 32)   Jesus stood still, and called them, and asked, "What do you want me to do for you?"

(Matthew 20 : 33)   They told him, "Lord, that our eyes may be opened."

(Matthew 20 : 34) Jesus, being moved with compassion, touched their eyes; and immediately their eyes received their sight, and they followed him.

Jesus Heals a Man Born Blind
Jn 9:1-12

(John 9 : 1) As he passed by, he saw a man blind from birth.

(John 9 : 2)   His disciples asked him, "Rabbi, who sinned, this man or his parents, that he was born blind?" (John 9 : 3) Jesus answered, "Neither did this man sin, nor his parents; but, that the works of God might be revealed in him.

(John 9 : 4)   I must work the works of him who sent me, while it is day. The night is coming, when no one can work.

(John 9 : 5)   While I am in the world, I am the light of the world."

(John 9 : 6)   When he had said this, he spat on the ground, made mud with the saliva, anointed the blind man's eyes with the mud,

(John 9 : 7)   and said to him, "Go, wash in the pool of Siloam" (which means "Sent"). So he went away, washed, and came back seeing.

(John 9 : 8)   The neighbors therefore, and those who saw that he was blind before, said, "Isn't this he who sat and begged?"

(John 9 : 9)   Others were saying, "It is he."

Still others were saying, "He looks like him."

He said, "I am he."

(John 9 : 10)   They therefore were asking him, "How were your eyes opened?"

(John 9 : 11)   He answered, "A man called Jesus made mud, anointed my eyes, and said to me, Go to the pool of Siloam, and wash.' So I went away and washed, and I received sight."

(John 9 : 12)   Then they asked him, "Where is he?" He said, "I don't know."

The Pharisees Investigate the Healing
Jn 9:13-34

(John 9 : 13)   They brought him who had been blind to the Pharisees.

(John 9 : 14)   It was a Sabbath when Jesus made the mud and opened his eyes.

(John 9 : 15)   Again therefore the Pharisees also asked him how he received his sight. He said to them, "He put mud on my eyes, I washed, and I see."

(John 9 : 16)   Some therefore of the Pharisees said, "This man is not from God, because he doesn't keep the Sabbath." Others said, "How can a man who is a sinner do such signs?" There was division among them.

(John 9 : 17)   Therefore they asked the blind man again, "What do you say about him, because he opened your eyes?" He said, "He is a prophet."

(John 9 : 18)   The Jews therefore did not believe concerning him, that he had been blind, and had received his sight, until they called the parents of him who had received his sight,

(John 9 : 19)   and asked them, "Is this your son, whom you say was born blind? How then does he now see?"

(John 9 : 20)   His parents answered them, "We know that this is our son, and that he was born blind;

(John 9 : 21)   but how he now sees, we don't know; or who opened his eyes, we don't know. He is of age. Ask him. He will speak for himself."

(John 9 : 22) His parents said these things because they feared the Jews; for the Jews had already agreed that if any man would confess him as Christ, he would be put out of the synagogue.

(John 9 : 23)   Therefore his parents said, "He is of age. Ask him."

(John 9 : 24)   So they called the man who was blind a second time, and said to him, "Give glory to God. We know that this man is a sinner."

(John 9 : 25)   He therefore answered, "I don't know if he is a sinner. One thing I do know: that though I was blind, now I see."

(John 9 : 26)   They said to him again, "What did he do to you? How did he open your eyes?"

(John 9 : 27)   He answered them, "I told you already, and you didn't listen. Why do you want to hear it again? You don't also want to become his disciples, do you?"

(John 9 : 28)   They insulted him and said, "You are his disciple, but we are disciples of Moses.

(John 9 : 29)   We know that God has spoken to Moses. But as for this man, we don't know where he comes from."

(John 9 : 30)   The man answered them, "How amazing! You don't know where he comes from, yet he opened my eyes.

(John 9 : 31)   We know that God doesn't listen to sinners, but if anyone is a worshiper of God, and does his will, he listens to him.

(John 9 : 32)   Since the world began it has never been heard of that anyone opened the eyes of someone born blind.

(John 9 : 33)   If this man were not from God, he could do nothing."

(John 9 : 34)   They answered him, "You were altogether born in sins, and do you teach us?" They threw him out.

Spiritual Blindness
Jn 9:35-41

(John 9 : 35)   Jesus heard that they had thrown him out, and finding him, he said, "Do you believe in the Son of God?"
(John 9 : 36)   He answered, "Who is he, Lord, that I may believe in him?"

(John 9 : 37)   Jesus said to him, "You have both seen him, and it is he who speaks with you."

(John 9 : 38)   He said, "Lord, I believe!" and he worshiped him.

(John 9 : 39)   Jesus said, "I came into this world for judgment, that those who don't see may see; and that those who see may become blind."

(John 9 : 40)   Those of the Pharisees who were with him heard these things, and said to him, "Are we also blind?"

(John 9 : 41)   Jesus said to them, "If you were blind, you would have no sin; but now you say, We see.' Therefore your sin remains.

The Good Shepherd and His Sheep
Jn 10:1-21

(John 10 : 1)   "Most certainly, I tell you, one who doesn't enter by the door into the sheep fold, but climbs up some other way, the same is a thief and a robber.

(John 10 : 2)   But one who enters in by the door is the shepherd of the sheep.

(John 10 : 3)   The gatekeeper opens the gate for him, and the sheep listen to his voice. He calls his own sheep by name, and leads them out.

(John 10 : 4)   Whenever he brings out his own sheep, he goes before them, and the sheep follow him, for they know his voice.

(John 10 : 5)   They will by no means follow a stranger, but will flee from him; for they don't know the voice of strangers."

(John 10 : 6)   Jesus spoke this parable to them, but they didn't understand what he was telling them.

(John 10 : 7)   Jesus therefore said to them again, "Most certainly, I tell you, I am the sheep's door.

(John 10 : 8)   All who came before me are thieves and robbers, but the sheep didn't listen to them.

(John 10 : 9)   I am the door. If anyone enters in by me, he will be saved, and will go in and go out, and will find pasture.

(John 10 : 10)   The thief only comes to steal, kill, and destroy. I came that they may have life, and may have it abundantly.

(John 10 : 11)   I am the good shepherd. The good shepherd lays down his life for the sheep.

(John 10 : 12)   He who is a hired hand, and not a shepherd, who doesn't own the sheep, sees the wolf coming, leaves the sheep, and flees. The wolf snatches the sheep, and scatters them.

(John 10 : 13)   The hired hand flees because he is a hired hand, and doesn't care for the sheep.

(John 10 : 14)   I am the good shepherd. I know my own, and I'm known by my own;

(John 10 : 15)   even as the Father knows me, and I know the Father. I lay down my life for the sheep.

(John 10 : 16) I have other sheep, which are not of this fold. I must bring them also, and they will hear my voice. They will become one flock with one shepherd.

(John 10 : 17) Therefore the Father loves me, because I lay down my life, that I may take it again.

(John 10 : 18) No one takes it away from me, but I lay it down by myself. I have power to lay it down, and I have power to take it again. I received this commandment from my Father."

(John 10 : 19) Therefore a division arose again among the Jews because of these words.

(John 10 : 20) Many of them said, "He has a demon, and is insane! Why do you listen to him?"

(John 10 : 21)   Others said, "These are not the sayings of one possessed by a demon. It isn't possible for a demon to open the eyes of the blind, is it?"

Further Conflict Over Jesus' Claims
Jn 10:22-42

(John 10 : 22)   It was the Feast of the Dedication at Jerusalem.

(John 10 : 23)   It was winter, and Jesus was walking in the temple, in Solomon's porch.

(John 10 : 24)   The Jews therefore came around him and said to him, "How long will you hold us in suspense? If you are the Christ, tell us plainly."

(John 10 : 25)   Jesus answered them, "I told you, and you don't believe. The works that I do in my Father's name, these testify about me.

(John 10 : 26)   But you don't believe, because you are not of my sheep, as I told you.

(John 10 : 27)   My sheep hear my voice, and I know them, and they follow me.

(John 10 : 28)   I give eternal life to them. They will never perish, and no one will snatch them out of my hand.

(John 10 : 29)   My Father, who has given them to me, is greater than all. No one is able to snatch them out of my Father's hand.

(John 10 : 30) I and the Father are one."

(John 10 : 31)   Therefore Jews took up stones again to stone him.

(John 10 : 32)   Jesus answered them, "I have shown you many good works from my Father. For which of those works do you stone me?"

(John 10 : 33)   The Jews answered him, "We don't stone you for a good work, but for blasphemy: because you, being a man, make yourself God."

(John 10 : 34)   Jesus answered them, "Isn't it written in your law, I said, you are gods?'

(John 10 : 35)   If he called them gods, to whom the word of God came (and the Scripture can't be broken),

(John 10 : 36)   do you say of him whom the Father sanctified and sent into the world, You blaspheme,' because I said, I am the Son of God?'

(John 10 : 37)   If I don't do the works of my Father, don't believe me.

(John 10 : 38)   But if I do them, though you don't believe me, believe the works; that you may know and believe that the Father is in me, and I in the Father."

(John 10 : 39)   They sought again to seize him, and he went out of their hand.

(John 10 : 40)   He went away again beyond the Jordan into the place where John was baptizing at first, and there he stayed.

(John 10 : 41)   Many came to him. They said, "John indeed did no sign, but everything that John said about this man is true."

(John 10 : 42)   Many believed in him there.

The Death of Lazarus
Jn 11:1-16

(John 11 : 1)   Now a certain man was sick, Lazarus from Bethany, of the village of Mary and her sister, Martha.

(John 11 : 2)   It was that Mary who had anointed the Lord with ointment, and wiped his feet with her hair, whose brother, Lazarus, was sick.

(John 11 : 3)   The sisters therefore sent to him, saying, "Lord, behold, he for whom you have great affection is sick."

John 11 : 4)   But when Jesus heard it, he said, "This sickness is not to death, but for the glory of God, that God's Son may be glorified by it."

(John 11 : 5)   Now Jesus loved Martha, and her sister, and Lazarus.

(John 11 : 6)   When therefore he heard that he was sick, he stayed two days in the place where he was.

(John 11 : 7)   Then after this he said to the disciples, "Let's go into Judea again."

(John 11 : 8)   The disciples told him, "Rabbi, the Jews were just trying to stone you, and are you going there again?" (John 11 : 9)   Jesus answered, "Aren't there twelve hours of daylight? If a man walks in the day, he doesn't stumble, because he sees the light of this world.

(John 11 : 10)   But if a man walks in the night, he stumbles, because the light isn't in him."

(John 11 : 11) He said these things, and after that, he said to them, "Our friend, Lazarus, has fallen asleep, but I am going so that I may awake him out of sleep."

(John 11 : 12) The disciples therefore said, "Lord, if he has fallen asleep, he will recover."

(John 11 : 13) Now Jesus had spoken of his death, but they thought that he spoke of taking rest in sleep.

(John 11 : 14) So Jesus said to them plainly then, "Lazarus is dead.

(John 11 : 15) I am glad for your sakes that I was not there, so that you may believe. Nevertheless, let's go to him."

(John 11 : 16) Thomas therefore, who is called Didymus, said to his fellow disciples, "Let's go also, that we may die with him."

Jesus Comforts the Sisters of Lazarus
Jn 11:17-37

(John 11 : 17) So when Jesus came, he found that he had been in the tomb four days already.

(John 11 : 18) Now Bethany was near Jerusalem, about fifteen stadia away.

(John 11 : 19) Many of the Jews had joined the women around Martha and Mary, to console them concerning their brother.

(John 11 : 20) Then when Martha heard that Jesus was coming, she went and met him, but Mary stayed in the house.

(John 11 : 21) Therefore Martha said to Jesus, "Lord, if you would have been here, my brother wouldn't have died.

(John 11 : 22) Even now I know that, whatever you ask of God, God will give you."

(John 11 : 23) Jesus said to her, "Your brother will rise again."

(John 11 : 24) Martha said to him, "I know that he will rise again in the resurrection at the last day."

(John 11 : 25) Jesus said to her, "I am the resurrection and the life. He who believes in me will still live, even if he dies.

(John 11 : 26) Whoever lives and believes in me will never die. Do you believe this?"

(John 11 : 27) She said to him, "Yes, Lord. I have come to believe that you are the Christ, God's Son, he who comes into the world."

(John 11 : 28) When she had said this, she went away, and called Mary, her sister, secretly, saying, "The Teacher is here, and is calling you."

(John 11 : 29) When she heard this, she arose quickly, and went to him.

(John 11 : 30) Now Jesus had not yet come into the village, but was in the place where Martha met him.

(John 11 : 31) Then the Jews who were with her in the house, and were consoling her, when they saw Mary, that she rose up quickly and went out, followed her, saying, "She is going to the tomb to weep there."

(John 11 : 32) Therefore when Mary came to where Jesus was, and saw him, she fell down at his feet, saying to him, "Lord, if you would have been here, my brother wouldn't have died."

(John 11 : 33) When Jesus therefore saw her weeping, and the Jews weeping who came with her, he groaned in the spirit, and was troubled,

(John 11 : 34) and said, "Where have you laid him?"

They told him, "Lord, come and see."

(John 11 : 35) Jesus wept.

(John 11 : 36) The Jews therefore said, "See how much affection he had for him!"

(John 11 : 37) Some of them said, "Couldn't this man, who opened the eyes of him who was blind, have also kept this man from dying?"

Jesus Raises Lazarus From the Dead
Jn 11:38-44

(John 11 : 38) Jesus therefore, again groaning in himself, came to the tomb. Now it was a cave, and a stone lay against it.

(John 11 : 39) "Jesus said, "Take away the stone."

Martha, the sister of him who was dead, said to him, "Lord, by this time there is a stench, for he has been dead four days."

(John 11 : 40) Jesus said to her, "Didn't I tell you that if you believed, you would see God's glory?"

(John 11 : 41) So they took away the stone from the place where the dead man was lying. Jesus lifted up his eyes, and said, "Father, I thank you that you listened to me.

(John 11 : 42) I know that you always listen to me, but because of the multitude that stands around I said this, that they may believe that you sent me."

(John 11 : 43) When he had said this, he cried with a loud voice, "Lazarus, come out!"

(John 11 : 44) He who was dead came out, bound hand and foot with wrappings, and his face was wrapped around with a cloth.

Jesus said to them, "Free him, and let him go."

The Plot to Kill Jesus
Jn 11:45-57

(John 11 : 45) Therefore many of the Jews, who came to Mary and saw what Jesus did, believed in him.

(John 11 : 46) But some of them went away to the Pharisees, and told them the things which Jesus had done.

(John 11 : 47) The chief priests therefore and the Pharisees gathered a council, and said, "What are we doing? For this man does many signs.

(John 11 : 48) If we leave him alone like this, everyone will believe in him, and the Romans will come and take away both our place and our nation."

(John 11 : 49) But a certain one of them, Caiaphas, being high priest that year, said to them, "You know nothing at all,

(John 11 : 50) nor do you consider that it is advantageous for us that one man should die for the people, and that the whole nation not perish."

(John 11 : 51) Now he didn't say this of himself, but being high priest that year, he prophesied that Jesus would die for the nation,

(John 11 : 52) and not for the nation only, but that he might also gather together into one the children of God who are scattered abroad.

(John 11 : 53) So from that day forward they took counsel that they might put him to death.

(John 11 : 54) Jesus therefore walked no more openly among the Jews, but departed from there into the country near the wilderness, to a city called Ephraim. He stayed there with his disciples.

(John 11 : 55) Now the Passover of the Jews was at hand. Many went up from the country to Jerusalem before the Passover, to purify themselves.

(John 11 : 56) Then they sought for Jesus and spoke one with another, as they stood in the temple, "What do you think that he isn't coming to the feast at all?"

(John 11 : 57) Now the chief priests and the Pharisees had commanded that if anyone knew where he was, he should report it, that they might seize him.

Jesus Anointed at Bethany
Jn 12:1-11 / Mt 26:6-12 / Mk 14:3-9

(John 12 : 1) Then six days before the Passover, Jesus came to Bethany, where Lazarus was, who had been dead, whom he raised from the dead.

(John 12 : 2) So they made him a supper there. Martha served, but Lazarus was one of those who sat at the table with him.

(John 12 : 3) Mary, therefore, took a pound of ointment of pure nard, very precious, and anointed the feet of Jesus, and wiped his feet with her hair. The house was filled with the fragrance of the ointment.

(John 12 : 4) Then Judas Iscariot, Simon's son, one of his disciples, who would betray him, said,

(John 12 : 5) "Why wasn't this ointment sold for three hundred denarii, and given to the poor?"

(John 12 : 6) Now he said this, not because he cared for the poor, but because he was a thief, and having the money box, used to steal what was put into it.

(John 12 : 7) But Jesus said, "Leave her alone. She has kept this for the day of my burial.

(John 12 : 8) For you always have the poor with you, but you don't always have me."

(Matthew 26 : 13)   Most certainly I tell you, wherever this Good News is preached in the whole world, what this woman has done will also be spoken of as a memorial of her."

(John 12 : 9) A large crowd therefore of the Jews learned that he was there, and they came, not for Jesus' sake only, but that they might see Lazarus also, whom he had raised from the dead.

(John 12 : 10) But the chief priests conspired to put Lazarus to death also,

(John 12 : 11) because on account of him many of the Jews went away and believed in Jesus.

(Matthew 26 : 6)   Now when Jesus was in Bethany, in the house of Simon the leper,

(Matthew 26 : 7)   a woman came to him having an alabaster jar of very expensive ointment, and she poured it on his head as he sat at the table.

(Matthew 26 : 8)   But when his disciples saw this, they were indignant, saying, "Why this waste?

(Matthew 26 : 9)   For this ointment might have been sold for much, and given to the poor."

(Matthew 26 : 10)   However, knowing this, Jesus said to them, "Why do you trouble the woman? Because she has done a good work for me.

(Matthew 26 : 11)   For you always have the poor with you; but you don't always have me.

(Matthew 26 : 12)   For in pouring this ointment on my body, she did it to prepare me for burial.

(Mark 14 : 3) While he was at Bethany, in the house of Simon the leper, as he sat at the table, a woman came having an alabaster jar of ointment of pure nard very costly. She broke the jar, and poured it over his head.

(Mark 14 : 4)   But there were some who were indignant among themselves, saying, "Why has this ointment been wasted?

(Mark 14 : 5) For this might have been sold for more than three hundred denarii, and given to the poor." They grumbled against her.

(Mark 14 : 6) But Jesus said, "Leave her alone. Why do you trouble her? She has done a good work for me.

(Mark 14 : 7)   For you always have the poor with you, and whenever you want to, you can do them good; but you will not always have me.

(Mark 14 : 8) She has done what she could. She has anointed my body beforehand for the burying.

(Mark 14 : 9)   Most certainly I tell you, wherever this Good News may be preached throughout the whole world, that which this woman has done will also be spoken of for a memorial of her."

Jesus Comes to Jerusalem as King
Lk 19:28-44 / Jn 12:12-19 / Mk 11:1-11 / Mt 21:1-11

(Luke 19 : 28)   Having said these things, he went on ahead, going up to Jerusalem.

(Luke 19 : 29)   It happened, when he drew near to Bethsphage and Bethany, at the mountain that is called Olivet, he sent two of his disciples,

(Luke 19 : 30)   saying, "Go your way into the village on the other side, in which, as you enter, you will find a colt tied, whereon no man ever yet sat. Untie it, and bring it.

(Luke 19 : 31)   If anyone asks you, Why are you untying it?' say to him: The Lord needs it.'"

(Luke 19 : 32)   Those who were sent went away, and found things just as he had told them.

(Luke 19 : 33)   As they were untying the colt, its owners said to them, "Why are you untying the colt?"

(Luke 19 : 34)   They said, "The Lord needs it."

(Luke 19 : 35)   They brought it to Jesus. They threw their cloaks on the colt, and set Jesus on them.

(John 12 : 14) Jesus, having found a young donkey, sat on it. As it is written,

(John 12 : 15) "Don't be afraid, daughter of Zion.

Behold, your King comes, sitting on a donkey's colt." (John 12 : 16) His disciples didn't understand these things at first, but when Jesus was glorified, then they remembered that these things were written about him, and that they had done these things to him.

(John 12 : 17) The multitude therefore that was with him when he called Lazarus out of the tomb, and raised him from the dead, was testifying about it.

(John 12 : 18) For this cause also the multitude went and met him, because they heard that he had done this sign.

(Luke 19 : 36)   As he went, they spread their cloaks on the road.

(Luke 19 : 37)   As he was now getting near, at the descent of the Mount of Olives, the whole multitude of the disciples began to rejoice and praise God with a loud voice for all the mighty works which they had seen,

(Luke 19 : 38)   saying, "Blessed is the King who comes in the name of the Lord!

(Mark 11 : 8)   Many spread their garments on the way, and others were cutting down branches from the trees, and spreading them on the road.

(Mark 11 : 9)   Those who went in front, and those who followed, cried out, "Hosanna! Blessed is he who comes in the name of the Lord!

(Mark 11 : 10)   Blessed is the kingdom of our father David that is coming in the name of the Lord! Hosanna in the highest!"

(John 12 : 19) The Pharisees therefore said among themselves, "See how you accomplish nothing. Behold, the world has gone after him."

(Luke 19 : 39)   Some of the Pharisees from the multitude said to him, "Teacher, rebuke your disciples!"

(Luke 19 : 40)   He answered them, "I tell you that if these were silent, the stones would cry out."

(Luke 19 : 41)   When he drew near, he saw the city and wept over it,

(Luke 19 : 42)   saying, "If you, even you, had known today the things which belong to your peace! But now, they are hidden from your eyes.

(Luke 19 : 43)   For the days will come on you, when your enemies will throw up a barricade against you, surround you, hem you in on every side,

(Luke 19 : 44)   and will dash you and your children within you to the ground. They will not leave in you one stone on another, because you didn't know the time of your visitation."

(Mark 11 : 1)   When they drew near to Jerusalem, to Bethsphage and Bethany, at the Mount of Olives, he sent two of his disciples,

(Mark 11 : 2)   and said to them, "Go your way into the village that is opposite you. Immediately as you enter into it, you will find a young donkey tied, on which no one has sat. Untie him, and bring him.

(Mark 11 : 3)   If anyone asks you, â˜Why are you doing this?' say, The Lord needs him;' and immediately he will send him back here."

(Mark 11 : 4)   They went away, and found a young donkey tied at the door outside in the open street, and they untied him.

(Mark 11 : 5)   Some of those who stood there asked them, "What are you doing, untying the young donkey?"

(Mark 11 : 6)   They said to them just as Jesus had said, and they let them go.

(Mark 11 : 7)   They brought the young donkey to Jesus, and threw their garments on it, and Jesus sat on it.

(Matthew 21 : 1)   When they drew near to Jerusalem, and came to Bethsphage, to the Mount of Olives, then Jesus sent two disciples,

(Matthew 21 : 2)   saying to them, "Go into the village that is opposite you, and immediately you will find a donkey tied, and a colt with her. Untie them, and bring them to me.

(Matthew 21 : 3)   If anyone says anything to you, you shall say, The Lord needs them,' and immediately he will send them."

(Matthew 21 : 4)   All this was done, that it might be fulfilled which was spoken through the prophet, saying,

(Matthew 21 : 5)   "Tell the daughter of Zion,

behold, your King comes to you,

humble, and riding on a donkey,

on a colt, the foal of a donkey."

(Matthew 21 : 6)   The disciples went, and did just as Jesus commanded them,

(Matthew 21 : 7)   and brought the donkey and the colt, and laid their clothes on them; and he sat on them.

(Matthew 21 : 8)   A very great multitude spread their clothes on the road. Others cut branches from the trees, and spread them on the road.

(Matthew 21 : 9)   The multitudes who went before him,

and who followed kept shouting,

"Hosanna to the son of David!

Blessed is he who comes in the name of the Lord!

Hosanna in the highest!"

(John 12 : 12) On the next day a great multitude had come to the feast. When they heard that Jesus was coming to Jerusalem,

(John 12 : 13) they took the branches of the palm trees, and went out to meet him, and cried out, "Hosanna! Blessed is he who comes in the name of the Lord, the King of Israel!"

(Matthew 21 : 10)   When he had come into Jerusalem, all the city was stirred up, saying, "Who is this?"

(Matthew 21 : 11)   The multitudes said, "This is the prophet, Jesus, from Nazareth of Galilee."

(Mark 11 : 11)   Jesus entered into the temple in Jerusalem. When he had looked around at everything, it being now evening, he went out to Bethany with the twelve.

Jesus Predicts His Death
Jn 12:20-36

(John 12 : 20) Now there were certain Greeks among those that went up to worship at the feast.

(John 12 : 21) These, therefore, came to Philip, who was from Bethsaida of Galilee, and asked him, saying, "Sir, we want to see Jesus."

(John 12 :22) Philip came and told Andrew, and in turn, Andrew came with Philip, and they told Jesus.

(John 12 : 23) Jesus answered them, "The time has come for the Son of Man to be glorified.

(John 12 : 24) Most certainly I tell you, unless a grain of wheat falls into the earth and dies, it remains by itself alone. But if it dies, it bears much fruit.

(John 12 : 25) He who loves his life will lose it. He who hates his life in this world will keep it to eternal life.

(John 12 : 26) If anyone serves me, let him follow me. Where I am, there will my servant also be. If anyone serves me, the Father will honor him.

(John 12 : 27) "Now my soul is troubled. What shall I say? Father, save me from this time?' But for this cause I came to this time.

(John 12 : 28) Father, glorify your name!" Then there came a voice out of the sky, saying, "I have both glorified it, and will glorify it again."

(John 12 : 29) The multitude therefore, who stood by and heard it, said that it had thundered. Others said, "An angel has spoken to him."

(John 12 : 30) Jesus answered, "This voice hasn't come for my sake, but for your sakes.

(John 12 : 31) Now is the judgment of this world. Now the prince of this world will be cast out.

(John 12 : 32) And I, if I am lifted up from the earth, will draw all people to myself."

(John 12 : 33) But he said this, signifying by what kind of death he should die.

(John 12 : 34) The multitude answered him, "We have heard out of the law that the Christ remains forever. How do you say, The Son of Man must be lifted up?' Who is this Son of Man?"

(John 12 : 35) Jesus therefore said to them, "Yet a little while the light is with you. Walk while you have the light, that darkness doesn't overtake you. He who walks in the darkness doesn't know where he is going.

(John 12 : 36) While you have the light, believe in the light, that you may become children of light." Jesus said these things, and he departed and hid himself from them.

Belief and Unbelief Among the Jews
Jn 12:37-50

(John 12 : 37) But though he had done so many signs before them, yet they didn't believe in him,

(John 12 : 38) that the word of Isaiah the prophet might be fulfilled, which he spoke,

"Lord, who has believed our report?

To whom has the arm of the Lord been revealed?"

(John 12 : 39) For this cause they couldn't believe, for Isaiah said again,

(John 12 : 40) "He has blinded their eyes and he hardened their heart,

lest they should see with their eyes,

and perceive with their heart,

and would turn,

and I would heal them."

(John 12 : 41) Isaiah said these things when he saw his glory, and spoke of him.

(John 12 : 42) Nevertheless even of the rulers many believed in him, but because of the Pharisees they didn't confess it, so that they wouldn't be put out of the synagogue,

(John 12 : 43) for they loved men's praise more than God's praise.

(John 12 : 44) Jesus cried out and said, "Whoever believes in me, believes not in me, but in him who sent me.

(John 12 : 45) He who sees me sees him who sent me.

(John 12 : 46) I have come as a light into the world, that whoever believes in me may not remain in the darkness. (John 12 : 47) If anyone listens to my sayings, and doesn't believe, I don't judge him. For I came not to judge the world, but to save the world.

(John 12 : 48) He who rejects me, and doesn't receive my sayings, has one who judges him. The word that I spoke, the same will judge him in the last day.

(John 12 : 49) For I spoke not from myself, but the Father who sent me, he gave me a commandment, what I should say, and what I should speak.

(John 12 : 50) I know that his commandment is eternal life. The things therefore which I speak, even as the Father has said to me, so I speak."

Jesus Curses a Fig Tree
Mk 11:12-14 / Mt 21:18-19

(Mark 11 : 12)   The next day, when they had come out from Bethany, he was hungry.

(Mark 11 : 13)   Seeing a fig tree afar off having leaves, he came to see if perhaps he might find anything on it. When he came to it, he found nothing but leaves, for it was not the season for figs.

(Mark 11 : 14)   Jesus told it, "May no one ever eat fruit from you again!" and his disciples heard it.

(Matthew 21 : 18)   Now in the morning, as he returned to the city, he was hungry.

> (Matthew 21 : 19)   Seeing a fig tree by the road, he came to it, and found nothing on it but leaves. He said to it, "Let there be no fruit from you forever!" Immediately the fig tree withered away.

Jesus drove out the Temple the Second Time
Mk 11:15-18 / Mt 21:12-17 / Lk 19:45-48
/ (Jn 2:13-17)

(Mark 11 : 15)   They came to Jerusalem, and Jesus entered into the temple, and began to throw out those who sold and those who bought in the temple, and overthrew the tables of the money changers, and the seats of those who sold the doves.

(Mark 11 : 16)   He would not allow anyone to carry a container through the temple.

(Mark 11 : 17)   He taught, saying to them, "Isn't it written, My house will be called a house of prayer for all the nations?' But you have made it a den of robbers!"

(Mark 11 : 18)   The chief priests and the scribes heard it, and sought how they might destroy him. For they feared him, because all the multitude was astonished at his teaching.

> (Matthew 21 : 12)   Jesus entered into the temple of God, and drove out all of those who sold and bought in the temple, and overthrew the money changers' tables and the seats of those who sold the doves.

> (Matthew 21 : 13)   He said to them, "It is written, My house shall be called a house of prayer,'but you have made it a den of robbers!"

(Matthew 21 : 14)   The blind and the lame came to him in the temple, and he healed them.

(Matthew 21 : 15)   But when the chief priests and the scribes saw the wonderful things that he did, and the children who were crying in the temple and saying, "Hosanna to the son of David!" they were indignant,

(Matthew 21 : 16)   and said to him, "Do you hear what these are saying?" Jesus said to them, "Yes. Did you never read, Out of the mouth of babes and nursing babies you have perfected praise?'"

(Matthew 21 : 17)   He left them, and went out of the city to Bethany, and lodged there.

> (Luke 19 : 45)   He entered into the temple, and began to drive out those who bought and sold in it,
>
> (Luke 19 : 46)   saying to them, "It is written, My house is a house of prayer, 'but you have made it a den of robbers'!"
>
> (Luke 19 : 47)   He was teaching daily in the temple, but the chief priests and the scribes and the leading men among the people sought to destroy him.
>
> (Luke 19 : 48)   They couldn't find what they might do, for all the people hung on to every word that he said.

The Fig Tree withered
Mk 11:19-26 / Mt 21:20-22

(Mark 11 : 19)   When evening came, he went out of the city.

(Mark 11 : 20)   As they passed by in the morning, they saw the fig tree withered away from the roots.

(Mark 11 : 21)   Peter, remembering, said to him, "Rabbi, look! The fig tree which you cursed has withered away."

(Mark 11 : 22)   Jesus answered them, "Have faith in God.

(Mark 11 : 23)   For most certainly I tell you, whoever may tell this mountain, Be taken up and cast into the sea,' and doesn't doubt in his heart, but believes that what he says is happening; he shall have whatever he says.

(Mark 11 : 24)   Therefore I tell you, all things whatever you pray and ask for, believe that you have received them, and you shall have them.

(Mark 11 : 25)   Whenever you stand praying, forgive, if you have anything against anyone; so that your Father, who is in heaven, may also forgive you your transgressions.

(Mark 11 : 26)   But if you do not forgive, neither will your Father in heaven forgive your transgressions."

(Matthew 21 : 20)   When the disciples saw it, they marveled, saying, "How did the fig tree immediately wither away?"

(Matthew 21 : 21)   Jesus answered them, "Most certainly I tell you, if you have faith, and don't doubt, you will not only do what was done to the fig tree, but even if you told this mountain, Be taken up and cast into the sea,' it would be done.

(Matthew 21 : 22)   All things, whatever you ask in prayer, believing, you will receive."

The Authority of Jesus Questioned
Mt 21:23-27 / Mk 11:27-33 / Lk 20:1-8

(Matthew 21 : 23)   When he had come into the temple, the chief priests and the elders of the people came to him as he was teaching, and said, "By what authority do you do these things? Who gave you this authority?"

(Matthew 21 : 24)   Jesus answered them, "I also will ask you one question, which if you tell me, I likewise will tell you by what authority I do these things.

(Matthew 21 : 25)   The baptism of John, where was it from? From heaven or from men?" They reasoned with themselves, saying, "If we say, From heaven,' he will ask us, Why then did you not believe him?'

(Matthew 21 : 26)   But if we say, From men,' we fear the multitude, for all hold John as a prophet."

(Matthew 21 : 27)   They answered Jesus, and said, "We don't know."

He also said to them, "Neither will I tell you by what authority I do these things.

(Mark 11 : 27)   They came again to Jerusalem, and as he was walking in the temple, the chief priests, and the scribes, and the elders came to him,

(Mark 11 : 28)   and they began saying to him, "By what authority do you do these things? Or who gave you this authority to do these things?"

(Mark 11 : 29)   Jesus said to them, "I will ask you one question. Answer me, and I will tell you by what authority I do these things.

(Mark 11 : 30)   The baptism of John was it from heaven, or from men? Answer me."

(Mark 11 : 31)   They reasoned with themselves, saying, "If we should say, From heaven;' he will say, Why then did you not believe him?'

(Mark 11 : 32)   If we should say, From men'" they feared the people, for all held John to really be a prophet. (Mark 11 : 33)   They answered Jesus, "We don't know."

Jesus said to them, "Neither do I tell you by what authority I do these things."

(Luke 20 : 1)   It happened on one of those days, as he was teaching the people in the temple and preaching the Good News, that the priests and scribes came to him with the elders.

(Luke 20 : 2)   They asked him, "Tell us: by what authority do you do these things? Or who is giving you this authority?"

(Luke 20 : 3)   He answered them, "I also will ask you one question. Tell me:

(Luke 20 : 4)   the baptism of John, was it from heaven, or from men?"

(Luke 20 : 5)   They reasoned with themselves, saying, "If we say, From heaven,' he will say, Why didn't you believe him?'

(Luke 20 : 6) But if we say, From men,' all the people will stone us, for they are persuaded that John was a prophet."

(Luke 20 : 7) They answered that they didn't know where it was from.

(Luke 20 : 8) Jesus said to them, "Neither will I tell you by what authority I do these things."

The Parable of the Two Sons
Mt 21:28-32

(Matthew 21 : 28)   But what do you think? A man had two sons, and he came to the first, and said, Son, go work today in my vineyard.'

(Matthew 21 : 29)   He answered, I will not,' but afterward he changed his mind, and went.

(Matthew 21 : 30)   He came to the second, and said the same thing. He answered, I go, sir,' but he didn't go.

(Matthew 21 : 31)   Which of the two did the will of his father?" They said to him, "The first." Jesus said to them, "Most certainly I tell you that the tax collectors and the prostitutes are entering into the Kingdom of God before you."

(Matthew 21 : 32)   For John came to you in the way of righteousness, and you didn't believe him, but the tax collectors and the prostitutes believed him. When you saw it, you didn't even repent afterward, that you might believe him.

The Parable of the Tenants
Mk 12:1-12 / Mt 21:33-46 / Lk 20:9-19

(Mark 12 : 1)   He began to speak to them in parables. "A man planted a vineyard, put a hedge around it, dug a pit for the wine press, built a tower, rented it out to a farmer, and went into another country.

(Mark 12 : 2)   When it was time, he sent a servant to the farmer to get from the farmer his share of the fruit of the vineyard.

(Mark 12 : 3)   They took him, beat him, and sent him away empty.

(Mark 12 : 4)   Again, he sent another servant to them; and they threw stones at him, wounded him in the head, and sent him away shamefully treated.

(Mark 12 : 5)   Again he sent another; and they killed him; and many others, beating some, and killing some.

(Mark 12 : 6)   Therefore still having one, his beloved son, he sent him last to them, saying, They will respect my son.'

(Mark 12 : 7) But those farmers said among themselves, This is the heir. Come, let's kill him, and the inheritance will be ours.'

(Mark 12 : 8)   They took him, killed him, and cast him out of the vineyard.

(Mark 12 : 9) What therefore will the lord of the vineyard do? He will come and destroy the farmers, and will give the vineyard to others.

(Matthew 21 : 33) "Hear another parable. There was a man who was a master of a household, who planted a vineyard, set a hedge about it, dug a wine press in it, built a tower, leased it out to farmers, and went into another country.

(Matthew 21 : 34)   When the season for the fruit drew near, he sent his servants to the farmers, to receive his fruit.

(Matthew 21 : 35)   The farmers took his servants, beat one, killed another, and stoned another.

(Matthew 21 : 36)   Again, he sent other servants more than the first: and they treated them the same way.

(Matthew 21 : 37)   But afterward he sent to them his son, saying, They will respect my son.'

(Matthew 21 : 38)   But the farmers, when they saw the son, said among themselves, â�˜This is the heir. Come, let's kill him, and seize his inheritance.'

(Matthew 21 : 39)   So they took him, and threw him out of the vineyard, and killed him.

(Matthew 21 : 40)   When therefore the lord of the vineyard comes, what will he do to those farmers?"

(Matthew 21 : 41)   They told him, "He will miserably destroy those miserable men, and will lease out the vineyard to other farmers, who will give him the fruit in its season."

(Matthew 21 : 42)   Jesus said to them, "Did you never read in the Scriptures,

The stone which the builders rejected,

the same was made the head of the corner.

This was from the Lord.

It is marvelous in our eyes?'

(Matthew 21 : 43)   "Therefore I tell you, the Kingdom of God will be taken away from you, and will be given to a nation producing its fruit.

(Matthew 21 : 44)   He who falls on this stone will be broken to pieces, but on whomever it will fall, it will scatter him as dust."

(Matthew 21 : 45)   When the chief priests and the Pharisees heard his parables, they perceived that he spoke about them.

(Matthew 21 : 46)   When they sought to seize him, they feared the multitudes, because they considered him to be a prophet.

(Mark 12 : 10)   Haven't you even read this Scripture:

The stone which the builders rejected,

the same was made the head of the corner.

(Mark 12 : 11)   This was from the Lord,

it is marvelous in our eyes'?"

(Mark 12 : 12)   They tried to seize him, but they feared the multitude; for they perceived that he spoke the parable against them. They left him, and went away.

(Luke 20 : 9)   He began to tell the people this parable. "Aman planted a vineyard, and rented it out to some farmers, and went into another country for a long time.

(Luke 20 : 10)   At the proper season, he sent a servant to the farmers to collect his share of the fruit of the vineyard. But the farmers beat him, and sent him away empty.

(Luke 20 : 11)   He sent yet another servant, and they also beat him, and treated him shamefully, and sent him away empty.

(Luke 20 : 12)   He sent yet a third, and they also wounded him, and threw him out.

(Luke 20 : 13)   The lord of the vineyard said, What shall I do? I will send my beloved son. It may be that seeing him, they will respect him.'

(Luke 20 : 14)   "But when the farmers saw him, they reasoned among themselves, saying, This is the heir. Come, let's kill him, that the inheritance may be ours.'

(Luke 20 : 15)   They threw him out of the vineyard, and killed him. What therefore will the lord of the vineyard do to them?

(Luke 20 : 16)   He will come and destroy these farmers, and will give the vineyard to others."

When they heard it, they said, "May it never be!"

(Luke 20 : 17)   But he looked at them, and said,

"Then what is this that is written,

The stone which the builders rejected,

the same was made the chief cornerstone?'

(Luke 20 : 18)   Everyone who falls on that stone will be broken to pieces,

but it will crush whomever it falls on to dust."

(Luke 20 : 19)   The chief priests and the scribes sought to lay hands on him that very hour, but they feared

> the people for they knew he had spoken this parable against them.

Paying Taxes to Caesar
Lk 20:20-26 / Mt 22:15-22 / Mk 12:13-17

(Luke 20 : 20)   They watched him, and sent out spies, who pretended to be righteous, that they might trap him in something he said, so as to deliver him up to the power and authority of the governor.

(Luke 20 : 21)   They asked him, "Teacher, we know that you say and teach what is right, and aren't partial to anyone, but truly teach the way of God.

(Luke 20 : 22)   Is it lawful for us to pay taxes to Caesar, or not?"

(Luke 20 : 23)   But he perceived their craftiness, and said to them, "Why do you test me?

(Luke 20 : 24)   Show me a denarius. Whose image and inscription are on it?"

They answered, "Caesar's."

(Luke 20 : 25)   He said to them, "Then give to Caesar the things that are Caesar's, and to God the things that are God's."

(Luke 20 : 26)   They weren't able to trap him in his words before the people. They marveled at his answer, and were silent.

(Matthew 22 : 15)   Then the Pharisees went and took counsel how they might entrap him in his talk.

(Matthew 22 : 16)   They sent their disciples to him, along with the Herodians, saying, "Teacher, we know that you are honest, and teach the way of God in truth, no matter whom you teach, for you aren't partial to anyone.

(Matthew 22 : 17)   Tell us therefore, what do you think? Is it lawful to pay taxes to Caesar, or not?"

(Matthew 22 : 18)   But Jesus perceived their wickedness, and said, "Why do you test me, you hypocrites?

(Matthew 22 : 19)   Show me the tax money."

They brought to him a denarius.

(Matthew 22 : 20)   He asked them, "Whose is this image and inscription?"

(Matthew 22 : 21)   They said to him, "Caesar's."

Then he said to them, "Give therefore to Caesar the things that are Caesar's, and to God the things that are God's."

(Matthew 22 : 22)   When they heard it, they marveled, and left him, and went away.

(Mark 12 : 13)   They sent some of the Pharisees and of the Herodians to him, that they might trap him with words.

(Mark 12 : 14)   When they had come, they asked him, "Teacher, we know that you are honest, and don't defer to anyone; for you aren't partial to anyone, but truly teach the way of God. Is it lawful to pay taxes to Caesar, or not?

(Mark 12 : 15)   Shall we give, or shall we not give?" But he, knowing their hypocrisy, said to them, "Why do you test me? Bring me a denarius, that I may see it."

(Mark 12 : 16)   They brought it.

He said to them, "Whose is this image and inscription?"

They said to him, "Caesar's."

(Mark 12 : 17)   Jesus answered them, "Render to Caesar the things that are Caesar's, and to God the things that are God's."

They marveled greatly at him.

The Resurrection and Marriage
Lk 20:27-40 / Mt 22:23-33 / Mk 12:18-27

(Luke 20 : 27)   Some of the Sadducees came to him, those who deny that there is a resurrection.

(Luke 20 : 28)   They asked him, "Teacher, Moses wrote to us that if a man's brother dies having a wife, and he is childless, his brother should take the wife, and raise up children for his brother.

(Luke 20 : 29)   There were therefore seven brothers. The first took a wife, and died childless.

(Luke 20 : 30)   The second took her as wife, and he died childless.

(Luke 20 : 31)   The third took her, and likewise the seven all left no children, and died.

(Luke 20 : 32)   Afterward the woman also died.

(Luke 20 : 33)   Therefore in the resurrection whose wife of them will she be? For the seven had her as a wife."

(Luke 20 : 34)   Jesus said to them, "The children of this age marry, and are given in marriage.

(Luke 20 : 35)   But those who are considered worthy to attain to that age and the resurrection from the dead, neither marry, nor are given in marriage.

(Luke 20 : 36)   For they can't die any more, for they are like the angels, and are children of God, being children of the resurrection.

(Luke 20 : 37)   But that the dead are raised, even Moses showed at the bush, when he called the Lord The God of Abraham, the God of Isaac, and the God of Jacob.'

(Luke 20 : 38)   Now he is not the God of the dead, but of the living, for all are alive to him."

(Luke 20 : 39)   Some of the scribes answered, "Teacher, you speak well."

(Luke 20 : 40)   They didn't dare to ask him any more questions.

(Matthew 22 : 23)   On that day Sadducees (those who say that there is no resurrection) came to him. They asked him,

(Matthew 22 : 24)   saying, "Teacher, Moses said, If a man dies, having no children, his brother shall marry his wife, and raise up seed for his brother.'

(Matthew 22 : 25)   Now there were with us seven brothers. The first married and died, and having no seed left his wife to his brother.

(Matthew 22 : 26)   In the same way, the second also, and the third, to the seventh.

(Matthew 22 : 27)   After them all, the woman died.

(Matthew 22 : 28)   In the resurrection therefore, whose wife will she be of the seven? For they all had her."

(Matthew 22 : 29)   But Jesus answered them, "You are mistaken, not knowing the Scriptures, nor the power of God.

(Matthew 22 : 30)   For in the resurrection they neither marry, nor are given in marriage, but are like God's angels in heaven.

(Matthew 22 : 31)   But concerning the resurrection of the dead, haven't you read that which was spoken to you by God, saying,

(Matthew 22 : 32)   I am the God of Abraham, and the God of Isaac, and the God of Jacob? God is not the God of the dead, but of the living."

(Matthew 22 : 33)   When the multitudes heard it, they were astonished at his teaching.

(Mark 12 : 18)   There came to him Sadducees, who say that there is no resurrection. They asked him, saying,

(Mark 12 : 19)   "Teacher, Moses wrote to us, If a man's brother dies, and leaves a wife behind him, and leaves no children, that his brother should take his wife, and raise up offspring for his brother.'

(Mark 12 : 20)   There were seven brothers. The first took a wife, and dying left no offspring.

(Mark 12 : 21)   The second took her, and died, leaving no children behind him. The third likewise;

(Mark 12 : 22)   and the seven took her and left no children. Last of all the woman also died.

(Mark 12 : 23)   In the resurrection, when they rise, whose wife will she be of them? For the seven had her as a wife."

(Mark 12 : 24)   Jesus answered them, "Isn't this because you are mistaken, not knowing the Scriptures, nor the power of God?

(Mark 12 : 25)   For when they will rise from the dead, they neither marry, nor are given in marriage, but are like angels in heaven.

(Mark 12 : 26)   But about the dead, that they are raised; haven't you read in the book of Moses, about the

Bush, how God spoke to him, saying, I am the God of Abraham, the God of Isaac, and the God of Jacob'

(Mark 12 : 27)   He is not the God of the dead, but of the living. You are therefore badly mistaken."

The Greatest Commandment
Mt 22:34-40 / Mk 12:28-34

(Matthew 22 : 34)   But the Pharisees, when they heard that he had silenced the Sadducees, gathered themselves together.

(Matthew 22 : 35)   One of them, a lawyer, asked him a question, testing him.

(Matthew 22 : 36)   "Teacher, which is the greatest commandment in the law?"

(Matthew 22 : 37)   Jesus said to him, "You shall love the Lord your God with all your heart, with all your soul, and with all your mind.'

(Matthew 22 : 38)   This is the first and great commandment.

(Matthew 22 : 39)   A second likewise is this, You shall love your neighbor as yourself.'

(Matthew 22 : 40)   The whole law and the prophets depend on these two commandments."

(Mark 12 : 28)   One of the scribes came, and heard them questioning together. Knowing that he had answered them well, asked him, "Which commandment is the greatest of all?"

(Mark 12 : 29)   Jesus answered, "The greatest is, Hear, Israel, the Lord our God, the Lord is one:

(Mark 12 : 30)   you shall love the Lord your God with all your heart, and with all your soul, and with all your mind, and with all your strength. 'This is the first commandment.

(Mark 12 : 31)   The second is like this, You shall love your neighbor as yourself. 'There is no other commandment greater than these."

(Mark 12 : 32)   The scribe said to him, "Truly, teacher, you have said well that he is one, and there is none other but he,

(Mark 12 : 33)   and to love him with all the heart, and with all the understanding, with all the soul, and with all the strength, and to love his neighbor as himself, is more important than all whole burnt offerings and sacrifices."

(Mark 12 : 34)   When Jesus saw that he answered wisely, he said to him, "You are not far from the Kingdom of God." No one dared ask him any question after that.

Whose Son Is the Messiah?
20:41-47pp — Mt 22:41–23:7; Mk 12:35-37

(Matthew 22 : 41)   Now while the Pharisees were gathered together, Jesus asked them a question,

(Matthew 22 : 42) saying, "What do you think of the Christ? Whose son is he?" They said to him, "Of David."

(Matthew 22 : 43)   He said to them, "How then does David in the Spirit call him Lord, saying,

(Matthew 22 : 44)   The Lord said to my Lord, sit on my right hand, until I make your enemies a footstool for your feet?'

(Matthew 22 : 45)   "If then David calls him Lord, how is he his son?"

(Matthew 22 : 46)   No one was able to answer him a word, neither did any man dare ask him any more questions from that day forward.

(Luke 20 : 41)   He said to them, "Why do they say that the Christ is David's son?

(Luke 20 : 42)   David himself says in the book of Psalms,

The Lord said to my Lord,

"Sit at my right hand,

(Luke 20 : 43)   until I make your enemies the footstool of your feet.'"

(Luke 20 : 44)   "David therefore calls him Lord, so how is he his son?"

(Mark 12 : 35)   Jesus responded, as he taught in the temple, "How is it that the scribes say that the Christ is the son of David?

(Mark 12 : 36)   For David himself said in the Holy Spirit,

The Lord said to my Lord,

"Sit at my right hand,

until I make your enemies the footstool of your feet."'

(Mark 12 : 37)   Therefore David himself calls him Lord, so how can he be his son?" The common people heard him gladly.

A Warning Against Hypocrisy
Mt 23"1-12 / Lk 20:45-47 / Mk 12:38-40

(Matthew 23 : 1)   Then Jesus spoke to the multitudes and to his disciples,

(Matthew 23 : 2)   saying, "The scribes and the Pharisees sat on Moses' seat.

(Matthew 23 : 3)   All things therefore whatever they tell you to observe, observe and do, but don't do their works; for they say, and don't do.

(Matthew 23 : 4)   For they bind heavy burdens that are grievous to be borne, and lay them on men's shoulders; but they themselves will not lift a finger to help them.

(Matthew 23 : 5)   But all their works they do to be seen by men. They make their phylacteries broad, enlarge the fringes of their garments,

(Matthew 23 : 6)   and love the place of honor at feasts, the best seats in the synagogues,

(Matthew 23 : 7)   the salutations in the marketplaces, and to be called Rabbi, Rabbi' by men.

(Luke 20 : 45)   In the hearing of all the people, he said to his disciples,

(Luke 20 : 46)   "Beware of the scribes, who like to walk in long robes, and love greetings in the marketplaces, the best seats in the synagogues, and the best places at feasts;

(Luke 20 : 47)   who devour widows' houses, and for a pretense make long prayers: these will receive greater condemnation."

(Matthew 23 : 8)   But don't you be called Rabbi,' for one is your teacher, the Christ, and all of you are brothers.

(Matthew 23 : 9)   Call no man on the earth your father, for one is your Father, he who is in heaven.

(Matthew 23 : 10)   Neither be called masters, for one is your master, the Christ.

(Matthew 23 : 11)   But he who is greatest among you will be your servant.

(Matthew 23 : 12)   Whoever exalts himself will be humbled, and whoever humbles himself will be exalted.

(Mark 12 : 38)   In his teaching he said to them, "Beware of the scribes, who like to walk in long robes, and to get greetings in the marketplaces,

(Mark 12 : 39)   and the best seats in the synagogues, and the best places at feasts:

(Mark 12 : 40)   those who devour widows' houses, and for a pretense make long prayers. These will receive greater condemnation."

Seven Woes on the Teachers of the Law and the Pharisees
Mt 23:13-39

(Matthew 23 : 13)   "Woe to you, scribes and Pharisees, hypocrites! For you devour widows' houses, and as a pretense you make long prayers. Therefore you will receive greater condemnation.

(Matthew 23 : 14)   "But woe to you, scribes and Pharisees, hypocrites! Because you shut up the Kingdom of Heaven against men; for you don't enter in yourselves, neither do you allow those who are entering in to enter.

(Matthew 23 : 15)   Woe to you, scribes and Pharisees, hypocrites! For you travel around by sea and land to make one proselyte; and when he becomes one, you make him twice as much of a son of Gehenna as yourselves.

(Matthew 23 : 16)   "Woe to you, you blind guides, who say, Whoever swears by the temple, it is nothing; but whoever swears by the gold of the temple, he is obligated.'

(Matthew 23 : 17)   You blind fools! For which is greater, the gold, or the temple that sanctifies the gold?

(Matthew 23 : 18)   Whoever swears by the altar, it is nothing; but whoever swears by the gift that is on it, he is obligated?'

(Matthew 23 : 19)   You blind fools! For which is greater, the gift, or the altar that sanctifies the gift?

(Matthew 23 : 20)   He therefore who swears by the altar, swears by it, and by everything on it.

(Matthew 23 : 21)   He who swears by the temple, swears by it, and by him who was livingin it.

(Matthew 23 : 22)   He who swears by heaven, swears by the throne of God, and by him who sits on it.

(Matthew 23 : 23)   "Woe to you, scribes and Pharisees, hypocrites! For you tithe mint, dill, and cumin, and have left undone the weightier matters of the law: justice, mercy, and faith. But you ought to have done these, and not to have left the other undone.

(Matthew 23 : 24)   You blind guides, who strain out a gnat, and swallow a camel!

(Matthew 23 : 25)   "Woe to you, scribes and Pharisees, hypocrites! For you clean the outside of the cup and of the platter, but within they are full of extortion and unrighteousness.

(Matthew 23 : 26)   You blind Pharisee, first clean the inside of the cup and of the platter, that its outside may become clean also.

(Matthew 23 : 27)   "Woe to you, scribes and Pharisees, hypocrites! For you are like whitened tombs, which outwardly appear beautiful, but inwardly are full of dead men's bones, and of all uncleanness.

(Matthew 23 : 28)   Even so you also outwardly appear righteous to men, but inwardly you are full of hypocrisy and iniquity.

(Matthew 23 : 29)   "Woe to you, scribes and Pharisees, hypocrites! For you build the tombs of the prophets, and decorate the tombs of the righteous,

(Matthew 23 : 30)   and say, If we had lived in the days of our fathers, we wouldn't have been partakers with them in the blood of the prophets.'

(Matthew 23 : 31)   Therefore you testify to yourselves that you are children of those who killed the prophets.

(Matthew 23 : 32)   Fill up, then, the measure of your fathers.

(Matthew 23 : 33)   You serpents, you offspring of vipers, how will you escape the judgment of Gehenna?

(Matthew 23 : 34)   Therefore behold, I send to you prophets, wise men, and scribes. Some of them you will kill and crucify; and some of them you will scourge in your synagogues, and persecute from city to city;

(Matthew 23 : 35)   that on you may come all the righteous blood shed on the earth, from the blood of righteous Abel to the blood of Zachariah son of Barachiah, whom you killed between the sanctuary and the altar.

(Matthew 23 : 36)   Most certainly I tell you, all these things will come upon this generation.

(Matthew 23 : 37)   "Jerusalem, Jerusalem, who kills the prophets, and stones those who are sent to her! How often I would have gathered your children together, even as a hen gathers her chicks under her wings, and you would not!

(Matthew 23 : 38)   Behold, your house is left to you desolate.

(Matthew 23 : 39)   For I tell you, you will not see me from now on, until you say, Blessed is he who comes in the name of the Lord!'"

The Widow's Offering
Mk 12:41-44 / Lk 21:1-4

(Mark 12 : 41)   Jesus sat down opposite the treasury, and saw how the multitude cast money into the treasury. Many who were rich cast in much.

(Mark 12 : 42)   A poor widow came, and she cast in two small brass coins, which equal a quadrans coin.

(Mark 12 : 43)   He called his disciples to himself, and said to them, "Most certainly I tell you, this poor widow gave more than all those who are giving into the treasury,

(Mark 12 : 44)   for they all gave out of their abundance, but she, out of her poverty, gave all that she had to live on."

(Luke 21 : 1)   He looked up, and saw the rich people who were putting their gifts into the treasury.

(Luke 21 : 2)   He saw a certain poor widow casting in two small brass coins.

(Luke 21 : 3)   He said, "Truly I tell you, this poor widow put in more than all of them,

(Luke 21 : 4)   for all these put in gifts for God from their abundance, but she, out of her poverty, put in all that she had to live on."

The Destruction of the Temple and Signs of the End Times
Mt 24:1-35 / Lk 21:5-28 & Lk 21:29-36 / Mk 13:1-31

(Matthew 24 : 1) Jesus went out from the temple, and was going on his way. His disciples came to him to show him the buildings of the temple.

(Luke 21 : 5)   As some were talking about the temple and how it was decorated with beautiful stones and gifts, he said,

(Luke 21 : 6)   "As for these things which you see, the days will come, in which there will not be left here one stone on another that will not be thrown down."

(Matthew 24 : 2)   But he answered them, "You see all of these things, don't you? Most certainly I tell you,

> there will not be left here one stone on another, that will not be thrown down."

(Matthew 24 : 3)   As he sat on the Mount of Olives, the disciples came to him privately, saying, "Tell us, when will these things be? What is the sign of your coming, and of the end of the age?"

(Matthew 24 : 4)   Jesus answered them, "Be careful that no one leads you astray.

(Matthew 24 : 5)   For many will come in my name, saying, I am the Christ,' and will lead many astray.

(Matthew 24 : 6)   You will hear of wars and rumors of wars. See that you aren't troubled, for all this must happen, but the end is not yet.

(Matthew 24 : 7)   For nation will rise against nation, and kingdom against kingdom; and there will be famines, plagues, and earthquakes in various places.

(Matthew 24 : 8) But all these things are the beginning of birth pains.

(Matthew 24 : 9)   Then they will deliver you up to oppression, and will kill you. You will be hated by all of the nations for my name's sake.

(Matthew 24 : 10)   Then many will stumble, and will deliver up one another, and will hate one another.

(Matthew 24 : 11) Many false prophets will arise, and will lead many astray.

(Matthew 24 : 12)   Because iniquity will be multiplied, the love of many will grow cold.

(Matthew 24 : 13)   But he who endures to the end, the same will be saved.

(Matthew 24 : 14)   This Good News of the Kingdom will be preached in the whole world for a testimony to all the nations, and then the end will come.

(Luke 21 : 7)   They asked him, "Teacher, so when will these things be? What is the sign that these things are about to happen?"

(Luke 21 : 8)   He said, "Watch out that you don't get led astray, for many will come in my name, saying, I am he,' and, The time is at hand.' Therefore don't follow them.

(Luke 21 : 9)   When you hear of wars and disturbances, don't be terrified, for these things must happen first, but the end won't come immediately."

(Luke 21 : 10)   Then he said to them, "Nation will rise against nation, and kingdom against kingdom.

(Mark 13 : 1)   As he went out of the temple, one of his disciples said to him, "Teacher, see what kind of stones and what kind of buildings!"

(Mark 13 : 2)   Jesus said to him, "Do you see these great buildings? There will not be left here one stone on another, which will not be thrown down."

(Mark 13 : 3)   As he sat on the Mount of Olives opposite the temple, Peter, James, John, and Andrew asked him privately,

(Mark 13 : 4)   "Tell us, when will these things be? What is the sign that these things are all about to be fulfilled?"

(Mark 13 : 5)   Jesus, answering, began to tell them, "Be careful that no one leads you astray.

(Mark 13 : 6)   For many will come in my name, saying, I am he!' and will lead many astray.

(Mark 13 : 7)   "When you hear of wars and rumors of wars, don't be troubled. For those must happen, but the end is not yet.

(Mark 13 : 8) For nation will rise against nation, and kingdom against kingdom. There will be earthquakes in various places. There will be famines and troubles. These things are the beginning of birth pains.

(Mark 13 : 9)   But watch yourselves, for they will deliver you up to councils. You will be beaten in synagogues. You will stand before rulers and kings for my sake, for a testimony to them.

(Mark 13 : 10)   The Good News must first be preached to all the nations.

(Mark 13 : 11) When they lead you away and deliver you up, don't be anxious beforehand, or premeditate what you will say, but say whatever will be given you in that hour. For it is not you who speak, but the Holy Spirit.

(Mark 13 : 12)   "Brother will deliver up brother to death, and the father his child. Children will rise up against parents, and cause them to be put to death.

(Mark 13 : 13) You will be hated by all men for my name's sake, but he who endures to the end, the same will be saved.

(Mark 13 : 14)   But when you see the abomination of desolation, spoken of by Daniel the prophet, standing where it ought not (let the reader understand), then let those who are in Judea flee to the mountains,

(Mark 13 : 15)   and let him who is on the housetop not go down, nor enter in, to take anything out of his house.

(Mark 13 : 16) Let him who is in the field not return back to take his cloak.

(Mark 13 : 17) But woe to those who are with child and to those who nurse babies in those days!

(Mark 13 : 18) Pray that your flight won't be in the winter.

(Mark 13 : 19)   For in those days there will be oppression, such as there has not been the like from the beginning of the creation which God created until now, and never will be.

(Mark 13 : 20)   Unless the Lord had shortened the days, no flesh would have been saved; but for the sake of the chosen ones, whom he picked out, he shortened the days.

(Mark 13 : 21)   Then if anyone tells you, Look, here is the Christ!' or, Look, there!' don't believe it.

(Mark 13 : 22)   For there will arise false christs and false prophets, and will show signs and wonders, that they may lead astray, if possible, even the chosen ones.

(Mark 13 : 23)   But you watch. "Behold, I have told you all things beforehand.

(Mark 13 : 24)   But in those days, after that oppression,

the sun will be darkened,

the moon will not give its light,

(Mark 13 : 25)   the stars will be falling from the sky,

and the powers that are in the heavens will be shaken.

(Mark 13 : 26)   Then they will see the Son of Man coming in clouds with great power and glory.

(Mark 13 : 27)   Then he will send out his angels, and will gather together his chosen ones from the four winds, from the ends of the earth to the ends of the sky.

(Mark 13 : 28)   "Now from the fig tree, learn this parable. When the branch has now become tender, and produces its leaves, you know that the summer is near;

(Mark 13 : 29) even so you also, when you see these things coming to pass, know that it is near, at the doors.

(Mark 13 : 30)   Most certainly I say to you, this generation will not pass away until all these things happen.

> (Mark 13 : 31) Heaven and earth will pass away, but my words will not pass away.

(Luke 21 : 11)   There will be great earthquakes, famines, and plagues in various places. There will be terrors and great signs from heaven.

(Luke 21 : 12)   But before all these things, they will lay their hands on you and will persecute you, delivering you up to synagogues and prisons, bringing you before kings and governors for my name's sake.

(Luke 21 : 13)   It will turn out as a testimony for you.

(Luke 21 : 14)   Settle it therefore in your hearts not to meditate beforehand how to answer,

(Luke 21 : 15)   for I will give you a mouth and wisdom which all your adversaries will not be able to withstand or to contradict.

(Luke 21 : 16)   You will be handed over even by parents, brothers, relatives, and friends. They will cause some of you to be put to death.

(Luke 21 : 17)   You will be hated by all men for my name's sake.

(Luke 21 : 18)   And not a hair of your head will perish.

(Luke 21 : 19)   "By your endurance you will win your lives.

(Luke 21 : 20) "But when you see Jerusalem surrounded by armies, then know that its desolation is at hand.

(Matthew 24 : 15)   "When, therefore, you see the abomination of desolation, which was spoken of through

Daniel the prophet, standing in the holy place (let the reader understand),

(Matthew 24 : 16)   then let those who are in Judea flee to the mountains.

(Matthew 24 : 17)   Let him who is on the housetop not go down to take out things that are in his house.

(Matthew 24 : 18)   Let him who is in the field not return back to get his clothes.

(Matthew 24 : 19)   But woe to those who are with child and to nursing mothers in those days!

(Matthew 24 : 20)   Pray that your flight will not be in the winter, nor on a Sabbath,

(Matthew 24 : 21)   for then there will be great oppression, such as has not been from the beginning of the world until now, no, nor ever will be.

(Matthew 24 : 22)   Unless those days had been shortened, no flesh would have been saved. But for the sake of the chosen ones, those days will be shortened.

(Matthew 24 : 23)   "Then if any man tells you, Behold, here is the Christ,' or, There,' don't believe it.

(Matthew 24 : 24)   For there will arise false christs, and false prophets, and they will show great signs and wonders, so as to lead astray, if possible, even the chosen ones.

(Matthew 24 : 25) "Behold, I have told you beforehand. (Matthew 24 : 26)   If therefore they tell you, Behold, he is in the wilderness,' don't go out; Behold, he is in the inner rooms,' don't believe it.

(Matthew 24 : 27)   For as the lightning flashes from the east, and is seen even to the west, so will be the coming of the Son of Man.

(Luke 21 : 21)   Then let those who are in Judea flee to the mountains. Let those who are in the midst of her depart. Let those who are in the country not enter therein.

(Luke 21 : 22)   For these are days of vengeance, that all things which are written may be fulfilled.

(Luke 21 : 23)   Woe to those who are pregnant and to those who nurse infants in those days! For there will be great distress in the land, and wrath to this people.

(Luke 21 : 24)   They will fall by the edge of the sword, and will be led captive into all the nations. Jerusalem will be trampled down by the Gentiles, until the times of the Gentiles are fulfilled.

(Luke 21 : 25)   There will be signs in the sun, moon, and stars; and on the earth anxiety of nations, in perplexity for the roaring of the sea and the waves;

(Luke 21 : 26)   men fainting for fear, and for expectation of the things which are coming on the world: for the powers of the heavens will be shaken.

(Luke 21 : 27)   Then they will see the Son of Man coming in a cloud with power and great glory.

(Luke 21 : 28)   But when these things begin to happen, look up, and lift up your heads, because your redemption is near."

(Matthew 24 : 28)   For wherever the carcass is, there is where the vultures gather together.

(Matthew 24 : 29)   But immediately after the oppression of those days, the sun will be darkened, the moon will not give its light, the stars will fall from the sky, and the powers of the heavens will be shaken;

(Matthew 24 : 30)   and then the sign of the Son of Man will appear in the sky. Then all the tribes of the earth will mourn, and they will see the Son of Man coming on the clouds of the sky with power and great glory.

(Matthew 24 : 31)   He will send out his angels with a great sound of a trumpet, and they will gather together his chosen ones from the four winds, from one end of the sky to the other.

(Luke 21 : 29)   He told them a parable. "See the fig tree, and all the trees.

(Luke 21 : 30)   When they are already budding, you see it and know by your own selves that the summer is already near.

(Luke 21 : 31)   Even so you also, when you see these things happening, know that the Kingdom of God is near.

(Luke 21 : 32)   Most certainly I tell you, this generation will not pass away until all things are accomplished.

(Luke 21 : 33)   Heaven and earth will pass away, but my words will by no means pass away.

(Luke 21 : 34)   "So be careful, or your hearts will be loaded down with carousing, drunkenness, and cares of this life, and that day will come on you suddenly.

(Luke 21 : 35)   For it will come like a snare on all those who dwell on the surface of all the earth.

(Luke 21 : 36)   Therefore be watchful all the time, praying that you may be counted worthy to escape all these things that will happen, and to stand before the Son of Man."

(Matthew 24 : 32)   "Now from the fig tree learn this parable. When its branch has now become tender, and produces its leaves, you know that the summer is near.

(Matthew 24 : 33)   Even so you also, when you see all these things, know that it is near, even at the doors.

(Matthew 24 : 34)   Most certainly I tell you, this generation will not pass away, until all these things are accomplished.

(Matthew 24 : 35)   Heaven and earth will pass away, but my words will not pass away.

The Day and Hour Unknown
Mt 24:36-51 / Mk 13:32-36 / (Lk 12:35-48)

(Matthew 24 : 36)   But no one knows of that day and hour, not even the angels of heaven ,but my Father only.

(Matthew 24 : 37) "As the days of Noah were, so will be the coming of the Son of Man.

(Matthew 24 : 38) For as in those days which were before the flood they were eating and drinking, marrying and giving in marriage, until the day that Noah entered into the ship,

(Matthew 24 : 39) and they didn't know until the flood came, and took them all away, so will be the coming of the Son of Man.

(Matthew 24 : 40) Then two men will be in the field: one will be taken and one will be left;

(Matthew 24 : 41) two women grinding at the mill, one will be taken and one will be left.

(Matthew 24 : 42) Watch therefore, for you don't know in what hour your Lord comes.

(Matthew 24 : 43) But know this, that if the master of the house had known in what watch of the night the thief was coming, he would have watched, and would not have allowed his house to be broken into.

(Matthew 24 : 44) Therefore also be ready, for in an hour that you don't expect, the Son of Man will come.

(Matthew 24 : 45) "Who then is the faithful and wise servant, whom his lord has set over his household, to give them their food in due season?

(Matthew 24 : 46) Blessed is that servant whom his lord finds doing so when he comes.

(Matthew 24 : 47) Most certainly I tell you that he will set him over all that he has.

(Matthew 24 : 48)   But if that evil servant should say in his heart, My lord is delaying his coming,'

(Matthew 24 : 49)   and begins to beat his fellow servants, and eat and drink with the drunkards,

(Matthew 24 : 50)   the lord of that servant will come in a day when he doesn't expect it, and in an hour when he doesn't know it,

(Matthew 24 : 51)   and will cut him in pieces, and appoint his portion with the hypocrites. There is where the weeping and grinding of teeth will be.

(Mark 13 : 32)   But of that day or that hour no one knows, not even the angels in heaven, nor the Son, but only the Father.

(Mark 13 : 33)   Watch, keep alert, and pray; for you don't know when the time is.

(Mark 13 : 34)   "It is like a man, traveling to another country, having left his house, and given authority to his servants, and to each one his work, and also commanded the doorkeeper to keep watch.

(Mark 13 : 35)   Watch therefore, for you don't know when the lord of the house is coming, whether at evening, or at midnight, or when the rooster crows, or in the morning;

(Mark 13 : 36)   lest coming suddenly he might find you sleeping.

What I tell you, I tell all: Watch."

The Parable of the Ten Virgins
Mt 25:1-13

(Matthew 25 : 1)   "Then the Kingdom of Heaven will be like ten virgins, who took their lamps, and went out to meet the bridegroom.

(Matthew 25 : 2)   Five of them were foolish, and five were wise.

(Matthew 25 : 3)   Those who were foolish, when they took their lamps, took no oil with them,

(Matthew 25 : 4)   but the wise took oil in their vessels with their lamps.

(Matthew 25 : 5)   Now while the bridegroom delayed, they all slumbered and slept.

(Matthew 25 : 6)   But at midnight there was a cry, Behold! The bridegroom is coming! Come out to meet him!'

(Matthew 25 : 7)   Then all those virgins arose, and trimmed their lamps.

(Matthew 25 : 8)   The foolish said to the wise, Give us some of your oil, for our lamps are going out.'

(Matthew 25 : 9)   But the wise answered, saying, What if there isn't enough for us and you? You go rather to those who sell, and buy for yourselves.'

(Matthew 25 : 10)   While they went away to buy, the bridegroom came, and those who were ready went in with him to the marriage feast, and the door was shut.

(Matthew 25 : 11)   Afterward the other virgins also came, saying, Lord, Lord, open to us.'

(Matthew 25 : 12)   But he answered, Most certainly I tell you, I don't know you.'

(Matthew 25 : 13)   Watch therefore, for you don't know the day nor the hour in which the Son of Man is coming.

The Parable of the Bags of Gold
Mt 25:14-30 / Lk 19:11-27

(Matthew 25 : 14)   "For it is like a man, going into another country, who called his own servants, and entrusted his goods to them.

(Matthew 25 : 15)   To one he gave five talents, to another two, to another one; to each according to his own ability. Then he went on his journey.

(Matthew 25 : 16)   Immediately he who received the five talents went and traded with them, and made another five talents.

(Matthew 25 : 17)   In the same way, he also who got the two gained another two.

(Matthew 25 : 18)   But he who received the one went away and dug in the earth, and hid his lord's money. (Matthew 25 : 19)   "Now after a long time the lord of those servants came, and reconciled accounts with them.

(Matthew 25 : 20)   He who received the five talents came and brought another five talents, saying, Lord, you delivered to me five talents. Behold, I have gained another five talents besides them.'

(Matthew 25 : 21)   "His lord said to him, Well done, good and faithful servant. You have been faithful over a few things, I will set you over many things. Enter into the joy of your lord.'

(Matthew 25 : 22)   "He also who got the two talents came and said, Lord, you delivered to me two talents. Behold, I have gained another two talents besides them.'

(Matthew 25 : 23)   "His lord said to him, Well done, good and faithful servant. You have been faithful over a few things, I will set you over many things. Enter into the joy of your lord.'

(Matthew 25 : 24)   "He also who had received the one talent came and said, Lord, I knew you that you are a hard man, reaping where you did not sow, and gathering where you did not scatter.

(Matthew 25 : 25)   I was afraid, and went away and hid your talent in the earth. Behold, you have what is yours.' (Matthew 25 : 26)   "But his lord answered him, You wicked and slothful servant. You knew that I reap where I didn't sow, and gather where I didn't scatter.

(Matthew 25 : 27)   You ought therefore to have deposited my money with the bankers, and at my coming I should have received back my own with interest.

(Matthew 25 : 28) Take away therefore the talent from him, and give it to him who has the ten talents.

(Matthew 25 : 29)   For to everyone who has will be given, and he will have abundance, but from him who doesn't have, even that which he has will be taken away.

(Matthew 25 : 30)   Throw out the unprofitable servant into the outer darkness, where there will be weeping and gnashing of teeth.'

(Luke 19 : 11)   As they heard these things, he went on and told a parable, because he was near Jerusalem, and they supposed that the Kingdom of God would be revealed immediately.

(Luke 19 : 12)   He said therefore, "A certain nobleman went into a far country to receive for himself a kingdom, and to return.

(Luke 19 : 13)   He called ten servants of his, and gave them ten mina coins, and told them, Conduct business until I come.'

(Luke 19 : 14)   But his citizens hated him, and sent an envoy after him, saying, We don't want this man to reign over us.'

(Luke 19 : 15)   "It happened when he had come back again, having received the kingdom, that he commanded these servants, to whom he had given the money, to be called to him, that he might know what they had gained by conducting business.

(Luke 19 : 16)   The first came before him, saying, Lord, your mina has made ten more minas.'

(Luke 19 : 17)   "He said to him, Well done, you good servant! Because you were found faithful with very little, you shall have authority over ten cities.'

(Luke 19 : 18)   "The second came, saying, Your mina, Lord, has made five minas.'

(Luke 19 : 19)   "So he said to him, And you are to be over five cities.'

(Luke 19 : 20)   Another came, saying, Lord, behold, your mina, which I kept laid away in a handkerchief,

(Luke 19 : 21)   for I feared you, because you are an exacting man. You take up that which you didn't lay down, and reap that which you didn't sow.'

(Luke 19 : 22)   "He said to him, Out of your own mouth will I judge you, you wicked servant! You knew that I am an exacting man, taking up that which I didn't lay down, and reaping that which I didn't sow.

(Luke 19 : 23)   Then why didn't you deposit my money in the bank, and at my coming, I might have earned interest on it?'

(Luke 19 : 24)   He said to those who stood by, Take the mina away from him, and give it to him who has the ten minas.'

(Luke 19 : 25)   "They said to him, Lord, he has ten minas!'

(Luke 19 : 26)   For I tell you that to everyone who has, will more be given; but from him who doesn't have, even that which he has will be taken away from him.

> (Luke 19 : 27) But bring those enemies of mine who didn't want me to reign over them here, and kill them before me.'"

The Sheep and the Goats
Mt 25:31-46

(Matthew 25 : 31) "But when the Son of Man comes in his glory, and all the holy angels with him, then he will sit on the throne of his glory.

(Matthew 25 : 32) Before him all the nations will be gathered, and he will separate them one from another, as a shepherd separates the sheep from the goats.

(Matthew 25 : 33) He will set the sheep on his right hand, but the goats on the left.

(Matthew 25 : 34) Then the King will tell those on his right hand, Come, blessed of my Father, inherit the Kingdom prepared for you from the foundation of the world;

(Matthew 25 : 35) for I was hungry, and you gave me food to eat. I was thirsty, and you gave me drink. I was a stranger, and you took me in.

(Matthew 25 : 36) I was naked, and you clothed me. I was sick, and you visited me. I was in prison, and you came to me.'

(Matthew 25 : 37) "Then the righteous will answer him, saying, Lord, when did we see you hungry, and feed you; or thirsty, and give you a drink?

(Matthew 25 : 38) When did we see you as a stranger, and take you in; or naked, and clothe you?

(Matthew 25 : 39) When did we see you sick, or in prison, and come to you?'

(Matthew 25 : 40) "The King will answer them, Most certainly I tell you, because you did it to one of the least of these my brothers, you did it to me.'

(Matthew 25 : 41) Then he will say also to those on the left hand, Depart from me, you cursed, into the eternal fire which is prepared for the devil and his angels;

(Matthew 25 : 42) for I was hungry, and you didn't give me food to eat; I was thirsty, and you gave me no drink;

(Matthew 25 : 43) I was a stranger, and you didn't take me in; naked, and you didn't clothe me; sick, and in prison, and you didn't visit me.'

(Matthew 25 : 44) "Then they will also answer, saying, Lord, when did we see you hungry, or thirsty, or a stranger, or naked, or sick, or in prison, and didn't help you?'

(Matthew 25 : 45) "Then he will answer them, saying, Most certainly I tell you, because you didn't do it to one of the least of these, you didn't do it to me.'

(Matthew 25 : 46) These will go away into eternal punishment, but the righteous into eternal life."

The Plot Against Jesus
Mt 26:1-5 / Mk 14:1-2 / Lk 21:37-38

(Matthew 26 : 1) It happened, when Jesus had finished all these words, that he said to his disciples,

(Matthew 26 : 2)   "You know that after two days the Passover is coming, and the Son of Man will be delivered up to be crucified."

(Luke 21 : 37)   Every day Jesus was teaching in the temple, and every night he would go out and spend the night on the mountain that is called Olivet.

(Luke 21 : 38)   All the people came early in the morning to him in the temple to hear him.

(Matthew 26 : 3)   Then the chief priests, the scribes, and the elders of the people were gathered together in the court of the high priest, who was called Caiaphas.

(Matthew 26 : 4)   They took counsel together that they might take Jesus by deceit, and kill him.

(Matthew 26 : 5)   But they said, "Not during the feast, lest a riot occur among the people."

(Mark 14 : 1)   It was now two days before the feast of the Passover and the unleavened

bread, and the chief priests and the scribes sought how they might seize him by deception, and kill him.

(Mark 14 : 2)   For they said, "Not during the feast, because there might be a riot of the people."

Judas Agrees to Betray Jesus
Lk 22:1-6 / Mk 14:10-11 / Mt 26:14-16

(Luke 22 : 1)   Now the feast of unleavened bread, which is called the Passover, drew near.

(Luke 22 : 2)   The chief priests and the scribes sought how they might put him to death, for they feared the people.

(Luke 22 : 3)   Satan entered into Judas, who was also called Iscariot, who was numbered with the twelve.

(Luke 22 : 4)   He went away, and talked with the chief priests and captains about how he might deliver him to them.

(Mark 14 : 10)   Judas Iscariot, who was one of the twelve, went away to the chief priests, that he might deliver him to them.

(Mark 14 : 11)   They, when they heard it, were glad, and promised to give him money. He sought how he might conveniently deliver him.

(Matthew 26 : 14)   Then one of the twelve, who was called Judas Iscariot, went to the chief priests,

---

(Matthew 26 : 15)   and said, "What are you willing to give me, that I should deliver him to you?" They weighed out for him thirty pieces of silver.

(Luke 22 : 5)   They were glad, and agreed to give him money.

(Luke 22 : 6)   He consented, and sought an opportunity to deliver him to them in the absence of the multitude.

(Matthew 26 : 16)   From that time he sought opportunity to betray him.

Preparation for the Last Supper
Lk 22:7-13 / Mk 14:12-16 / Mt 26:17-19

(Luke 22 : 7)   The day of unleavened bread came, on which the Passover must be sacrificed.

(Luke 22 : 8)   He sent Peter and John, saying, "Go and prepare the Passover for us, that we may eat."

(Luke 22 : 9)   They said to him, "Where do you want us to prepare?"

(Luke 22 : 10)   He said to them, "Behold, when you have entered into the city, a man carrying a pitcher of water will meet you. Follow him into the house which he enters.

(Luke 22 : 11)   Tell the master of the house, The Teacher says to you, "Where is the guest room, where I may eat the Passover with my disciples?"'

(Luke 22 : 12)   He will show you a large, furnished upper room. Make preparations there."

(Luke 22 : 13)   They went, found things as he had told them, and they prepared the Passover.

(Mark 14 : 12)   On the first day of unleavened bread, when they sacrificed the Passover, his disciples asked him, "Where do you want us to go and prepare that you may eat the Passover?"

(Mark 14 : 13)   He sent two of his disciples, and said to them, "Go into the city, and there you will meet a man carrying a pitcher of water. Follow him,

(Mark 14 : 14)   and wherever he enters in, tell the master of the house, The Teacher says, "Where is the guest room, where I may eat the Passover with my disciples?"'

(Mark 14 : 15)   He will himself show you a large upper room furnished and ready. Get ready for us there."

(Mark 14 : 16)   His disciples went out, and came into the city, and found things as he had said to them, and they prepared the Passover.

(Matthew 26 : 17)   Now on the first day of unleavened bread, the disciples came to Jesus, saying to him, "Where do you want us to prepare for you to eat the Passover?"

(Matthew 26 : 18)   He said, "Go into the city to a certain person, and tell him, The Teacher says, "My time is at hand. I will keep the Passover at your house with my disciples."'"

(Matthew 26 : 19)   The disciples did as Jesus commanded them, and they prepared the Passover.

Jesus Washes His Disciples' Feet
Jn 13:1-17

(John 13 : 1)   Now before the feast of the Passover, Jesus, knowing that his time had come that he would depart from this world to the Father, having loved his own who were in the world, he loved them to the end.

(John 13 : 2)   During supper, the devil having already put into the heart of Judas Iscariot, Simon's son, to betray him,

(John 13 : 3)   Jesus, knowing that the Father had given all things into his hands, and that he came from God, and was going to God,

(John 13 : 4)   arose from supper, and laid aside his outer garments. He took a towel, and wrapped a towel around his waist.

(John 13 :5)   Then he poured water into the basin, and began to wash the disciples' feet, and to wipe them with the towel that was wrapped around him.

(John 13 : 6)   Then he came to Simon Peter. He said to him, "Lord, do you wash my feet?"

(John 13 : 7)   Jesus answered him, "You don't know what I am doing now, but you will understand later."

(John 13 : 8)   Peter said to him, "You will never wash my feet!"

Jesus answered him, "If I don't wash you, you have no part with me."

(John 13 : 9)   Simon Peter said to him, "Lord, not my feet only, but also my hands and my head!"

(John 13 : 10)   Jesus said to him, "Someone who has bathed only needs to have his feet washed, but is completely clean. You are clean, but not all of you."

(John 13 : 11)   For he knew him who would betray him, therefore he said, "You are not all clean."

(John 13 : 12)   So when he had washed their feet, put his outer garment back on, and sat down again, he said to them, "Do you know what I have done to you?

(John 13 : 13)   You call me, Teacher' and Lord.' You say so correctly, for so I am.

(John 13 : 14)   If I then, the Lord and the Teacher, have washed your feet, you also ought to wash one another's feet.

(John 13 : 15)   For I have given you an example, that you also should do as I have done to you.

(John 13 : 16)   Most certainly I tell you, a servant is not greater than his lord, neither one who is sent greater than he who sent him.

(John 13 : 17)   If you know these things, blessed are you if you do them.

The Last Super
Lk 22:14-20 / Mk 14:22-25 / Mt 26:20
& Mt 26:26-29

(Luke 22 : 14)   When the hour had come, he sat down with the twelve apostles.

(Luke 22 : 15)   He said to them, "I have earnestly desired to eat this Passover with you before I suffer,

(Luke 22 : 16)   for I tell you, I will no longer by any means eat of it until it is fulfilled in the Kingdom of God."

(Luke 22 : 17)   He received a cup, and when he had given thanks, he said, "Take this, and share it among yourselves,

(Luke 22 : 18)   for I tell you, I will not drink at all again from the fruit of the vine, until the Kingdom of God comes."

(Luke 22 : 19)   He took bread, and when he had given thanks, he broke it, and gave to them, saying, "This is my body which is given for you. Do this in memory of me."

(Luke 22 : 20)   Likewise, he took the cup after supper, saying, "This cup is the new covenant in my blood, which is poured out for you.

(Mark 14 : 22)   As they were eating, Jesus took bread, and when he had blessed, he broke it, and gave to them, and said, "Take, eat. This is my body."

(Mark 14 : 23)   He took the cup, and when he had given thanks, he gave to them. They all drank of it.

(Mark 14 : 24)   He said to them, "This is my blood of the new covenant, which is poured out for many.

(Mark 14 : 25)   Most certainly I tell you, I will no more drink of the fruit of the vine, until that day when I drink it anew in the Kingdom of God."

(Matthew 26 : 20)   Now when evening had come, he was reclining at the table with the twelve disciples.

(Matthew 26 : 26)   As they were eating, Jesus took bread, gave thanks for it, and broke it. He gave to the disciples, and said, "Take, eat; this is my body."

(Matthew 26 : 27)   He took the cup, gave thanks, and gave to them, saying, "All of you drink it,

(Matthew 26 : 28)   for this is my blood of the new covenant, which is poured out for many for the remission of sins.

(Matthew 26 : 29)   But I tell you that I will not drink of this fruit of the vine from now on, until that day when I drink it anew with you in my Father's Kingdom."

Jesus Predicts His Betrayal
Jn 13:18-30 / Mt 26:21-25 / Lk 22:21-23
/ Mk 14:17-21

(John 13 : 18)   I don't speak concerning all of you. I know whom I have chosen. But that the Scripture may be fulfilled, He who eats bread with me has lifted up his heel against me.'

(John 13 : 19)   From now on, I tell you before it happens, that when it happens, you may believe that I am he.

(John 13 : 20)   Most certainly I tell you, he who receives whomever I send, receives me; and he who receives me, receives him who sent me."

(Matthew 26 : 21)   As they were eating, he said, "Most certainly I tell you that one of you will betray me."

(Matthew 26 : 22)   They were exceedingly sorrowful, and each began to ask him, "It isn't me, is it, Lord?"

(Matthew 26 : 23)   He answered, "He who dipped his hand with me in the dish, the same will betray me.

(Matthew 26 : 24)   The Son of Man goes, even as it is written of him, but woe to that man through whom the Son of Man is betrayed! It would be better for that man if he had not been born."

(Matthew 26 : 25)   Judas, who betrayed him, answered, "It isn't me, is it, Rabbi?"

He said to him, "You said it."

> (John 13 : 21)   When Jesus had said this, he was troubled in spirit, and testified, "Most certainly I tell you that one of you will betray me."
>
> (John 13 : 22)   The disciples looked at one another, perplexed about whom he spoke.

(John 13 : 23)   One of his disciples, whom Jesus loved, was at the table, leaning against Jesus' breast.

(John 13 : 24)   Simon Peter therefore beckoned to him, and said to him, "Tell us who it is of whom he speaks."

(John 13 : 25)   He, leaning back, as he was, on Jesus' breast, asked him, "Lord, who is it?"

(John 13 : 26)   Jesus therefore answered, "It is he to whom I will give this piece of bread when I have dipped it." So when he had dipped the piece of bread, he gave it to Judas, the son of Simon Iscariot.

(John 13 : 27)   After the piece of bread, then Satan entered into him.

Then Jesus said to him, "What you do, do quickly."

(John 13 : 28)   Now no man at the table knew why he said this to him.

(John 13 : 29)   For some thought, because Judas had the money box, that Jesus said to him, "Buy what things we need for the feast," or that he should give something to the poor.

(John 13 : 30)   Therefore having received that morsel, he went out immediately. It was night.

(Luke 22 : 21)   But behold, the hand of him who betrays me is with me on the table.

(Luke 22 : 22)   The Son of Man indeed goes, as it has been determined, but woe to that man through whom he is betrayed!"

(Luke 22 : 23)   They began to question among themselves, which of them it was who would do this thing.

(Mark 14 : 17)   When it was evening he came with the twelve.

(Mark 14 : 18)   As they sat and were eating, Jesus said, "Most certainly I tell you, one of you will betray me he who eats with me."

(Mark 14 : 19)   They began to be sorrowful, and to ask him one by one, "Surely not I?" And another said, "Surely not I?"

(Mark 14 : 20)   He answered them, "It is one of the twelve, he who dips with me in the dish.

(Mark 14 : 21)   For the Son of Man goes, even as it is written about him, but woe to that man by whom the Son of Man is betrayed! It would be better for that man if he had not been born."

About Who is Greater
Lk 22:24-30

(Luke 22 : 24)   There arose also a contention among them, which of them was considered to be greatest.

(Luke 22 : 25)   He said to them, "The kings of the nations lord it over them, and those who have authority over them are called benefactors.'

(Luke 22 : 26)   But not so with you. But one who is the greater among you, let him become as the younger, and one who is governing, as one who serves.

(Luke 22 : 27)   For who is greater, one who sits at the table, or one who serves? Isn't it he who sits at the table? But I am in your midst as one who serves.

(Luke 22 : 28)   But you are those who have continued with me in my trials.

(Luke 22 : 29)   I confer on you a kingdom, even as my Father conferred on me,

(Luke 22 : 30)   that you may eat and drink at my table in my Kingdom. You will sit on thrones, judging the twelve tribes of Israel."

Jesus Predicts Peter's Denial
Jn 13:31-38 / Lk 22:31-38 / Mt 26:31-35
/ Mk 14:27-31

(John 13 : 31) When he had gone out, Jesus said, "Now the Son of Man has been glorified, and God has been glorified in him.

(John 13 : 32)   If God has been glorified in him, God will also glorify him in himself, and he will glorify him immediately.

(John 13 : 33)   Little children, I will be with you a little while longer. You will seek me, and as I said to the Jews, Where I am going, you can't come,' so now I tell you.

(John 13 : 34)   A new commandment I give to you, that you love one another, just like I have loved you; that you also love one another.

(John 13 : 35)   By this everyone will know that you are my disciples, if you have love for one another."

(John 13 : 36)   Simon Peter said to him, "Lord, where are you going?" Jesus answered, "Where I am going, you can't follow now, but you will follow afterwards."

(John 13 : 37)   Peter said to him, "Lord, why can't I follow you now? I will lay down my life for you."

(John 13 : 38)   Jesus answered him, "Will you lay down your life for me? Most certainly I tell you, the rooster won't crow until you have denied me three times.

(Luke 22 : 31)   The Lord said, "Simon, Simon, behold, Satan asked to have you, that he might sift you as wheat,

(Luke 22 : 32)   but I prayed for you, that your faith wouldn't fail. You, when once you have turned again, establish your brothers."

(Luke 22 : 33)   He said to him, "Lord, I am ready to go with you both to prison and to death!"

(Luke 22 : 34)   He said, "I tell you, Peter, the rooster will by no means crow today until you deny that you know me three times."

(Matthew 26 : 31)   Then Jesus said to them, "All of you will be made to stumble because of me tonight, for it is written, I will strike the shepherd, and the sheep of the flock will be scattered.'

(Matthew 26 : 32)   But after I am raised up, I will go before you into Galilee."

(Matthew 26 : 33)   But Peter answered him, "Even if all will be made to stumble because of you, I will never be made to stumble."

(Matthew 26 : 34)   Jesus said to him, "Most certainly I tell you that tonight, before the rooster crows, you will deny me three times."

(Matthew 26 : 35)   Peter said to him, "Even if I must die with you, I will not deny you." All of the disciples also said likewise.

(Luke 22 : 35)   He said to them, "When I sent you out without purse, and wallet, and shoes, did you lack anything?"

They said, "Nothing."

(Luke 22 : 36)   Then he said to them, "But now, whoever has a purse, let him take it, and likewise a wallet. Whoever has none, let him sell his cloak, and buy a sword.

(Luke 22 : 37)   For I tell you that this which is written must still be fulfilled in me: He was counted with transgressors.' For that which concerns me has an end."

(Luke 22 : 38)   They said, "Lord, behold, here are two swords." He said to them, "That is enough."

(Mark 14 : 27)   Jesus said to them, "All of you will be made to stumble because of me tonight, for it is written, I will strike the shepherd, and the sheep will be scattered.' (Mark 14 : 28)   However, after I am raised up, I will go before you into Galilee."

(Mark 14 : 29)   But Peter said to him, "Although all will be offended, yet I will not."

(Mark 14 : 30)   Jesus said to him, "Most certainly I tell you, that you today, even this night, before the rooster crows twice, you will deny me three times."

(Mark 14 : 31)   But he spoke all the more, "If I must die with you, I will not deny you." They all said the same thing.

Jesus Comforts His Disciples
Jn 14:1-4

(John 14 : 1)   "Don't let your heart be troubled. Believe in God. Believe also in me.

(John 14 : 2)   In my Father's house are many homes. If it weren't so, I would have told you. I am going to prepare a place for you.

(John 14 : 3)   If I go and prepare a place for you, I will come again, and will receive you to myself; that where I am, you may be there also.

(John 14 : 4)   Where I go, you know, and you know the way."

Jesus the Way to the Father
Jn 14:5-14

(John 14 : 5)   Thomas said to him, "Lord, we don't know where you are going. How can we know the way?" (John 14 : 6)   Jesus said to him, "I am the way, the truth, and the life. No one comes to the Father, except through me.

(John 14 : 7)   If you had known me, you would have known my Father also. From now on, you know him, and have seen him."

(John 14 : 8)   Philip said to him, "Lord, show us the Father, and that will be enough for us."

(John 14 : 9)   Jesus said to him, "Have I been with you such a long time, and do you not know me, Philip? He who has seen me has seen the Father. How do you say, Show us the Father?'

(John 14 : 10)   Don't you believe that I am in the Father, and the Father in me? The words that I tell you, I speak not from myself; but the Father who lives in me does his works.

(John 14 : 11)   Believe me that I am in the Father, and the Father in me; or else believe me for the very works' sake.

(John 14 : 12)   Most certainly I tell you, he who believes in me, the works that I do, he will do also; and he will do greater works than these, because I am going to my Father.

(John 14 : 13)   Whatever you will ask in my name, that will I do, that the Father may be glorified in the Son.

(John 14 : 14)   If you will ask anything in my name, I will do it.

Jesus Promises the Holy Spirit
Jn 14:15-31

(John 14 : 15)   If you love me, keep my commandments.

(John 14 : 16)   I will pray to the Father, and he will give you another Counselor, that he may be with you forever,

(John 14 : 17)   the Spirit of truth, whom the world can't receive; for it doesn't see him, neither knows him. You know him, for he lives with you, and will be in you.

(John 14 : 18)   I will not leave you orphans. I will come to you.

(John 14 : 19)   Yet a little while, and the world will see me no more; but you will see me. Because I live, you will live also.

(John 14 : 20)   In that day you will know that I am in my Father, and you in me, and I in you.

(John 14 : 21)   One who has my commandments, and keeps them, that person is one who loves me. One who loves me will be loved by my Father, and I will love him, and will reveal myself to him."

(John 14 : 22)   Judas (not Iscariot) said to him, "Lord, what has happened that you are about to reveal yourself to us, and not to the world?"

(John 14 : 23)   Jesus answered him, "If a man loves me, he will keep my word. My Father will love him, and we will come to him, and make our home with him.

(John 14 : 24)   He who doesn't love me doesn't keep my words. The word which you hear isn't mine, but the Father's who sent me.

(John 14 : 25)   I have said these things to you, while still living with you.

(John 14 : 26)   But the Counselor, the Holy Spirit, whom the Father will send in my name, he will teach you all things, and will remind you of all that I said to you.

(John 14 : 27)   Peace I leave with you. My peace I give to you; not as the world gives, give I to you. Don't let your heart be troubled, neither let it be fearful.

(John 14 : 28)   You heard how I told you, I go away, and I come to you.' If you loved me, you would have rejoiced, because I said I am going to my Father;' for the Father is greater than I.

(John 14 : 29)   Now I have told you before it happens so that, when it happens, you may believe.

(John 14 : 30)   I will no more speak much with you, for the prince of the world comes, and he has nothing in me.

(John 14 : 31)   But that the world may know that I love the Father, and as the Father commanded me, even so I do. Arise, let us go from here.

The Parable of the True Vine and Branches
Jn 15:1-17

(John 15 : 1) "I am the true vine, and my Father is the farmer.

(John 15 : 2) Every branch in me that doesn't bear fruit, he takes away. Every branch that bears fruit, he prunes, that it may bear more fruit.

(John 15 : 3) You are already pruned clean because of the word which I have spoken to you.

(John 15 : 4) Remain in me, and I in you. As the branch can't bear fruit by itself, unless it remains in the vine, so neither can you, unless you remain in me.

(John 15 : 5) I am the vine. You are the branches. He who remains in me, and I in him, the same bears much fruit, for apart from me you can do nothing.

(John 15 : 6) If a man doesn't remain in me, he is thrown out as a branch, and is withered; and they gather them, throw them into the fire, and they are burned.

(John 15 :7) If you remain in me, and my words remain in you, you will ask whatever you desire, and it will be done for you.

(John 15 : 8) "In this is my Father glorified, that you bear much fruit; and so you will be my disciples.

(John 15 : 9) Even as the Father has loved me, I also have loved you. Remain in my love.

(John 15 : 10) If you keep my commandments, you will remain in my love; even as I have kept my Father's commandments, and remain in his love.

(John 15 : 11) I have spoken these things to you, that my joy may remain in you, and that your joy may be made full.

(John 15 : 12) "This is my commandment, that you love one another, even as I have loved you.

(John 15 : 13) Greater love has no one than this, that someone lay down his life for his friends.

(John 15 : 14) You are my friends, if you do whatever I command you.

(John 15 : 15) No longer do I call you servants, for the servant doesn't know what his lord does. But I have called you friends, for everything that I heard from my Father, I have made known to you.

(John 15 : 16) You didn't choose me, but I chose you, and appointed you, that you should go and bear fruit, and that your fruit should remain; that whatever you will ask of the Father in my name, he may give it to you.

(John 15 : 17) "I command these things to you, that you may love one another.

The World Hates the Disciples
Jn 15:18-25

(John 15 : 18) If the world hates you, you know that it has hated me before it hated you.

(John 15 : 19) If you were of the world, the world would love its own. But because you are not of the world, since I chose you out of the world, therefore the world hates you.

(John 15 : 20) Remember the word that I said to you: A servant is not greater than his lord.'If they persecuted me, they will also persecute you. If they kept my word, they will keep yours also.

(John 15 : 21) But all these things will they do to you for my name's sake, because they don't know him who sent me.

(John 15 : 22) If I had not come and spoken to them, they would not have had sin; but now they have no excuse for their sin.

(John 15 : 23) He who hates me, hates my Father also.

(John 15 : 24) If I hadn't done among them the works which no one else did, they wouldn't have had sin. But now have they seen and also hated both me and my Father.

(John 15 : 25) But this happened so that the word may be fulfilled which was written in their law, They hated me without a cause.'

Jesus goes and send the Holy Spirit
Jn 15:26-27 & Jn 16:1-15

(John 15 : 26) "When the Counselor has come, whom I will send to you from the Father, the Spirit of truth, who proceeds from the Father, he will testify about me.

(John 15 : 27) You will also testify, because you have been with me from the beginning.

(John 16 : 1) "These things have I spoken to you, so that you wouldn't be caused to stumble.

(John 16 : 2) They will put you out of the synagogues. Yes, the time comes that whoever kills you will think that he offers service to God.

(John 16 : 3) They will do these things because they have not known the Father, nor me.

(John 16 : 4) But I have told you these things, so that when the time comes, you may remember that I told you about them. I didn't tell you these things from the beginning, because I was with you.

(John 16 : 5) But now I am going to him who sent me, and none of you asks me, Where are you going?'

(John 16 : 6) But because I have told you these things, sorrow has filled your heart.

(John 16 : 7) Nevertheless I tell you the truth: It is to your advantage that I go away, for if I don't go away, the Counselor won't come to you. But if I go, I will send him to you.

(John 16 : 8) When he has come, he will convict the world about sin, about righteousness, and about judgment;

(John 16 : 9) about sin, because they don't believe in me;

(John 16 : 10) about righteousness, because I am going to my Father, and you won't see me any more;

(John 16 : 11) about judgment, because the prince of this world has been judged.

(John 16 : 12) "I have yet many things to tell you, but you can't bear them now.

(John 16 : 13) However when he, the Spirit of truth, has come, he will guide you into all truth, for he will not speak from himself; but whatever he hears, he will speak. He will declare to you things that are coming.

(John 16 : 14) He will glorify me, for he will take from what is mine, and will declare it to you.

(John 16 : 15) All things whatever the Father has are mine; therefore I said that he takes of mine, and will declare it to you.

The Disciples' Grief Will Turn to Joy
Jn 16:16-33 & Jn 17:1-5

(John 16 : 16) A little while, and you will not see me. Again a little while, and you will see me."

(John 16 : 17) Some of his disciples therefore said to one another, "What is this that he says to us, A little while, and you won't see me, and again a little while, and you will see me;' and, Because I go to the Father?'"

(John 16 : 18) They said therefore, "What is this that he says, A little while?' We don't know what he is saying."

(John 16 : 19) Therefore Jesus perceived that they wanted to ask him, and he said to them, "Do you inquire among yourselves concerning this, that I said, A little while, and you won't see me, and again a little while, and you will see me?'

(John 16 : 20) Most certainly I tell you, that you will weep and lament, but the world will rejoice. You will be sorrowful, but your sorrow will be turned into joy.

(John 16 : 21) A woman, when she gives birth, has sorrow, because her time has come. But when she has delivered the child, she doesn't remember the anguish any more, for the joy that a human being is born into the world.

(John 16 : 22) Therefore you now have sorrow, but I will see you again, and your heart will rejoice, and no one will take your joy away from you.

(John 16 : 23) "In that day you will ask me no questions. Most certainly I tell you, whatever you may ask of the Father in my name, he will give it to you.

(John 16 : 24) Until now, you have asked nothing in my name. Ask, and you will receive, that your joy may be made full.

(John 16 : 25) I have spoken these things to you in figures of speech. But the time is coming when I will no more speak to you in figures of speech, but will tell you plainly about the Father.

(John 16 : 26) In that day you will ask in my name; and I don't say to you, that I will pray to the Father for you,

(John 16 : 27) for the Father himself loves you, because you have loved me, and have believed that I came from God.

(John 16 : 28) I came from the Father, and have come into the world. Again, I leave the world, and go to the Father."

(John 16 : 29) His disciples said to him, "Behold, now you speak plainly, and speak no figures of speech.

(John 16 : 30) Now we know that you know all things, and don't need for anyone to question you. By this we believe that you came from God."

(John 16 : 31) Jesus answered them, "Do you now believe?

(John 16 : 32) Behold, the time is coming, yes, and has now come, that you will be scattered, everyone to his own place, and you will leave me alone. Yet I am not alone, because the Father is with me.

(John 16 : 33) I have told you these things, that in me you may have peace. In the world you have oppression; but cheer up! I have overcome the world."

(John 17 : 1) Jesus said these things, and lifting up his eyes to heaven, he said, "Father, the time has come. Glorify your Son, that your Son may also glorify you;

(John 17 : 2) even as you gave him authority over all flesh, he will give eternal life to all whom you have given him.

(John 17 : 3) This is eternal life, that they should know you, the only true God, and him whom you sent, Jesus Christ.

(John 17 : 4) I glorified you on the earth. I have accomplished the work which you have given me to do.

(John 17 : 5) Now, Father, glorify me with your own self with the glory which I had with you before the world existed.

Jesus Prays for His Disciples
Jn 17:6-19

(John 17 : 6) I revealed your name to the people whom you have given me out of the world. They were yours, and you have given them to me. They have kept your word.

(John 17 : 7) Now they have known that all things whatever you have given me are from you,

(John 17 : 8) for the words which you have given me I have given to them, and they received them, and knew for sure that I came from you, and they have believed that you sent me.

(John 17 : 9) I pray for them. I don't pray for the world, but for those whom you have given me, for they are yours.

(John 17 : 10) All things that are mine are yours, and yours are mine, and I am glorified in them.

(John 17 : 11)   I am no more in the world, but these are in the world, and I am coming to you. Holy Father, keep them through your name which you have given me, that they may be one, even as we are.

(John 17 : 12)   While I was with them in the world, I kept them in your name. Those whom you have given me I have kept. None of them is lost, except the son of destruction, that the Scripture might be fulfilled.

(John 17 : 13)   But now I come to you, and I say these things in the world, that they may have my joy made full in themselves.

(John 17 : 14)   I have given them your word. The world hated them, because they are not of the world, even as I am not of the world.

(John 17 : 15)   I pray not that you would take them from the world, but that you would keep them from the evil one.

(John 17 : 16)   They are not of the world even as I am not of the world.

(John 17 : 17)   Sanctify them in your truth. Your word is truth.

(John 17 : 18)   As you sent me into the world, even so I have sent them into the world.

(John 17 : 19)   For their sakes I sanctify myself, that they themselves also may be sanctified in truth.

Jesus Prays for All Believers
Jn 17:20-26 / Mk 14:26 / Mt 26:30

(John 17 : 20)   Not for these only do I pray, but for those also who believe in me through their word,

(John 17 : 21)   that they may all be one; even as you, Father, are in me, and I in you, that they also may be one in us; that the world may believe that you sent me.

(John 17 : 22)   The glory which you have given me, I have given to them; that they may be one, even as we are one;

(John 17 : 23)   I in them, and you in me, that they may be perfected into one; that the world may know that you sent me, and loved them, even as you loved me. (John 17 : 24)   Father, I desire that they also whom you have given me be with me where I am, that they may see my glory, which you have given me, for you loved me before the foundation of the world.

(John 17 : 25)   Righteous Father, the world hasn't known you, but I knew you; and these knew that you sent me.

(John 17 : 26)   I made known to them your name, and will make it known; that the love with which you loved me may be in them, and I in them."

(Mark 14 : 26) When they had sung a hymn, they went out to the Mount of Olives.

(Matthew 26 : 30) When they had sung a hymn, they went out to the Mount of Olives.

Jesus Prayed at Gethsemane
Mk 14:32-42 / Jn 18:1-2 / Lk 22:39-46
/ Mt 26:36-46

(Mark 14 : 32) They came to a place which was named Gethsemane. He said to his disciples, "Sit here, while I pray."

(Mark 14 : 33) He took with him Peter, James, and John, and began to be greatly troubled and distressed.

(Mark 14 : 34) He said to them, "My soul is exceedingly sorrowful, even to death. Stay here, and watch." (Mark 14 : 35) He went forward a little, and fell on the ground, and prayed that, if it were possible, the hour might pass away from him.

(Mark 14 : 36) He said, "Abba, Father, all things are possible to you. Please remove this cup from me. However, not what I desire, but what you desire."

(Mark 14 : 37) He came and found them sleeping, and said to Peter, "Simon, are you sleeping? Couldn't you watch one hour?

(Mark 14 : 38) Watch and pray, that you may not enter into temptation. The spirit indeed is willing, but the flesh is weak."

(Mark 14 : 39) Again he went away, and prayed, saying the same words.

(Mark 14 : 40)   Again he returned, and found them sleeping, for their eyes were very heavy, and they didn't know what to answer him.

(Mark 14 : 41)   He came the third time, and said to them, "Sleep on now, and take your rest. It is enough. The hour has come. Behold, the Son of Man is betrayed into the hands of sinners.

(Mark 14 : 42)   Arise, let us be going. Behold, he who betrays me is at hand."

(John 18 : 1)   When Jesus had spoken these words, he went out with his disciples over the brook Kidron, where there was a garden, into which he and his disciples entered.

(John 18 : 2)   Now Judas, who betrayed him, also knew the place, for Jesus often met there with his disciples.

(Luke 22 : 39)   He came out, and went, as his custom was, to the Mount of Olives. His disciples also followed him.

(Luke 22 : 40)   When he was at the place, he said to them, "Pray that you don't enter into temptation."

(Luke 22 : 41)   He was withdrawn from them about a stone's throw, and he knelt down and prayed,

(Luke 22 : 42)   saying, "Father, if you are willing, remove this cup from me. Nevertheless, not my will, but yours, be done."

(Luke 22 : 43)   An angel from heaven appeared to him, strengthening him.

(Luke 22 : 44)   Being in agony he prayed more earnestly. His sweat became like great drops of blood falling down on the ground.

(Luke 22 : 45)   When he rose up from his prayer, he came to the disciples, and found them sleeping because of grief,

(Luke 22 : 46)   and said to them, "Why do you sleep? Rise and pray that you may not enter into temptation."

(Matthew 26 : 36)   Then Jesus came with them to a place called Gethsemane, and said to his disciples, "Sit here, while I go there and pray."

(Matthew 26 : 37)   He took with him Peter and the two sons of Zebedee, and began to be sorrowful and severely troubled.

(Matthew 26 : 38)   Then he said to them, "My soul is exceedingly sorrowful, even to death. Stay here, and watch with me."

(Matthew 26 : 39)   He went forward a little, fell on his face, and prayed, saying, "My Father, if it is possible, let this cup pass away from me; nevertheless, not what I desire, but what you desire."

(Matthew 26 : 40)   He came to the disciples, and found them sleeping, and said to Peter, "What, couldn't you watch with me for one hour?

(Matthew 26 : 41)   Watch and pray, that you don't enter into temptation. The spirit indeed is willing, but the flesh is weak."

(Matthew 26 : 42)   Again, a second time he went away, and prayed, saying, "My Father, if this cup can't pass away from me unless I drink it, your desire be done."

(Matthew 26 : 43)   He came again and found them sleeping, for their eyes were heavy.

(Matthew 26 : 44)   He left them again, went away, and prayed a third time, saying the same words.

(Matthew 26 : 45)   Then he came to his disciples, and said to them, "Sleep on now, and take your rest. Behold, the hour is at hand, and the Son of Man is betrayed into the hands of sinners.

(Matthew 26 : 46)   Arise, let's be going. Behold, he who betrays me is at hand."

Jesus Arrested
Lk 22:47-53 / Jn 18:3-14 / Mk 14:43-52 / Mt 26:47-56

(Luke 22 : 47)   While he was still speaking, behold, a multitude, and he who was called Judas, one of the twelve, was leading them. He came near to Jesus to kiss him.

(John 18 : 3) Judas then, having taken a detachment of soldiers and officers from the chief priests and the Pharisees, came there with lanterns, torches, and weapons.

(John 18 : 4) Jesus therefore, knowing all the things that were happening to him, went out, and said to them, "Who are you looking for?"

(John 18 : 5) They answered him, "Jesus of Nazareth."

Jesus said to them, "I am he."

Judas also, who betrayed him, was standing with them.

(John 18 : 6) When therefore he said to them, "I am he," they went backward, and fell to the ground.

(John 18 : 7) Again therefore he asked them, "Who are you looking for?"

They said, "Jesus of Nazareth."

(John 18 : 8) Jesus answered, "I told you that I am he. If therefore you seek me, let these go their way,"

(John 18 : 9) that the word might be fulfilled which he spoke, "Of those whom you have given me, I have lost none."

(Luke 22 : 48) But Jesus said to him, "Judas, do you betray the Son of Man with a kiss?"

(Mark 14 : 44) Now he who betrayed him had given them a sign, saying, "Whomever I will kiss, that is he. Seize him, and lead him away safely."

(Mark 14 : 45) When he had come, immediately he came to him, and said, "Rabbi! Rabbi!" and kissed him.

(Mark 14 : 46)   They laid their hands on him, and seized him.

(Luke 22 : 49)   When those who were around him saw what was about to happen, they said to him, "Lord, shall we strike with the sword?"

(John 18 : 10)   Simon Peter therefore, having a sword, drew it, and struck the high priest's servant, and cut off his right ear. The servant's name was Malchus.

(John 18 : 11)   Jesus therefore said to Peter, "Put the sword into its sheath. The cup which the Father has given me, shall I not surely drink it?"

(Luke 22 : 50)   A certain one of them struck the servant of the high priest, and cut off his right ear.

(Luke 22 : 51)   But Jesus answered, "Let me at least do this" and he touched his ear, and healed him.

(Matthew 26 : 52)   Then Jesus said to him, "Put your sword back into its place, for all those who take the sword will die by the sword.

(Matthew 26 : 53)   Or do you think that I couldn't ask my Father, and he would even now send me more than twelve legions of angels?

(Matthew 26 : 54)   How then would the Scriptures be fulfilled that it must be so?"

(Matthew 26 : 55)   In that hour Jesus said to the multitudes, "Have you come out as against a robber with swords and clubs to seize me? I sat daily in the temple teaching, and you didn't arrest me.

(Luke 22 : 52)   Jesus said to the chief priests, captains of the temple, and elders, who had come against him, "Have you come out as against a robber, with swords and clubs?

(Luke 22 : 53)   When I was with you in the temple daily, you didn't stretch out your hands against me. But this is your hour, and the power of darkness."

(Matthew 26 : 56)   But all this has happened, that the Scriptures of the prophets might be fulfilled." Then all the disciples left him, and fled.

(John 18 : 12)   So the detachment, the commanding officer, and the officers of the Jews, seized Jesus and bound him,

(John 18 : 13)   and led him to Annas first, for he was father-in-law to Caiaphas, who was high priest that year.

(John 18 : 14)   Now it was Caiaphas who advised the Jews that it was expedient that one man should perish for the people.

(Mark 14 : 43)   Immediately, while he was still speaking, Judas, one of the twelve, came and with him a multitude with swords and clubs, from the chief priests, the scribes, and the elders.

(Mark 14 : 47)   But a certain one of those who stood by drew his sword, and struck the servant of the high priest, and cut off his ear.

(Mark 14 : 48)   Jesus answered them, "Have you come out, as against a robber, with swords and clubs to seize me?

(Mark 14 : 49)   I was daily with you in the temple teaching, and you didn't arrest me. But this is so that the Scriptures might be fulfilled."

(Matthew 26 : 47)   While he was still speaking, behold, Judas, one of the twelve, came, and with him a great multitude with swords and clubs, from the chief priest and elders of the people.

(Matthew 26 : 48)   Now he who betrayed him gave them a sign, saying, "Whoever I kiss, he is the one. Seize him."

(Matthew 26 : 49)   Immediately he came to Jesus, and said, "Hail, Rabbi!" and kissed him.

(Matthew 26 : 50)   Jesus said to him, "Friend, why are you here?"

> Then they came and laid hands on Jesus, and took him.
>
> (Matthew 26 : 51)   Behold, one of those who were with Jesus stretched out his hand, and drew his sword, and struck the servant of the high priest, and struck off his ear.

> (Mark 14 : 50)   They all left him, and fled.

(Mark 14 : 51)   A certain young man followed him, having a linen cloth thrown around himself, over his naked body. The young men grabbed him,

(Mark 14 : 52)   but he left the linen cloth, and fled from them naked.

Jesus Before the Sanhedrin
Mk14:53-65 / Jn 18:15-24 / Mt 26:57-68

(Mark 14 : 53)   They led Jesus away to the high priest. All the chief priests, the elders, and the scribes came together with him.

(John 18 : 15)   Simon Peter followed Jesus, as did another disciple. Now that disciple was known to the high priest, and entered in with Jesus into the court of the high priest;

(John 18 : 16)   but Peter was standing at the door outside. So the other disciple, who was known to the high priest, went out and spoke to her who kept the door, and brought in Peter.

(John 18 : 17)   Then the maid who kept the door said to Peter, "Are you also one of this man's disciples?" He said, "I am not."

(John 18 : 18)   Now the servants and the officers were standing there, having made a fire of coals, for it was cold. They were warming themselves. Peter was with them, standing and warming himself.

(Mark 14 : 54)   Peter had followed him from a distance, until he came into the court of the high priest. He was sitting with the officers and warming himself in the light of the fire.

(John 18 : 19)   The high priest therefore asked Jesus about his disciples, and about his teaching.

(John 18 : 20)   Jesus answered him, "I spoke openly to the world. I always taught in synagogues, and in the temple, where the Jews always meet. I said nothing in secret.

(John 18 : 21)   Why do you ask me? Ask those who have heard me what I said to them. Behold, these know the things which I said."

(John 18 : 22)   When he had said this, one of the officers standing by slapped Jesus with his hand, saying, "Do you answer the high priest like that?"

(John 18 : 23)   Jesus answered him, "If I have spoken evil, testify of the evil; but if well, why do you beat me?"

(John 18 : 24)   Annas sent him bound to Caiaphas, the high priest.

(Mark 14 : 55)   Now the chief priests and the whole council sought witnesses against Jesus to put him to death, and found none.

(Mark 14 : 56)   For many gave false testimony against him, and their testimony didn't agree with each other.

(Mark 14 : 57)   Some stood up, and gave false testimony against him, saying,

(Mark 14 : 58)   "We heard him say, I will destroy this temple that is made with hands, and in three days I will build another made without hands.'"

(Mark 14 : 59)   Even so, their testimony did not agree.

(Mark 14 : 60)   The high priest stood up in the midst, and asked Jesus, "Have you no answer? What is it which these testify against you?"

(Mark 14 : 61)   But he stayed quiet, and answered nothing. Again the high priest asked him, "Are you the Christ, the Son of the Blessed?"

(Mark 14 : 62)   Jesus said, "I am. You will see the Son of Man sitting at the right hand of Power, and coming with the clouds of the sky."

(Mark 14 : 63)   The high priest tore his clothes, and said, "What further need have we of witnesses?

(Mark 14 : 64)   You have heard the blasphemy! What do you think?" They all condemned him to be worthy of death.

(Mark 14 : 65) Some began to spit on him, and to cover his face, and to beat him with fists, and to tell him, "Prophesy!" The officers struck him with the palms of their hands.

(Matthew 26 : 57)   Those who had taken Jesus led him away to Caiaphas the high priest, where the scribes and the elders were gathered together.

(Matthew 26 : 58)   But Peter followed him from a distance, to the court of the high priest, and entered in and sat with the officers, to see the end.

(Matthew 26 : 59)   Now the chief priests, the elders, and the whole council sought false testimony against Jesus, that they might put him to death;

(Matthew 26 : 60)   and they found none. Even though many false witnesses came forward, they found none. But at last two false witnesses came forward,

(Matthew 26 : 61)   and said, "This man said, I am able to destroy the temple of God, and to build it in three days.'"

(Matthew 26 : 62) The high priest stood up, and said to him, "Have you no answer? What is this that these testify against you?"

(Matthew 26 : 63)   But Jesus held his peace. The high priest answered him, "I adjure you by the living God, that you tell us whether you are the Christ, the Son of God."

(Matthew 26 : 64)   Jesus said to him, "You have said it. Nevertheless, I tell you, after this you will see the Son of Man sitting at the right hand of Power, and coming on the clouds of the sky."

(Matthew 26 : 65)   Then the high priest tore his clothing, saying, "He has spoken blasphemy! Why do we need any more witnesses? Behold, now you have heard his blasphemy.

(Matthew 26 : 66)   What do you think?"

They answered, "He is worthy of death!"

(Matthew 26 : 67)   Then they spit in his face and beat him with their fists, and some slapped him,

(Matthew 26 : 68)   saying, "Prophesy to us, you Christ! Who hit you?"

Peter Disowns Jesus
Lk 22:54-62 / Jn 18:25-27 / Mk14:66-72
/ Mt 26:69-75

(Luke 22 : 54)   They seized him, and led him away, and brought him into the high priest's house. But Peter followed from a distance.

(Luke 22 : 55)   When they had kindled a fire in the middle of the courtyard, and had sat down together, Peter sat among them.

(Luke 22 : 56)   A certain servant girl saw him as he sat in the light, and looking intently at him, said, "This man also was with him."

(Luke 22 : 57)   He denied Jesus, saying, "Woman, I don't know him."

(Luke 22 : 58)   After a little while someone else saw him, and said, "You also are one of them!" But Peter answered, "Man, I am not!"

(Luke 22 : 59)   After about one hour passed, another confidently affirmed, saying, "Truly this man also was with him, for he is a Galilean!"

(John 18 : 25)   Now Simon Peter was standing and warming himself. They said therefore to him, "You aren't also one of his disciples, are you?" He denied it, and said, "I am not."

(John 18 : 26)   One of the servants of the high priest, being a relative of him whose ear Peter had cut off, said, "Didn't I see you in the garden with him?"

(Luke 22 : 60)   But Peter said, "Man, I don't know what you are talking about!" Immediately, while he was still speaking, a rooster crowed.

(Luke 22 : 61)   The Lord turned, and looked at Peter. Then Peter remembered the Lord's word, how he said to him, "Before the rooster crows you will deny me three times."

(Luke 22 : 62)   He went out, and wept bitterly.

(John 18 : 27)   Peter therefore denied it again, and immediately the rooster crowed.

(Mark 14 : 66)   As Peter was in the courtyard below, one of the maids of the high priest came,

(Mark 14 : 67)   and seeing Peter warming himself, she looked at him, and said, "You were also with the Nazarene, Jesus!"

(Mark 14 : 68)   But he denied it, saying, "I neither know, nor understand what you are saying." He went out on the porch, and the rooster crowed.

(Mark 14 : 69)   The maid saw him, and began again to tell those who stood by, "This is one of them."

(Mark 14 : 70)   But he again denied it.

After a little while again those who stood by said to Peter, "You truly are one of them, for you are a Galilean, and your speech shows it."

(Mark 14 : 71)   But he began to curse, and to swear, "I don't know this man of whom you speak!"

(Mark 14 : 72)   The rooster crowed the second time. Peter remembered the word, how that Jesus said to him, "Before the rooster crows twice, you will deny me three times." When he thought about that, he wept.

(Matthew 26 : 69)   Now Peter was sitting outside in the court, and a maid came to him, saying, "You were also with Jesus, the Galilean!"

(Matthew 26 : 70)   But he denied it before them all, saying, "I don't know what you are talking about."

(Matthew 26 : 71)   When he had gone out onto the porch, someone else saw him, and said to those who were there, "This man also was with Jesus of Nazareth."

(Matthew 26 : 72)   Again he denied it with an oath, "I don't know the man."

(Matthew 26 : 73)   After a little while those who stood by came and said to Peter, "Surely you are also one of them, for your speech makes you known."

(Matthew 26 : 74)   Then he began to curse and to swear, "I don't know the man!" Immediately the rooster crowed.

(Matthew 26 : 75)   Peter remembered the word which Jesus had said to him, "Before the rooster crows, you will deny me three times." He went out and wept bitterly.

The Guards Mock Jesus
Lk 22:63-65

(Luke 22 : 63)   The men who held Jesus mocked him and beat him.

(Luke 22 : 64)   Having blindfolded him, they struck him on the face and asked him, "Prophesy! Who is the one who struck you?"

(Luke 22 : 65)   They spoke many other things against him, insulting him.

Jesus Before the Chief Priest
Lk 22:66-71

(Luke 22 : 66)   As soon as it was day, the assembly of the elders of the people was gathered together, both chief priests and scribes, and they led him away into their council, saying,

(Luke 22 : 67)   "If you are the Christ, tell us." But he said to them, "If I tell you, you won't believe,

(Luke 22 : 68)   and if I ask, you will in no way answer me or let me go.

(Luke 22 : 69)   From now on, the Son of Man will be seated at the right hand of the power of God."

(Luke 22 : 70)   They all said, "Are you then the Son of God?" He said to them, "You say it, because I am."

(Luke 22 : 71)   They said, "Why do we need any more witness? For we ourselves have heard from his own mouth!"

Judas Hangs Himself
Mt 27:1-10

(Matthew 27 : 1)   Now when morning had come, all the chief priests and the elders of the people took counsel against Jesus to put him to death:

(Matthew 27 : 2)   and they bound him, and led him away, and delivered him up to Pontius Pilate, the governor.

(Matthew 27 : 3) Then Judas, who betrayed him, when he saw that Jesus was condemned, felt remorse, and brought back the thirty pieces of silver to the chief priests and elders,

(Matthew 27 : 4)   saying, "I have sinned in that I betrayed innocent blood." But they said, "What is that to us? You see to it."

(Matthew 27 : 5)   He threw down the pieces of silver in the sanctuary, and departed. He went away and hanged himself.

(Matthew 27 : 6)   The chief priests took the pieces of silver, and said, "It's not lawful to put them into the treasury, since it is the price of blood."

(Matthew 27 : 7)   They took counsel, and bought the potter's field with them, to bury strangers in.

(Matthew 27 : 8)   Therefore that field was called "The Field of Blood" to this day.

(Matthew 27 : 9)   Then that which was spoken through Jeremiah the prophet was fulfilled, saying,

"They took the thirty pieces of silver,

the price of him upon whom a price had been set,

whom some of the children of Israel priced,

(Matthew 27 : 10)   and they gave them for the potter's field, as the Lord commanded me."

Jesus Before the Pilate
Jn 18:28-40 / Lk 23:1-7 / Mt 27:11-14 / Mk 15:1-2

(John 18 : 28)   They led Jesus therefore from Caiaphas into the Praetorium. It was early, and they themselves didn't enter into the Praetorium, that they might not be defiled, but might eat the Passover.

(Luke 23 : 1)   The whole company of them rose up and brought him before Pilate.

(Luke 23 : 2)   They began to accuse him, saying, "We found this man perverting the nation, forbidding paying taxes to Caesar, and saying that he himself is Christ, a king."

(John 18 : 29)   Pilate therefore went out to them, and said, "What accusation do you bring against this man?"

(John 18 : 30)   They answered him, "If this man weren't an evildoer, we wouldn't have delivered him up to you."

(John 18 : 31)   Pilate therefore said to them, "Take him yourselves, and judge him according to your law." Therefore the Jews said to him, "It is not lawful for us to put anyone to death,"

(John 18 : 32)   that the word of Jesus might be fulfilled, which he spoke, signifying by what kind of death he should die.

(John 18 : 33)   Pilate therefore entered again into the Praetorium, called Jesus, and said to him, "Are you the King of the Jews?"

(John 18 : 34)   Jesus answered him, "Do you say this by yourself, or did others tell you about me?"

(John 18 : 35)   Pilate answered, "I'm not a Jew, am I? Your own nation and the chief priests delivered you to me. What have you done?"

(John 18 : 36)   Jesus answered, "My Kingdom is not of this world. If my Kingdom were of this world, then my servants would fight, that I wouldn't be delivered to the Jews. But now my Kingdom is not from here."

(John 18 : 37)   Pilate therefore said to him, "Are you a king then?" Jesus answered, "You say that I am a king. For this reason I have been born, and for this reason I have come into the world, that I should testify to the truth. Everyone who is of the truth listens to my voice."

(John 18 : 38)   Pilate said to him, "What is truth?" When he had said this, he went out again to the Jews, and said to them, "I find no basis for a charge against him.

(John 18 : 39)   But you have a custom, that I should release someone to you at the Passover. Therefore do you want me to release to you the King of the Jews?"

(John 18 : 40)   Then they all shouted again, saying, "Not this man, but Barabbas!" Now Barabbas was a robber.

(Luke 23 : 3)   Pilate asked him, "Are you the King of the Jews?" He answered him, "So you say."

(Luke 23 : 4)   Pilate said to the chief priests and the multitudes, "I find no basis for a charge against this man."

(Luke 23 : 5)   But they insisted, saying, "He stirs up the people, teaching throughout all Judea, beginning from Galilee even to this place."

(Luke 23 : 6) But when Pilate heard Galilee mentioned, he asked if the man was a Galilean.

(Luke 23 : 7) When he found out that he was in Herod's jurisdiction, he sent him to Herod, who was also in Jerusalem during those days.

(Matthew 27 : 11) Now Jesus stood before the governor: and the governor asked him, saying, "Are you the King of the Jews?" Jesus said to him, "So you say."

(Matthew 27 : 12) When he was accused by the chief priests and elders, he answered nothing.

(Matthew 27 : 13)   Then Pilate said to him, "Don't you hear how many things they testify against you?"

(Matthew 27 : 14) He gave him no answer, not even one word, so that the governor marveled greatly.

(Mark 15 : 1)   Immediately in the morning the chief priests, with the elders and scribes, and the whole council, held a consultation, and bound Jesus, and carried him away, and delivered him up to Pilate.

(Mark 15 : 2)   Pilate asked him, "Are you the King of the Jews?"

He answered, "So you say."

Jesus Before Herod
Lk 23:8-12

(Luke 23 : 8)   Now when Herod saw Jesus, he was exceedingly glad, for he had wanted to see him for a long time, because he had heard many things about him. He hoped to see some miracle done by him.

(Luke 23 : 9)   He questioned him with many words, but he gave no answers.

(Luke 23 : 10)   The chief priests and the scribes stood, vehemently accusing him.

(Luke 23 : 11)   Herod with his soldiers humiliated him and mocked him. Dressing him in luxurious clothing, they sent him back to Pilate.

(Luke 23 : 12)   Herod and Pilate became friends with each other that very day, for before that they were enemies with each other.

Jesus Before the Pilate again
Lk 23:13-16

(Luke 23 : 13)   Pilate called together the chief priests and the rulers and the people,

(Luke 23 : 14)   and said to them, "You brought this man to me as one that perverts the people, and see, I have examined him before you, and found no basis for a charge against this man concerning those things of which you accuse him.

(Luke 23 : 15)   Neither has Herod, for I sent you to him, and see, nothing worthy of death has been done by him.

(Luke 23 : 16)   I will therefore chastise him and release him."

The Soldiers Mock Jesus
Jn 19:1-3

(John 19 : 1)   So Pilate then took Jesus, and flogged him.

(John 19 : 2)   The soldiers twisted thorns into a crown, and put it on his head, and dressed him in a purple garment.

(John 19 : 3)   They kept saying, "Hail, King of the Jews!" and they kept slapping him.

Jesus Handed to Cruxifiction
Jn 19:4-16 / Mt 27:15-31 / Lk 23:17-25
/ Mk 15:3-20

(John 19 : 4)   Then Pilate went out again, and said to them, "Behold, I bring him out to you, that you may know that I find no basis for a charge against him."

(John 19 : 5)   Jesus therefore came out, wearing the crown of thorns and the purple garment. Pilate said to them, "Behold, the man!"

(Mark 15 : 3)   The chief priests accused him of many things.

(Mark 15 : 4)   Pilate again asked him, "Have you no answer? See how many things they testify against you!"

(Mark 15 : 5)   But Jesus made no further answer, so that Pilate marveled.

(Matthew 27:15) Now at the feast the governor was accustomed to release to the multitude one prisoner, whom they desired.

(Matthew 27 : 16) They had then a notable prisoner, called Barabbas.

(Matthew 27 : 17) When therefore they were gathered together, Pilate said to them, "Whom do you want me to release to you? Barabbas, or Jesus, who is called Christ?"

(Matthew 27 : 18) For he knew that because of envy they had delivered him up.

(Matthew 27 : 19) While he was sitting on the judgment seat, his wife sent to him, saying, "Have nothing to do with that righteous man, for I have suffered many things this day in a dream because of him."

(Matthew 27 : 20) Now the chief priests and the elders persuaded the multitudes to ask for Barabbas, and destroy Jesus.

(Matthew 27 : 21) But the governor answered them, "Which of the two do you want me to release to you?"

They said, "Barabbas!"

(Matthew 27 : 22) Pilate said to them, "What then shall I do to Jesus, who is called Christ?" They all said to him, "Let him be crucified!"

(John 19 : 6) When therefore the chief priests and the officers saw him, they shouted, saying, "Crucify! Crucify!"

Pilate said to them, "Take him yourselves, and crucify him, for I find no basis for a charge against him."

> (Luke 23 : 17)   Now he had to release one prisoner to them at the feast.

(Luke 23 : 18)   But they all cried out together, saying, "Away with this man! Release to us Barabbas!"

(Luke 23 : 19)   one who was thrown into prison for a certain revolt in the city, and for murder.

(Luke 23 : 20)   Then Pilate spoke to them again, wanting to release Jesus,

(Luke 23 : 21)   but they shouted, saying, "Crucify! Crucify him!"

(Luke 23 : 22)   He said to them the third time, "Why? What evil has this man done? I have found no capital crime in him. I will therefore chastise him and release him."

(Luke 23 : 23)   But they were urgent with loud voices, asking that he might be crucified. Their voices and the voices of the chief priests prevailed.

(John 19 : 7)   The Jews answered him, "We have a law, and by our law he ought to die, because he made himself the Son of God."

(John 19 : 8)   When therefore Pilate heard this saying, he was more afraid.

(John 19 : 9)   He entered into the Praetorium again, and said to Jesus, "Where are you from?" But Jesus gave him no answer.

(John 19 : 10) Pilate therefore said to him, "Aren't you speaking to me? Don't you know that I have power to release you, and have power to crucify you?"

(John 19 : 11) Jesus answered, "You would have no power at all against me, unless it were given to you from above. Therefore he who delivered me to you has greater sin."

(John 19 : 12) At this, Pilate was seeking to release him, but the Jews cried out, saying, "If you release this man, you aren't Caesar's friend! Everyone who makes himself a king speaks against Caesar!"

(John 19 : 13) When Pilate therefore heard these words, he brought Jesus out, and sat down on the judgment seat at a place called "The Pavement," but in Hebrew, "Gabbatha."

(John 19 : 14) Now it was the Preparation Day of the Passover, at about the sixth hour. He said to the Jews, "Behold, your King!"

(John 19 : 15) They cried out, "Away with him! Away with him! Crucify him!"

Pilate said to them, "Shall I crucify your King?"

The chief priests answered, "We have no king but Caesar!"

(Matthew 27 : 23) But the governor said, "Why? What evil has he done?" But they cried out exceedingly, saying, "Let him be crucified!"

(Matthew 27 : 24)   So when Pilate saw that nothing was being gained, but rather that a disturbance was starting, he took water, and washed his hands before the multitude, saying, "I am innocent of the blood of this righteous person. You see to it."

(Matthew 27 : 25)   All the people answered, "May his blood be on us, and on our children!"

(Matthew 27 : 26) Then he released to them Barabbas, but Jesus he flogged and delivered to be crucified.

(Luke 23 : 24)   Pilate decreed that what they asked for should be done.

(Luke 23 : 25)   He released him who had been thrown into prison for insurrection and murder, for whom they asked, but he delivered Jesus up to their will.

(John 19 : 16)   So then he delivered him to them to be crucified. So they took Jesus and led him away.

(Mark 15 : 5)   But Jesus made no further answer, so that Pilate marveled.

(Mark 15 : 6)   Now at the feast he used to release to them one prisoner, whom they asked of him.

(Mark 15 : 7)   There was one called Barabbas, bound with those who had made insurrection, men who in the insurrection had committed murder.

(Mark 15 : 8)   The multitude, crying aloud, began to ask him to do as he always did for them.

(Mark 15 : 9)   Pilate answered them, saying, "Do you want me to release to you the King of the Jews?"

(Mark 15 : 10)   For he perceived that for envy the chief priests had delivered him up.

(Mark 15 : 11)   But the chief priests stirred up the multitude, that he should release Barabbas to them instead.

(Mark 15 : 12)   Pilate again asked them, "What then should I do to him whom you call the King of the Jews?"

(Mark 15 : 13)   They cried out again, "Crucify him!"

(Mark 15 : 14)   Pilate said to them, "Why, what evil has he done?"

But they cried out exceedingly, "Crucify him!"

(Mark 15 : 15)   Pilate, wishing to please the multitude, released Barabbas to them, and handed over Jesus, when he had flogged him, to be crucified.

(Mark 15 : 16) The soldiers led him away within the court, which is the Praetorium; and they called together the whole cohort.

(Mark 15 : 17) They clothed him with purple, and weaving a crown of thorns, they put it on him.

(Mark 15 : 18) They began to salute him, "Hail, King of the Jews!"

(Mark 15 : 19) They struck his head with a reed, and spat on him, and bowing their knees, did homage to him.

(Mark 15 : 20) When they had mocked him, they took the purple off of him, and put his own garments on him. They led him out to crucify him.

(Matthew 27 : 27) Then the governor's soldiers took Jesus into the Praetorium, and gathered the whole garrison together against him.

(Matthew 27 : 28) They stripped him, and put a scarlet robe on him.

(Matthew 27 : 29) They braided a crown of thorns and put it on his head, and a reed in his right hand; and they kneeled down before him, and mocked him, saying, "Hail, King of the Jews!"

(Matthew 27 : 30) They spat on him, and took the reed and struck him on the head.

(Matthew 27 : 31) When they had mocked him, they took the robe off of him, and put his clothes on him, and led him away to crucify him.

The Crucifixion of Jesus
Lk 23:26-31 / Mk 15:21-22 / Mt 27:32-33
/ Jn 19:17-18

(Luke 23 : 26)   When they led him away, they grabbed one Simon of Cyrene, coming from the country, and laid on him the cross, to carry it after Jesus.

(Mark 15 : 21)   They compelled one passing by, coming from the country, Simon of Cyrene, the father of Alexander and Rufus, to go with them, that he might bear his cross.

(Mark 15 : 22) They brought him to the place called Golgotha, which is, being interpreted, "The place of a skull."

(Luke 23 : 27) A great multitude of the people followed him, including women who also mourned and lamented him.

(Luke 23 : 28) But Jesus, turning to them, said, "Daughters of Jerusalem, don't weep for me, but weep for yourselves and for your children.

(Luke 23 : 29)   For behold, the days are coming in which they will say, Blessed are the barren, the wombs that never bore, and the breasts that never nursed.'

(Luke 23 : 30)   Then they will begin to tell the mountains, Fall on us!' and tell the hills, Cover us.'

(Luke 23 : 31)   For if they do these things in the green tree, what will be done in the dry?"

(Matthew 27 : 32)   As they came out, they found a man of Cyrene, Simon by name, and they compelled him to go with them, that he might carry his cross.

(Matthew 27 : 33)   They came to a place called "Golgotha," that is to say, "The place of a skull."

(John 19 : 17)   He went out, bearing his cross, to the place called "The Place of a Skull," which is called in Hebrew, "Golgotha,"

(John 19 : 18)   where they crucified him, and with him two others, on either side one, and Jesus in the middle.

Jesus's First Word while on the Cross
Mk 15:23-25 / Jn 19:23-24 / Lk 23:34-37
/ Mt 27:34-36

(Mark 15 : 25)   It was the third hour, and they crucified him.

(John 19 : 23)   Then the soldiers, when they had crucified Jesus, took his garments and made four parts, to every soldier a part; and also the coat. Now the coat was without seam, woven from the top throughout.

(John 19 : 24)   "Then they said to one another, "Let's not tear it, but cast lots for it to decide whose it will be,"

that the Scripture might be fulfilled, which says,

"They parted my garments among them. For my cloak they cast lots."

Therefore the soldiers did these things.

(Luke 23 : 34)   Jesus said, "Father, forgive them, for they don't know what they are doing." Dividing his garments among them, they cast lots.

(Luke 23 : 35)   The people stood watching. The rulers with them also scoffed at him, saying, "He saved others. Let him save himself, if this is the Christ of God, his chosen one!"

(Luke 23 : 36)   The soldiers also mocked him, coming to him and offering him vinegar,

(Luke 23 : 37)   and saying, "If you are the King of the Jews, save yourself!"

(Matthew 27 : 34) They gave him sour wine to drink mixed with gall. When he had tasted it, he would not drink.

(Matthew 27 : 35)   When they had crucified him, they divided his clothing among them, casting lots,

(Matthew 27 : 36)   and they sat and watched him there.

> (Mark 15 : 23) They offered him wine mixed with myrrh to drink, but he didn't take it.
>
> (Mark 15 : 24) Crucifying him, they parted his garments among them, casting lots on them, what each should take.

The Title on the Cross and the Insulted by Others Jn 19:18-22 / Lk 23:32-33 & Lk 23:38 / Mt 27:37-43 / Mk 15:26-32

(John 19 : 19) Pilate wrote a title also, and put it on the cross. There was written, "JESUS OF NAZARETH, THE KING OF THE JEWS."

(John 19 : 20) Therefore many of the Jews read this title, for the place where Jesus was crucified was near the city; and it was written in Hebrew, in Latin, and in Greek.

(John 19 : 21) The chief priests of the Jews therefore said to Pilate, "Don't write, The King of the Jews,' but, he said, I am King of the Jews.'"

(John 19 : 22) Pilate answered, "What I have written, I have written."

(Luke 23 : 32) There were also others, two criminals, led with him to be put to death.

(Luke 23 : 33) When they came to the place that is called The Skull, they crucified him there with the criminals, one on the right and the other on the left.

(John 19 : 18) where they crucified him, and with him two others, on either side one, and Jesus in the middle.

(Matthew 27 : 37) They set up over his head the accusation against him written, "THIS IS JESUS, THE KING OF THE JEWS."

(Matthew 27 : 38)   Then there were two robbers crucified with him, one on his right hand and one on the left.

(Matthew 27 : 39) Those who passed by blasphemed him, wagging their heads,

(Matthew 27 : 40)   and saying, "You who destroy the temple, and build it in three days, save yourself! If you are the Son of God, come down from the cross!"

(Matthew 27 : 41)   Likewise the chief priests also mocking, with the scribes, the Pharisees, and the elders, said,

(Matthew 27 : 42) "He saved others, but he can't save himself. If he is the King of Israel, let him come down from the cross now, and we will believe in him.

(Matthew 27 : 43) He trusts in God. Let God deliver him now, if he wants him; for he said, I am the Son of God.'"

(Luke 23 : 38)   An inscription was also written over him in letters of Greek, Latin, and Hebrew: "THIS IS THE KING OF THE JEWS."

(Mark 15 : 26)   The superscription of his accusation was written over him, "THE KING OF THE JEWS."

(Mark 15 : 27)   With him they crucified two robbers; one on his right hand, and one on his left.

(Mark 15 : 28)   The Scripture was fulfilled, which says, "He was numbered with transgressors."

(Mark 15 : 29)   Those who passed by blasphemed him, wagging their heads, and saying, "Ha! You who destroy the temple, and build it in three days,

(Mark 15 : 30)   save yourself, and come down from the cross!"

(Mark 15 : 31) Likewise, also the chief priests mocking among themselves with the scribes said, "He saved others. He can't save himself.

(Mark 15 : 32)   Let the Christ, the King of Israel, now come down from the cross, that we may see and believe him." Those who were crucified with him insulted him.

Jesus's Second Word while on the Cross
Jn 19:25-27

(John 19 : 25)   But there were standing by the cross of Jesus his mother, and his mother's sister, Mary the wife of Clopas, and Mary Magdalene.

(John 19 : 26)   Therefore when Jesus saw his mother, and the disciple whom he loved standing there, he said to his mother, "Woman, behold your son!"

(John 19 : 27)   Then he said to the disciple, "Behold, your mother!" From that hour, the disciple took her to his own home.

Jesus's Third Word while on the Cross
Lk 23:39-44 / Mt 27:44

(Luke 23 : 39)   One of the criminals who was hanged insulted him, saying, "If you are the Christ, save yourself and us!"

(Luke 23 : 40) But the other answered, and rebuking him said, "Don't you even fear God, seeing you are under the same condemnation?

(Luke 23 : 41) And we indeed justly, for we receive the due reward for our deeds, but this man has done nothing wrong."

(Luke 23 : 42)   He said to Jesus, "Lord, remember me when you come into your Kingdom."

(Luke 23 : 43)   Jesus said to him, "Assuredly I tell you, today you will be with me in Paradise."

(Luke 23 : 44)   It was now about the sixth hour, and darkness came over the whole land until the ninth hour.

(Matthew 27 : 44) The robbers also who were crucified with him cast on him the same reproach.

Jesus's Fourth Word while on the Cross
Mk 15:33-36 / Mt 27:45-49

(Mark 15 : 33)   When the sixth hour had come, there was darkness over the whole land until the ninth hour.

(Mark 15 : 34)   At the ninth hour Jesus cried with a loud voice, saying, "Eloi, Eloi, lama sabachthani?" which is, being interpreted, "My God, my God, why have you forsaken me?"

(Mark 15 : 35) Some of those who stood by, when they heard it, said, "Behold, he is calling Elijah."

(Mark 15 : 36)   One ran, and filling a sponge full of vinegar, put it on a reed, and gave it to him to drink, saying, "Let him be. Let's see whether Elijah comes to take him down."

(Matthew 27 : 45)   Now from the sixth hour there was darkness over all the land until the ninth hour.

(Matthew 27 : 46)   About the ninth hour Jesus cried with a loud voice, saying, "Eli, Eli, lima

> sabachthani?" That is, "My God, my God, why have you forsaken me?"
>
> (Matthew 27 : 47) Some of them who stood there, when they heard it, said, "This man is calling Elijah."
>
> (Matthew 27 : 48) Immediately one of them ran, and took a sponge, and filled it with vinegar, and put it on a reed, and gave him a drink.
>
> (Matthew 27 : 49) The rest said, "Let him be. Let's see whether Elijah comes to save him."

Jesus's Fifth, Sixth, and Seventh Word while on the Cross
Jn 19:28-30 / Mk 15:37 / Lk 23:45-46 / Mt 27:50

(John 19 : 28) After this, Jesus, seeing that all things were now finished, that the Scripture might be fulfilled, said, "I am thirsty."

(John 19 : 29) Now a vessel full of vinegar was set there; so they put a sponge full of the vinegar on hyssop, and held it at his mouth.

(John 19 : 30) When Jesus therefore had received the vinegar, he said, "It is finished." He bowed his head, and gave up his spirit.

> (Mark 15 : 37) Jesus cried out with a loud voice, and gave up the spirit.

> (Luke 23 : 45) The sun was darkened, and the veil of the temple was torn in two.

(Luke 23 : 46) Jesus, crying with a loud voice, said, "Father, into your hands I commit my spirit!" Having said this, he breathed his last.

> (Matthew 27 : 50) Jesus cried again with a loud voice, and yielded up his spirit.

The Earthquake and the Curtain torn in Two
Mt 27:51-56 / Lk 23:47-49 / Mk 15:38-41

(Matthew 27 : 51)   Behold, the veil of the temple was torn in two from the top to the bottom. The earth quaked and the rocks were split.

(Matthew 27 : 52) The tombs were opened, and many bodies of the saints who had fallen asleep were raised;

(Matthew 27 : 53)   and coming out of the tombs after his resurrection, they entered into the holy city and appeared to many.

(Matthew 27 : 54) Now the centurion, and those who were with him watching Jesus, when they saw the earthquake, and the things that were done, feared exceedingly, saying, "Truly this was the Son of God."

(Matthew 27 : 55) Many women were there watching from afar, who had followed Jesus from Galilee, serving him.

(Matthew 27 : 56) Among them were Mary Magdalene, Mary the mother of James and Joses, and the mother of the sons of Zebedee.

(Luke 23 : 47) When the centurion saw what was done, he glorified God, saying, "Certainly this was a righteous man."

(Luke 23 : 48) All the multitudes that came together to see this, when they saw the things that were done, returned home beating their breasts.

(Luke 23 : 49) All his acquaintances, and the women who followed with him from Galilee, stood at a distance, watching these things.

the to

(Mark 15 : 38) The veil of the temple was torn in two from top to the bottom.

(Mark 15 : 39) When the centurion, who stood by opposite him, saw that he cried out like this and breathed his last, he said, "Truly this man was the Son of God!"

(Mark 15 : 40) There were also women watching from afar, among whom were both Mary Magdalene, and

Mary the mother of James the less and of Joses, and Salome;

(Mark 15 : 41) who, when he was in Galilee, followed him, and served him; and many other women who came up with him to Jerusalem.

The Burial of Jesus
Jn 19:31-42 / Lk 23:50-56 / Mk 15:42-43
& Mk 15:46-47 / Mt 27:57-61

(John 19 : 31)   Therefore the Jews, because it was the Preparation Day, so that the bodies wouldn't remain on the cross on the Sabbath (for that Sabbath was a special one), asked of Pilate that their legs might be broken, and that they might be taken away.

(John 19 : 32) Therefore the soldiers came, and broke the legs of the first, and of the other who was crucified with him;

(John 19 : 33) but when they came to Jesus, and saw that he was already dead, they didn't break his legs.

(John 19 : 34) However one of the soldiers pierced his side with a spear, and immediately blood and water came out.

(John 19 : 35) He who has seen has testified, and his testimony is true. He knows that he tells the truth, that you may believe.

(John 19 : 36) For these things happened, that the Scripture might be fulfilled, "A bone of him will not be broken."

(John 19 : 37) Again another Scripture says, "They will look on him whom they pierced."

(Luke 23 : 50)   Behold, a man named Joseph, who was a member of the council, a good and righteous man

(Luke 23 : 51)   (he had not consented to their counsel and deed), from Arimathaea, a city of the Jews, who was also waiting for the Kingdom of God:

(Luke 23 : 52)   this man went to Pilate, and asked for Jesus' body.

(Mark 15 : 44) Pilate marveled if he were already dead; and summoning the centurion, he asked him whether he had been dead long.

(Mark 15 : 45) When he found out from the centurion, he granted the body to Joseph.

(John 19 : 38)   After these things, Joseph of Arimathaea, being a disciple of Jesus, but secretly for fear of the Jews, asked of Pilate that he might take away Jesus' body. Pilate gave him permission. He came therefore and took away his body.

(John 19 : 39) Nicodemus, who at first came to Jesus by night, also came bringing a mixture of myrrh and aloes, about a hundred Roman pounds.

(John 19 : 40)   So they took Jesus' body, and bound it in linen cloths with the spices, as the custom of the Jews is to bury.

(John 19 : 41)   Now in the place where he was crucified there was a garden. In the garden was a new tomb in which no man had ever yet been laid.

(Mark 15 : 46) He bought a linen cloth, and taking him down, wound him in the linen cloth, and laid him in a tomb which had been cut out of a rock. He rolled a stone against the door of the tomb.

(John 19 : 42)   Then because of the Jews' Preparation Day (for the tomb was near at hand) they laid Jesus there.

(Matthew 27 : 59)   Joseph took the body, and wrapped it in a clean linen cloth,

(Matthew 27 : 60)   and laid it in his own new tomb, which he had cut out in the rock, and he rolled a great stone to the door of the tomb, and departed.

(Luke 23 : 53)   He took it down, and wrapped it in a linen cloth, and laid him in a tomb that was cut in stone, where no one had ever been laid.

(Luke 23 : 54)   It was the day of the Preparation, and the Sabbath was drawing near.

(Luke 23 : 55)   The women, who had come with him out of Galilee, followed after, and saw the tomb, and how his body was laid.

(Luke 23 : 56)   They returned, and prepared spices and ointments. On the Sabbath they rested according to the commandment.

(Mark 15 : 42)When evening had now come, because it was the Preparation Day, that is, the day before the Sabbath,

(Mark 15 : 43) Joseph of Arimathaea, a prominent council member who also himself was looking for the Kingdom of God, came. He boldly went in to Pilate, and asked for Jesus' body.

(Mark 15 : 47) Mary Magdalene and Mary, the mother of Joses, saw where he was laid.

(Matthew 27 : 57) When evening had come, a rich man from Arimathaea, named Joseph, who himself was also Jesus' disciple came.

(Matthew 27 : 58) This man went to Pilate, and asked for Jesus' body. Then Pilate commanded the body to be given up.

> (Matthew 27 : 61)   Mary Magdalene was there, and the other Mary, sitting opposite the tomb.

The Guard at the Tomb
Mt 27:62-66

(Matthew 27 : 62)   Now on the next day, which was the day after the Preparation Day, the chief priests and the Pharisees were gathered together to Pilate,

(Matthew 27 : 63) saying, "Sir, we remember what that deceiver said while he was still alive: After three days I will rise again.'

(Matthew 27 : 64) Command therefore that the tomb be made secure until the third day, lest perhaps his disciples come at night and steal him away, and tell the people, He is risen from the dead;' and the last deception will be worse than the first."

(Matthew 27 : 65) Pilate said to them, "You have a guard. Go, make it as secure as you can."

(Matthew 27 : 66) So they went with the guard and made the tomb secure, sealing the stone.

Jesus Has Risen
Mk 16:1-3 / Mt 25:1-8 / Lk 24:1-12 / Jn 20:1-10

(Mark 16 : 1) When the Sabbath was past, Mary Magdalene, and Mary the mother of James, and Salome, bought spices, that they might come and anoint him.

(Mark 16 : 2) Very early on the first day of the week, they came to the tomb when the sun had risen.

(Mark 16 : 3) They were saying among themselves, "Who will roll away the stone from the door of the tomb for us?"

(Matthew 28 : 1) Now after the Sabbath, as it began to dawn on the first day of the week, Mary Magdalene and the other Mary came to see the tomb.

(Matthew 28 : 2) Behold, there was a great earthquake, for an angel of the Lord descended from the sky, and came and rolled away the stone from the door, and sat on it.

(Matthew 28 : 3) His appearance was like lightning, and his clothing white as snow.

(Matthew 28 : 4) For fear of him, the guards shook, and became like dead men.

(Matthew 28 : 5) The angel answered the women, "Don't be afraid, for I know that you seek Jesus, who has been crucified.

(Matthew 28 : 6) He is not here, for he has risen, just like he said. Come, see the place where the Lord was lying.

> (Luke 24 : 1)   But on the first day of the week, at early dawn, they and some others came to the tomb, bringing the spices which they had prepared.
>
> (Luke 24 : 2)   They found the stone rolled away from the tomb.

(Luke 24 : 3)   They entered in, and didn't find the Lord Jesus' body.

(Luke 24 : 4)   It happened, while they were greatly perplexed about this, behold, two men stood by them in dazzling clothing.

(Luke 24 : 5)   Becoming terrified, they bowed their faces down to the earth.

They said to them, "Why do you seek the living among the dead?

(Luke 24 : 6)   He isn't here, but is risen. Remember what he told you when he was still in Galilee,

(Luke 24 : 7) saying that the Son of Man must be delivered up into the hands of sinful men, and be crucified, and the third day rise again?"

(Luke 24 : 8)   They remembered his words,

(Matthew 28 : 7)   Go quickly and tell his disciples, He has risen from the dead, and behold, he goes before you into Galilee; there you will see him.' Behold, I have told you." (Matthew 28 : 8) They departed quickly from the tomb with fear and great joy, and ran to bring his disciples word.

(John 20 : 1) Now on the first day of the week, Mary Magdalene went early, while it was still dark, to the tomb, and saw the stone taken away from the tomb.

(Luke 24 : 9) returned from the tomb, and told all these things to the eleven, and to all the rest.

(Luke 24 : 10) Now they were Mary Magdalene, Joanna, and Mary the mother of James. The other women with them told these things to the apostles.

(Luke 24 : 11) These words seemed to them to be nonsense, and they didn't believe them.

(Luke 24 : 12)   But Peter got up and ran to the tomb. Stooping and looking in, he saw the strips of linen lying by themselves, and he departed to his home, wondering what had happened.

(John 20 : 2) Therefore she ran and came to Simon Peter, and to the other disciple whom Jesus loved, and said to them, "They have taken away the Lord out of the tomb, and we don't know where they have laid him!"

(John 20 : 3) Therefore Peter and the other disciple went out, and they went toward the tomb.

(John 20 : 4) They both ran together. The other disciple outran Peter, and came to the tomb first.

(John 20 : 5)   Stooping and looking in, he saw the linen cloths lying, yet he didn't enter in.

(John 20 : 6)   Then Simon Peter came, following him, and entered into the tomb. He saw the linen cloths lying,

(John 20 : 7)   and the cloth that had been on his head, not lying with the linen cloths, but rolled up in a place by itself.

(John 20 : 8)   So then the other disciple who came first to the tomb also entered in, and he saw and believed.

(John 20 : 9)   For as yet they didn't know the Scripture, that he must rise from the dead.

(John 20 : 10)   So the disciples went away again to their own homes.

Jesus Appears to Mary Magdalene
Jn 20:11-18 / Mt 28:9-11 / Mk 16:4-11

(John 20 : 11)   But Mary was standing outside at the tomb weeping. So, as she wept, she stooped and looked into the tomb,

(John 20 : 12)   and she saw two angels in white sitting, one at the head, and one at the feet, where the body of Jesus had lain.

(John 20 : 13)   They told her, "Woman, why are you weeping?" She said to them, "Because they have taken away my Lord, and I don't know where they have laid him."

(John 20 : 14)   When she had said this, she turned around and saw Jesus standing, and didn't know that it was Jesus.

(John 20 : 15)   Jesus said to her, "Woman, why are you weeping? Who are you looking for?" She, supposing him to be the gardener, said to him, "Sir, if you have carried him away, tell me where you have laid him, and I will take him away."

(John 20 : 16)   Jesus said to her, "Mary."

She turned and said to him, "Rabboni!" which is to say, "Teacher!"

(John 20 : 17)   Jesus said to her, "Don't hold me, for I haven't yet ascended to my Father; but go to my brothers, and tell them, I am ascending to my Father and your Father, to my God and your God.'"

(Matthew 28 : 10)   Then Jesus said to them, "Don't be afraid. Go tell my brothers that they should go into Galilee, and there they will see me."

(John 20 : 18)   Mary Magdalene came and told the disciples that she had seen the Lord, and that he had said these things to her.

(Mark 16 : 10)   She went and told those who had been with him, as they mourned and wept.

(Mark 16 : 11)   When they heard that he was alive, and had been seen by her, they disbelieved.

(Matthew 28 : 9)   As they went to tell his disciples, behold, Jesus met them, saying,

(Mark 16 : 4)   for it was very big. Looking up, they saw that the stone was rolled back.

(Mark 16 : 5)   Entering into the tomb, they saw a young man sitting on the right side, dressed in a white robe, and they were amazed.

(Mark 16 : 6)   He said to them, "Don't be amazed. You seek Jesus, the Nazarene, who has been crucified. He has risen. He is not here. Behold, the place where they laid him!

(Mark 16 : 7)   But go, tell his disciples and Peter, He goes before you into Galilee. There you will see him, as he said to you.'"

(Mark 16 : 8)   They went out, and fled from the tomb, for trembling and astonishment had come on them. They said nothing to anyone; for they were afraid.

(Mark 16 : 9)   Now when he had risen early on the first day of the week, he appeared first to Mary Magdalene, from whom he had cast out seven demons.

The Guards' Report
Mt 28:11-15

(Matthew 28 : 11) Now while they were going, behold, some of the guards came into the city, and told the chief priests all the things that had happened.

(Matthew 28 : 12) When they were assembled with the elders, and had taken counsel, they gave a large amount of silver to the soldiers,

(Matthew 28 : 13) saying, "Say that his disciples came by night, and stole him away while we slept.

(Matthew 28 : 14) If this comes to the governor's ears, we will persuade him and make you free of worry."

(Matthew 28 : 15) So they took the money and did as they were told. This saying was spread abroad among the Jews, and continues until this day.

On the Road to Emmaus
Lk 24:13-32 / Mk 16:12

(Luke 24 : 13)   Behold, two of them were going that very day to a village named Emmaus, which was sixty stadia from Jerusalem.

(Luke 24 : 14) They talked with each other about all of these things which had happened.

(Luke 24 : 15) It happened, while they talked and questioned together, that Jesus himself came near, and went with them.

(Luke 24 : 16) But their eyes were kept from recognizing him.

(Luke 24 : 17)   He said to them, "What are you talking about as you walk, and are sad?"

(Luke 24 : 18)   One of them, named Cleopas, answered him, "Are you the only stranger in Jerusalem who doesn't know the things which have happened there in these days?"

(Luke 24 : 19)   He said to them, "What things?"

They said to him, "The things concerning Jesus, the Nazarene, who was a prophet mighty in deed and word before God and all the people;

(Luke 24 : 20)   and how the chief priests and our rulers delivered him up to be condemned to death, and crucified him.

(Luke 24 : 21)   But we were hoping that it was he who would redeem Israel. Yes, and besides all this, it is now the third day since these things happened.

(Luke 24 : 22)   Also, certain women of our company amazed us, having arrived early at the tomb;

(Luke 24 : 23)   and when they didn't find his body, they came saying that they had also seen a vision of angels, who said that he was alive.

(Luke 24 : 24)   Some of us went to the tomb, and found it just like the women had said, but they didn't see him."

(Luke 24 : 25)   He said to them, "Foolish men, and slow of heart to believe in all that the prophets have spoken!

(Luke 24 : 26)   Didn't the Christ have to suffer these things and to enter into his glory?"

(Luke 24 : 27)   Beginning from Moses and from all the prophets, he explained to them in all the Scriptures the things concerning himself.

(Luke 24 : 28)   They drew near to the village, where they were going, and he acted like he would go further.

(Luke 24 : 29)   They urged him, saying, "Stay with us, for it is almost evening, and the day is almost over." He went in to stay with them.

(Luke 24 : 30)   It happened, that when he had sat down at the table with them, he took the bread and gave thanks. Breaking it, he gave to them.

(Luke 24 : 31)   Their eyes were opened, and they recognized him, and he vanished out of their sight.

(Luke 24 : 32)   They said one to another, "Weren't our hearts burning within us, while he spoke to us along the way, and while he opened the Scriptures to us?"

(Mark 16 : 12)   After these things he was revealed in another form to two of them, as they walked, on their way into the country.

Simon returned to tell the disciples about Jesus
Lk 24:33-35

(Luke 24 : 33)   They rose up that very hour, returned to Jerusalem, and found the eleven gathered together, and those who were with them,

(Luke 24 : 34)   saying, "The Lord is risen indeed, and has appeared to Simon!"

(Luke 24 : 35)   They related the things that happened along the way, and how he was recognized by them in the breaking of the bread.

Jesus appeared to the Disciples
Lk 24:36-43 / Jn 20:19-23 / Mk 16:13-14

(Luke 24 : 36)   As they said these things, Jesus himself stood among them, and said to them, "Peace be to you."

(Luke 24 : 37)   But they were terrified and filled with fear, and supposed that they had seen a spirit.

(Luke 24 : 38) He said to them, "Why are you troubled? Why do doubts arise in your hearts?

(Luke 24 : 39)   See my hands and my feet, that it is truly me. Touch me and see, for a spirit doesn't have flesh and bones, as you see that I have."

(Luke 24 : 40)   When he had said this, he showed them his hands and his feet.

(John 20 : 21)   Jesus therefore said to them again, "Peace be to you. As the Father has sent me, even so I send you."

(John 20 : 22)   When he had said this, he breathed on them, and said to them, "Receive the Holy Spirit!

(John 20 : 23)   If you forgive anyone's sins, they have been forgiven them. If you retain anyone's sins, they have been retained."

(Luke 24 : 41)   While they still didn't believe for joy, and wondered, he said to them, "Do you have anything here to eat?"

(Luke 24 : 42)   They gave him a piece of a broiled fish and some honeycomb.

(Luke 24 : 43)   He took them, and ate in front of them.

(Mark 16 : 13)   They went away and told it to the rest. They didn't believe them, either.

(Mark 16 : 14)   Afterward he was revealed to the eleven themselves as they sat at the table, and he rebuked them for their unbelief and hardness of heart, because they didn't believe those who had seen him after he had risen.

(John 20 : 19)   When therefore it was evening, on that day, the first day of the week, and when the doors were locked where the disciples were assembled, for fear of the Jews, Jesus came and stood in the midst, and said to them, "Peace be to you."

(John 20 : 20)   When he had said this, he showed them his hands and his side. The disciples therefore were glad when they saw the Lord.

Jesus Appears to Thomas
Jn 20:24-29

(John 20 : 24)   But Thomas, one of the twelve, called Didymus, wasn't with them when Jesus came.

(John 20 : 25)   The other disciples therefore said to him, "We have seen the Lord!" But he said to them, "Unless I see in his hands the print of the nails, and put my hand into his side, I will not believe."

(John 20 : 26) After eight days again his disciples were inside, and Thomas was with them. Jesus came, the doors being locked, and stood in the midst, and said, "Peace be to you."

(John 20 : 27)   Then he said to Thomas, "Reach here your finger, and see my hands. Reach here your hand, and put it into my side. Don't be unbelieving, but believing."

(John 20 : 28)   Thomas answered him, "My Lord and my God!"

(John 20 : 29)   Jesus said to him, "Because you have seen me,you have believed. Blessed are those who have not seen, and have believed."

Jesus and the Miraculous Catch of Fish
Jn 21:1-14

(John 21 : 1)   After these things, Jesus revealed himself again to the disciples at the sea of Tiberias. He revealed himself this way.

(John 21 : 2)   Simon Peter, Thomas called Didymus, Nathanael of Cana in Galilee, and the sons of Zebedee, and two others of his disciples were together.

(John 21 : 3)   Simon Peter said to them, "I'm going fishing." They told him, "We are also coming with you." They immediately went out, and entered into the boat. That night, they caught nothing.

(John 21 : 4)   But when day had already come, Jesus stood on the beach, yet the disciples didn't know that it was Jesus.

(John 21 : 5)   Jesus therefore said to them, "Children, have you anything to eat?"

They answered him, "No."

(John 21 : 6)   He said to them, "Cast the net on the right side of the boat, and you will find some." They cast it therefore, and now they weren't able to draw it in for the multitude of fish.

(John 21 : 7)   That disciple therefore whom Jesus loved said to Peter, "It's the Lord!" So when Simon Peter heard that it was the Lord, he wrapped his coat around him (for he was naked), and threw himself into the sea.

(John 21 : 8)   But the other disciples came in the little boat (for they were not far from the land, but about two hundred cubits away), dragging the net full of fish.

(John 21 : 9)   So when they got out on the land, they saw a fire of coals there, and fish laid on it, and bread.

(John 21 : 10)   Jesus said to them, "Bring some of the fish which you have just caught."

(John 21 : 11)   Simon Peter went up, and drew the net to land, full of great fish, one hundred fifty-three; and even though there were so many, the net wasn't torn.

(John 21 : 12)   Jesus said to them, "Come and eat breakfast." None of the disciples dared inquire of him, "Who are you?" knowing that it was the Lord.

(John 21 : 13)   Then Jesus came and took the bread, gave it to them, and the fish likewise.

(John 21 : 14)   This is now the third time that Jesus was revealed to his disciples, after he had risen from the dead.

Jesus Reinstates Peter
Jn 21:15-23 / Lk 24:44-48 / Mk 16:15-18

(John 21 : 15)   So when they had eaten their breakfast, Jesus said to Simon Peter,

"Simon, son of Jonah, do you love me more than these?

He said to Him, "Yes, Lord, you know that I have affection for you."

He said to him, :Feed my lambs"

(John 21 : 16)   He said to him again a second time, "Simon, son of Jonah, do you love me?" He said to him, "Yes, Lord; you know that I have affection for you."

He said to him, "Tend my sheep."

(John 21 : 17)   He said to him the third time, "Simon, son of Jonah, do you have affection for me?"

Peter was grieved because he asked him the third time, "Do you have affection for me?"

He said to him, "Lord, you know everything. You know that I have affection for you."

Jesus said to him, "Feed my sheep.

(John 21 : 18) Most certainly I tell you, when you were young, you dressed yourself, and walked where you wanted to. But when you are old, you will stretch out your hands, and another will dress you, and carry you where you don't want to go."

(John 21 : 19)   Now he said this, signifying by what kind of death he would glorify God. When he had said this, he said to him, "Follow me."

(John 21 : 20)   Then Peter, turning around, saw a disciple following. This was the disciple whom Jesus sincerely loved, the one who had also leaned on Jesus' breast at the supper and asked, "Lord, who is going to betray You?"

(John 21 : 21)   Peter seeing him, said to Jesus, "Lord, what about this man?"

(John 21 : 22)   Jesus said to him, "If I desire that he stay until I come, what is that to you? You follow me."

(John 21 : 23)   This saying therefore went out among the brothers, that this disciple wouldn't die. Yet Jesus didn't say to him that he wouldn't die, but, "If I desire that he stay until I come, what is that to you?"

(Luke 24 : 44)   He said to them, "This is what I told you, while I was still with you, that all things which are written in the law of Moses, the prophets, and the psalms, concerning me must be fulfilled."

(Luke 24 : 45)   Then he opened their minds, that they might understand the Scriptures.

(Luke 24 : 46)   He said to them, "Thus it is written, and thus it was necessary for the Christ to suffer and to rise from the dead the third day,

(Luke 24 : 47)   and that repentance and remission of sins should be preached in his name to all the nations, beginning at Jerusalem.

(Luke 24 : 48)   You are witnesses of these things.

(Mark 16 : 15) He said to them, "Go into all the world, and preach the Good News to the whole creation.

(Mark 16 : 16) He who believes and is baptized will be saved; but he who disbelieves will be condemned.

(Mark 16 : 17) These signs will accompany those who believe: in my name they will cast out demons; they will speak with new languages;

(Mark 16 : 18) they will take up serpents; and if they drink any deadly thing, it will in no way hurt them; they will lay hands on the sick, and they will recover."

The Great Commission
Mt 28:16-20

(Matthew 28 : 16)   But the eleven disciples went into Galilee, to the mountain where Jesus had sent them.

(Matthew 28 : 17)   When they saw him, they bowed down to him, but some doubted.

(Matthew 28 : 18)   Jesus came to them and spoke to them, saying, "All authority has been given to me in heaven and on earth.

(Matthew 28 : 19)   Go, and make disciples of all nations, baptizing them in the name of the Father and of the Son and of the Holy Spirit,

(Matthew 28 : 20)   teaching them to observe all things that I commanded you. Behold, I am with you always, even to the end of the age." Amen.

The Ascension of Jesus
Lk 24:49-53 / Mk 16:19-20 / Jn 21:24-25
& Jn 20:30-31

(Luke 24 : 49)   Behold, I send out the promise of my Father on you. But wait in the city of Jerusalem until you are clothed with power from on high."

(Luke 24 : 50)   He led them out as far as Bethany, and he lifted up his hands, and blessed them.

(Mark 16 : 19)   So then the Lord, after he had spoken to them, was received up into heaven, and sat down at the right hand of God.

(Luke 24 : 51)   It happened, while he blessed them, that he withdrew from them, and was carried up into heaven.

(Luke 24 : 52) They worshiped him, and returned to Jerusalem with great joy,

(Luke 24 : 53)   and were continually in the temple, praising and blessing God. Amen.

(Mark 16 : 20) They went out, and preached everywhere, the Lord working with them, and confirming the word by the signs that followed. Amen.

(John 21 : 24) This is the disciple who testifies about these things, and wrote these things. We know that his witness is true.

(John 21 : 25)   There are also many other things which Jesus did, which if they would all be written, I suppose that even the world itself wouldn't have room for the books that would be written.

(John 20 : 30) Therefore Jesus did many other signs in the presence of his disciples, which are not written in this book;

(John 20 : 31) but these are written, that you may believe that Jesus is the Christ, the Son of God, and that believing you may have life in his name.